ALSO BY SEAN R. FRAZIER

The Call of Chaos (The Forgotten Years Book 1)

The Coming Storm (The Forgotten Years Book 2)

Descent into Madness (The Forgotten Years Book 3)

Ascent into Light (The Forgotten Years Book 4)

PRAISE FOR SEAN R. FRAZIER

"This epic urban fantasy is filled with magic, sarcasm, and a little gun slinging. Ellyne is the heroine I'd love to be besties with!"

Mandy Lawson, author of the Lora Kate London Series

"An imaginative, fast-paced and fun read!"

Matthew Cesca, author of The Forbidden Scrolls Trilogy

"Never underestimate a gunslinger. Or a Mage on the run."

K. M. Warfield, author of the Heroes of Avoch series

"Nothing short of a magical adventure; full of action, thrills and conspiracies."

Trey Stone, author of At the Gate

"Author Sean R. Frazier uses stellar worldbuilding and a vivid imaginative drive to immerse readers in a captivating blend of magic, prophecy, and survival. The unique concept of magic as a restraint rather than a boon added depth to the story's dynamics, creating an interesting dystopian vibe that bucks the trend of typical urban fantasy works everywhere."

Readers' Favorite Review

MAGE BREAKER

MAGE BREAKER

SEAN R. FRAZIER

Published in the United States by Creative James Media.

www.creativejamesmedia.com

978-1-956183-56-6 (trade paperback)

First U.S. Edition 2023

To Kristin, Gillian, and Tanith. Your support means the world to me, and I love you three more than anything.

CHAPTER ONE

SPITTLE SPRAYED from the man's mouth as Ellyne pounded her fist into his jaw. She thought she saw a tooth fly out. The sound and sensation of impact were two experiences she knew too well and, while she may not have reveled in the experience, were much like old friends she simply bumped into often.

"Did your mother raise you wrong, were you born in a barn, or are you simply a terrible person who makes the worst decisions?" she asked.

Groaning quietly, the man said nothing, still reeling from her punch. His mop-like black hair hung over his eyes and, though she couldn't see them, Ellyne imagined they held the look of shock. He touched his tongue and inspected the blood on his finger briefly before wiping it on his blue jacket and balling his hands into fists.

"You're gonna die," he growled through gritted teeth.

Thoughtfully, Ellyne replied, "Someday, yes." She looked around, noting two particularly seedy individuals rising from their chairs. The bald one wore a "Transgressors" T-shirt that was at least one size too small. The shirt would probably have fit him if he worked out a few times.

The other man was a tall, wiry sort donned in a green sleeveless shirt and a black kimler, or what many people called a "man skirt." Try as he might—and he was trying ridiculously hard— he wasn't pulling off the look. It didn't help the mean scowl he attempted to muster beneath his patchy stubble. How old was this kid?

"Three on one?" She sized up the competition and saw no weapons—probably their best decision of the night. She held her palms out in front of her. "Listen, guys, I honestly didn't mean to nearly break his jaw. And, to be fair, I *did* ask him nicely to remove his hand from my thigh. So, really, it's his fault."

None of the three men made a move, seemingly surprised at the sudden confrontation, and exchanged uneasy glances with one another.

"How about we call it even and just forget it ever happened?"

The rest of the bar patrons had pretty much ceased whatever they were doing so they could focus on the fight at hand. Most of them seemed like well-meaning folk with no desire to get in the middle of an altercation between four troublemakers.

But they certainly didn't want to miss a good ass-kicking, no matter who was involved. Even Victor, the bartender, appeared riveted to the scene, clutching a glass in one hand and a beer bottle in the other. The only noise, other than Ellyne speaking, came from the numerous video screens set on various channels ranging from sports to the local news. Apparently, there was a brawl at one of the games, and there was a dangerous, wanted mage on the run from the Ilserate.

"No," the spindly one said, "we can't forget. Our memories ain't good for that."

"Wait . . . so you *could* forget, or you won't? I'm confused. Because, if you say—"

"You know what I mean!"

"Are you sure you know what you're getting into? You seem confused."

Even if she *did*, in fact, understand what the boy was trying to say, it didn't matter because she wasn't listening. Her attention was focused on the area around her—the tables, the chairs, bottles, briefcases, and even loose change. Everything could be useful in some way. Not only was it fun to troll the bad guys, but it was a good stalling tactic while she figured everything out. Fortunately, it never took her long.

Her kick was accurate and swift, striking the wiry one in the chest and knocking him over a table. Several glasses shattered on the ground as the patrons jumped from their seats, dodging various spilled liquids. Unfortunately, she was able to determine the man was wearing nothing underneath his kimler.

The distraction gave an opening for an attack and the bald man swung his meaty fist. Ellyne's vision clouded as pain shot through her face. She steadied herself and rubbed her jaw as her sight quickly cleared.

"I hope you enjoyed that," she said with a smirk slowly appearing on her face.

"Oh, I did, lady."

"That's the only one you get."

Predictably, he followed up with the same punch. Ellyne grabbed a nearby chair and held it before her. The man's fist slipped in between the slats on the back, becoming entangled. Seizing the opportunity, she twisted the chair and stepped to the side, both swinging the man forward and, if her guess was correct, snapping his right arm. He slammed into a table, scattering more patrons as the wood splintered violently.

The wiry one was up again, standing next to mop head and sizing her up. Ellyne's jaw hurt, but it was nothing a few shots of squama juice couldn't cure. She ignored the urge to rub it. There was no sense giving these thugs the satisfaction.

They both attacked at once, yelling various insults at her.

She grabbed a handful of coins from a nearby table and tossed them at the two men who, surprisingly, cowered at the harmless impact. The distraction proved useful, and she saw her chance.

"You're new at this, aren't you?" Ellyne laughed, jumping into the fray, dodging attacks and countering with her own. She may have been outnumbered, but her skill was incomparable, and it wasn't long before she got the upper hand.

In mere moments, the fight was over, and all three adversaries were left groaning on the ground. One of them clutched his hand, having broken several fingers and another favored his arm. She gave herself a brief look, largely to see if any their blood had spattered on her jacket or trousers.

When Ellyne was satisfied, she picked up a wallet and sifted through it until she found what she needed, then discarded it on top of its groaning owner. She deftly made her way through the wreckage over to the counter to settle the bill.

"Well, that looked like fun, Ellyne."

"Yes, Victor." She sat on a stool and inspected the pay card. "A thousand laughs."

Victor's eyes settled on the card Ellyne held between her fingers as she, too, appeared to be scrutinizing it.

"A gold pay card, eh?" he asked, the wonder in his voice painfully obvious.

"It does seem a bit odd," she mused, turning the card over in her hand. It appeared legitimate. "Where would common rabble like that," she motioned to the wiry man "get a gold pay card?"

"The most obvious answer," Victor began, "is probably—"

"Stolen," Ellyne suggested. "I can't imagine he would have a high enough balance to acquire a gold pay card. But I guess I've seen weirder."

"Yep, stolen," he agreed.

Around the room, she saw funds changing hands as

people scanned one another's pay cards. They pointed to various things and nodded. Even those who apparently lost their hard-earned tiks appeared jovial.

Ellyne pointed to the three men who still hadn't gotten off the floor. "They're really sorry about the mess." She held the pay card up so Victor could scan it, then he punched in a few numbers. She saw him hesitate, then punch in a few more, and she laughed. She didn't blame him for skimming a little extra off the top.

When he was done, she tossed the card over her shoulder. "Didn't I ask you to stop letting patrons place wagers?"

"I did, Ellyne, I promise! But you know . . . old habits die hard. And, besides, it's good for business. Half these fools come in here just for the daily events."

"I don't get in fights *that* often . . . do I? Weekly, maybe, but *daily*?"

Victor nodded, wearing the biggest shit-eating grin on his face. "At least one a week, little lady. My bar's become an entertainment venue. Oh, wait. Hold still." He used his thumb to wipe something, presumably blood, off her jacket. "Wouldn't want to ruin your style."

"Of course. This *is* my favorite jacket, after all."

"It's your only jacket."

"Black leather suits me, don't you think?"

"Yes, very much so. It matches your trousers and boots. Why ruin the look with the white tank top? Why not just complete the black ensemble?"

Ellyne laughed. She let Victor get away with far more than anyone else. Sometimes, she felt Victor was her only friend, but she also figured he'd ignore her if she wasn't a regular in his establishment. "I have other clothes, Victor, but these are my fightin' clothes!"

Victor laughed and filled a glass with squama juice and ice, setting it in front of her. "Darlin' . . . *all* your clothes are fightin' clothes."

She sneered playfully at him and quickly downed the drink. Victor refilled it the moment she set it back down on the bar. "Good afternoon!" he shouted to three people who just walked in. He greeted them as they stepped up to the bar, leaving Ellyne alone. She listened to the news on one of the screens above her.

". . . experts say flocia use is at an all-time high and this may cause problems. A Kithrak spokesperson has said they may have to increase their fees in order to meet such a high demand. That would mean more time spent in a T-Helm for most people."

"Of course, they will," she grumbled, staring into her drink. It was an alluring brown color and she liked the way the ice swirled when she poked the cubes with her finger. "Hey, Victor, are you hearing this?"

Victor finished up with his new customers and strolled back toward Ellyne. "Hearing what? Oh, the whole flocia crisis?"

"Yeah, flocia crisis number five hundred and one. There's a new crisis every week. Wasn't there too much last month? Now there may not be enough?"

"Sounds about right. I have no idea how that whole system works."

"I don't think the Kithrak even know how the whole system works."

"Maybe. But we really do use a lot of magic. I mean, pretty much *everything* runs on magic these days—vehicles, the Metro, these digital screens—everything."

"Do you remember before? When everything didn't?"

"I try not to."

"Why don't the Kithrak simply open up the source— what's it called?"

"The Teranyne?"

"Yeah, that. Why don't they just open it up and let it regulate itself?"

"Ellyne, do you not pay attention?" Victor snapped his fingers inches from her face. She wanted to break them out of sheer irritation. "You know as well as I do, if magic flow was left unchecked, it would destroy everything. The Kithrak have the power and knowledge to control it and prevent it from washing over us in a flood of fire and . . . well, pain and stuff."

"I guess." She tore at a cocktail napkin, creating tiny bits of fluffy confetti. "I mean, that's what we're told, but sometimes I wonder if the old ways were better."

"The Legacy Age? Better? Have you forgotten the pollution? The finite resources? The overwhelming poverty?"

"And have *you* forgotten the Flocia Wars?"

"Ellyne, what's your point?"

"My point is . . ." She turned around and drew her revolver in one smooth motion, pointing it at the three men who now stood unsteadily before her. All three held their wands outstretched, pointed at her. She fired a shot, shattering the wand in the mop-haired man's hand. "Don't even think about it, skab. Next time, it won't be your wand I destroy."

All three backed away slowly, speechless, until they got halfway across the room. They turned and almost collided with the door before opening it and scurrying out.

More money changed hands around the bar.

She inspected her golden firearm before slipping it back into the holster at her hip and situating her jacket over it.

"You still have nightmares?"

She stared down into her drink. "Most nights, yeah."

"Ellyne, that conflict was twenty years ago."

"Feels like it was yesterday. It was a horror—all of it. I mean, what's humanity to do when people suddenly discover magical powers and then some alien race shows up shortly after?"

"It's a lot to consider."

"That's a gross understatement. People freak out. They lose whatever shred of rational thought they had to begin with, and they go full bananas." She fell silent for a moment, reliving everything in one flash of insight. "We lost so much."

"But look what we gained! And the price we pay is small —so small! Five minutes a day in a Taranom T-Helm thing. That's insignificant, in my opinion."

Five minutes? It seemed like just yesterday it was only thirty seconds. When had it gotten so long?

"Maybe. It feels like a con." She brushed a few blond strands of hair away from her face.

"You think everything's a con," Victor laughed, pulling a glass from underneath the bar.

"That's because everything *is* a con."

She let the rest of her juice slide smoothly past her lips and down her throat, nodded to Victor and headed for the front door as several customers clapped and cheered. Ellyne turned around and bowed deeply, exaggerating every movement. Louder cheers and howls erupted from the crowd.

Grinning as she stepped out the door, a flaxen-haired dog nearly knocked her over as it galloped down the sidewalk and turned a corner, trailing its leash behind it. She heard several people swear at the animal from nearby.

The street was busy for a Tuesday afternoon—busier than she preferred it to be. Didn't anyone work anymore?

"Sheesh," she remarked under her breath. "You'd think everyone was on permanent vacation."

Ellyne chuckled, the fact that she didn't hold a job was an irony not lost on her. Working was for suckers, and she had no desire to be one of the mindless masses, always scurrying from one place to another. Working was what people did to earn money to pay for her . . . services.

And goons like those three in Victor's bar were always the perfect targets for her skills. Not only did she skim some money from those bozos, but if anyone needed hired muscle, that little show back there was the perfect advertisement for her skills.

That wasn't all she could do, though. She was capable of so much more. Of course, everyone's needs varied. Those screwheads didn't deserve to die for their idiocy, though there was a time somewhere in her past, she would have ended their lives and never given it a second thought.

The city was littered with screens, each panel broadcasting something different—whether it was the news, an advertisement, or general information about something mundane like traffic flow. It seemed a majority of them were broadcasting more news about the escapee. Ellyne had no time for such things . . . unless someone presented her with financial compensation to care.

Karnascus was basically a living city. Monitored and controlled by an artificial intelligence, it could essentially operate itself. The AI, known as JASN, kept everything from traffic to streetlights running smoothly. Of course, this was all possible because of flocia.

The Metro breezed past, fifteen feet above the street. Hovering above the rail using magic, it made virtually no sound. The only indication anyone had of its presence was the wind it produced. Ellyne recalled the first days of the Metro after the Ilserate government converted it from mechanical to flocia. There were many accidents and deaths caused by its lack of noise so it was elevated to avoid unfortunate collisions with pedestrians.

Ellyne turned left and casually strolled down the sidewalk, dodging people who were obviously in a terrible hurry to get to wherever it was they were going—probably somewhere useless. Many walked, but some rode on hoversticks and yet others used magic to simply float to wherever they were headed. There were some sights she simply never got used to.

She passed an Instaportal as someone stepped inside and

vanished. Anyone who had tiks burning a hole in their pocket used this method of travel. Teleportation was the quickest and safest way to get anywhere, but it was also the priciest and, years ago, it was far less reliable. But there hadn't been an accident in at least, what, a couple of years? The only thing she was sure of was nobody could pay her enough tiks to use one.

There was no coming back from an Instaportal malfunction. In fact, many magical mishaps could cause serious injury or death. And no amount of magic could cure death. Sure, she'd heard stories of Kithrak mages who were rumored to command so much power they could bring a person back to life, but she didn't put stock in tall tales. In fact, she suspected those rumors were probably started by the Kithrak themselves, in an effort to display just how powerful they were.

Still, she wondered how much they'd charge for such a service. How long would someone have to spend in a T-Helm for that payment?

"Sure, they'll bring you back to life, then you spend the rest of it paying them back," she mumbled to herself. "I think I'd rather stay dead than be in debt to those bastards."

Times certainly were simpler before the Kithrak showed up twenty years ago. The sudden appearance of an alien race was enough to cause panic across the entire planet, but their arrival in Karnascus nearly tore the city—and humanity —apart.

The arrival of aliens would have been more than enough chaos for Ellyne's liking, but they also brought with them flocia—magic in its raw form. And once panicking humans figured out how to tap into it, things got a whole lot worse.

Ellyne remembered the Flocia Wars vividly and all too often. She instinctively rubbed her left shoulder, unable to feel the scar under her jacket and shirt, but she knew it was there. The ache still flared up from time to time, and she still had the bullet—a keepsake and a reminder of the past . . . and the hope of revenge.

"Hey! Watch it!"

Ellyne nearly knocked a man off his hoverstick. She wasn't sure if it was her lack of attention or his bad driving that caused the near collision but, whatever the cause, she felt like pushing him off anyway.

The man sneered at her as he passed, then gazed at the data pad he held in one hand while clutching a cup of something in the other. Ellyne sighed, feeling momentarily lost. She hadn't had a job in weeks and, even though she wasn't hurting for coin, the boredom often got to her. One could be entertained by bar fights and booze for only so long.

Of the screens around her, three were advertisements and the other showed information relating to building demolition. It never surprised Ellyne just how little useful data there was to glean from any of the public screens. Sure, at first, they had been integral resources with a purpose. It had only taken a couple of years for them to devolve into commercialism, propaganda, and vapid pop songs on repeat.

As she got closer, she could read the screen better. Crews were demolishing a damaged building on Sunset today. Sunset was only two blocks away. For a moment, Ellyne thought about investigating. A building implosion was better entertainment than she got most days, but she thought better of it.

Just as she turned to leave, the screen flickered. It was quick enough to make Ellyne wonder if she'd actually seen it, but then it happened once more.

"Caution! Traffic Ahead!"

She did a double take, staring at the sign which showed its original demolition message. She muttered under her breath, "If you mean a congested sidewalk, then you're not wrong. Looks like JASN needs to fix this screen."

The sun's last rays bathed the city in a golden glow and

the air was still hot, but Ellyne shrugged it off as she pushed her way through the throng of bodies on the sidewalk. She always found it amusing that, in a time of such high magic, people still walked. Usually, that was because they lacked the magical talent or device to travel any other way. Or they simply didn't want to pay the toll to do so. She herself enjoyed walking and, since she had nowhere particular to be, there was no reason to travel otherwise.

The information on a nearby sign flickered and, this time, Ellyne was sure she saw it change.

"Unexpected delays."

"Proceed with caution."

Those were traffic warnings, but this wasn't a traffic-focused screen. So why would a sidewalk screen broadcast traffic warnings?

She tapped a man on the shoulder and pointed to the screen. "Did you see that? On the screen?"

"See what? Look, I'm in a hurry, miss."

The encounter was brief, and the man walked faster, obviously hoping to avoid another dialogue with her. Ellyne sighed and turned the corner into an empty alley, eventually emerging onto another crowded sidewalk. She turned right and slipped into her apartment building.

Her space was on the top floor of the building—the fourth floor. Living high above the din of the streets below was liberating, but the four flights of stairs often made her wish she lived closer to ground level.

As always, she exited the stairwell on the first floor, walked to the end of the hallway, and scaled the fire escape outside. She never used the front door anymore—not since the first time she caught three thugs hiding in her apartment, waiting for her. She never found out who they were working for but, then, she hadn't actually asked them. Upon reaching the fourth story, she leapt to her rusted balcony and peeked in her window.

From her vantage point, she saw nothing out of place in her bedroom. She didn't keep a tidy apartment, believing it to be a waste of time, but she knew very well the proper place for every object, and she would have known if something had been moved. Her hairbrush, for example, was always in the same place on her dresser, pointing the same direction. The handle hung precariously off the side of the dresser and would have been disturbed upon opening the bedroom door.

The brush wasn't the only object set out this way, but it was the first one she inspected every time. Her little triggers aside, the room largely looked as if it had already been ransacked. Most children probably kept their bedrooms cleaner than she did. This was an assumption, as she didn't actually know any children. The window made no noise as she slowly pushed it up and slid inside.

This was all her standard procedure, of course. This level of caution quickly got old, but it had saved her life on multiple occasions. She pissed off a lot of people and word traveled fast. Eventually, a few of them found their way here, hoping to ambush her. It was impossible to remain hidden from everyone forever, so caution was paramount.

Not counting the bathroom, her apartment had only two rooms—the bedroom and a hybrid living room/kitchen. If anyone was in her apartment, they would be in the next room. Nobody had yet chosen to hide in her bathroom.

Ellyne pushed open the door and brazenly burst into the living room, expecting it to be empty as it almost always was.

She didn't know who was more shocked—her or the girl on the couch.

CHAPTER
TWO

THE KID SCREAMED and leapt from the sofa; her hands outstretched in front of her. Ellyne knew full well this was not a gesture of surrender but rather, it was the way a lot of mages placed their hands for the most opportune spellcasting. Consequently, her revolver was in her hand and pointed at the intruder.

A moment of tense silence followed where their breathing was the only sound in the room. Ellyne pulled back the gun's hammer with her thumb and clicked it into place—usually just for effect, but always a satisfying sound.

"You've got five seconds to—"

"Okay, uh, just wait a second," the girl stammered nervously. Her hands shook, but Ellyne knew what a mage—even a nervous mage—could do. "My name is Nicole Saranuin, and I came here to find you." She slowly brushed strands of black hair out of her face. "I didn't actually expect to, you know."

"Know what?"

"Meet you. I mean, I was told you lived here, and I really hoped I would get to meet you, but I wasn't sure but here we both are and I can't believe I actually found you this is incredible!"

The girl rambled so quickly that her words ran together in one confusing sentence. Still, while her mouth rambled a mile a minute, her green eyes held worry and fear. No, this intruder wasn't a danger.

She was scared.

Ellyne sighed and rolled her eyes. Most people would have already had a bullet in them by now, but she didn't feel particularly threatened. Relaxing slightly, but still pointing her gun at the girl for good measure, she said, "Slow the hell down. I can barely understand what you're saying."

Nicole took a deep breath and exhaled. "Can I sit down?"

"No."

"Very well." She lowered her hands to her sides, fidgeting and tugging on her red, knee-length skirts. Ellyne chuckled when she realized the girl's garb resembled that of an urban fairy tale princess. She looked horribly out of place and, on the streets, would certainly stick out in a crowd.

She took another deep breath, exhaling slowly. "I'm sorry to just break into your apartment like this. To be fair, you have no magical wards to keep out intruders. I mean, you're basically inviting thieves, so it's really your fault."

"I'm not interested in your assessment of my home security," Ellyne sneered.

"I'm just saying, if you—"

"This is the part where I get bored and tell you to leave or put a bullet in you. Why are you here?"

"Oh . . . right. I mean, I'm sorry. I have nowhere else to go and no one else to turn to."

"But why are you here?"

"Anyway, as I said, my name is Nicole and I need your help." She glanced around nervously and shifted her weight before finally looking back at the couch."

"Of course you do."

"So . . . can we talk?" Nicole asked, starting to sit down.

"We *are* talking. And don't get comfortable. You're not staying," Ellyne growled while subtly flourishing her weapon.

"Without you pointing your gun at me, I mean. I don't wish to hurt you—hey is that the gun? I mean *the* gun?"

"What do you mean?"

"Your revolver!" Nicole motioned to the shiny, golden pistol currently pointed at her. "Is that the weapon you used in the Flocia Wars? I mean, I was sort of skeptical if it was even real—or that *you* were even real—but there it is and here you are! It's gorgeous!"

Ellyne growled, then sighed. She holstered her weapon, now one hundred percent certain of one thing: the black-haired pipsqueak wasn't going to harm her past merely talking her to death. She ran her fingers through her short blonde hair, trying to think of where this should go next.

"I read all about them—the wars, I mean. Most people who go through school have. It's all part of the standard curriculum. Naturally, you're mentioned a lot. But more like a legend than something real."

"If you're trying to flatter me—"

"Oh, no! I wouldn't—" She sighed and looked thoughtful for a moment. "I mean, yeah, I sort of am. I'm sorry, I'm really nervous because you're you and I'm—"

"I've changed my mind." Ellyne gestured to the battered, threadbare black suede couch as she sat on the vintage steamer trunk that served as coffee table nearby. "Please have a seat if it'll help you calm down so this can end quicker."

Truthfully, she should've escorted this girl out of her apartment. Anyone else would have already been dead or fled in fear. The difference between her and everyone else who had previously broken in was, by now, the intruder would have tried to kill her without being so chatty.

And Ellyne was a slight bit curious. It certainly wasn't the worst thing that could've happened, but it was up there on her list.

"I mean, you *are* Ellyne Thandaral, aren't you?" She sat on the couch, awkwardly repositioning herself several times. "*The* Ellyne Thandaral—the Golden Gunslinger?"

"That's all in the past, kid. That person isn't around anymore. I'd prefer the past remains just that—the past. Also, my name's not eh-leene. It's pronounced El-leen-ya."

Disappointment painted Nicole's round face.

"I'm not a hero, kid."

"I'm not a kid. I'm twenty-five years old."

"Still a kid."

"Even if I were a child, I'm mature for my age. I imagine you were much the same."

She stifled a laugh. How did this girl think she could compare them? Ellyne saw no similarities. "Okay, now that we've had our little chat, it's time for you to go."

"Go? No, wait—I'm sorry if I offended you. I really am. Please don't make me leave! I have nowhere safe to go. I need your help."

Ellyne grabbed Nicole's arm and dragged her to the front door. "I'm sorry, but I can't help you." Nicole struggled in her grip, but Ellyne was much stronger. "Now, I think it's time you were going."

She opened the door and was about to drag Nicole out into the hallway when a blast of force threw her against the wall outside her apartment. She yelped and spots filled her vision as she struggled to remain standing. Shock, disbelief, and terror overcame her for a brief moment. Her right hand instinctively went to draw her revolver, but she resisted the urge. She had to remain calm. If this Nicole had the upper hand, Ellyne had to keep a cool head.

"Oh shit," Nicole gasped. "I'm sorry! I didn't mean to do that! Well, I did mean to do that, but I didn't mean to hit you that hard. I just wanted you to back off. Are you okay? Please tell me you're okay!"

"I'm fine." Ellyne's back screamed in agony as she stumbled back into the apartment, massaging the back of her head and shutting the door behind them.

"Are you sure?"

"Yes!" she growled, trying not to look frail as she collapsed on the couch. "I'm sure I'm fine. I'm not particularly jovial at the moment, though." She adjusted a rather worn-out throw pillow under her head and tried to process what just happened.

This girl probably could've killed her—without so much as a thought. She hadn't, so Ellyne wasn't concerned with that. No, it was the power the girl used.

Additionally, there had been no warning—no words, incantations, or silly hand motions that mages used to cast their magic. Likewise, she hadn't used a wand or any other similar enchanted magic device. Ellyne made it a point to be well-educated about the dangers magic posed and what just happened fit none of the molds. Either this girl was lucky, or she was . . . something else entirely.

Nicole stood awkwardly while Ellyne worked to regain her senses. "If you'd allow me, I could—"

"No!" The urge to draw her pistol returned. "I don't want your help, especially if it involves your filthy magic. Just give me another minute or two and then we can talk about how you need to leave me alone."

"Can I sit on the couch?"

"No, you cannot." Ellyne rubbed her temples to hopefully minimize the throbbing in her head. She wondered if the wall outside suffered any damage. More importantly, she wondered if the landlord would find out and charge her to fix it. That wasn't in her budget this month . . . or any month. There were better things to spend her money on . . . like squama juice.

"Oh, hey, your screen just turned on."

"What?"

"Your screen—it just turned on by itself."

Ellyne squinted, steadying her vision until the two floaty screens merged into one. Sure enough, it was powering up. She didn't remember the last time she'd actually turned the thing on. Last year? The year before? It came with the apartment and wasn't something she normally used—much like the front door.

"I thought I unplugged it," she muttered, stumbling off the couch and propping herself up on the makeshift coffee table with a disdainful snort. She approached the screen and pushed the power button to turn it off, then returned to the couch. A throbbing headache was bubbling up from within her.

"You could've just used the remote—"

"I also could've just shot the damned thing—do you ever stop talking and asking questions?"

"I'm sorry. I really don't get to talk to people very often or really get out into the city. I'm sort of new at this."

"That I believe. And what about blasting people into walls? Are you new at that?"

Nicole cast her eyes towards her red boots and fidgeted with her skirt some more. The guilt she had practically dripped off her. "No, not so much."

"That I also believe." With a little relaxation, Ellyne managed to wrangle the headache down to a dull thud with some deep breaths and distraction techniques. She was used to such things. In the days before everything ran off magic, a couple pills would've done the deed, but now everything was spells and potions and bullshit she wanted to stay away from. She didn't trust magic. There was always a price.

She was also out of pain relievers.

Not only did she distrust magic, but those who used it. This, of course, meant that pretty much everyone was suspect. People used it to varying degrees and those who couldn't conjure spells naturally used devices—enchanted items, wands and the like. The three goons in Victor's bar were prime examples of untalented. The untalented, often called skabs, either couldn't learn magic or were too lazy to try. So, they used enchanted wands to focus whatever power they could muster, even if there wasn't much to muster.

It didn't matter the reason; the rage and jealousy were always there. Ellyne, on the other hand, preferred to be as far away from flocia or magic or whatever the hell anyone wanted to call it.

"It's on again."

"What?"

"Your screen—it turned itself on again. Is it broken? I've never heard of a screen—even a broken one—turning itself on. Usually, they just shut themselves down or, if they're the fancier models, repair themselves by siphoning flocia from—"

"Shh!" Ellyne put her hand over Nicole's mouth. After a couple of seconds, the girl finally stopped her blathering, and she removed it.

"What?" she silently mouthed.

The screen hanging on the wall popped and sizzled, then sprang to life JASN's symbol—an inverted green triangle inside a purple circle—appeared, then disappeared, leaving the screen black and empty.

"You're friends with The Keeper?"

"What? No. Of course not. And keep your voice down."

JASN's symbol appeared again, this time in the upper left corner of the screen, followed by text.

Warning: Trespassers Will Be Shot On Sight.

"What trespassers? He doesn't mean *me*, does he? You're not going to shoot me, are you?"

"Settle your tiara, princess, I'm not going to shoot you. As long as you don't throw me into any more walls."

Please, no soliciting.

"Why is The Keeper broadcasting on a screen in your apartment?

"Beats me, but it can't be good."

The message blinked once as if for emphasis before it disappeared. Ellyne remained calm but her concern increased. What the hell was going on? Was JASN malfunctioning? If the city's Keeper was having issues of some kind, that could throw Karnascus into utter chaos. JASN's predecessor, JAKE had been exactly that—chaos. At least until he was decommissioned, and JASN was put into service.

Nicole looked from the screen to Ellyne and back again, her confusion mixing with panic. "Does it always do this?"

Ellyne understood her feelings but kept her exterior cool and collected. "No idea. I never use it."

"Well, why's The Keeper broadcasting messages on it?"

Ellyne sighed, knowing no amount of vague explanations would satisfy the curious girl. "I told you I don't know. But the fact that it's happening isn't filling me with warm fuzzies right about now."

Keep your head and arms inside the building at all times.

Ellyne looked out the window. The street below was deserted except for three dark figures entering the building as a metro train sped by, its unmistakable blinking lights quickly disappearing into the dusk.

She immediately darted around the room, filling pockets with as much ammunition as she could find. "Time to go, kid" she said, hastily grabbing a dagger from an end table and tucking it into her jacket.

The screen went dark and powered down.

"Go? Go where?"

"Anywhere but here, kid. No, not that way." Nicole was about to open the door, but Ellyne shook her head and pointed to the window.

Nicole stared at her, dumbfounded. "You . . . you want *me* to climb out the window?"

"I don't *want* you to do anything. What you do is your choice. But there are three individuals making their way up here at this very moment. In my experience, that's not usually a good thing."

"I could teleport us out of here, no problem."

"That's up to you. I have no issue with it except for the part where you mentioned the word 'us'." She had one foot on the narrow ledge outside the window. "I'll be going this way. Whatever you decide, you'd best make it quick. They looked like they were in a hurry."

"Are you sure they're after us?"

"Don't know, but I'm not waiting around to find out, and you shouldn't either."

She ducked out the window and shimmied across the ledge to the fire escape. The rickety metal stairs rattled as she took them two at a time until she leapt down into the alley. Nicole was nowhere to be found, but that was her problem—Ellyne couldn't wait around for her to catch up. Besides, the girl could probably take care of herself.

She looked up at her window, hoping to see Nicole squeezing out onto the ledge. "Dammit, kid, c'mon."

"Why are we waiting around?"

Ellyne spun around to face Nicole, who had a huge grin on her face. She opened her mouth to say something, thought better of it and, instead, hurried off into the dark alley without a word. She was too busy trying to puzzle out what was going on. Nicole followed, thankfully remaining quiet.

Ordinarily, someone tracked her down to get revenge for someone she'd killed or even merely pissed off. But she hadn't run a job in weeks, so it didn't quite add up. Why would someone be looking for her now?

The Ilserate traditionally left her alone—she was essentially a war hero to many people. But she would've been naïve to assume the government wasn't at least keeping tabs on her. It could *always* be the Ilserate.

The Techno Guild had never moved against her. In fact, they were aggressively trying to recruit her. She would've been a perfect Technician.

But the Teranyne Order . . . they were always a wild card. Those zealots worshiped magic like a god. They would probably *eat* flocia if they could. And they weren't harmless. Their order was always suspect when something like this happened. But even they hadn't acted against her for months.

No, none of those were probably the answer, but there was always one individual she could inevitably trace everything back to whenever something like this happened.

"Marik," she muttered. "He must still be afraid of me after all these years. Good. He should be." She ran her tongue over her bottom right molar, felt the smooth ever-cold metal, and smiled. They would meet again and, when that happened, she would pay him the same respect he'd given her. She would knock out one of his teeth and leave him lying on the ground, bleeding. But Ellyne would finish the job—something Marik failed to do.

"So, where are we going? And who's Marik?"

"Somewhere safe." Ellyne had nearly forgotten Nicole was behind her, becoming lost in her own thoughts of revenge. She turned down a nearby street and into another alley, sticking to the shadows when she could. "And don't worry about Marik."

"Where is everyone? The streets are so empty."

Ellyne peered around a corner into the desolate avenue. "Have you never been out at night?"

"I mean, yeah, I have . . . actually, no. No I really haven't."

They scurried across the open street and into another alley where Ellyne paused. "Most people stay home and use their T-Helms at night. As I understand it, the effort and the flocia replenishment are exhausting."

Something wasn't adding up. How did she not know

anything about the day-to-day functioning of the city? "Oh, that makes sense."

"Don't you do the same?"

Nicole's face twisted up, almost as if she was trying to hide something. "Oh, uh . . . yeah, sort of. It's complicated."

"Of course it is. Why shouldn't it be? Sorry I asked." She pointed across the street. "We're close. Just around the corner and across the street."

"Where? In that dump?" Nicole pointed to a building that looked like it would collapse if someone nearby sneezed.

"Two doors down. That one's unsafe. The city condemned it after I . . . well, after some things happened. Now's our chance!"

Ellyne darted across the street and up to the building's door.

"A bar?"

"Victor's is the safest place we can be. Plus, he's foolish enough to trust me with a key to the joint." Ellyne fished out a small, silver key and quickly unlocked the door, thankful for the fact that Victor didn't magically ward the bar. He once joked about how he wished the place would burn down so he could claim the insurance money. Maybe the two were related.

The lock clicked and the door swung open. Ellyne gestured for Nicole to enter but she hesitated, looking uncomfortable.

"I've . . . never been in a bar before."

"And, what, you're afraid alcohol bottles are going to attack you?" Ellyne laughed but Nicole remained awkward and quiet. "Look, it's not the alcohol you need be concerned about, it's the *people*. But the bar's deserted so get your ass inside before someone sees us."

Nicole reluctantly ducked inside, and Ellyne locked the door behind them. The bar was dark, and all screens were off.

If it were daytime, this would make the worst hideout, since everyone knew they could find her here.

After a quick glance around, Ellyne finally processed what Nicole had said. "Wait a minute. You've never been in a bar? And you're twenty-eight?"

"Twenty-five. And, no, I've never been in a bar." Nicole sneered as she sat at one of the tables, poking at a hole in the booth's cheap vinyl. "There are lots of places I haven't been."

"Get a drink?"

"No thank you."

"No, I want you to get me a drink."

Nicole's face displayed both confusion and contempt. "You don't get to command me like—"

"Relax, kid, it was a joke. But I *am* going to get a drink. You sure you don't want one? Wait, you've probably never had one, right?"

"Right."

"Suit yourself." Ellyne strode behind the bar and poured a straight shot of squama juice, quickly downing it and pouring herself another. She made a mental note to settle up with Victor in the morning. Ellyne might be one to help herself to his beverages, but she wasn't a thief.

"So now what?"

"Well, now we lay low and figure out just what the hell is going on. But we should probably make our way upstairs, away from street level and windows." Ellyne opened a door, revealing a narrow staircase leading up. "Since I don't know who those goons were, I don't know what they want. And I don't know how determined they are."

Nicole followed Ellyne's lead and took the stairs to the second floor. They emerged into a large, fully furnished room. The curtains on all the windows were drawn and there was but one small screen hanging on the wall.

"You say you don't know who those people were or what they want?"

"No clue. I didn't get a look at their faces, but I don't think I've stepped on anyone's private parts lately. They could be working for someone who holds a ridiculously long grudge, I guess."

Irony. Ellyne had held her grudge against Marik for over ten years. To her defense, though, he did try to kill her. That wasn't something she was going to quickly forget.

"I might."

"Might what?" Ellyne asked.

"I might know who they are."

CHAPTER
THREE

"OKAY, SPILL." Ellyne leaned forward on the couch, facing Nicole in her chair. The sooner she learned about the situation, the sooner she could get her life back to a more peaceful state. "Tell me what you know about whoever's after us."

"Not us."

"No, they clearly were after us. I've had a lot of experience with this type of situation. People don't usually bust into my apartment building in the middle of the night just to have coffee and cookies with someone else."

"No, I mean, they're not after *us*. They came for *me*."

"Well, that's a first. Okay, then, elaborate please."

"I'm . . . I'm in trouble. I'm a wanted fugitive and those men came to your apartment tonight to apprehend me. I doubt they knew you would be involved."

"Shit." Ellyne shook her head in disbelief. "You're a criminal? Oh wait—are you *the* fugitive I saw on the screens today?"

"No! I mean, maybe? I mean, no, I haven't committed a crime . . . except my escape was probably a crime now that I think of it. But, before that, I did nothing."

Ellyne stifled a frustrated laugh. Every passing minute—

every word Nicole uttered—complicated matters. But she recalled the true fear she'd seen in the girl's eyes when she tried to make her leave the apartment. She said she needed Ellyne's help and had nowhere to go. At least, that's about what Ellyne *thought* she remembered. Honestly, it was tough to make sense of most things she said because of all the rambling and carrying on.

"If you're being hunted or pursued or whatever, maybe you should go to law enforcement for help. It sounds way safer than seeking out a washed-up war veteran."

"No, I can't! The enforcers are controlled by the Ilserate . . . and the Ilserate is exactly who I'm trying to avoid!"

"Wait. Hold on, there." Ellyne jumped off the couch and peeked out two of the windows. Thankfully, the streets were still deserted and there was no sign of the pursuers. "You mean to tell me the people who are looking for you are working for the *Ilserate*?"

"Yes."

"Look, you've got to go. I don't want any part of that." She inspected the curtains to make sure they covered both windows entirely and then turned back to Nicole. "I've been working for years to keep the Ilserate off my back. I don't need any more government altercations."

"So . . . the thing about that is, uh, it's not just them," Nicole added quietly, gazing down at her boots.

"They've caused far too many problems for me in the past —wait, what did you say?"

"It's not just the government. The Techno Guild is also after me."

"The Technos, too? Good lord, girl, you're in a shit heap of trouble."

Nicole nodded in agreement before adding, "And the Teranyne Order."

"Of course, they are. Might as well piss off the entire trifecta." Ellyne laughed. She didn't know what else to do.

"What did you do to paint a target on your head for all three factions?"

"I . . . it's complicated. I'm not even entirely sure myself."

"I definitely didn't sign up for this." She plopped back down on the couch, feeling the squama juice's minor effects start to take hold and wishing she'd guzzled a few more shots. "Never did I say to myself 'Self, today you're going to get caught up in a shit show and become a target for all three factions in Karnascus.'"

Silence followed as Nicole fidgeted uneasily, gazing into her lap. Ellyne wrestled with her conscience. Her first instinct was to dump the girl and lay low until it blew over. Whatever this problem was, it was Nicole's. Frankly, she couldn't care less which faction apprehended her. Each one was on Ellyne's shit list for multiple reasons and there was no lesser of three evils.

I wonder if there's any kind of reward for handing her over. That would solve the problem while simultaneously fixing some of my own. Maybe just drop her off with the first patrol that we come across.

"I'm sorry," she stammered, her quiet voice cracking slightly. Suddenly, Nicole looked every bit the diminutive girl Ellyne accused her of being. With her head bowed, she picked at something on her skirts, nervously moving her finger over it repeatedly. "It's just . . . I'm scared."

"You should be. If the Ilserate, Technos, and Teranynes are all after you, you're pretty much screwed."

"Which is why I came to find you." Nicole sniffed. Was she crying? "I heard I could trust you."

Ellyne rolled her eyes. This was all getting rather ridiculous. "Okay, I'll bite," she said, already annoyed with herself for continuing the drama. But she didn't know how to handle a crying Nicole and curiosity was one of her classier flaws. "What happened?"

Nicole sniffed again and wiped her eyes dry before setting

her gaze back on Ellyne. For a moment, a glimmer of hope passed across her face which further annoyed Ellyne. Simply asking questions didn't indicate a desire to help. It was best that Nicole understood this.

"I escaped from the Ilserate, and they want me back. They think I command immeasurable magical power. Everyone in the government who knows about me—which apparently isn't many people—thinks I can command flocia better than anyone else and they don't want to let that power go."

"So, then, do you?" Ellyne immediately recalled how easily Nicole unleashed a force to knock her into the wall—wordless and motionless.

Nicole wiped away another tear from her cheek and then dried her hand on her clothes. She sniffed one more time and finally composed herself. It was Ellyne's turn to feel awkward. What did most people do in a situation like this? Pat her on the shoulder? Hug her? No, she wouldn't be doing that.

"Yes. And both the Technos and the Teranynes know this, too. They probably have spies within the government—"

"Or someone squealed for a payout."

"Or that."

Ellyne paced, seriously considering going back downstairs and getting another drink. She pushed several wisps of blond hair away from her face and resisted the urge to hit something.

"Well, shit."

"I know you're angry." Nicole looked very much like a child who was about to be punished by her parents.

Ellyne swore under her breath, grumbling and growling to herself.

"I seriously didn't think they would pick up my trail so soon. I thought I had more time."

"Yeah, well, you were wrong."

"Well, moaning and grumbling about it won't do us any good."

"Wrong!" Ellyne shouted, slamming her fists down on a nearby counter. "It helps a lot and right now it's keeping me from doing all kinds of things you'll regret later."

Anger seethed within her. All the work—all the meticulous dealings and back-alley transactions she'd performed for years so she could disappear from everyone's crosshairs were supremely destroyed by one little girl in less than an hour.

"There's a reason I'm so difficult to find, kiddo. Sure, I walk among everyone, drink in their presence, fight them, maybe even kill them, but at the end of the day they don't know who I *really* am."

"Why do you hide? Why don't you want them to know you're Ellyne Thandaral, the celebrated hero of the—"

"Because, inevitably, someone comes snooping or asks questions and causes trouble for me . . . like you, for example." She returned to the couch, propping her forehead on her hands and resting her elbows on legs spread apart to take up as much space as she could. "But that's all moot and now I need to figure out what I should do next."

"You mean what *we* should do next, right?"

Ellyne remained silent for a moment, tangling with her emotions. "Right," she grumbled.

"And what *are* we to do next? We can't stay here forever."

Ellyne slipped her gun out of its holster and held it up to the light, its brilliant golden hue almost sparkling. She found, by staring at her weapon, she could focus better. And, of course, it was a good way to outright shoot someone when they weren't expecting it. It clicked as she released the chamber, noting all eight bullets were loaded. It was by all accounts an antique but that made it no less deadly, especially with the specific modifications she applied or had applied for her by someone else.

"No, we can't. However, getting here was about as far as

my plan went. At least now I know what I'm up against. I'm not happy about all this, but I can't prepare for the unknown." She slapped the chamber back into the gun. It made a whizzing sound as she spun it, still admiring it until the cylinder stopped.

What she said was true, though—about her plan. This was pretty much it. At least, here, they were in relative safety and, if they had to, they could at least spend a night or two. Victor would be cool with it unless she attracted unwanted attention.

She *always* attracted unwanted attention.

"We'll sleep here tonight." She reclined on the couch, stretching to purposely take up all the space. It was a familiar bed—one she'd used several times when things turned sour. "That'll give me time to think things through and hopefully come up with a plan of some kind. We'll have to stay up here tomorrow until nightfall, of course. We can't walk the city streets or even go near the bar downstairs."

They sat in silence for a while as Ellyne desperately tried to devise a course of action that would keep the heat off her. If she'd been asked what her worst possible scenario would be it might've come pretty close to this, except she couldn't have imagined Nicole. No, Nicole simply made it all worse than she could've planned for.

Strategy and planning weren't her strengths. Sure, during the war, it was thanks to her cunning that her forces had managed to overcome the Ilserate's bots and free her comrades. And that allowed them to capture the government's fortifications and release their regional control on the flow of flocia.

But that was a long time ago and, if she was being honest, the course of action had been straightforward. Bots were notoriously flawed, and each model had certain . . . shortcomings. The same held true for newer bots. They were all cheaply made but could still fire hundreds of bullets a minute. Well, some of them could, anyway. Except they didn't fire bullets anymore, did they? Only antiques used such outdated weaponry.

Not a day went by that she didn't question whether she was on the right side of history. The lesser of two evils was still evil. You couldn't put the flocia back in its source. Still, the idea sounded nice.

"Don't you need a T-Helm or something?"

"What?" Nicole snapped out of whatever trance she'd apparently been in. Whatever thoughts were preoccupying her, they must have been terrifying. Being on just one faction's shit list was bad enough, but all three was nightmare fuel.

Or maybe the girl simply didn't know the level of danger she was truly in. *They* were truly in.

"You know, a Taranom? Don't you wear T-Helms like everyone else?"

"Oh, um . . . like I said, no, I actually don't."

"Wait, so how do you get away without wearing a T-Helm? Don't the Kithrak shut you off from the Source for not paying your dues?"

"You'd think so, right? I mean, I thought so, but it turns out they either can't or don't or I don't know."

She was getting chatty again. Ellyne's head hurt with just the thought of another long, rambling diatribe. Still, this was an intriguing nugget—that she never used a T-Helm. How could she forego payment when everyone else had to ante up at the end of the day or week or whenever?

"I assume, then, that the Kithrak are probably after you, too."

"Oh shit!" Nicole yelled, eyes wide, and immediately covered her mouth. "Oh, I'm sorry. I didn't mean to swear. It's just . . . I never thought about that! But, yes, I suppose they, too, would like to find me."

"Fortunate number four. So, is there anyone who *doesn't* want you dead or under their control?"

"You don't," Nicole replied timidly.

"You don't know that." Ellyne regretted uttering those words—they were spoken out of frustration and anger. Wanting to be rid of someone in your life wasn't the same as wishing harm on them. "I don't want any part of you," she continued, mumbling to herself now, "and that somehow makes me your greatest ally."

"I'm sorry, what?"

"So, you're supposed to be the most powerful mage?" Ellyne asked, briskly changing the subject while simultaneously trying to sort things out. "A fifteen-year-old girl?"

"I'm twenty-five."

"Whatever. You're not only the most powerful mage on the planet, but you also command magic without paying the Kithrak for it. So, yeah, I'd say that paints a target directly on your pretty little face . . . and on my back. If I were anyone else, yeah, I'd want to see you dead or controlled. You're dangerous . . . to everyone because you *can't* be controlled. It sounds like you're basically a powerful weapon without any owner."

"I really thought you'd want to help me," Nicole said, tears beginning to well up in her eyes. "I've heard the stories. You're supposed to be a hero. Don't heroes always do the right thing?"

"Not always." Ellyne reclined, sprawling out and staring up at the plain white ceiling, trying to keep her temper in check. "Magic and I don't get along. I want nothing to do with flocia or the magic it produces, yet you've dragged me into your world consisting of nothing but that."

She quickly glanced at Nicole who fidgeted, picking at one of her fingernails and keeping her gaze at the floor. Ellyne might have felt sorry for her had she not been trying to temper her own anger.

"Furthermore, because you're being hunted by everyone and everything on the planet, now I am too."

The screen hanging on the wall briefly flickered to life, garnering both Ellyne's and Nicole's attention. They looked at each other.

"Shit, not again," Ellyne cursed as they both stared at the screen with an eerie silence.

The screen remained dark for what seemed like forever as the anticipation built. Both women were well aware this wasn't normal and, after the screen in Ellyne's apartment exhibited the same behavior, they knew something important was about to happen.

"What is going on?" Nicole whispered.

"How should I know? You're the one who uses magic."

The device sprang to life as splotches of random colors covered the screen until it went mostly black again. Mostly—except for the familiar green inverted triangle inside a purple circle in the upper left corner.

Nicole looked at Ellyne who immediately saw the deep concern within her. "The Keeper again?"

Ellyne grunted, her hand instinctively going to rest on her gun.

"Warning: Squatters Will Be Evicted."

"The hell?" Ellyne stared at the words as they blinked twice, then disappeared. She shrugged and let her hand off the revolver at her hip and flexed her fingers, trying to relax while puzzling out the possible meaning behind it.

Nicole, too, appeared confused but she looked at Ellyne who shrugged again and stared at the screen, hoping for more.

"Warning: Squatters Will Be Evicted."

And then it hit her. Ellyne gasped and rushed to one of the windows, peeking out carefully from behind the curtains. The streets below were empty. Not even an Ilserate bot wandered by. Their patrols were sporadic and uncommon anyway, but she was accustomed to spotting one every now and then. In fact, the absolute emptiness on the street was worrisome.

Then one of the screens on the street below sprang to life. There was no symbol of JASN, no splotchy colors—nothing except an arrow pointing right that blinked twice and disappeared.

She shut the curtain and backed away as if the window would bite her. The curiosity and hesitation she once felt were quickly replaced by irritation. JASN had warned them of danger previously but, this time, there was no peril to be seen. Why was the city's AI talking directly to them, and what did it want?

"What is it?" Nicole asked, peeking out from behind the counter in the kitchen area. Ellyne chuckled at how ridiculous she looked—the most powerful mage ever half-hiding from nothing behind a counter.

"We're . . . we're leaving."

"Why?"

"Don't ask questions. Let's go."

"Where are we going?"

Ellyne replied with only an annoyed glare as she ushered Nicole down the staircase.

The bar downstairs was still empty and quiet as they spilled out into the main room. She took a long pull from the nearest bottle of squama juice, emptying it entirely.

"Really? A drink?" Nicole whispered, the exasperation coming through nicely.

Ellyne moved to the front of the bar and looked out the windows but still saw no signs of activity. "You're not the boss of me, kid."

They lingered behind the bar, waiting for something— anything—to happen. Ellyne couldn't decide whether to be tense or irritated.

"I've never heard of a city AI operating this way before," she whispered. "Maybe it's malfunctioning?"

"Sure," Nicole laughed, "it's malfunctioning only for us. Makes total sense."

"Okay, you have a point. But what if it's the Ilserate leading us into a trap?"

"I thought about that. But if it meant us harm, it wouldn't have warned us back in your apartment, right?"

"Also a good point," Ellyne conceded, "unless it's working for one particular faction and doesn't want anyone else interfering."

Nicole was silent, but Ellyne could see fresh worry on her face. Suddenly, she wished she hadn't thought of that last bit.

A right-pointing arrow appeared on a screen across the street, blinked twice, then disappeared.

"That's our cue. Time to go."

CHAPTER
FOUR

"WHERE ARE WE GOING?" Nicole asked, keeping her voice low.

"Don't ask questions, kid."

"Why are we leaving?"

"What did I just tell you?"

"I don't understand."

"Stop with the questions already!"

"Ha! That wasn't a question!"

Ellyne's frustration mounted within her. "Now's the perfect time to shut up," she growled, inspecting the empty street. The streetlights did well to illuminate the city in darkness—a feature Ellyne would have rather done without on most nights. Of course, they were powered by flocia which created a strange, glowing orb or some shit inside the light's glass enclosure. Not that it mattered, of course, since the only thing that *did* matter was skulking in the shadows became supremely difficult in their presence.

Which was precisely the point of having streetlights, obviously. Of course, before they were magic-powered, streetlights would malfunction and light bulbs would die. The city often took forever and a day to fix them, so walking around at night was far more pleasant back then. Even as a kid she recognized the advantage, not that she had a reason to melt into the darkness back then . . . usually.

"Let's go."

Ellyne locked the door behind them as they headed the direction the screen had indicated. She was ready for whatever danger might present itself, knowing full well this still could be a trap.

"Aren't you cold?" Nicole asked as a chilly breeze kicked up.

Summer days usually ranged from hot to stifling, but summer nights were either pleasant or bordering on cold. "It's why I wear a jacket, kid. Besides, you're only wearing that . . . flimsy dress thing. I figure *you* would be cold."

"I probably would be, but I created a magical enchantment that regulates the temperature around me to whatever I want. It's simple but effective. I can extend it around you if you want. It wouldn't be—"

"No."

"Okay." She sounded almost hurt, but Ellyne couldn't be bothered. A jacket worked just as well as any magic, and it didn't require a T-Helm to use.

"Why do you wear that, anyway? The only practical piece of clothing you have is your boots, but I can't say I'm fond of that shade of red."

"The Ilserate provided my clothes—said I should look like the princess I am. This was the most suitable set of clothes I could find to . . . well, to escape, I guess."

"Well, that explains that. We really need to get you something else to wear so you don't stick out so badly."

"I mean, I kind of like it. They're pretty."

"And completely impractical. If we're going to run around the city and possibly get into a fight, you need better clothes. Though I suppose you don't really need to fight, do you? I guess that's one point for you."

Nicole laughed. "So, where are we going?"

"That way." Ellyne pointed to an alley across the street. In a moment of serendipity, a nearby screen briefly displayed a green arrow pointing the same direction. "Don't ask questions," she repeated when Nicole was about to say something. Those three words were quickly becoming her mantra. She was intensely curious about this situation, but following the arrows seemed the only way to find possible answers and, hopefully, to avoid danger.

They hurried through a familiar open space. Ellyne had seen it used often as a performance area for musical acts and various theatrical productions. In fact, she'd attended a Transgressors concert here a while ago. She'd also seen Flotsam live but left early when a brawl broke out. Of course, she started it, but she had long forgotten why.

"We're following directions from JASN? Why?"

When they had crossed into the alley, Ellyne backed Nicole up against a wall and growled. "Listen, kid, we've already been over this. I don't know. I don't know what's going on with any of this. The only thing I know is The Keeper's sending us directions to something and it seems a better course of action to follow them than to sit and wait to be discovered. But that's all I know, so now you're up to speed."

Nicole huffed. Her frustration was palpable, but Ellyne could also see she was scared—probably terrified inside. She may have been fifteen or twenty-five or whatever, but she essentially *was* a child, and Ellyne never had been good with kids—even when she herself was one.

A fog began to settle in as they cautiously made their way through the now gloomy, dark city streets, following The Keeper's sporadic signals. Ellyne found herself questioning their benefactor more and more now that she had some time to think about it. As far as she was aware, JASN never interacted directly with Karnascus citizens. JASN was an AI, programmed to control traffic lights and screens and, well, pretty much everything that ran the city. He could act dynamically to situations that arose, but his messages were directed at the entire city—not just one or two individuals.

So the question was, why was he helping them? Or *was* he helping them?

"Shit," Ellyne muttered to herself, tired of tossing questions around inside her brain. "Come on." She urged Nicole to follow her after she looked around a building and found the next street was empty. She darted around the corner but quickly realized Nicole wasn't behind her.

The girl was standing in plain view, staring—at what Ellyne knew not.

"What are you doing?" Ellyne whispered, controlling her urge to yell.

"It's beautiful!"

"What's beautiful?"

"All of it!" Nicole gestured to everything around them, grinning like a fool. "The city is a wondrous place—the buildings, the lights . . . even the streets! I hadn't noticed until now —I guess evading pursuers causes you not to notice these things."

Ellyne looked around them. The buildings were a hodgepodge of older and modern architecture, some with curved, elegant edges and others with the traditional, stocky square look. Some were adorned with colorful lights in windows and doorways while others appeared to be crumbling into the also-disintegrating streets.

Everything did sort of have its own unique beauty . . . if one could get past the dirty façade.

"We really don't need to be standing out in the street so that everyone can find us."

"I know, I'm sorry. I did mention I've never been out of the Ilserate compound, right?"

"You might have, but let's admire the exquisite nature of this crap pile from a more covert vantage point, okay?"

"You're right. I promise it won't happen again."

They scurried back into the shadows, keeping close to the buildings and out of plain view. Ellyne was surprised they hadn't encountered any bot patrols or sketchy people, and they managed to avoid the gaze of everyone they'd seen thus far. She was thankful for the fog this night.

A nearby screen sprang to life.

"Warning: Congestion Ahead!"

It flashed three times before disappearing and going dark once more. Ellyne looked around and, not seeing anyone or anything in the immediate vicinity, continued down the street The Keeper had directed them to. Another screen across the street on the second story of a building flashed the same message, then went dark.

Ellyne motioned to Nicole. "Stay here," she whispered, creeping up to the corner of the intersection. Further down the street she could see an approaching patrol—three bots and an enforcer. Ordinarily, she wouldn't give them a second thought, but she also wouldn't be traveling with the world's most wanted mage. No, she couldn't simply saunter past this one.

Citizens weren't usually given permission to travel the streets at night. There was no curfew, but if you loitered, a patrol would inevitably harangue you. These interactions often ended in violence—violence, Ellyne suspected, instigated by the patrols.

This group made no haste moving through the avenue, lazily inspecting storefronts and apartment buildings for anything or anyone amiss. It was largely a holdover from the days when people would use magic for nefarious purposes—theft, destruction, murder, and the like.

Sure, those activities were still a regular occurrence, but they were certainly nowhere near the frequency they had been in the past. People eventually became accustomed to their power level and realized they weren't unique in that aspect. There was always someone more powerful than you.

In other words, many rogue magic-users had their asses handed to them by other mages or, eventually, by the enforcers. Once everyone got used to the level of lethality, much of the associated crime quietly disappeared. These days, only the very desperate—or very crafty—resorted to crime.

And there were still a lot of them.

Ellyne continued observing the patrol. The three bots were standard bronze models—almost skeletal-looking torsos that ended in a disc-like platform that hovered a foot off the ground. Their heads were small, faceless rectangles which she always found sort of creepy, even though they were supposedly designed for the opposite effect.

But it was their arms you had to worry about. Each arm was a spindly metal limb that ended in a mockery of a hand with anywhere from one to five wands taking the place of any fingers. Those wands could shoot a variety of pre-programmed spells ranging from a stunning spell to a spell that could turn someone inside-out.

What spells they could actually lob at someone were never standard and she suspected it was up to the actual enforcer in charge to decide which they'd like their bots to cast. So, yeah, it wasn't the bots you had to worry about so much as the nature of the enforcer.

And this enforcer was a Kithrak.

"Well, that's fantastic," she muttered and ducked back around the corner.

Kithrak varied wildly in appearance, but they were, as far as Ellyne knew, relatively humanoid-shaped to begin with. Many of them apparently thought it better to try to blend in with the human populace and, using magic, altered their appearance to look as much the part as they could. Some succeeded, others failed. Still others failed spectacularly.

That's how Ellyne understood it, anyway. She normally didn't pay much attention because, to her, any Kithrak was something to be avoided. They proclaimed themselves flocia's peaceful stewards, but she didn't trust them.

This particular Kithrak seemed to have the image down pretty well, but its limbs were a little too long and it had a third eye planted in its forehead. She suspected some features were just too difficult to conceal—or they simply didn't feel the need.

The second explanation was more likely true, because most Kithrak were more adept at magic than even the most skilled humans. They didn't merely thrive on magic, they *lived* off magic. Flocia was, in effect, their lifeblood. Ellyne wasn't completely sure of the connection's specifics, but she wouldn't have been a damned bit surprised if they were *made* of flocia.

And that's when it all fell into place. Did they want Nicole because they were truly afraid of her? Could she far outperform them in the magical arts? That would be something to maybe prod in the future. Right now, this patrol was the problem, as it was directly in their path and barely moving.

Nicole was beside her, her face perplexed.

"Patrol," Ellyne mouthed without sound, pointing to around the corner.

Nicole held her hands in front of her, palms up and fingers pointing at the sky. She looked at them, then at Ellyne and grinned.

Ellyne swore she saw sparks crackle from Nicole's wonderfully manicured fingernails. She shook her head and gently pushed Nicole's hands down to her sides. If Nicole was truly *that* powerful, yeah, this patrol would be flaming garbage in a matter of seconds but usually, where there was one patrol, there was at least another nearby. And she didn't feel like fighting every enforcer in the precinct.

At least, not tonight.

Surely there was another way. They could move through a side street and take a detour, but what if that landed them in front of another patrol? No. The Keeper specifically sent them this way. Or was JASN trying to get them captured?

"Watch for cross traffic!"

The screen showing these words was tough to see, but the message became clear once Ellyne spotted the five shadowy figures coming down the street approaching from the other direction. As they came closer into view, she heard them laughing and carrying on—obnoxious and loud as if they'd had too much squama juice or torflower ale.

"Let's hang back and sit this one out," she whispered, urging Nicole back down the street they came from. They hunkered down behind a dumpster, peeking out to watch. Nicole appeared confused, but Ellyne reassured her. "Wait and watch."

It wasn't long before the patrol found their purpose and moved more quickly toward the group of drunken louts who, upon seeing the patrol, became slightly belligerent. When the two groups finally met up on the left side of the intersection, they stopped. Ellyne could hear low voices met by a softer, more soothing tone from the Kithrak. Aside from mumbling, she couldn't make out anything that was said.

But it wasn't long until the spells began to fly. She thought she saw the first spell come from one of the humans, but it mattered little as the area erupted in a cacophony of explosions coupled with a ferocious light show. It would be sorted out later and, even if the enforcer was to blame, would be swept under the rug.

She grabbed Nicole's arm. "Come on, now's our chance!"

Ellyne scurried around the corner with Nicole in tow, making sure to keep an eye on the combat. The humans, at least two of them using wands, appeared clumsy and largely inept. They would be no problem for the patrol, but it didn't matter to Ellyne since she and Nicole would be long gone by the time the action wrapped up.

Several errant spells whizzed past them, striking buildings nearby and scorching the walls or taking chunks out of the brick. A nearby screen flashed an arrow pointing left and they were about to turn down a side street when another patrol materialized out of nowhere, blocking their escape. Two Kithrak, flanked by five bots now stood in their way.

The Kithrak wore confused looks, obviously not expecting them to be in the area.

Please don't let them recognize us. Please don't let them recognize us.

The two Kithrak looked at each other, then back at them. "You, Nicole Saranuin, are under arrest for crimes against Karnascus, and you, whoever you are, are also under arrest for aiding a criminal!"

"Aw hell," Ellyne growled.

Her revolver was in her hand instantly, the cold metal against her palm, providing her with familiar comfort. Instinct took over, just as it always did.

But before she could pull back the hammer and fire a shot, a blast of force leveled the patrol, knocking them to the ground and shoving them violently backward. Two Kithrak and five bots rolled, bounced, and clattered down the street as if they were common garbage being blown by the wind, finally coming to a stop probably fifty feet from them.

"Most powerful mage, huh?"

Nicole nodded. The grin on her lips told Ellyne all she needed to know—the girl had very much enjoyed that.

Ellyne had to admit she had, too.

The enforcers tried to clear the cobwebs and get to their feet as most of the bots sparked and smoked, largely motionless. That blast, while incapacitating the machines, hadn't killed the enforcers, so they must have some kind of magical wards around them for protection. At least, that's what Ellyne's limited magical knowledge told her.

Which meant they'd soon recover, and this place would be swarming with more in no time.

Nicole's fingertips glowed with a blue, pulsing energy, matching the same glow that now appeared in her eyes. Ellyne felt the ground beneath her start to rumble.

She grabbed the girl's arm and tugged, but Nicole didn't budge. The rumbling beneath her feet intensified. "Not today, Nicole. It's time to go. We don't need a full-on battle." She slipped her revolver back into its holster.

She tugged harder and shook her until Nicole finally came to, the blue pulsing light fading gradually before vanishing entirely.

"Right. Sorry!"

They hurried down a small, poorly paved street that ran behind several restaurants. Though the shops were all closed, Ellyne swore she could detect the lingering smell of something tasty and her stomach growled in response.

There were no screens nearby to direct them, so they simply continued forward, hoping they went the right way. Ellyne wasn't sure they were headed in the right direction but, if she was being honest, she'd rather not rely on the city's AI to direct them to safety—if that's even where they were being led.

Even the AI was powered by magic.

"Two enforcer patrols led by Kithraks," Nicole muttered. "What are the odds?"

"The Ilserate must really want you back. I've only ever seen a handful of Kithrak-led forces, and never two in the same week let alone the same night."

"They only send out Kithrak mages on missions of the utmost importance."

"Then that first patrol was definitely sent out to find you, wasn't it?"

"Probably."

"Shit."

Ellyne walked faster, largely resisting the urge to run. Nicole kept up with her but still appeared to be sightseeing. Certainly, the city would have been a wondrous thing to someone whose entire world was a series of government buildings—prison cells in disguise.

"You, uh . . . you handled that patrol really well," Ellyne reluctantly admitted, cursing herself for letting Nicole wear her down.

"Huh? Oh, thank you."

They spilled out into an open plaza of sorts. During the day, this area was probably teeming with people, entertainers, and small vendor carts. Several of the streetlights were dark— a blessing Ellyne was thankful for. But she expected to see some direction from JASN and, when none appeared, she froze. Nicole, too, appeared to be scanning the area for a sign with a concerned look on her face.

"What now?" Nicole asked.

"We keep moving."

"Where?"

To Ellyne, it didn't matter. They had to stay on the move to avoid patrols. Wherever they went, JASN could presumably find them. The problem was, Ellyne herself was hesitant. If for some reason The Keeper had lost track of them, it couldn't alert them to danger. They might stumble into a larger Ilserate force. For all she knew, the Technos and the Teranynes could have scouts out looking for them, too.

Ellyne slinked back into the shadows, keeping an eye on the plaza. "I think I'm beginning to understand why everyone's looking for you."

"Why's that?"

"You threw magic around like it was a toy. I've seen only a few people ever best a Kithrak in a magic duel but never so swift and decisively. You had them on their asses before they could attack. You handled magic much like the Kithrak themselves."

Ellyne didn't recall this part of the city. She peered out into the empty area ahead. To call it a park was a vast overstatement. There was a gazebo at the center but no plant life or leisure equipment of any kind. It was likely just another construct to do business.

Still nothing.

"Not only were you fast," she continued, "but you were powerful. Those Kithrak probably had all kinds of magical protections around them, and you sent them flying like it was your job."

"They did. I could see their wards," Nicole said, beaming.

"You could *see* them?"

"Yeah, couldn't you?"

"That's not how it works." Actually, Ellyne wasn't sure how it worked, but she was pretty certain it wasn't like that. "Look, I don't use magic but, from what I've learned, you don't just get to *see* wards and protections other people have. You have to do some kind of poking and prodding with magic or cast some kind of counter spell, right?"

"I don't."

"I'm not even sure it mattered. You so quickly overpowered them I don't really think their wards—"

"If they hadn't already had protections cast on themselves and their bots, my spell would have turned them to ash."

"You could've outright killed them?"

"I didn't mean to . . . I sort of reacted before I thought it through. I didn't really intend it to be that powerful."

"Remind me never to piss you off," Ellyne said with a chuckle, despite being serious.

Every screen in the area remained dark, but Ellyne finally saw what she needed to see. "We're leaving."

"But I don't—"

"There." She pointed across the plaza. A light that had

once been dark now flickered rhythmically. The pattern had been easy enough for her to discern—it was an old, coded way of communicating without words. It was, in fact, a method Ellyne herself had used many times during the wars.

Clever.

Slinking through darkness only illuminated by starlight, they cautiously moved across the open plaza, looking every direction for danger and, thankfully, finding none. They came to a stop under the streetlight which eventually ceased its flickering and went dark.

"Now what?" Nicole asked somewhat impatiently. Ellyne shared her irritation with this whole situation.

"We're here."

"Here? Where's here? At least we could've stopped at a candy store or something, but this is just another street with more buildings and—"

Metal grinding on metal interrupted Nicole's tirade as a sewer grate in front of them slowly slid open. Ellyne stared into the dark hole as the grinding finished, revealing a passage.

Nicole, too, stared into the darkness. They looked at each other, then back to the now fully open sewer grate.

Nicole stepped back and pointed toward the ground. "Gross," she spat, a look of disgust plastered on her face.

Ellyne caught a whiff of the escaping air and wrinkled her nose. She gestured to the dark passage and tried not to grimace. "After you."

CHAPTER
FIVE

"IT SMELLS like rotting feet down here," Ellyne choked. This was her first trip to the Karnascus sewers and, if all went as planned, her last.

Nicole gagged as she hopped off the crude metal ladder that was built into the slimy, crumbling brick wall of the dark passage.

"Taking a Metro would've been a lot easier you know." Nicole sputtered, holding her nose. She dry heaved for effect. Or maybe it was genuine. "And far more sanitary, for sure."

"Yeah, well, the trains don't really go the way we're going. Besides, I've had a couple of bad experiences on the Metro, so I'd rather avoid it."

"No way, you?" Nicole laughed sarcastically. "What happened? Did you have to punch a bunch of people? Maybe blow some stuff up?"

Ellyne felt a lump in her throat and her irritation rose. "Something like that, yeah. Come on, let's move."

The tunnel was dark except for a flickering light up ahead. This was old city territory—neglected and probably largely forgotten since before the discovery of flocia. Chances were good it operated mostly magic-free which, as far as Ellyne was concerned, was a decent excuse to be slogging through the sewer.

Light sprang from Nicole's palm, taking the shape of a winged, twinkling ball that cast shadows in every direction with its blue-hued illumination. "No reason to walk in the dark and risk stepping in . . . well, anything down here." She inspected the bottom of her left boot and nearly lost her balance.

Ellyne rolled her eyes and headed for the flickering light up ahead. This time, there was no hidden message within and no screens on which to broadcast, so it was all she could do to simply hope The Keeper was still directing them.

The passage was little more than a crudely dug tunnel someone had at one time pushed some bricks up against. The ground, too, was brick with a large, ancient-looking pipe running through the middle. Ellyne wondered just how often these old sewers were even used anymore when most of inhabitants of Karnascus probably had magic-based bathrooms. It was certainly one aspect of magic she herself couldn't avoid.

Rumor had it, whenever someone flushed the toilet, whatever was in it was whisked away to another dimension or somewhere off-planet or wherever. While she didn't trust the system, she did find the humor in possibly shitting in someone else's parallel universe or whatever that would be called. Either way, it wasn't something she wished to dwell on.

Currently, this place was in that same category.

The flickering lamp was at a crossroads where they could go forward, left, or right. A quick inspection revealed a traditional light bulb hanging in the fixture.

The moment they arrived the light went dark.

"Which way now?" Nicole sounded funny and Ellyne quickly discovered she was still pinching her nose closed. The visual made her crack a smile.

Ellyne herself tried to deal with the odors as best she could, preferring to have both her hands free in case danger presented itself. She wondered if Nicole could cast spells while holding her nose.

"To the right," she said, pointing to another barely visible flickering light. She cursed the lack of screens, for once appreciating their purpose, but it was a sewer and what would anyone expect? She considered them lucky The Keeper had any control down here at all.

They passed several lamps that were completely dark, so Ellyne's confidence in JASN was still solid. She simply wished she knew *where* it was leading them.

And why would've been nice, too.

Nicole's magical illumination was just enough to keep them from tripping or stepping in anything vile. Several times however, the light flickered and dimmed, but eventually returned to its normal level of brightness. While Nicole seemed puzzled by this, Ellyne wasn't surprised. Magic wasn't always reliable.

Especially not around her.

They had just reached the next lamp when Ellyne stopped, waiting for the next light to appear. There were only two paths forward, but she could see no clear indicator pointing them in the right direction.

"I'm going to smell like this horrible place forever," Nicole whined. "No amount of soap and no number of showers will get this stench off."

"Shh!"

"I think it's basically part of me now. Part of me, part of my clothes, part of every—"

"Shh! Quiet!"

"What?"

Ellyne forced her hand over the girl's mouth. She pushed it away but, to Ellyne's relief, she said not another word. She looked confused, though, and Ellyne feared she might speak up at any moment.

"We're not alone," Ellyne whispered, pointing to the tunnel to the right.

"Not alone? Who would be lurking under the city in the sewers?"

Ellyne tilted her head and raised an eyebrow, wondering just how naïve Nicole really was. "Well, *we* are."

"Okay, but besides us?"

"Who . . . or what."

"What do you mean?"

There was a moment of solace—a brief slice of calm—before instinct took over. In one fluid moment, Ellyne's gun was in her hand with the hammer pulled and a bullet escaped the chamber. The shot echoed so loudly throughout the tunnel that she resisted the urge to cup her hands over her ears. The brief flash of light illuminated a wider area than Nicole's magic—revealing something humanoid, mid jump, thrown violently backward into the wall where it slumped, motionless.

"What the shit was that?" Nicole shouted, quickly cupping her hand over her own mouth. "Sorry . . . language."

Ellyne paid her no mind as she slowly approached the shadowy foe, gun drawn and pointed at it. "Come over here," she whispered.

Nicole shook her head violently. "Nuh uh."

"I need your light, damn it."

Ellyne knelt, poking whatever it was with the barrel of her revolver. When it remained still and she was confident it was dead, she motioned Nicole over with her hand. As the girl and her light moved closer, the corpse's features became clearer, and more terrifying.

It was human. Or, at one time, it *had been* human. But its form was twisted, gnarled like a tree made of bones and flesh. Its face was misshapen and angry, missing some teeth and its nose entirely. In Nicole's inadequate magical illumination, she had a difficult time scrutinizing it as closely as she would've liked.

"Can you turn the light up?"

Almost before she finished her question, Nicole's light intensified, shedding proper illumination about the cavern as if were daylight.

She wished she hadn't asked.

"Why didn't you make it this bright from the start?"

"Uh, I don't know. I guess I thought we were trying to be sneaky. I didn't want to give away . . . what would you call it? Our position?"

Ellyne huffed, but at least she could now see the body in detail. "What in the name of the gods are you?" Ellyne didn't believe in the gods—many people didn't. Once magic came along, the old gods became largely irrelevant to much of the populace. Sure, some still clung to them like a safety net, but Ellyne had never been one for miracles and spirituality. Though that didn't stop her from invoking their names from time to time.

Prodding the corpse further produced no new information. It was a grotesque mockery of life. Had it adapted to something down in the sewers that mutated it?

She stood, her right knee popping loudly. That was something she'd needed to do for hours, now, and it brought much-welcomed relief. "Did magic cause this?"

"Probably."

"Probably? Aren't you the expert?"

"I've been through all the magical schooling the Ilserate could provide me—even some taught to me by Kithrak—yet nothing like this was ever mentioned. I mean, I skipped class sometimes because I overslept but it would be supremely coincidental if those few days were lessons about something like this. Don't you think?"

Ellyne could do nothing but stare at her, confused and unsure even what to say next.

"Magic . . . doesn't really work that way. There are no set boundaries for magic or what people can use it for. A mage can excel at levitation and simultaneously be terrible at the simplest things like an illusion. Not everyone has a talent for everything."

"What about you?"

"Me? I'm good at everything." Nicole beamed, apparently proud of herself.

"I figured."

"Magic is organic for me. Just as peoples' skills with flocia vary so, too, do their methods. Some people have to remember motions and words to cast spells while others do it all mentally without much thought. Still, others can conjure magic without really thinking. And, of course, there are the untalented who need a device like a wand to channel flocia for magical effects."

"Skabs."

"Yeah, skabs." Nicole looked a little closer at the corpse, obviously repulsed. "Wow, it smells terrible. The Ilserate let me have a dog once—I named him Rufus. He rolled in something in the courtyard and—"

"Focus."

"Right. I mean, I guess magic could've caused such an effect to twist the body like this. I can't really see any other explanation. But it's magic I'm unfamiliar with—maybe an older form not practiced anymore."

"Or only practiced by a scant few."

"Or that."

Ellyne could tell Nicole was both as curious and repulsed as she was, but neither wanted to linger over this dead abomination and spend any more time down in the sewer tunnel than they had to.

"So, this guy probably pissed someone off, they hurled

some kind of magic at him, and he comes down here to live in exile. That would make sense. I guess he could've attacked us for any number of reasons." She slipped her gun back into its holster at her hip. "We should get going."

It made sense, but it also didn't sit right with her. Nicole appeared more disgusted than worried, so Ellyne tried not to dwell on it.

"Which way?" she asked.

"That way." Ellyne pointed to a now flickering light in the distance.

"Took it long enough."

"Damned AI." Ellyne started in the direction of the light with Nicole at her side. She thought about asking her to dim it but, at this point, it didn't matter. If there were any more . . . oddities down here, a brighter light might give them away sooner, but they would hopefully be able to see the danger sooner also. "Maybe it's got a sense of humor . . . or it led us into this encounter intentionally."

"Why would it do that?" Nicole asked.

"What if it's not on our side?"

"Are you always this suspicious?"

"No. Sometimes I'm more suspicious."

Nicole giggled. She snatched her floating light out of the air and held it before her. "Hold out your hand."

"No." Ellyne folded her arms in front of her, feeling the leather of her jacket pull tightly on her skin.

"You really don't trust magic, do you?"

"Nicole, now isn't the time for this. We need to get to safety and figure everything out. We were just attacked by something in a sewer of all places, and we have no idea where we're headed."

"If you let me place this light in your hand, I can show you just how wondrous magic is. I can show you what you're missing."

"No thanks. I do just fine without it. Now, let's go."

Nicole sighed, acquiescing. She let the light flutter back into the air and the two walked in silence as they approached the next light.

Ellyne's frustration mounted every time the girl flaunted her magic. She was already uneasy with the amount of flocia carelessly thrown around daily, but the added irritation when someone tried to force it on her piled onto that. It would have been entirely different if it were a choice.

She got the question constantly—why she doesn't use magic? Did she feel left out not using magic when everyone else did? Didn't she know how great magic was? She'd long since stopped explaining or entertaining the notions and, instead, resorted to telling people to shove it. That worked better and the conversations were shorter.

If she didn't know better, she'd swear everyone was addicted to flocia. And maybe they were. People were odd animals.

"Oh look, we're here," Nicole said sarcastically. "And it looks just like the last place we were. Funny, that. This is the absolute worst tour ever. I'd like my money back."

That squeezed a chuckle out of Ellyne. Apparently, when Nicole wasn't being hyper and annoying, she could be funny.

"Well, wherever *here* is, it's the end of the line," Ellyne added.

This last lamp hung in a dead end. The sewer pipe disappeared into a wall but there was nowhere for them to continue following. However, the very moment Ellyne noticed metal rungs behind her, a hatch opened in the ceiling, flooding the area in a pale green light that mingled oddly with Nicole's blue illumination.

"Well, that's convenient," Nicole muttered, staring upward.

"And, hopefully, the end of all this covert sneaking around bullshit. Come on."

Ellyne went first, grabbing the cold, somewhat slimy

metal rungs imbedded into the wall. She felt the desire to take several showers after this was all over . . . whenever that would be. And possibly burn all her clothes. Hopefully, the slime on the rungs was only moss or harmless condensation.

She climbed out of the decrepit, neglected sewer and into a room that couldn't have been more opposite. The walls were smooth, metallic, and covered with blinking lights, gauges, and screens. It was as if she had emerged from a dark age and into the future—jarring and not necessarily pleasant, but at least it smelled better.

"Oh, this is cool!" Nicole exclaimed, climbing out of the hatch which promptly sealed behind her.

"I guess we're not going back that way, not that I want to." Ellyne looked around. They were at the end of a hallway. Ahead of them she saw what looked like a door, but not the variety she was used to with hinges and a doorknob. "And I guess we've only got one way to go anyway." She pointed to the end of the hall.

Nicole was still busy marveling at the hall itself. Ellyne had to admit, it was impressive. What could warrant so much technology in one place, though? It was then that she saw the numerous familiar triangle-in-circle symbols plastered all over the screens. The Keeper lived here.

And then she felt it—almost like static electricity. It began with the hair on her head and flowed through her, raising goosebumps on her arms.

"Shit," she muttered. "Damn it, not now."

She tried to relax, breathing deep with her eyes closed while the lights dimmed and flickered and several of the screens malfunctioned, distorting and blinking wildly. Even Nicole's mote of light acted erratically, swooping and bouncing off the walls.

Ellyne fell to one knee, her hands over her ears to try to shut out the noise—the deafening din created by the considerable magic in the room.

"Concentrate," she muttered under her breath. "Don't let this happen. Make it flow *through* you instead of building up inside. Don't push it out all at once. Relax. Breathe, damn it!"

"Ellyne? Are you okay?"

Ellyne shrieked, feeling the pressure within her building to unbearable levels. Nicole jumped back, surprised, worried, and afraid.

"Keep it together," she whispered. You've beaten this before and it's no different this time."

Ellyne shrieked again. Her head felt as if it would burst at any moment. It would be so easy—so simple to just expel it all at once.

And so catastrophic.

"You are not a dam. You are a pipe—a conduit."

"I don't understand," Nicole sputtered. "What's going on?"

She breathed. She concentrated. For what seemed like an eternity, Ellyne teetered on the very edge of the sharpest knife, torn between salvation and destruction.

The pressure began to decrease. She felt it leave her body as if she were exhaling for minutes all at once. Her panic subsided and, eventually, everything around her returned to normal. She spent several more minutes on one knee, recovering, while Nicole watched her nervously, still afraid but quiet. Ellyne finally stood, catching her breath and leaned against the wall.

"What . . . what happened?"

"Nothing."

"That wasn't *nothing*." Nicole's face cycled from fear to intense curiosity. "The surge of flocia I just felt was incredible —like nothing I've ever sensed before! I've never pulled that much at one time. How did—are you sick?"

"Yeah, something like that. Now drop it."

Nicole looked as if she wanted to continue pushing but

Ellyne shot her a fierce glance and the girl obviously thought better of it, but the disappointment was obvious.

"Come on." Ellyne headed to the other end of the hall. "Let's see what's on the other side."

Nicole hesitated, still quite obviously turning over in her mind every question she could formulate but asking none of them. Ellyne, now having regained most of her strength, approached the end of the hall.

The "door" appeared to be solid metal. When Ellyne got close, it slid open with a whooshing sound, revealing an octagonal room beyond.

"I guess we're expected," she muttered.

Screens, blinking lights, and switches covered literally every inch of the room, including the ceiling. Everywhere she looked Ellyne could see a different part of the city. She recognized several locations, but most of them were new to her which, considering her relatively limited travel distance in Karnascus, wasn't a surprise.

Nicole sidled up next to her, mouth agape. "Uh," she stammered, "what is this? Some kind of control room?"

In the center of the room was a high-backed office chair on wheels. It faced away from them so, if there was someone sitting in it, Ellyne couldn't see who it was.

"Hey there!" Nicole shouted and waved. Ellyne knocked her hand down and glared. "What?"

"Just . . . let me handle this, okay?"

Nicole nodded, obviously disappointed.

"Um . . . hello?"

"How is that better than what I said?"

Nicole had a point. Ellyne had no idea how to talk to an AI. Likewise, she didn't know if an AI was capable of a conversation in the first place. This, combined with the plethora of questions running through her head, annoyed her. She should be intensely curious and excited but, instead, she was irritated. Mystery and intrigue were tiresome concepts she had neither time nor patience for.

"Enough of this shit," she muttered. "Why have you brought us here?"

"To help you, of course!"

CHAPTER
SIX

"WHO THE HELL ARE YOU?" Ellyne asked, her hand resting on her holstered weapon.

The dark-skinned boy in the chair grinned and tented his fingers in front of him.

"Are you," Nicole stammered, "are you JASN?"

"Me? Yes! Er, I mean, no . . . not quite." He pushed his frizzy, abundant hair away from his face and smiled some more. "It's complicated."

"Well, uncomplicate it." Ellyne's patience was running thin.

"Okay, so, JASN is The Keeper of the city, right? Well, I'm . . . JASN's keeper, I guess." He got up and approached them, his slippers scuffing along the floor. He offered his hand to Nicole who happily shook it. Ellyne decided otherwise.

"My name's Derek," he continued. "This room is JASN's hub. I call it the cortex. From here, I can monitor everything in the city, including JASN itself."

"Wait," Ellyne interrupted. "Hold on. You, a kid, keep JASN running?"

"I mean, I'm almost twenty-three. Don't let the appearance fool you. But yes. I tweak the AI and keep him functioning."

"Him?"

"Well, yeah. I mean, I can't keep calling him 'it' can I?"

"Why you?"

"Because I built him."

Ellyne found herself speechless. She'd always assumed a team of nerdy scientists was behind something as complex as JASN. Well, nerdy scientists and talented mages—probably Kithrak. Something like a magic-based AI always seemed well beyond the capabilities of humans. Certainly, they'd never achieved artificial sentience before the Age of Magic.

"I know what you're thinking." Derek rose from his chair. "How can one stunningly handsome man be responsible for such a marvelous creation." He gestured around the room with a cheesy grin on his lips. "It's simple. JASN is based off me. I used a piece of my own brain to create him. It wasn't only a stroke of genius on my part but, and I hate to admit this, also a rather simple solution."

He was taller than Ellyne had anticipated. He also wasn't the skinny, pimply nerd she thought he'd be. In fact, he looked as though he might need to get out of that chair a little more often.

"The Keeper, here, is essentially part code, part magic, and part living construct."

Nicole gasped, seemingly awestruck as she gazed around the room, her mouth agape.

"Right? Like I said, a stroke of genius!"

"It's fantastic!" the girl mumbled, unable to pry her wide eyes away from the spectacle.

Ellyne grew irritated with the small talk. "All right, *stroke of genius.* You mind telling us why you've been helping us? Why you brought us here? And why you made us travel through the disgusting sewer tunnels?"

"That . . . is a little harder to explain. Here, let me get you guys something to sit on." Ellyne swore she sensed the slightest tingle run down her arms as he flourished his hand in the air and two plush, overstuffed chairs materialized behind them. "Please, have a seat!"

Nicole promptly reclined in hers, adjusting her skirts and getting comfortable.

"I'd rather stand," Ellyne muttered, crossing her arms.

"Suit yourself."

"Do continue. What's your interest in us?"

"Well aren't you just all business and seriousness and stuff?" Derek laughed, waving his hand again. This time, his chair scooted across the floor and scooped him up. "So, this one, here . . ." he stared at Nicole.

"Oh, I'm Nicole . . . Nicole Saranuin."

"Right. And you?"

"Ellyne."

"Ellyne . . ."

"Just Ellyne."

"Fair enough . . . *just Ellyne*. It would seem Nicole, here, has caused quite a stir as of late."

"We know."

"Do you, though? Because I'm not sure you *actually* know what you think you do."

Nicole shifted uneasily in her chair. For a moment, Ellyne wondered if she had some information she wasn't sharing, but she dismissed this notion on account of the fact the girl couldn't ever stop talking and probably sucked at keeping secrets.

"What are you getting at?"

"It's simple. JASN monitors Karnascus. I monitor JASN. What he sees, I see . . . and I see a whole lot going on. Everyone, and I do mean *everyone* is looking for her."

"Like I said, we know." Boredom was quickly replacing Ellyne's curiosity. For such an all-seeing, all-knowing vibe

Derek gave off, he didn't appear to have any information they didn't already possess.

Derek sighed and pushed a few buttons on the arm of his chair. A holographic screen sprang to life in front of him and he began moving things around and tapping on other things. Ellyne didn't understand what he was doing but it intrigued her.

"So," he began, "I know you're aware that every faction in the city is looking for you. I'd wager, in a few days, the citizens themselves will also be looking for you—if things don't go well for the Ilserate."

"You think the government will enlist everyone to find her?"

"Why wouldn't they? Such a thing probably won't sit well with the likes of the Technicians or the Teranynes, but it'll be the Kithrak who reap the biggest benefit from the situation."

"The Ilserate and the Kithrak . . . working together?"

"Is that so difficult to believe? But here's the *real* question —who's *actually* pulling the strings?"

Ellyne was about to ask how Derek knew so much but the answer was obvious. Any skepticism she had melted away quickly, given the vast resources Derek had at his disposal.

As if to further solidify himself as the expert, he flourished his hand in the air several times. Each motion produced a new image in the air until they littered the area in front of him with live, moving visuals.

"These are just a few of the patrols out and about right now, hunting for her." He pointed to Nicole. "As you no doubt already noticed, they aren't your average Ilserate night patrols."

"Yeah, we found out the hard way."

Nicole leaned forward, obviously scrutinizing each image. "How many patrols are there?"

"The actual number's irrelevant." Derek moved the

images around, organizing them in a neater fashion for better viewing.

A large screen nearby sprang to life.

"Caution: Two-hundred and fifteen traffic disruptions detected."

"Or apparently, according to JASN, the number is *very* relevant," Derek replied, the sarcasm easily detectable.

"Two-hundred and seventeen."

"We get the idea." Derek fiddled with the controls on his armrest for a moment. "Anyway, from what I've seen, normal night patrols number about twenty-five to thirty."

"And aren't normally led by a Kithrak," Ellyne added, more to herself than to the rest of the room.

"See? Now you're catching on." Derek winked awkwardly and laughed. "Normal patrols are a couple of bots and *maybe* an Ilserate mage—if there's been notable strife in the area previously. I mean, look at this particular patrol group, here."

He picked one of the hovering images and enlarged it, bringing it to the forefront. Nicole gasped and Ellyne's eyes went wide.

"Exactly. That's *three* Kithrak and ten bots in one patrol! Why would they need such a force to quell thieves or to stop a fight?"

Ellyne recognized the area immediately. "We just came from there."

"And it was an impressive encounter." His eyes turned to Nicole who suddenly looked very small and afraid. "I have to admit, I enjoyed watching you hand the patrols their own asses. But, if I'm being honest, the odds against you are overwhelming."

Nicole shrunk in her chair. Ellyne wasn't sure, but she thought the girl was crying. She knew she should do something to try and comfort her but what would that be, exactly?

"There's no way out," Nicole sobbed. "I thought I could escape the government but there's no way I can evade everyone and everything!"

"Look," Ellyne said, turning to Nicole, "there's always a way out. Things aren't *that* bad."

"Well, actually," Derek interrupted, "they are."

Ellyne glared at him so hard she would've shot lasers out of her eyes if she could have. Part of her wanted to put a bullet in him—somewhere nonlethal but painful. He quickly backed off and diverted his attention to the many live images playing out in front of him as if something important just happened.

Which left Ellyne with absolutely no idea how to comfort Nicole. The truth was, Derek was largely correct—Nicole couldn't hide forever. Sure, if she were hiding from just the Technicians or Teranynes or even just the Ilserate it probably would've been relatively simple, but this was ridiculous. Soon, everyone in Karnascus would know Nicole's face and would be out looking for her.

It looked bleak, and Ellyne was beginning to wonder if it was all worth it. So, Nicole was powerful—big deal. Life would go on. Life always went on. The desires of one faction weren't monumental in the big picture and, on the plus side, it may not be such a bad thing if the factions all decided to duke it out with one another. In fact, that may have some benefits.

Derek cleared his throat. When nobody responded, he awkwardly did it again until Ellyne finally acknowledged him.

"The Ilserate want their property back—that much is obvious. But why were you even there in the first place?"

Nicole sniffed, wiping her eyes again. Her breathing was rapid and shallow, on the verge of hyperventilation. It was several minutes before she calmed down enough to do anything but sob.

"I've lived within the Ilserate since I could remember. They basically raised me."

"But *why*?"

"They think I'm the secret to understanding flocia and magic. They realize that, yes, humans can use magic, but no one truly understands it. The Kithrak have always been in charge, feeding us magic but only just enough to keep us using it without truly gaining knowledge about it."

"Sounds like the government wishes to wrest control from the Kithrak, doesn't it?" Derek pondered, still watching the many images playing out in front of them.

Ellyne wandered about the room, still eschewing the chair Derek had provided. "According to Nicole, she's the most powerful magic-user ever to have lived."

"I think she's right," Derek replied. "I've never seen even a Kithrak handle flocia so easily and fluidly as she does. I can understand why they'd like to capture her."

Nicole shot Derek an accusing and somewhat puzzled look.

"I've been . . . observing you since you escaped," he said, nervously.

"Well, that's certainly not creepy." Nicole stated sarcastically. She sounded mostly calm, now, but she looked fragile— as if she would burst out in tears again at any moment. Ellyne found the contrast unsettling.

"Maybe," Derek chuckled. "But, without my help, where would you be? Your escape was pretty sloppy, and you were lucky. But without my help—and JASN's—you wouldn't have made it far."

"Okay, then, why would you help me? What are you after?"

Both were poignant questions Ellyne herself was going to ask.

"Because I have no love for the Ilserate. See, everyone thinks The Keeper is just some automaton that keeps Karnascus operating smoothly and, while that is indeed his main function, only a few individuals know about me. While JASN keeps the city running smoothly, I keep JASN running smoothly. What JASN sees, I can see, and I've seen some pretty shady things. JASN won't judge, but I'd be happy to."

Ellyne held up her hand to interrupt. "Wait," she said. "You're going out of your way to help one individual? To what? Get back at someone?"

"You could say that, yes."

She folded her arms across her chest and rolled her eyes. "No. No way. There's more to this. Spill it."

"Okay, okay," Derek giggled. "You're really good, you know that?"

Ellyne smirked briefly. "It's what I'm told."

"So, yeah, there is indeed a bit more to it that I was going to explain anyway. Listen, I definitely believe in helping people so that much is true. However, the Kithrak have something they call the *Skarash Ascalore* prophecy—"

"Wait," Ellyne laughed. "A prophecy?"

"I sense skepticism in your voice. You don't believe in prophecies?"

"Only the desperate and the foolish believe in prophecies," she scoffed.

"Well," Derek continued, "you may be right, but the Kithrak *do* believe this prophecy. They believe there is one who will command unbelievable power over them. This one individual will rise against them, overthrow them, ruin their civilization, and free their people from enslavement."

The room was silent as Ellyne considered Derek's words. Nicole appeared to be doing the same.

"Enslavement?" Ellyne asked.

"Obviously," he continued, "the Kithrak think—"

"They think that individual is me." Nicole stood and fidgeted, tugging at the hem of one of her skirts. "I guess that sort of explains a lot."

Ellyne gazed at the many images floating in front of Derek. He really *could* keep an eye on the entire city. That gave them a monumental advantage. "And if all the other factions know this . . . then they would obviously each like to get their hands on her."

"The Kithrak most of all, obviously." Derek zoomed in on another patrol—one passing by the sewer entrance they'd escaped through. "Though the Kithrak probably prefer to simply kill you, of course. Maybe study you, then kill you."

Nicole shuddered as the color ran out of her face. "You said enslavement. I don't understand, though. Nobody here in Karnascus is a slave."

"Aren't they, though?" Derek typed something in on a holographic keyboard and an image of a T-Helm appeared. "This—the Taranom or T-Helm or whatever you want to call it. Is this not a tool of enslavement?"

"But no one's *forced* to use a T-Helm. They can simply go without using magic."

"They really can't, though. Magic is everywhere and flocia powers everything. People are *addicted* to magic, unable to live without it. And, by accordance, they must use a T-Helm to repay their debts to the Kithrak. Surely you see this."

"And if they don't," Ellyne added, "then the Kithrak block them from flocia, right?"

"Exactly. No T-Helm, no magic. People are slaves to flocia and, by extension, slaves to the Kithrak. But nobody seems to care because it's far better than going without magic."

"Are we even sure the factions know about this prophecy?"

"I doubt they do, Ellyne. It wouldn't surprise me if they simply knew of Nicole's power and wanted her for their own petty reasons. If the Ilserate knew, they probably wouldn't be cooperating with the Kithrak anymore."

"Unless they had no choice in the matter."

"Now you're catching on. Which would mean—"

"Which would mean the Ilserate and the Kithrak are working together!" Nicole was excited about her revelation, which Ellyne found preferable to her being a tear-soaked mess.

"Or the Kithrak control the Ilserate from the inside," Ellyne suggested. She wished she could share Nicole's enthusiasm. The truth was, this was getting messier by the minute.

"Exactly!" Even Derek seemed excited. "There are no taps into the government buildings so JASN isn't allowed in. I've been working to sneak his feed inside so I can get a glimpse of what goes on but, I have to say, their magical protections are exquisite—far better than my meager capabilities."

"Meager?" Nicole gestured around the room. "You built all this! How can you call this meager?"

"I built JASN, yes, but there is far more code than conjuring involved with it. The Ilserate is just the opposite. It's a hardened structure, but I haven't given up. With enough time, I can probably find a way to poke a hole in their security. It's just going to take a while."

"Then I suggest you keep trying," Ellyne agreed. "That could make the difference."

"Agreed. But for now, we need to get you two somewhere safe."

"What about here?" Nicole asked.

"Definitely not. I'm already putting myself in danger by bringing you here in the first place. We need to find an isolated spot for you two to lay low for a while until we can figure something out."

"We had a good spot, actually."

"Where? The bar? Hardly. Look here."

Derek brought up a live image of Victor's. The bar itself was as they had left it—dark and empty—but as Derek zoomed out across the street, the image showed three patrols in the area, loitering in the vicinity—obviously waiting for something.

"They know she's with you and they know where you like to hang out."

"Well, shit," Ellyne spat. "I was hoping they wouldn't figure that out. This complicates things."

"I don't think there's anywhere safe inside the city."

"Are you suggesting hiding out in a farmhouse somewhere remote or maybe a cave?" Ellyne laughed but quickly realized the gravity of the situation when Derek didn't laugh along with her.

"Or somewhere else. Cerilis is nearby and Ilserate presence there is minimal, I hear. Maybe you can ally with the Teranyne Order or the Techno Guild—slowly build their trust and then use them against—"

"Against the world?"

"Well, yeah, that does sound difficult. But what other options are there?"

"Find us somewhere relatively safe here in Karnascus. We'll figure out what to do from there." *Or maybe I can just drop Nicole off and wash my hands of the whole damned thing. This has gotten out of control.*

"Okay, give me a few minutes. I'll find a safe house for you guys."

Derek went to work, fingers furiously typing on the holographic keyboard, while Ellyne tried to formulate even the beginning of a plan.

Ellyne tried to disguise the worry on her face. "Don't worry, Nicole, we'll figure something out."

"This is like that one show with the detective—her name is Loren Winstead—who always gets herself into the worst situations and comes up with the most ridiculous solutions that somehow always work out and she solves the case. You ever see that show? It's called 'Parts Unknown'! I watched it all the time growing up."

Neither Ellyne nor Derek responded.

"Oh, wait, I guess you probably haven't seen it since you don't watch screens at all. Aren't you bored all the time without stuff to do?"

Ellyne heard her but Nicole's voice was more like a bird chirping in the distance—something she could easily ignore while she tried to think. Easy to ignore, yes, but she still wished the girl would zip it and let her think.

It reminded her of battle—the constant gunshots, explosions, and magic sounds that, while background noise, never ceased. It was all something she'd learned to tune out but that didn't mean it still wasn't a distracting nuisance.

She remembered all too vividly the Battle of Grand Hill. At least, that's what they called it once it was all over—once it was in the history books. It was little more than a group of mages intent on asserting their magical dominance and holing up in a small town atop a plateau.

She recalled her unit fighting uphill with magic and guns and sometimes even rocks and sticks, gaining ground inch by inch over the span of days and weeks. Gunfire and spells relentlessly polluted her ears day and night, sometimes with no intended target. Back then, people were drunk with magical power and though magic gave them the right to do what they wanted. Some people still believed this notion.

In the end, it had been Ellyne who resolved the conflict. In the end, it was *always* Ellyne, charging forward with her revolver and her blade, puncturing enemies with bullets and tearing into them with cold steel. She was the best at her bloody craft.

"I think I've found an acceptable location," Derek said, bringing Ellyne back into the here and now. "It's not a fancy hotel, but I don't think anyone will come looking for you for a while. It should give us some time."

"Great," Ellyne replied, trying to leave her thoughts behind. "So where is it?"

"Well . . . that's the downside. It's across town."

Ellyne gazed at the image Derek was currently scrutinizing. The apartment building looked shockingly nice—almost new, even. The fact that it was such a long distance was indeed a problem, though. Traversing the city now, with the enhanced patrols, was more dangerous than before.

"Looks okay to me."

"It's been abandoned for a while . . . on account of the residents all being . . . dead."

"Wait, what?" Nicole shouted. "What do you mean, dead?"

"Oh, yeah, I guess that's the other downside. As you can see, it's only a complex of sixteen apartments and the building is pristine but the reason for that is because nobody's lived in it for a while. There was a series of murders."

"How many murders?" Nicole asked quietly, sounding almost as if she didn't want to know.

"Wait," Ellyne interrupted. "Let me guess . . . sixteen murders."

"The lady wins the prize."

Nicole looked ill, staring at the image of the building. "That's horrible!"

"No argument, here." Derek tapped on some holographic buttons and dragged three images around. "Take a closer look."

One image slowly rotated, revealing what appeared to be a simple two-story building with trees and grass on all sides. In fact, it appeared to be the only building on the block.

Ellyne approached the image and watched it closely. "Two floors and, what, eight apartments per floor?"

"Appears that way."

"Does JASN have any vision points nearby? I'd really prefer a live look."

"Oh, this *is* a live look, actually." The image zoomed out from above, revealing the terrain around the area. Ellyne believed she was looking at the edge of the city.

"What? How?"

"Oh, it's a new system I've been working on. JASN now

has little mini-JASNs. Well, not really, but that's what I call them."

"Your point?"

"Oh, they're drones. JASN uses them to view Karnascus from above or wherever. I convinced one of the mages in the Ilserate to develop an invisibility charm. It's not much more than a light-refraction spell and it's not perfect, but it gets the job done—mostly."

"Mostly?" Nicole perked up, apparently intrigued by magic-talk.

"Right—mostly. See, if they move too fast, they shimmer . . . and sometimes they just shimmer for no reason. Anyway, several people have reported seeing ghosts. Fortunately, their concerns are promptly dismissed."

Ellyne laughed. In the Age of Magic, when virtually anything is possible through flocia, she found it amusing that people still resorted to their superstitions.

Nicole laughed along with her. "You know, given enough time, I could most likely develop a more effective charm. In fact, I could probably boost The Keeper's capabilities by—"

"If we were staying to chit-chat, Nicole, that'd be fantastic. But we're on the run, remember? If we stay here, it's only a matter of time before someone stumbles upon us," Ellyne reminded her quickly. She was antsy to get moving.

"Oh yeah, right." The smile disappeared from her lips, replaced with concern and fear. Not the reaction Ellyne had hoped for, but it didn't much matter. "So, we're really going to stay in this . . . murder house?"

"Looks more like a murder shack," Derek laughed.

Neither Nicole nor Ellyne saw the humor.

"Tough room." He sighed, punching a few more holographic buttons and frowning. "Look, it's the best I got right now. None of the factions go anywhere near it, so it's off their radar. They won't be bothering you. At least not for a while. What more can you ask for?"

Ellyne looked at Nicole whose face showed signs of another sobbing fit.

Perfect. I'm able to give a morale-boosting speech to a bunch of leatherneck idiots about to face unimaginable odds, but I have no idea what to say to a . . . how old did she say she was?

"We'll make it work." She nodded to Derek who nodded back. "Nicole, I'm sure it's not that bad. We'll be safe."

"I've programmed your route into The Keeper. He'll direct you while I keep watch and make any changes to avoid unexpected . . . complications."

Ellyne turned to a still worried Nicole and, with great effort, tempered her voice to a more soothing demeanor. "Listen, Nicole. We'll be safe. Besides, you're the most powerful mage on the planet. What have we got to fear?" She winked and grinned.

"Oh," Derek said, holding up a hand to get their attention. "About that . . . I wouldn't go throwing around flocia too much."

"Why's that?" Ellyne groaned, bracing herself for the inevitable disappointing information she knew she was going to receive.

"Well, you see, the Ilserate have ways of monitoring powerful flocia fluctuations. If Nicole here goes and decimates half a city block, they'll know. Then they'll come after you. They sort of transmitted this information on unsecured channels." Derek looked relatively pleased.

"What the shit?" Ellyne balled her fists. She really wished there was something nearby she could destroy that wasn't expensive. "What's the purpose of that?"

"Only one purpose—"

"To find me, right?" Nicole asked.

"Now the *other* lady wins the prize."

Ellyne's urge to destroy something grew but, while an inner fire raged, her exterior was stoic and calm as always. "Let's get out of here before we get any more bad news."

Nicole nodded.

Derek opened a door on the other side of the room and motioned for them to enter. "Be careful out there," he said. "I'm beginning to think there's more at work here than we know."

"And there's the added bad news," Ellyne muttered.

"I'm just trying to help."

"I know, and I thank you for your . . . and *his* assistance." She gestured around them at the buttons, lights, and screens.

"You hear that, buddy? I think she likes you!"

A simple smiley face appeared on all the screens, blinked three times, then disappeared as everything returned to normal.

"I think he likes you, too," Derek whispered. "Now get going!"

Ellyne and Nicole hurried through the door which closed behind them, leaving them in a dimly lit hallway with a few, tiny blinking lights.

Ellyne immediately felt very much alone.

THE SUN WOULDN'T BE UP for another few hours. This gave them plenty of time to use the cover of night before people congested the sidewalks and vehicles filled the streets. If they were lucky, they'd arrive at the murder shack just before sunup.

Murder shack. At first, Ellyne hated the term but she almost found it funny now. Regardless, she really needed to stop referring to it as such. Nicole was already on edge, scared of her own shadow, and there was no need to make things worse.

But this was all new territory, wasn't it? This wasn't at all like the battles in which she'd motivated her companions and inspired them to fight. Violence and bloodshed aside, she almost preferred a battle to skulking around the city at night, hoping to avoid their pursuers. At least, in a war, there were fewer tears.

"Let's get moving," Ellyne whispered as they spilled out onto the street. The doorway behind them shimmered, distorting the air around it until it solidified into smooth stone.

Nicole nodded and they hurried down the street, passing

a small group of people loitering outside a bar. It certainly wasn't against the law to be out at night and several businesses thrived after dark, but most people had reasons to stay indoors.

Taranoms were reason number one, of course. T-Helms were most conveniently used at the end of the day and often left people feeling drained as Ellyne understood it. Most people settled in for the night at that point.

Another reason was the rumors of patrols concocting stories and inventing reasons to arrest people, and she could easily envision that happening. But she also believed people were not to be trusted with magic. She'd fought for years to establish security and ultimately lost, and now she was forced into an existence where every simpleton could conjure up a fireball at will.

It was an existence where the law was just as dangerous as lawlessness. If you found yourself caught in between the two you were no better off than if you were on either side. Fighting fire with fire always resulted in more fire. It was a damn shame nobody realized this.

And that was the final reason not to be roaming the city at night. People and magic were both dangerous, and a largely deserted city at night became a playground for all kinds of ugly things.

"It would be so much easier if I could just teleport us."

"Over my dead body." Ellyne kept her gaze up and around them. She caught sight of a patrol further down the street, but it turned a corner and disappeared. "Besides, the Ilserate would find us."

"It's so frustrating!" Nicole balled her fists and growled. "What good is magic if I'm not allowed to use it?"

"Welcome to my world," Ellyne muttered to herself.

It had to be scary for her—being so vulnerable. Knowing how powerful she was but being unable to utilize that power. Ellyne could see it written all over the girl's face. To be so dependent on something and then to have it yanked away . . . she wondered if that's how it felt to those who neglected their T-Helms and were cut off from flocia until they paid their dues.

Ellyne had never used magic so she wasn't sure she could relate fully. Maybe if squama juice suddenly disappeared, she'd understand more.

The thought brought a tiny grin to her lips. She shouldn't have found it amusing—that the only thing she was attached to was a good, strong drink—but it made her feel secure, the fact nobody could take anything important away from her.

Several individuals had tried. All of them were dead, save one, and Marik Kalamoor's time would come. She owed him that much.

She once again ran her tongue over the crude metal replacement for her lower right molar and resisted the urge to rub the scar on her left shoulder. Both were unfortunate reminders of his treachery. Unfortunate yes, but also motivation.

Their paths would cross again.

They wound through city streets and alleys, keeping to the darker places and watching for The Keeper's telltale signs of aid. JASN held true, directing them through safe areas and warning them of danger. Neither the AI nor Derek were perfect, however, and there were several times they nearly stumbled into an unsavory situation, or a patrol materialized in a nearby spot that was a little too close.

It occurred to Ellyne that the Ilserate, if they so desired, could probably tap into JASN's systems. Or maybe they couldn't. Or maybe they thought they already had? She wondered how good Derek really was and how long he could keep up his subterfuge.

The very thought chilled her blood. If the Ilserate found out, what would happen to Derek? What would happen to her and Nicole? Hopefully, he was as smart and sneaky as he thought he was. Nobody could afford to let the Ilserate have complete control over The Keeper.

For that matter, what if Derek decided to abuse his power? Essentially, that's what he was doing by helping them, but what if he turned against them? What if he already was? He'd be a powerful enemy.

Are you ever going to fully trust anyone?

"So, this is what it's like," Nicole grumbled.

"What what's like?"

"What it's like to, you know, be you."

"What're you on about now?"

"You don't use magic. I *can't* use magic. This is what it's like to be you."

"You have no idea what it's like to be me."

"Tell me."

Ellyne grabbed Nicole and dragged her into a recessed doorway. This was definitely neither the place nor the time to discuss this, but she knew the girl wouldn't shut up unless something was said.

"Listen, I live my life perfectly fine without magic. Your situation and mine are nothing alike. You've come to rely too much on magic and, when it's pulled out from under you, you crumble. I, on the other hand, have *never* relied on magic and can live a perfectly happy life without it."

Nicole was speechless. She obviously hadn't expected a diatribe of this magnitude.

"You act as if, by not being able to use magic, you lead a doomed existence. This is precisely the problem! Everyone relies too much on magic and they lose their shit when it gets taken away whereas I exist with or without it. I am tethered to nothing. So, no, our situations are entirely different."

"So, you're happy then? Without magic?"

"I've never used magic. I've never known any other way so, yes, I'm perfectly content. And I sure as hell don't want to wear one of those ugly T-Helms."

The look on Nicole's face showed a pensive introspection, as if Ellyne had truly given her something to ponder. Hopefully it would keep her quiet for a while. They still had a lot of ground to cover and no real plan of action once they got there.

Ellyne's mind never stopped working. It always considered their options and struggled to come up with their next course of action. Despite its constant hard work, it had not yet given her any insight as to where they should go or what they should do once they got to their safe house.

Sure, they could lay low for a couple of days, maybe a week at most, but what then? Maybe Derek would be able to help but she couldn't count on him. She didn't *want* to count on him. She couldn't deny his aid was incredibly helpful, but she also felt somewhat vulnerable relying on it.

She could be asleep, relaxing in her own bed right now but instead, here she was, traipsing about the city at night, dodging patrols so they could go hide out in a murder shack, cowering like vermin in the dark, hoping nobody turned on the lights.

"This has been fun and all, but let's keep moving."

Nicole nodded, apparently satisfied with the conversation they'd just had. Ellyne hoped she wouldn't bring it up again, but she had no illusions.

That wasn't to say Ellyne, on occasion, wasn't curious what it was like to use magic for everything. The difference was probably night and day. She was curious, yes, but she had no desire to live that lifestyle. Besides, there were very specific, insurmountable obstacles that stood in the way of such a thing—not the least of which was the fact she didn't own a T-Helm and had no plans to.

The sun cast its first rays upon the city and, as if they had been waiting for this very thing, people appeared on the sidewalks, venturing outside their homes and going about whatever business they had. She wasn't familiar with this section of the city, but she could've probably predicted everyone's patterns back around her apartment. She was a dedicated people-watcher which, now that she thought about it, could be construed as a little creepy.

With the emergence of all the people from their slumbers, the patrols would probably lessen or disappear. This meant they could make the rest of their trek without being too concerned if ordinary citizens weren't yet on alert. But she had no illusions—they were still wanted by the Ilserate, and each faction was still hunting for them.

The only advantage now was the fact they could blend in a lot easier with the crowds. Until those crowds were also looking for them. She assumed this would happen eventually, which was why they couldn't simply be out and about during the day.

"Is that it?" Nicole pointed ahead of them.

"Looks like it."

Derek had used The Keeper's drones to show them the general lay of the land, but he hadn't zoomed out enough to give them the full picture. Ellyne felt more apprehension with each step that brought her closer.

The ten-foot-high fence surrounding the area ended in coiled barbed wire at the top. As they approached, she could see the various warning and caution signs hung about the area. They varied from "crime scene" to "biohazard." A couple even read "flocia leak" which gave Ellyne pause. Was such a thing a possibility? Could flocia leak into the environment somehow without being used for magical effect? It wasn't something she'd ever considered, nor was it something she wanted to think about.

Everything on the other side of the fence appeared normal. The apartment building was still in pristine condition. The various landscaping was a bit out of control due to neglect, but the plants in the area appeared to thrive, overgrowing everything.

But it was readily apparent that nobody lived here and hadn't for quite some time.

"Let's go around back." Ellyne pointed along the fence. "Hopefully we can avoid attracting any unwanted attention."

Nicole nodded and followed her lead. Ellyne was disappointed to find no breaches in the fence, so the various warning signs must have adequately deterred people. Either that or everyone already knew the murder shack's bad reputation.

And they were going to spend the night in it.

"Hey, look," Nicole said. "Someone's thrown some things over the barbed wire and piled up a bit of garbage."

"To get in? Why would anyone do that?"

"Free place to live? Or free stuff I guess."

Maybe the signs weren't doing their jobs after all.

"Looks like we might be sharing the place with someone else." Ellyne inspected the situation. A tattered blanket and some twisted sheet metal had both been placed over the barbed wire atop the fence. The pile at the base was little more than a few bricks and some trash. It was obvious someone wanted in, but the real question was whether they made it.

"So, how do we do this?"

"I guess, ordinarily, you'd just magic yourself to the other side."

"Ordinarily, I wouldn't be attempting to break into a murder shack in the first place."

Ellyne laughed. Nicole joined her.

"Fair point. I don't have anything to cut through this fence, and I doubt that's a great idea in the first place. Someone else was kind enough to do most of the work for us, so I guess we climb."

To her surprise, Nicole didn't argue. Instead, she started climbing.

"Looks like you've climbed fences before," Ellyne joked, beginning her own ascent.

"Yeah, well, I did lots of things while stuck in the Ilserate. I can't say my clothes are helping, though."

"Why *are* you wearing those clothes, anyway?"

"I like them. They're comfortable but not practical, I guess. But I also was forced to wear what the government provided. And since I was always paraded around like an asset, I guess they always wanted me to look my best."

"The Ilserate controlled even what you wore? That's ridiculous."

"Looking back on it—just during the short time I've been free of them—yeah, it seems ridiculous now. But, before I escaped, it felt normal. It was all I knew."

"I hate them more every time you talk about them."

Once they reached the top of the fence, Ellyne moved to climb over the top, but Nicole cut her off and effortlessly made the transition. "Slowpoke," she laughed as she hopped to the ground.

Ellyne landed beside her, scowling. This wasn't supposed to be a fun playground romp.

Walking among the trees and through what used to be a small garden was a pleasant change from the city streets. Sure, it looked and felt different, but it also *smelled* different. Every fragrance sent beautiful messages that painted a picture of flowers and grass and slightly crisper air. She could get used to this.

They found a sidewalk underneath leaves, dirt, and grass and followed it through an overgrown ornamental archway, eventually approaching a door at the rear of the building. To Ellyne's surprise, it was unlocked.

Convenient, yet worrisome.

"Before we go in," she whispered, "I need you to stick close to me. We're going to have to sweep the area for any potential hostiles."

"What if we find some . . . you know, hostiles?"

"We'll figure that out if it. happens Just stick with me and don't use your magic unless it's absolutely necessary, okay?"

Nicole nodded and they entered the building.

Once they were safe, Nicole laid back on the couch and slipped off her boots. "I don't remember how long it's been since I got some sleep, but I think I'm way past due."

"You and me both." Ellyne reclined in the plush chair. It was brown with an ugly striped pattern, but nothing mattered except it was relatively comfortable. She'd certainly had worse sleeping accommodations in the past.

"I wish these were more than one-room apartments. I would've liked at least a simple bed."

"I think we're just lucky to be alone. I'm not in the mood for social obligations. I guess the murder shack's not so bad. Whatever happened here, it appears things were taken care of."

"The basement was creepy, though."

"It's a basement with basement things like old junk and locked doors."

Nicole yawned. "I guess so."

"Never been in a basement before?"

"Now that you mention it . . . no. I mean, not like that one. It was filthy."

"Stick with me and you'll see all the fancy sights."

Nicole snorted and mumbled something that sounded like gibberish to Ellyne who surmised she was nearly asleep already.

It had to be scary for her—to not be able to use her magic. These were thoughts Ellyne had difficulty grasping but was beginning to understand a little more. Magic was Nicole's only protection. When taken away, she must have felt exposed. Whereas Ellyne didn't even need her gun or blade to protect herself, Nicole was damn near helpless without magic.

While she felt she should stay awake and keep watch for danger, her eyelids sagged under their own weight, and she felt her body relax. Sleep would overtake her whether she welcomed it or not.

When she opened her eyes again, the room was dark. Her left shoulder popped as she yawned and stretched, scanning the room briefly before remembering where she was. There was just enough ambient city light combined with dim moonlight to see the couch was empty.

"Nicole? Hey, Nicole?"

When there was no answer, she got up. Once she realized she was alone, Ellyne felt irritation set in. Maybe Nicole went to another apartment to be alone.

She paced a moment, wondering if she should try to find the girl. This could all be nothing or it could be something . . . something bad. Maybe this was the perfect opportunity for Ellyne to disappear and wash her hands of this whole mess.

"I'll be damned if I'm playing babysitter," she grumbled, leaning against the window. "Son of a bitch, what are you doing outside?"

She turned from the window, dashed into the hallway, and headed down the stairs, swearing under her breath. How foolish could this girl be to stand outside, wide open and vulnerable? If *anyone* saw her, they were screwed.

She hurried through the small lobby, out the front doors of the building and crossed the garden, finally stopping next to Nicole.

"What are you doing out here?" she growled, grabbing Nicole's arm. "It's not a good idea to be just standing out here in the open. If a patrol came by and saw you—"

"There haven't been any patrols—not in this area." She gazed at the sky, never taking her eyes off the stars. "I woke up a couple of hours ago. I watched, but didn't see any patrols so, after a while I got bored, and I thought it would be okay to get some fresh air. And it's beautiful out here. I've never seen such a lovely moon."

"It was reckless. If there *had* been a patrol, and they had snatched you, I wouldn't have known what happened."

Ellyne breathed in deeply and tried to calm herself, reveling in the fresh scent of the night air. She had to admit, it was nice to experience such tranquility—a stark contrast from her apartment in the city where she couldn't see most of the stars and the air smelled like other people. "I don't care what —wait, no patrols? Really?"

"Nope. Not a one."

"That's odd." Ellyne looked up. Though the city lights still polluted the view, there were fewer in this area, so more stars were visible. "I wonder why. Probably because nobody comes around this place. Not that I blame them."

"It's peaceful. I could get used to it."

"So, the murder shack's not so bad anymore, is it?"

"No," Nicole giggled, "it's not too bad. But we can't stay here forever."

"No, we can't."

Nicole leisurely paced, kicking at the dirt and inspecting something she picked up off the ground. Ellyne began to wonder if she'd ever actually been outside among nature before. The city didn't lend itself to many plants but there were certain areas that held parks or, at the very least, a tree or two—maybe a bush as well. The government compounds, though . . . she wouldn't be surprised if the only plants they had were plastic.

"That's called a rock," she snickered.

"Oh really?" Nicole replied sarcastically. "I had no idea."

The stars were truly pretty and, without much of a moon to spoil them, they twinkled even brighter. Ellyne herself rarely paid attention to their radiant beauty, largely taking them for granted. But it was also a luxury to be able to look up when you were accustomed to always looking around you.

"I've been thinking . . . maybe we can leave the city altogether—find a smaller town. At the very least, we could establish a new life for you, and I could possibly return to Karnascus once you're settled. Maybe the Ilserate wouldn't come looking for you."

Nicole said nothing. Ellyne sighed. This was a difficult conversation to have, but she couldn't be expected to take care of Nicole forever. With Nicole's magical ability, surely she could survive on her own.

Unless, of course, the Ilserate found her . . . or the Kithrak.

"Damn it," she swore under her breath, turning around. "Look, I'm sorry, it's just—"

Nicole had her back to Ellyne and said nothing, simply staring ahead. Ellyne knew the idea wouldn't go over well—she figured Nicole would be hurt but what was she to do? Her life had no room for anyone else, and certainly not for the most powerful—and wanted—mage on the planet.

"I promise we'll figure it all out," she continued. "You'll be safe."

Nicole remained silent. Just about the time Ellyne was about to stomp up to her and tell her to grow up, she slowly backed up, still looking ahead of her.

"Nicole, what is it? What's wrong?"

The girl said nothing, but stopped next to Ellyne, slowly raised her finger and pointed.

Ellyne's eyes followed her finger and stopped on a dark shape crouching next to a bush nearby. "Shit," she whispered.

"What is it?"

"I don't know, but it's not alone."

Ellyne pointed out two more humanoid-shaped shadows in the distance. They didn't move like normal people. In fact, they seemed more like . . . that weird creature she killed in the sewers beneath Karnascus.

"Where are they coming from?"

"I don't know, but they're between us and the apartments."

"Do you think we can get past them?"

As if to answer her question, one of the figures paused and growled. Its yellow eyes possessed a dull glow, and they were fixed on Ellyne and Nicole.

"I'm betting on no."

CHAPTER EIGHT

ELLYNE'S REVOLVER was in her hand the moment the shadowy creature advanced. In less than a second after, her shot shattered the night's silence and it lay dead with a bullet in its head.

Two more came at them from the same direction, lumbering like animals on all fours and making savage, guttural noises as they approached.

Two more shots rang out and they both fell. Ellyne pulled the gun's hammer back and watched for more. The hammer pulled itself back automatically, but she sometimes enjoyed the satisfaction of cocking it herself.

"Now's our chance. Go!"

Nicole sprinted across the grass toward the apartment building and Ellyne followed behind to cover her. She heard screams from every direction.

"I think we've found the cause of the murders!" she shouted. "No wonder they blocked off the area!"

"What do we do?"

"Just get inside! We'll figure it out from there."

"We probably should have heeded the warning signs."

"You're not wrong, but they never mentioned hungry mutants."

One of the creatures lunged at Ellyne. She simultaneously slid underneath and put a bullet in it, ending up on her feet and never missing a stride.

Something collided with her from the side and knocked her down. She rolled across the grass several times and jumped to her feet, gun still in her hand.

There were four of them, now, crawling along the ground between Ellyne and Nicole. Saliva dripped from protruding tusk-like fangs as they approached.

"Keep running! I've got this!"

She fired off three rapid shots, dropping one target with each bullet. The fourth shot, however, was an empty click. She pulled the trigger again and received another empty click for her efforts.

"Damn. Never reloaded after the sewer. No time now!"

It lunged and Ellyne dodged, barely avoiding its claws. Claws! It had claws!

"What the hell are you things?"

She holstered her weapon and drew her blade. Barely larger than a dagger, she knew it wasn't enough to protect her as several more drooling monsters closed in.

She counted five of them. Certainly not the best odds but she'd squared off against five men before. Then again, these weren't men. Well, not anymore.

She pressed a button on the dagger's crossguard, felt a familiar pop from within as the springs activated, and watched the blade extend out to an additional three feet.

"Now that's more like it."

Ellyne skewered one beast as it lunged for her, dropping it and removing her blade. She slashed at another, but it dodged backward. There were six of them, now, on all sides of her. She watched Nicole barely get through the front door and slam it behind her as two of them clawed to get in, desperately ramming themselves into the door and scratching at it.

"Great. She's safe. Now what?" She wondered if Nicole would risk her safety and use magic to save her even though she told her not to. At this point, she wasn't sure if she'd be mad.

Her sword bit into the flesh of the nearest creature. It wailed and snarled through clenched teeth as blood dripped from the wound.

They all still appeared largely human but parts of them were twisted and vile. And while they acted savage and mindless, they displayed a modicum of intelligence and restraint—even some basic strategy. They must have once been human, but what happened to them?

Ellyne's stomach turned and she trembled as sweat beads appeared on her forehead. She struggled to hold her sword and remain upright as she desperately lashed out with her blade, missing one monster but clumsily impaling another.

The creature bellowed before choking on its own blood and falling on her sword. Too weak to pull it free, she left it stuck in the creature's corpse and stumbled toward the building.

"What's happening?" she gurgled. "Did one of them wound me? Why do I feel so weak? Are they venomous?"

One of them tackled her from behind. Ellyne rolled onto her back and meekly wrestled with it as it clawed at her and snapped its jaws. The others quickly closed in as she struggled to wrest herself free of her attacker's clutches. Panic set in as she thrashed and screamed.

Her right arm tingled, feeling warm as if she had slept on it wrong. That warmth soon intensified, becoming an almost painfully hot sensation. She screamed, squirming furiously against her attacker until she found her opportunity.

With a thunderous crack, her fist and the creature collided, collapsing its skull, sending it sailing through the air and creating a shockwave that flung the others in all directions. It shook the trees and flattened smaller shrubs in the immediate area.

Ellyne's mind cleared and her muscles strengthened as the nausea subsided. She grabbed her sword and hurried to the building.

"Nicole! Open up!" she yelled, pounding her fist on the metal door.

The door flew open. Ellyne slipped inside and pressed herself against it as Nicole locked it. Then she sank to her knees to catch her breath.

"I thought you were dead!"

Ellyne gasped for air. She felt both exhausted and energized at the same time. "I thought I was, too."

"What do we do now?"

With shaky fingers, Ellyne drew her revolver, kicked out the cylinder, and removed the cartridge. She replaced it with a fully loaded cartridge and slapped the cylinder back into place.

"That's the first thing we do."

"Okay, then what?"

"Then we pass out."

"Hey! Hey, Ellyne, wake up. Oh good. I was so worried you were hurt. You passed out and I thought maybe you were dying or dead or something, but you weren't bleeding so I just let you sleep but, wow, you slept for quite a while!"

When Ellyne opened her eyes, the first thing she saw was Nicole's face, positioned over her and grinning like a fool. She blinked several times to try and focus as Nicole's voice faded in and out.

"Stop," she stammered weakly.

"Stop what? I'll gladly stop whatever you want just tell me!"

"Talking . . . stop talking."

Ellyne lay on the floor for several minutes as her

strength gradually returned. When she was able to move, she sat up gingerly and propped herself against the door, noticing the beams of sun currently shining through the windows.

She closed her eyes and rested her head against the door with a dull clunk. "How long?"

"How long what?"

"How long was I out?"

"Uh, I'm not sure, but I think it's just about ten o'clock."

Ellyne sighed. "That didn't go as I'd planned."

Nicole sat beside her. It was painfully apparent how nervous and frightened she was, but also how relieved and thankful. "I thought you might not wake up. After what you did out there—"

"After what I did?" In an instant, it all came back to her, memories flooding back like a dam bursting, each one vying for her attention. "Shit. What *did* I do?"

"I was going to ask the same thing."

"And I was hoping you would know. It was like magic, which would be . . . impossible."

Nicole's smile disappeared and her face became that of unyielding, unfeeling stone. "That was no magic I've ever seen," she said. "Never have I witnessed something so raw and untamed. No, that was absolutely not magic." She looked almost frightened.

"Not magic? Then you tell me—what the hell was it? Because, last time I checked, I didn't have the ability to send out skull-shattering shockwaves from my fist. I feel ill just thinking about having used magic. I feel gross."

That was the truth. Until now, she'd never used magic. Not only was it an unpleasant feeling, it was downright revolting.

"I told you, that wasn't magic. That was something far more undisciplined and arcane and . . . savage."

Ellyne sat up a bit, repositioning herself on the cold, hard floor to avoid her legs falling asleep. She wasn't sure she should keep asking questions she didn't want the answers to.

"Fine," she growled, "what's more raw than magic?"

"Flocia. Pure flocia."

"Same thing—just as disgusting."

"No, it's not!" Nicole scooted to face Ellyne better. In the short time she had known this girl, her face had never appeared this serious. Having nearly died last night apparently had that effect. "Flocia is the *source* of magic."

"I know that already, but it's magic."

"Flocia is the raw power that comes from the source—from within the Teranyne itself. Magic is basically refined flocia—processed and distilled in a way to make it useful to us. Nobody uses flocia straight from the source."

"Why? Because it's dangerous?" Ellyne made air quotes with her fingers when she said the last word. Then she snorted and scoffed.

"No, that's not it at all."

"Then why?"

"Because nobody *can* use flocia. Nobody! Not even the Kithrak! Not even . . . me."

"Do I detect a bit of jealousy?"

"What? No!"

"Come on, you know you are." She playfully poked Nicole in the side and smirked. Apparently, Nicole wasn't the only unicorn in their little group, and, for some reason, Ellyne found this too amusing not to mention. It had been quite a while since she had anyone around to tease.

"I am not!" Nicole pouted. "Besides, all the theoretical magical research tells us it's not possible anyway. Magic is a way to distill flocia into a form that can be commanded—like hammering steel into something useful."

"Well," Ellyne laughed, "apparently theoretical magical research is bullshit." She slowly stood on shaky legs and carefully took a few steps. True, the situation was humorous, but she was ultimately masking her contempt for what she had possibly done. Using anything related to magic frightened her on many levels.

And disgusted her for several more.

Her strength returned quickly once she got up and moved. Nicole remained seated against the wall, obviously turning everything over in her head, trying to puzzle out what just happened, how, and why.

She found herself doing the same thing, though. She'd known for some time she was . . . unique, but this was a surprise.

"Given everything I know about flocia," Nicole muttered, "you should be dead. The amount of sheer power I sensed when it happened was . . . immense. You should probably be dead *twice*."

"Many people have said I'm hard to kill."

"How do you even live a life that makes people say that?"

"I apparently piss off a lot of people."

Nicole apparently had no rebuttal. She almost looked as if she'd short-circuited somehow.

"Anyway, that's their problem. I'm a damned ray of sunshine." She gazed out the window. This whole area had looked foreboding and dark last night but, with the sun currently doing its thing, it didn't look so bad.

She could see the corpses from here, though. Those things . . . they must have been like the creature they encountered in the sewer tunnel. But what were they?

Ellyne rubbed her temples to try and ease the dull throbbing. Given what she'd done, and the fact she should be dead according to Nicole, she figured escaping with a slight headache was a fortunate occurrence.

"If you've got a headache, I know a spell to make it go away."

"No. I'll be fine."

She reached into a jacket pocket and pulled out a small

bottle. After dry swallowing two pills, she slipped the bottle back into the pocket.

"Wow! I haven't seen a bottle of pain killers in . . . well, maybe ever!"

"Yeah yeah, magic and blah blah. I'm old school. Besides, if you channel magic, the Ilserate will probably be busting down this door shortly thereafter."

"I forgot. Yeah, there is that." Nicole's face turned sad.

Ellyne gasped and turned from the window, sliding quickly down the wall until she sat next to Nicole again.

"What is it? What did you see?"

"If the Ilserate's watching for powerful magic . . . do you think they could have sensed whatever it was I did?"

"Oh shit." Nicole gasped and covered her mouth. "Sorry, language."

Ellyne smirked. She always found it humorous when the girl swore.

"I don't know how their monitoring system works or what it can detect. I'd say it's possible. But, if they noticed, then why aren't they here already?"

"Good question. Maybe they're scared. If what you said is true—and it's something far out of the ordinary—then maybe they're just trying to wrap their corrupt little heads around what happened."

"That's possible. But they had to notice, right?" It was Nicole's turn to stand and pace the floor. "I mean, a burst of flocia all at once like that should've registered on their, well, whatever they use to detect stuff like that. One time, when I was really young, I got bored and I left my room and—"

The girl was rambling again. Ellyne rolled her eyes and sighed. "I don't need a history lesson, Nicole. I just need to know, is it possible?"

"I'd say yes."

"Then we're leaving. If they're wasting time getting their shit together, then we're going to take advantage of their hesitation. If such an occurrence is powerful and unique, then you can bet they'll assume it's you, even if they don't know what the hell to do about it. But they'll probably bring a larger force."

They were out the front door in the blink of an eye, running under the overgrown arch and through the garden which was now littered with numerous corpses. Ellyne ignored her morbid curiosity and resisted the urge to stop and inspect one of them. "I guess we know why this building was abandoned!"

"If those things live here, though, is it really abandoned?"

"Just keep running!"

Nicole looked terrified. She was doing everything she could not to notice any of the dead creatures as they passed each one. Ellyne couldn't blame her, but her own curiosity was piqued. There was something here—something that, apparently, wasn't common knowledge—something she couldn't let go of.

"We'll need to find somewhere else safe once we get out of here." Ellyne pointed to the fence up ahead. Her mind worked furiously to think of a plan. Damn it, why was she so bad at plans and strategy? She'd been skilled during the Flocia Wars, hadn't she? But war didn't apply to every situation, did it?

They didn't make it to the fence. The air before them shimmered and, in a heartbeat, they were surrounded.

"Stop where you are! The Ilserate commands it!"

Ellyne's revolver was in her hand a split second later.

"Now now, let's not be hasty. We don't crave confrontation; we are merely here to collect our . . . property."

"I know that voice."

Ellyne scanned the area around her. Four Ilserate mages, four Ilserate bots and . . .

"Marik."

"Nice to see you again, Ellyne. Alive and well, I see." He

stared at her, through one green eye and one blue eye, his face as smug as ever.

She leveled her gun at him. Every fiber of her being told her to pull the trigger, to shoot the man dead where he stood, but to do so would most likely mean her demise. Even then, it still might be worth it. She once again found herself running her tongue over the chunk of metal in her jaw, reminded of his treachery. It would be so delicious if she could make him pay right then and there.

"No thanks to you, Marik."

"Ah, yes," he laughed. "Still bitter about the past I see?"

"I tend to remember those who double-cross me and then try to kill me. Fortunately, you seem to be inept at both."

"Charming . . . as always."

"Still bald, I see. I guess magic can't regrow hair, huh?"

Marik scowled. Ellyne grinned.

Two of the Ilserate agents had their wands pointed at them while the other two held their hands ready to cast spells. The bots, of course, stood motionless, docile until commanded.

"As per the agreement you and the Ilserate have, we will leave you alone this time. But should you steal our property again, we will consider that agreement void and may possibly, promptly, pay you another visit.

Each time he uttered a word that began with the letter "p", fine drops of spittle formed a tiny cloud in front of him. He always over-aspirated that letter. Yet another thing Ellyne found annoying about him, not to mention gross. That alone was reason to kill him.

"Property? You act as if she's not a human being. She even has a name! It's . . . it's, uh—"

"My name is *Nicole*," she growled.

"Yes, yes, you have a name, but you still belong to the government. I don't know how you managed to escape last time but I assure you it won't happen again."

"Now hold on, Marik—"

Marik held his hands up, facing Ellyne. She knew enough about magic and about him to know he had a spell loaded and ready to cast at her. Ordinarily, she wouldn't even bat an eye at the threat of magic, but he knew her better than anyone, which meant he knew how best to beat her.

He'd done it once before.

She felt helpless.

"Ellyne, if you interfere I will kill you right here—this time not with a bullet which, obviously, didn't do the job the first time. I'm sure you know I've got a litany of magical protection to render your little toy gun harmless."

He had always been skilled at making someone feel miniscule with a mere word or two. Another entry in her ever-growing list of reasons to kill the man.

As much as it frustrated her, she knew he was right. She could empty all eight bullets into him, and they would most likely have no effect. One more reason she detested magic. Especially right now.

She slipped the gun back into its holster, slowly and begrudgingly, still trying to think her way out of this. It was then that she realized the easiest solution took care of two problems.

"Fine," she said, removing her hand from her gun. "You know what? Fine. You're actually doing me a favor." She grabbed Nicole and shoved her forward. "She's all yours."

"Wait, what?" Nicole shrieked. Two of the Ilserate mages immediately swooped in and grabbed her, immobilizing her hands. She struggled but to no avail.

"You can have her." They didn't know. If Marik even suspected what Ellyne had done last night, he would've hinted at it. He could never resist playing that game. If he didn't know, then she could resume her quiet life. "The only thing she's done is complicate my life and talk incessantly.

And now that you have her, you can go back to leaving me the hell alone and I can go back to forgetting you exist."

She knew she couldn't forget but it was far better if Marik believed that.

"Excellent," he gloated. "You're smarter than I gave you credit for, Ellyne. See that you keep your nose out of Ilserate business in the future and we'll have no further altercations."

"If it means never having to see you again, Marik, you can bet on it." She ran her tongue over the metal tooth again.

Without words or warning, Marik disappeared with the rest of the Ilserate agents, taking Nicole with them—probably to the main government compound. Wherever they went, Ellyne didn't care as long as it wasn't here.

It was as if a great weight was removed from her shoulders. She no longer had to live life on the run. She could return to her apartment and her stool at Victor's. Maybe someone would have a job for her by now.

A shot or two of squama juice or maybe some torflower ale sounded perfect. Both sounded even better. Possibly while listening to The Transgressors or Rebel Soul on full volume. Anything to put this behind her and get back to some normalcy.

She scaled the fence with ease. It would be nice to be able to walk once again unhindered during daylight without having to constantly look behind her for danger—more than normal, anyway.

She dropped to the ground on the other side of the fence and wiped her dusty hands on her black trousers. Damn, it felt good.

She thought she heard the faint buzzing of a drone somewhere above her.

CHAPTER
NINE

"HERE YOU GO, MY MAN!" Victor placed a glass on the bar and poured some Charnonin ale in it. "Enjoy!"

A thin, weasely man with greasy brown hair snatched the glass and nodded. "Thanks, my friend!"

"Seems a bit fancy for you. Are you celebrating something?"

"You could say that."

Ellyne watched as the patron settled at a table across from a woman. They struck up a conversation that she listened in on briefly, until boredom overtook her.

He looked like a businessman—wearing a respectable suit and shiny leather shoes with his hat lying on the table. He was obviously one of the many drones that wandered back and forth from one worthless endeavor to something less important on a daily basis. Maybe this guy worked for a bank and this lady was a client, completely unsuspecting of his intentions to bilk her out of her hard-earned tiks.

Or maybe *she* was playing him. As far as Ellyne was concerned, it didn't matter. Besides, chances were really high they were simply meeting up in a bar on a date or something else equally mundane.

The woman flicked her brown hair and mumbled something to the man who replied. She wore a conservative, floral dress and full makeup. An elegant, ornate wand sat on her hip, attached to her thin belt.

"Hi," Ellyne mumbled to herself. "My name's Tatania. I love long strolls on the beach under the moonlight." She paused and giggled, wondering if she'd had too much alcohol until she took another swig of her ale.

"My name's Rufus," she continued, exaggerating a man's voice. "I'm so glad our mutual friend set us up on this date. I've been so lonely since my inflatable doll popped last week."

Ellyne snorted and swallowed more ale, enjoying the tingle as it went down. People were always seeking out other people to justify their meaningless lives, completely mired in magic and the establishment that controlled it. They all thought magic made them powerful or important. The truth was, magic made them just as important as the next person. They were all uniquely alike.

"So where did you disappear to?"

Ellyne snapped out of her trance as Victor refilled her glass.

"Did someone hire you for a job?"

"Something like that, yeah." She stared into the honey-colored beverage, swirling it in her cup to make the foam on the top froth a bit more.

"How'd it go?"

"Sideways."

"Sorry to hear that. I guess not everything can go our way, eh?"

Ellyne took a large gulp, letting the cold smoothness drizzle down her throat, leaving the bitter aftertaste as the only memory from the drink. "Sometimes, life is better when a job ends poorly."

Victor appeared confused. "I don't understand."

"You'll have to trust me."

Victor laughed. "Well, you're the gunslinger, so I defer to you. But answer me this if you will. Why do you drink that hog piss? There are plenty of better-quality ales out there."

"It's bitter."

"Just like you!" Victor laughed again as he passed through the door to the back room.

"Just like me," she sighed.

She'd had a day or so to mull over recent events. Several things came to light, not the least of which was encountering those creatures, whatever they were. Derek was certainly a surprise, and whatever happened to Ellyne back at the apartment building—supposedly touching flocia—that memory still made her ill. She couldn't wrap her head around such a thing.

But Nicole was a completely different issue altogether. She was glad to be rid of the girl. Nicole was nothing but trouble, bringing all the factions down on Ellyne at once in the span of a few minutes. Screw that.

Things were back to normal, though, and that's what mattered. Ellyne was again free to move about the city unhindered. Let the Techs, Mages, Ilserate, and Kithrak all fight over Nicole. They could all kill one another in spectacular fashion without Ellyne getting involved. That was all she wanted, wasn't it?

The couple at the table behind her were still there, talking and carrying on. Ellyne threw a quick glance their direction and immediately noted the lady's wand was missing. She slowly turned her head to watch them out of the corner of her eye, now curious, even though she knew the direction this was probably headed.

Neither of them said a word for a good ten seconds and both looked nervous to the point of trembling. The woman flicked her hair and laughed as Ellyne noticed a bead of sweat run down the man's cheek.

"So, it's like that is it?" she mused.

Ellyne dove over the bar just as the first two spells whizzed over her head, shattering several bottles of liquor on the wall.

"Damn it!" she heard the man whisper. "I told you we should've acted sooner!"

"Indeed, you should have!" Ellyne muttered to herself.

In one smooth motion she stood, drew her pistol, and fired at the man. Her bullet went wide left, and he waved his hands, conjuring another spell that also missed, impacting the wall and sending bits of wood in all directions.

She ducked behind the bar again as several patrons gasped and shouted. Ellyne heard the door open and close multiple times as she presumed some of them fled into the streets.

"If you come with us peacefully," the woman shouted, "we promise we won't harm you! The Teranyne Order simply wants to ask you some questions."

"The last time I trusted the mages, things didn't go so well!"

"Have it your way!" the man laughed.

Victor poked his head out from the back room. She mouthed the words "get back" and motioned him to stay put.

The front door opened, feet scuffled, and then it shut again.

"Alright, let's try this again."

Ellyne popped up from behind the counter again but held her fire. "Well. This is awkward."

Three members of the Techno Guild, each with shocked looks on their faces, had their guns pointed at the mages. The moment they saw Ellyne, neither group could decide at whom to point their weapons. If anything, she wished she could take a picture before chaos ensued.

The rest of the patrons had apparently seen fit to clear out.

"We didn't come here to start trouble with you, mages,"

one of the Techs said, gun pointed squarely at the man. "We're here for her." He pointed to Ellyne, as if there was any mystery about who he meant.

"Well, see," the woman said, her wand in her hand. "So are we."

Ellyne ducked back behind the counter. Victor remained in his back room, peaking out at her. She shrugged and gave him a puzzled look. This was precisely what she wanted to avoid. And Nicole had to get her tangled up in this messy web of intrigue and mystery and . . . irritation.

"But Nicole's out of the picture," she mumbled, "so why are they bothering with me?"

She heard gunfire followed by the sound of various spells. Maybe, if she were fortunate, these bozos would kill off one another and she could loot the bodies. All the spoils, none of the work. The enemy of my enemy and all that.

"She's coming with us!" a man yelled.

"Like hell she is!" another man argued.

More gunfire echoed throughout the room, followed by explosions and muttered words as spells were cast and thrown. If she was being truthful, she'd probably feel compelled to give Victor whatever tiks she got out of this to pay for his bar being torn apart.

"This is ridiculous," she mumbled, loading a bullet in the empty chamber as the fight continued on the other side of the bar. She heard one of the men yelp.

"Shit!" another man yelled. "Decker's down!"

Ellyne reached up onto the counter, feeling around for her glass. She awkwardly grabbed it and swallowed the remaining contents.

Victor saw her. He knew what she was about to do and shook his head, motioning for her to slip into the back room with him. She smirked and stood up, immediately firing a shot and catching one of the Techs in the stomach.

"Now that's more like it," she laughed, flourishing her weapon.

The remaining Technician, his face now ghostly pale, turned his attention to her. The two mages followed suit, but nobody made a move, apparently waiting on someone else to go first as the moment dragged on uncomfortably.

"So, who wants to go first?"

The Tech and the two Teranynes froze, unsure if they should even respond.

"What are you hoping to gain, here?" Ellyne asked calmly, her eyes darting between the different targets. Whereas her three adversaries alternated pointing their weapons at their various enemies, she held her gun by her head, pointed up at the ceiling.

All three instantly trained their weapons on her. The male mage held his hands out, ready to cast a spell. He was steady and calm whereas the woman's wand and the Tech's gun quivered.

The woman cleared her throat and kept an eye both on the Tech and Ellyne. "Where is," she started, her voice cracking slightly. "Where is the girl?"

"Not here, obviously."

The longer this played out, the better she felt. Of these three individuals, the male mage appeared to be the only person who seemed remotely competent. The two dead Techs didn't matter, but the remaining Tech looked as though he might die of heart failure at any moment. Even if he fired a shot, he'd never hit with such an unsteady hand.

And the gun he held gave her a chuckle. Sure, the Technicians eschewed magic, claiming to be purists but Ellyne knew the truth—they used magic when it was convenient. They didn't cast spells, but they relied on devices powered by magic—whether or not they admitted it.

This man's gun was no different. It was a Schnick 427. Otherwise known as the "Companion," it was currently the best-selling firearm Schnick produced, holding twelve bullets in a clip.

It also had a semiautomatic firing enchantment cast on it and probably a self-cleaning spell as well. So much for the famous Technician magic hatred.

"Then where is she?"

"By now, somewhere deep in the Ilserate compound—probably the basement."

"Shit," the male mage spat.

"We're already on bad terms with them, right?" the woman whispered.

"You're lying," the Tech growled. "She's here somewhere, isn't she?"

She could tell from the man's tone that he didn't truly believe what he was saying. "Honestly, I'm glad to be rid of her. Now if you'd like to register your complaints with the government, you're certainly welcome to do so. Otherwise, I'd appreciate it if you would stop trashing my friend's establishment."

"Well, if the girl isn't here," the mage continued, "then you need to come with us."

"You and I both know that's not going to happen."

Before she could react, the mage thrust his hands in front of him and shot a spell at her. It hit her square in the chest and she staggered backward, gasping for breath. Her arms stiffened and her legs shook, struggling to keep her standing.

A defiant growl escaped her lips as she dropped to one knee behind the counter, struggling to hold onto her weapon.

"Did you kill her?" the woman asked.

"Simple stunning spell. She'll be immobile for several minutes at least."

"You mages back off. She's coming with *me!*"

"I highly doubt that."

A gunshot followed by a woman's scream and the sound of a spell filled Ellyne's ears as she recovered. Her limbs tingled and began to respond as she took a few deep breaths, and finally stood.

"I'm done with all of you."

"Wait," the male mage stammered, "how—"

"Because your spellcasting sucks."

She fired on the male mage—the last person standing—striking him in the head. He collapsed instantly and joined the rest of them on the floor.

She inspected what was now basically a murder scene. The tingling in her extremities eventually gave way to an odd warmth that washed over her and then vanished.

Victor appeared beside her and scratched his head. "That was . . . a bit beyond your normal altercations, Ellyne."

She sighed. "Indeed."

"What did you do to piss off *both* the Teranynes and the Technicians?"

"Not much, but it's a long story."

When Ellyne finally no longer needed the counter for support, she holstered her gun and relaxed. She grabbed her empty cup and held it out to Victor.

"Fill 'er up one more time? That was thirsty work."

"It's a good thing that mage's spells were so weak," Victor replied, pouring more ale into Ellyne's glass. "I thought you were screwed when he hit you."

"So did I," she laughed nervously and downed the entire glass. "Yeah . . . definitely a good thing he was so . . . inept." She turned to Victor. He appeared dumbfounded of all things —not worried, concerned, or even afraid. He was an odd man. "Look, Victor, I probably shouldn't be here."

"To be honest, I'm surprised you still are," he laughed. "Go on, get out. I'll take care of this mess. No one's going to fret over a couple of dead mages and Technos."

"Except the Teranyne Order and Technicians Guild," she smirked.

"Well, yeah, them. But I can handle them easily enough. Besides, they largely killed one another."

"Just . . . be careful, Victor. I feel like there's something more serious going on here. Something we're not seeing."

Victor grabbed a nearby mop and was just about to get to work. "What do you mean?"

"I'm not really sure. It's just a hunch."

"A hunch?" He paused, looking around the empty bar, and sighed. "I don't like your hunches, Ellyne. Your hunches are more solid than most peoples' facts."

"Yeah, neither do I." She headed to the door but paused. "Hey, Victor?"

"What now?"

"Thank you."

He nodded and got to work cleaning up as Ellyne slipped out the front door and onto the sidewalk.

Outside, the sun still shone, and people were still milling about as it was only slightly past six o'clock. Ordinarily, Ellyne would stay at Victor's until it was dark out but, given the circumstances, this was the best way to go.

She stopped just outside the door, unsure of her next move. Obviously, she needed a place to stay but where? Once word of what just happened made its way back to the Teranynes or the Technos—or both—they would probably come looking for her. Was it safe to go back to her apartment? Was *anywhere* safe?

"Damn you, Nicole, for dragging me into this."

What she really wanted was a hot shower and then to forget any of this ever happened. Only one of those was going to happen this night, and it would have to be somewhere other than her apartment. She couldn't risk Victor's bar incurring yet more destruction, either. No, she needed somewhere remote to hide out.

"I hope it still has running water."

By the time Ellyne arrived at the murder shack, she had

essentially lost all concept of time. The sun wasn't up yet but she didn't recall how long it had been since sunset. She effortlessly traversed the fence and passed the corpses of the horrid creatures she'd dispatched during her last visit, which felt like mere hours ago.

She slipped inside the building just as two of the monsters rounded the corner, sniffing the air and inspecting the area. From the safety of a window, she watched as they meandered about, stumbling and moving their misshapen bodies in curious, unnatural ways that made them look almost . . . broken.

"I was hoping I'd killed them all," she whispered, transfixed.

It was difficult to look away. These creatures were both grotesque and riveting. What were they? And why had she not seen one before their sewer encounter? It was true—Ellyne needed a place to lay low—but that wasn't the only reason she returned. Her instincts told her there was something to be discovered—something she'd missed the other night.

It also had hot water, much to Ellyne's relief. The place may have been deserted, but the magic used to circulate water was apparently still active.

Once she secured the door, she hurried to get out of her clothes and stepped into the shower, letting the warm jets spray from above, seemingly feeling each drop that cascaded down her body. She stood under the water with her eyes closed for several minutes as the tension in her muscles slowly melted away.

"I suppose soap and shampoo would be too much to ask for," she mumbled. Indeed, she saw neither. "Hot water alone will have to suffice. It's better than nothing."

Ellyne had no idea how long she stood under the water, trying to keep her mind from revisiting the events of the last three days. It was the only peace she'd had but it was short-lived.

Eventually, those thoughts resurfaced, as she knew they would. They crept back in and gnawed at the back of her head, stubbornly refusing to be ignored. She sighed and turned off the water.

After wiping the condensation off the mirror, she stared at herself. She looked tired. She *felt* tired. "There's more to this. What am I missing? Or am I just losing it?"

Grabbing a nearby towel, she beat the dust out of it and dried off, briefly considering sleeping naked rather than put on her old clothes. It was never really an option, however, because being prepared was often far more important than comfort.

She reluctantly got dressed, strapped her weapon to her hip and sunk down deep into the squishy couch cushions at the same time a plume of dust exploded around her.

The sun was setting when she woke up, surprised she'd fallen asleep and slept for as long as she had. She certainly didn't feel well-rested or refreshed, and her neck was stiff from falling asleep while sitting up. She took this time to try and settle the thoughts within her mind.

Everything about the room was frozen in time—dusty and completely undisturbed, as if whoever lived here simply disappeared one day. If this building lay empty for so long, why hadn't anyone moved in? Why was it fenced off? So much for clearing her mind.

"Of course!" she said, hopping up from the couch. "Those . . . things must have something to do with it." Her footsteps as she paced the small room were the only sounds other than her voice. She often thought out loud, as she called it. In fact, thinking out loud had resulted in several brawls throughout the years. People tended to get angry when you thought bad things about them . . . out loud.

She combed her fingers through her hair and closed her eyes. "What am I missing?" She paused and let her mind wander for a moment until it ended up in the building's basement.

"Of course!" she shouted and ran into the hallway. She found the stairs leading to the basement and hurried down them, flicking a light switch at the bottom.

When the lights flickered to life, they painted the same scene Ellyne had seen before—a dull basement with heating and cooling equipment, and lots of pipes and cables. She saw shelves with various stools and containers as well as a work bench. But on the far wall, in the corner, was the door—simple and nondescript but, as she found out last time, locked.

"Why are you locked when nothing else is?"

She strode across the room and instinctively turned the handle, but it was unyielding. She hadn't expected it to suddenly be unlocked this time, but stranger things had happened—just recently, in fact.

"Well, I don't think anyone's going to evict me for destruction of property."

Stepping back, she drew her revolver, cocked it, and looked away as she fired a shot at the spot where the latch bolt would be. The door shattered, flinging splinters of wood in all directions. The doorknob clattered onto the concrete floor.

"My very own unlocking spell," she quipped, shoving her weapon back into its holster. "Best magic around."

The door swung inward, creaking on its tired hinges as Ellyne nudged it open, trying hard to conceal her movements and noise though she assumed nobody was around to hear them. The room beyond was dark and though she fumbled around for a light switch she found nothing. The scant light from behind her did little to illuminate the room beyond but, from here, she thought she saw shelves.

"Well," she mused, "if nothing's jumped out and latched onto my face by now, I guess there's no danger." She moved further into the room with her hand cautiously resting on the door. No danger now didn't equate to no danger later.

Her boot kicked something and she nearly tripped. She caught herself just as something brushed her left cheek, causing her to jump back and point her gun into the darkness. It was shortly thereafter she realized there was a string hanging from the ceiling.

"Way to stay cool Ellyne," she muttered, putting her weapon away again and now fumbling for the string in the dark. Several seconds later, her fingers finally grasped it and she tugged on it. A conventional, Legacy Age, light bulb flickered briefly overhead and then went dark.

A second tug yielded no reaction from the bulb. "Third time's a charm," she sighed tugging yet again. This time, it flickered and hummed, struggling to do its job and briefly illuminating the room. During the small blasts of light, Ellyne tried to scrutinize the room's contents but still couldn't get a good enough look.

When the light bulb finally stabilized, Ellyne could indeed see the walls were lined with shelves and each shelf was piled high with equipment that looked to be nothing more than jumbles of wires, plastic, and metal haphazardly poking out in all directions. The overflowing shelves begat piles of the same refuse littering the floor.

"What is this?" She nudged some of the discarded tech with her boot. "Looks like a computer graveyard or something—old Legacy Age technology, maybe. But why is it in the basement of an abandoned apartment building?"

She sifted through some more of it, using her blade to scoot the various bits of junk around the floor until something caught her eye. She knelt, picked it up, and turned it over a few times.

"This is part of a T-Helm," she muttered, inspecting it closer. While she certainly wasn't an expert on the devices, having avoided them like a bad disease, this was an unmistakable piece of one. Closer inspection revealed more of the same in both the piles and on the shelves.

She tossed the plastic remnant onto the floor. "It's a Taranom graveyard, but what's all of this doing down here, and who put it here?"

The questions came at Ellyne swiftly, piling up just like the shattered T-Helm detritus before her.

"Where are the owners?"

She stood in the middle of the room for several moments, looking at the junk, and looking *past* the junk as her mind desperately tried to reassemble a puzzle that was more missing pieces than anything else.

"Wait a minute."

An idea came to her and she rushed out of the room. Hurrying up the stairs, she burst into the first of the living areas. "Okay," she murmured, searching the room, "where are you?"

Searching all sixteen rooms didn't take her long but, when she was finished, she came up empty. "Sixteen rooms and not one T-Helm among them."

No residents, no T-Helms, but the rooms were all full of abandoned personal effects.

"What the hell happened here?"

People never went anywhere without their T-Helms. Magic was life and, without a T-Helm, there was no magic. It was an addiction nobody could resist, so why would someone go without?

"It stands to reason someone would forego a T-Helm if they didn't use magic." She paced the width of the small apartment, staring at the floor. "Or if they somehow transcended the need for one, but I don't see that as very probable."

She stopped in her tracks as the third possibility barged into her thoughts.

"What if they had no choice?"

Ellyne made her way down to the front door. The memory was still fresh in her mind—what she'd done by supposedly channeling flocia. It was right inside this door where she'd collapsed after her narrow escape. Nicole's explanation of the event didn't sit well with her, but that wasn't why she found herself inspecting the door.

"Ugh," she muttered. "Nicole. What a mess."

She ran her fingers over the door but something caught her eye or, rather, the lack of something. She opened it and noticed two things.

First, the door was unnaturally heavy. She remembered it being metal, which seemed an odd choice, but closer inspection revealed it to be *solid* metal. The hinges were reinforced and sturdy.

Second, both the hinges and the locking mechanism were on the *outside* and the door opened outward.

"I'm not well-read on construction techniques," she said, running her fingers over the cold metal, "but that's a really unconventional way to hang a door."

It was then that her fingers found the dents and several deep scratches.

"Someone obviously wanted out really badly. I'm beginning to think the term 'murder shack' isn't quite so amusing anymore."

She stood in the doorway for several minutes, simply processing everything. The conclusion she reached was a simple one—a conclusion she often reached.

She had no desire to get involved.

"I can't stay here. Even my apartment is safer than this horror factory."

"TO HELL with all of it—the murder shack, the Kithrak, what's her name . . . all of it. I'm done."

The streets were clearing out as Ellyne traveled them, her head ducked to avoid notice. Her apartment may not be the safest place to hide out but at least she knew the dangers she would face there. People with wands or guns she could handle, but she'd prefer not to face any more of those subhuman creatures again. If she never saw another one it'd be too soon. Hopefully, she never would.

"I haven't seen the last of them, have I?" she mumbled to herself.

Try as she might, she couldn't stop her mind from wandering, from working out the puzzles she'd unwittingly stumbled upon. She loved a good challenge, it was true, but enjoyed the simple life too much to be drawn into this . . . whatever it was.

Was it already too late to avoid entanglement? She'd washed her hands of the girl and left the murder shack behind. There was nothing more she knew to remove herself from.

Several small drops of rain pelted her, followed by a few

more until a light drizzle fell from the sky. Ellyne's first instinct was to cower under an awning somewhere until it stopped, but she saw no point. It wasn't a heavy downpour, and it was harmless. Getting wet was the least of her concerns.

The feeling of lying in her own bed again was foremost in her mind. It seemed like she'd been away for years, which was silly, but accurate. She needed a good, long rest without distractions—some peace and downtime to relax and put all this out of her mind.

That was unlikely to happen if anyone came knocking on her door, which it appeared they inevitably would. The very thought was annoying, but not as annoying as the other thoughts, all of which centered around . . . what was her name?

"Nicole . . . damn it." Apparently, not using her name didn't make anything easier.

Every time she tried to distract herself, her thoughts eventually went back to the girl. Yes, she was thankful to be done with that whole situation. But her mind still haunted her, niggling at her with notions and ideas and plans and . . . shame.

She gave her up at the first sign of conflict. She simply handed Nicole over to Marik, that asshole. She was possibly just as annoyed with herself for giving up the girl as she was for giving Marik what he wanted.

But she'd also gotten what *she* wanted, right? She was free of entanglements and no longer had to deal with a chatty little girl.

But was she really? Sure, the Ilserate and Kithrak may not be breathing down her neck anymore, but that last altercation in Victor's bar sort of disproved that whole idea of freedom from entanglements. She was still very much on the run and would be for the foreseeable future.

And if Nicole was this super-powerful mage breaker thing

from a prophecy, what would happen to her? If Derek was right and the Kithrak feared her that much, surely they would dispose of her if the Ilserate could be convinced to allow them . . . or forced to allow them.

There were a lot of ifs, and Ellyne wasn't sure she put any stock in prophecies or mystical human doomsday weapons, but perception was reality and, if this was the Kithrak's perception, that would make them very desperate.

Ellyne stepped in a puddle, splashing water onto herself, but she barely noticed.

She wished it would stop there, but there was more. Though she tried to deny it, there was guilt. She'd handed Nicole over to the government, and that was bad enough, but she'd also betrayed . . . a friend? And, now that she was thinking about it, had she condemned Nicole to death?

"Shit." She froze, standing in the rain and completely unsure what she should do. Paralyzed by indecision, she growled and let each rain drop hit her. She wanted to punch something. "Damn it!" she howled, startling a pedestrian across the street who quickened their pace a bit. "She's not even here and she's still in my head."

Her words were met with only the gentle tapping of the rain falling on everything around her.

"Fine," she continued, and looked around her. "Where's a freakin' camera?"

Ellyne stomped down the sidewalk, anger rising within her. She knew JASN could see her. Surely there was a camera nearby. "I know you can see me, Derek! I know you're watching!"

She spotted a camera hanging from a light post next to a small grassy area with a bench and ran over to it. Jumping onto the bench, she waved her arms and hopped up and down to hopefully get Derek's attention. Certainly, she looked foolish but, thankfully, the area was already deserted.

"Look over here, damn it! Come on! Right here!"

The camera moved. She thought she could hear the sound of it as it turned to focus in on her. It was possible JASN was simply scanning the area and Derek wasn't even paying attention.

"That's right. Look at the foolish, grown-ass woman flailing about on a city bench!"

The camera stopped once it got to her.

"Derek, JASN, whoever—I need your help." She waited for a response, staring at a nearby screen, but it remained dark. "Come on, Derek! I need your help!"

Still nothing. There were only five screens nearby that she saw, and they all remained dark. Growling, she dropped her arms to her sides, her frustration mounting.

"Nicole needs your help!"

More time passed with no response. Defeated, Ellyne sat on the bench, trying to plan her next move as the rain continued to fall. She watched as the drops splashed into a nearby puddle. The first step was to undo what had been done, but that was a major undertaking. Was there even a practical way to get the factions off her back in the first place? They obviously weren't leaving her alone even after she handed over Nicole.

That wasn't even the place to start. Her mind raced, considering all the problems she had currently. Some were her fault but others, like those subhumans back at the murder shack, were not. She had a sneaking suspicion they were a part of this puzzle somehow and she didn't like that prospect.

"Fine," she pouted, standing. "I guess I'll just do it the hard way."

She was about to start shooting things when she saw a reflection in a puddle and looked up. JASN's symbol appeared on a nearby screen hanging on the outside wall of a restaurant.

She rushed to get closer.

"Derek! Is that you?"

"Warning: Distraction can cause accidents. Exercise caution."

"Derek, I need to talk to you. I've got some information you might find useful!"

"Caution: Beware of pickpockets."

"Cut the crap, Derek. Nicole's in danger!"

"Warning: You're an asshole."

"Very funny. Okay, fine—I get it. I'm sorry! I screwed up. Now get off your ass and let me in or I'll find my own way in, and you're not going to like my methods."

The words on the screen were replaced by the familiar triangle and circle which promptly morphed into a green arrow pointing left.

Ellyne curtsied sarcastically and hurried in the arrow's direction, turning right when she spotted the next arrow.

The rain fell harder, now, but her spirits lifted a bit, having finally gotten Derek's attention. If anyone could help her, he could. He would have access and knowledge to help her determine exactly what her next move was. She just hoped her faith in him wasn't misplaced. She hoped he was the genius she thought he was. She also hoped he wasn't holding a grudge.

It wasn't long before the arrows took her to an alley. Deserted and dark, it ended in a wall and was bereft of any screens. She looked around but saw no sign of JASN.

"If you tricked me . . ."

Before she could finish her thought, the wall at the end of the alley shifted, shimmered, and then disappeared altogether, revealing stairs leading down. Without hesitation, she hurried down them as the wall reappeared behind her.

"Well, I've never seen anything like that before," she mused. Her tooth hurt—the metal tooth. She had minor problems with it since it was implanted. She assumed most people probably paid for someone to cast a spell to regenerate a tooth or something, but she didn't have that option. It wasn't anything more than a slightly annoying ache and, besides, it only acted up when she was around powerful magic. Even then, it wasn't every time.

She had known what she was getting into, though. The metal was special, and it reacted badly to magic sometimes. It was all intentional. It was also how she knew there was an abundance of powerful magic about the dimly lit corridor in which she now found herself.

"Could I get a little more light in here, please?"

Ellyne expected to see another corridor filled with lights and gizmos but, instead, was greeted with what resembled the sewer tunnel from earlier. At the end of the tunnel was a metal door, however, so she knew she was in the right place.

It could be a trap. She was always suspicious but was even more cautious now that JASN or Derek or whoever seemed to be angry with her. However, if she were being honest, she wasn't so thrilled with herself at the moment either. But she needed help to sort things out, even if such a thing wasn't her usual course of action.

To her surprise, once she reached the door, it opened, receding into the ground and revealing another screen-covered room at the center of which sat Derek, looking simultaneously angry and smug. This was going to be an unpleasant conversation.

"Thanks for finally letting me in. Do all your rooms look like this?"

"Yes. JASN has more than one node in the city. I change locations depending on my mood . . . or when someone keeps relentlessly nagging me for help."

"Well, if you would've answered me the first time, I wouldn't have had to nag you." Ellyne walked further into the room, at which point the door sealed itself.

"Well, if *you* hadn't screwed up in the first place, this wouldn't be an issue!" Derek had a scowl on his face that could possibly kill. Until now, she hadn't known how truly angry he was, but his face said it all. "So, yeah, here we are, and it's your fault."

Ellyne felt her cheeks get hot with shame and frustration, as if she were a young girl being admonished by her parents. When was the last time she'd thought about them?

"Not only did you surrender your friend—someone who was relying on you—to the Ilserate, you handed over the mage breaker to them! You essentially gave the Ilserate a weapon that could not only be used against the Kithrak, but that could also be used against the general populace!"

What could she say? Ellyne knew she made a mess of the situation, but she hadn't given it this much thought until now. She'd only ever considered Nicole to be an asset—just as the Ilserate had, which made her just as rotten as the government. Nicole was more than just a force or object to be manipulated, but she'd only considered the girl to be nothing more than a pest—something to be rid of.

"We aren't friends," she finally admitted, although she wasn't sure how true that was anymore.

"Oh really? It sort of looked like that to me."

"No," Ellyne argued, "she came to me for help. I didn't ask for any of this. That doesn't make us friends."

Derek looked at her sternly. "Sure, that's convenient. Say what you will, but I know you can't continue an existence when your only supposed friend is a bottle of booze. Nicole came to you, needing help, and she trusted you. That sounds like friendship to me, and—"

"I gave her up." Saying the words really hit home. It felt like the air in the room was squeezing her.

"You gave her up. You handed her back to the very people she escaped from. She came to you for help, and you ditched her at the first confrontation."

"Listen," she said, regaining some of her composure while wrestling with her emotions, "yeah, I screwed up and I was being selfish."

"Yep.

"And I betrayed someone who . . . thought she was my friend."

"While not one-hundred percent accurate," Derek acknowledged, "you're on the right track."

"And now," Ellyne scowled, frowning at Derek's statement, "the Ilserate have their weapon back, which is less than optimal. Consequently, I need to get Nicole back."

"Now you're talking!" he said excitedly, his eyes lighting up with the prospect of positive things happening.

"I can't let the Ilserate keep control of her."

"And," Derek sighed, "she's your friend, damn it." His irritation was obvious.

Ellyne rolled her eyes. "Let's not rush things. I've operated alone for a long time."

"Fine. What do you need?"

"First of all, where did they take her?"

"I mean, that's obvious enough, isn't it? We both know she's back at the Ilserate compound."

"Painfully obvious, yes. But the government compound is a big place, and there are other buildings sprinkled throughout Karnascus, right?"

Ellyne approached the screens, hoping to get a better view of the images Derek was tinkering with. His fingers worked furiously, moving different pictures and videos around in the air and typing on a keyboard Ellyne couldn't see.

"I pieced together footage of the whole scene. JASN caught it from several different angles, including one of his drones."

She reluctantly watched it play out again as she and Marik talked, then as she eventually handed over Nicole and walked away. At the time she'd been so happy to be rid of her but now, she had never felt more ashamed, remorseful and . . . sad.

"Okay, I get it. What I did was despicable. But where did they take her?"

"Oh, the main Ilserate compound, of course."

"Then why did you make me watch that?"

Derek grinned an all-knowing grin.

"Fine, I guess I deserved it."

"Look—"

Ellyne held up her hand to stop Derek. An idea popped into her head—a question she needed an answer to before they proceeded.

"Why are you so interested in all this? I mean, I understand many people have no love for the government or the Kithrak . . . or the factions for that matter, but you seem extra invested in this whole thing. You're legitimately pissed that I let Nicole go, and not simply because I was being an asshole, I'd wager."

"I, uh—" Derek stammered, hesitating.

"Yeah, I thought so. Spill it."

Derek sighed and his shoulders slumped. "Fine," he said. "Because Nicole represents both a significant danger and a significant resource."

"To whom?"

"To me. To all the . . . Kithrak."

Ellyne's gun was in her hand quicker than any time in the past. She pulled back the hammer with her thumb until it clicked, staring down its barrel.

"Don't move," she growled. "I'll give you one chance to explain yourself, and if I don't like your answer, then—"

"Whoa. Whoa. There's no need for—"

"Not fast enough."

"Okay, okay." Derek held up his hands, palms out in front of him. He swallowed hard, obviously choosing his next words carefully. "I'm a Kithrak."

"I figured that out already. Explain yourself and why I shouldn't put a hole in you."

"Because I'm on your side."

"How do you figure?" Ellyne reminded herself of Derek's help, which was the only thing that stayed her hand.

"I've . . . I've been helping you, haven't I?"

"I'm no stranger to betrayal. We're friends from way back. So, how am I actually sure you *have* been helping me? You're a Kithrak. You could be simply using Nicole and me to get what you want. Maybe you're upset because Nicole's in Ilserate hands and not Kithrak custody."

"I'm upset the mage breaker is in custody at all!" he shrieked angrily.

Ellyne motioned with her gun as he yelled, causing him to immediately back down. His frustration was curious—he seemed genuinely concerned, but not for his own purposes. Ellyne always thought she could get a good read on most people, but Derek was . . . complicated. He didn't fit in with the other Kithrak she'd encountered.

If Nicole was as powerful as she was supposed to be, it made sense to keep her safe from all factions. Even then, Ellyne still wasn't sure what role she herself had to play in all this, and Derek's motives were still suspect.

This was getting far messier than Ellyne would have liked. She longed for the simple days when it was obvious who to shoot. But then, that was an illusion, wasn't it? She'd spent all her time in the Flocia Wars trying to destroy magic. When that wasn't possible, the goal turned to restricting magic—all under the guise of fighting for the Ilserate alongside Marik so people could be free.

It was a lie, of course. The Ilserate were just as bad as the Kithrak, and all they wanted was to control flocia. And Marik . . . well, he jumped ship and allied with the Kithrak once he saw defeat on the horizon. She thought about her shoulder and ran her tongue over the metal in her jaw, wishing to someday be done with that response to Marik.

"I'm going to choose to trust you," she said, slowly lowering her revolver. "For now."

Derek sighed as if he'd been holding his breath. Ellyne wondered if he'd soiled himself.

"You can put your hands down now." She accepted her reputation preceded her but was curious why a Kithrak would be afraid of her and . . . a gun.

"Oh, right!" Derek slowly lowered his hands and resumed typing and manipulating the images before him. Within seconds he acted as if their standoff never happened.

Ellyne approached, still suspicious, watching as he pulled up images of Ilserate buildings. She recognized most of them, having walked among many of them as an Ilserate puppet. A few were new or had been remodeled, but the compound looked largely the same as it had during the wars.

"So . . . you, uh . . . don't look like a Kithrak." There was no harm in finessing some information out of him, was there?

"You're right, I don't." Derek responded matter-of-factly, directing all his attention to the images and text that appeared and disappeared at a ridiculous rate. "There are lots of others who look almost human like me. We're meant to assimilate into human culture which is, admittedly, ridiculously easy without the extra eyes or arms."

"So why, then?"

"Why what?" With all the images, videos, and text moving across his vision at such a phenomenal rate, Ellyne wondered how he even kept a conversation with her.

"Why are you helping me?"

"I'm helping you because you're helping *her*." He paused for a moment, scrutinizing something before swiping it away, only to be replaced with another something. "Or, at least, you *were* helping her."

"I'm helping her now."

"Good!" He called up an image and flipped it around so it

faced Ellyne. "This," he continued, "is the Kithrak prophecy about the mage breaker."

"Okay. It's an open book with illegible chicken scratch."

"It's a Kithrak text written in the Kithrak tongue. You might be the first and only human to see it. We Kithrak speak your language, but we have our own."

"Makes sense."

"History tells of my people's humble beginnings. It's a bunch of garbage you don't need to know and I'd bet half of it is historically inaccurate. The short version is the Kithrak, like all species, began as a simple society with no technology or magic."

"That's not surprising."

"Exactly," Derek said, still working on his invisible keyboard. "But, whereas humans developed over a long period of time, the Kithrak discovered flocia and harnessed it naturally. With even the first, simple incantation, our advancement skipped ahead several hundred years."

"That seems rather convenient. Discovering the ability to lift rocks doesn't sound like hundreds of years of evolution. Are you sure your texts aren't lying about that part?"

"See, that's the thing," Derek chuckled. "Ancient Kithrak didn't simply stumble onto our first spell after trial and error —they were *taught*."

"Taught? By whom?"

"By flocia."

"Okay, whatever," Ellyne said, unsure how to process this information. "Can we fast forward to the part that's relevant to me?"

"Subtle." He typed for a few seconds and made some wild motions with his hands. The book's pages flipped several times before stopping on a page that glowed red. "This," he continued, "is the particular part about the mage breaker."

"Nicole."

"Yes. Above all else, my people fear losing magic or

merely losing control of magic. Both are akin to an apocalyptic event for the Kithrak. We believe we will sink back to the pre-flocia society."

"And your people believe that this . . . mage breaker . . . that it's Nicole? They believe it that strongly?"

"There is debate within certain castes as to whether she is but, yes—she's widely seen as the most powerful mage on the planet. She's maybe the most powerful mage ever. And it's not just her extraordinary power, but the very ways she uses magic. Even the most skilled Kithrak can't do what she can."

Ellyne recalled how Nicole used magic to throw her against the wall outside her apartment. Such a thing seemed commonplace to most but, to Ellyne, it was anything but. It jarred her even now to think about it. She wondered if this is how the Kithrak felt about the whole mage breaker situation. Fear was an intense motivator, and it could make someone do desperate things.

"The Kithrak are truly afraid of her," Ellyne whispered.

"Very afraid," Derek added. "They believe she, as the mage breaker, can take control of flocia from us."

"Then let's break her out of there. How do we do that though?"

"The Ilserate compound has their own isolated, internal network. They don't connect to the same net JASN does. They've taken paranoia to the highest degree."

"I see . . . sort of. But elaborate a bit because I really don't get it."

"JASN has no visibility inside the compound. Therefore, I have no visibility inside the compound, which means we're going in blind. I can't see in, but they also can't see out."

"Well, that complicates things. What do you suggest?" Ellyne asked a frown appearing on her lips.

Derek looked shocked she'd even asked him what to do. "Me? I was hoping you had a plan. You're more familiar with the Ilserate than I am."

"Why the hell would I have a plan?"

"Seriously? I've read all kinds of things about you. You're the Golden Gunslinger—the Juggernaut of the Faril Offensive! You commanded troops in battle and pulled off amazing victories! Surely you're used to making plans."

Ellyne growled, pacing the floor. Despite what her record said, she felt different. She was much better at improvisation.

"So, we have two options, then. One, we go in totally blind and shoot up the place. I've done that before. It's not pretty. Two, we find a way to get JASN access to the Ilserate compound's network. Also not pretty, I'm guessing, but probably less dangerous."

"No, definitely not pretty, or easy. But certainly not impossible. I have an idea. If you give me some time, I can create a device that can hopefully bridge their internal network with JASN, giving us full visibility and access."

"How long will that take?"

"Hopefully not longer than a day. Maybe less. Without knowing specifics about their security protocols, I have to essentially plan for every contingency."

"I don't want to wait that long." Ellyne strode toward the door, all of a sudden feeling the urgency. There was no telling what the Ilserate would do to Nicole now that others knew about her skill and ability. Chances were high that the Technicians Guild and the Teranyne Order were also making plans to apprehend her. "You do what you do best and I'll do what I do best."

"What's that?"

"Improvising . . . and possibly shooting some people," she said with a thoughtful smirk brightening her face.

ELEVEN

THE OFFICER'S uniform was itchy as hell, and it was all Ellyne could do to keep from scratching every inch of her body. She didn't remember it being this uncomfortable during the war. Perhaps sitting in a closet for a decade or two had been problematic.

She was glad she hadn't burned it like she originally planned. Simply knowing she had an Ilserate commander's uniform in her apartment was bad enough. She hated it. She hated it every time she thought about it, and living with it in her possession was unpleasant. But, for once, she was happy to have it.

"Hopefully, this is the last time I ever have to see this thing," she muttered, passing the normal throng of people muscling their way to and from work or wherever people went daily. Many of them gave her a wide berth but those who weren't paying attention looked shocked when they bumped into her. Ilserate officers weren't individuals someone wanted to tangle with.

Except, recently, Ellyne made a career of doing just that. The pay was crappy, but the hours were good and there was immense job satisfaction.

Ilserate uniforms had changed very little since she served in their army. Everything was still green—the shirt, the trousers, the coat . . . even the ugly little cap she wore atop her head. She suspected the shade of green was currently darker but that was about the only noticeable deviation. With any luck, nobody would question her.

She suddenly longed for her normal clothes. Just the simple fact she'd had to do something with her hair to facilitate the cap annoyed her. She'd burn the damned thing if it weren't on her head.

The duffel bag she carried with her made it more difficult to navigate the crowds. It was also green. Who chose green for everything? Many of the fights during the Flocia Wars took place *in cities* where there wasn't much green to begin with. Maybe green uniforms weren't selling well and the government got a massive discount.

Ellyne waited with everyone else at the corner for the light to change, watching the various vehicles zip by her. Now would be a great time for JASN to change the traffic lights in her favor so she could keep moving. Unfortunately, he didn't seem to be in the giving mood.

She became acutely aware of one particular man who wouldn't take his eyes off her duffel bag. Every time she looked at him, he averted his gaze and pretended to be grooving to whatever music he was supposed to be listening to in his oversized blue headphones.

He was pale—abnormally pale. She figured thinking about stealing from an Ilserate officer could instill a certain level of fear in someone. Yet he still seemed committed to the cause. Many civilians may not have taken notice, but he was painfully bad at seeming inconspicuous.

"Hey," she whispered, leaning in a bit and gripping the duffel bag tightly. "It'll only take me a couple of seconds to break your clavicle if you decide to start shit. If you don't know what a clavicle is, then I can show you, but it won't be a pleasant lesson."

The man turned even paler, if that was possible. The shock on his face told her all she needed to know, and she had to suppress the grin she felt forming.

"And nobody around here will bat an eye," she continued. "If I were you, I'd walk away now, before I break something just for fun."

The man promptly did as Ellyne suggested, scurrying away quickly as if she had an infectious disease. She felt almost disappointed. A fight would have worked out some pent-up aggression as a result of wearing this horrible uniform. Ugh, it was also too warm. Did the Ilserate hate everything about comfort?

If only those two Technicians waiting for her back at her apartment knew what they really died for. She acknowledged going back was a dangerous idea but a proper disguise, no matter how ridiculous and uncomfortable, was important. They hadn't even expected her to show up.

The light changed and she hurried across the street, turning a corner after the next block. In the distance, atop a hill, she could see the main Ilserate building—a stark, silver tower they called The Citadel. It was the tallest structure in Karnascus and the phallic comparisons were every bit as obvious. Most of them had probably already been made, repeated in bars or business meetings and laughed at by children. Even if you were pro-government, it was too good an opportunity to pass up.

"Come on, Derek, we're running out of time," she mumbled, partly to herself, partly to him.

He'd promised to have a solution ready for her by the time she got to the facility, and time was running out. He also promised to give her instructions but, thus far, she'd neither seen nor heard anything. Maybe she moved faster than he did.

Before she learned he was a Kithrak, she might not have been so suspicious. Knowing what she'd just learned, however, doubt seeped in through the cracks. What if this was a setup?

She continued down the sidewalk. This street led straight to the gates of the Ilserate compound and, the problem was, she wasn't sure how she was going to get past them. That was only problem number one. Problem number two was finding Nicole. Problem number three wasn't hers. It was the Ilserate's.

"Pretty sure there are all kinds of problems in there I'm not considering," she muttered.

Her frustration mounted. Things were so much easier with a bullet . . . or eight. Sneaking and espionage were not her areas of expertise. They weren't even interesting! What fun was screwing someone over in a colossal manner if you couldn't gloat about it to their faces? Before they died, of course.

"Derek, if you're going to do something, you've got maybe five minutes. Move your ass."

Sidewalk traffic eased as she got closer to the Ilserate compound while street traffic increased. Most Ilserate officials, workers, and troops used government transports to conduct business and apparently wouldn't be caught dead walking, while most citizens had few reasons to be in this area and would be scrutinized.

Which, surprisingly, was a good thing. When the nearest screen briefly flashed her a message, no one else was around to see it. The only problem was, it was an arrow pointing up.

"How am I supposed to go up? I can't fly, Derek."

"Caution: thunderstorms likely."

"What?" Ellyne looked up in time to catch something as she saw a drone speed away. "Efficient."

She wasn't the computer genius Derek was, but she knew enough to recognize a drive chip. She'd need to get to a computer to use it, but that wouldn't be too hard. She'd been in The Citadel enough to know her way around, assuming they hadn't remodeled the place. Good thing the government was cheap and rarely spent money if they didn't have to. She slipped the chip into the breast pocket of her jacket.

The gates got nearer as she walked, still unsure of what to do when she actually got there. She didn't have a government ID card anymore, and they would surely search her before she was allowed through.

"Hey!"

She snapped out of her trance to see a transport truck had stopped next to her. The man driving it was staring at her. Because the truck lacked any doors, it was even more obvious.

"Hey, pretty lady! Need a ride?"

"That's Commander to you, Private!" She hadn't missed a thing after all these years. Ellyne couldn't remember how many times she'd had to utter that phrase to put a misbehaving brat in his or her place. Unfortunately, she did need a ride.

"Shit. My apologies, Commander!" He raised his right palm, facing out, to his forehead in a salute.

"Also, yes, Private. I could use a ride." She walked in front of the vehicle and climbed into the passenger seat next to the soldier. "Thank you, Private."

"Why were you walking, ma'am?"

"Out for fresh air. Lost track of time." It wasn't the greatest excuse, but her thoughts were focused on more important things, one of which was trying to ignore the overwhelming odor of this man's body spray.

He was young—probably no older than twenty years. Unless he'd seen her in a photo or read about her, she wasn't in much danger of being recognized. But Nicole had sought her out and she was, what, twenty also? No, twenty-three. It didn't matter. She still needed to be cautious.

The truck lurched forward until they stopped outside the main gates. The sturdy, latticed patterns were made of steel and probably riddled with enchantments.

No, *definitely* riddled with enchantments. Ellyne felt her entire body tingle and reverberate with energy. She closed her eyes and concentrated on relaxing, breathing in and out slowly. Now was not the time for something . . . whatever it was, to happen.

"Excuse me."

She felt the tingly warmth within her start to fade—no, not fade so much as disperse itself throughout her body. It was still there, but she only barely felt it. That was going to be annoying. Hopefully it would go away at some point. More importantly, she would need to figure out why it kept happening.

"Excuse me, ma'am!"

One of the men stationed at the gate was trying to get her attention.

"I'm sorry, Private," she said, clearing her throat. "I was just going over today's tasks in my head. Got lost there for a moment. Busy day ahead!" Ellyne laughed nervously.

"Great. I just need to see your identification."

Shit.

She looked at the front of her ugly green jacket and feigned shock. Then she pretended to search her pockets.

"I appear to either have lost it or left it on my desk. Been so busy lately I've been forgetting things!" She laughed and continued pretending to search.

"I can check the records to determine if you're authorized. What's your name, commander?"

Ellyne's brain went into overdrive. Shooting this guy would have been so much easier.

"Oh, it's Kendra. Kendra Vantz."

Kendra Vantz led her Frozen Hellions squad during the Wars. They once teamed up with Ellyne's Iron Wolves to take

New Faranon from the Kithrak. She was a shrewd woman, a brilliant strategist and the ultimate badass.

She'd also been dead for twelve years. Hopefully this guy didn't know that.

"Let me check real fast."

"Hey!" a man's voice shouted. Another truck had pulled up behind them and several more behind it. Ellyne couldn't get a good look at the guy yelling. "Can you get a move-on already? We're in a hurry!"

"I just need to check this—"

"I don't care what you need, Private! This is time-sensitive material we got in here! If you want to explain to your bosses why this delivery was late, be my guest but I'm not taking the heat for it!"

"Excuse me, Private," Ellyne said, attempting to sound soothing. "I understand protocol, but I assure you, I've got access." She made eyes at him or, at least, she tried. "I wouldn't want such a good soldier like yourself to get into trouble, now. But I understand. We're all just doing our jobs."

Hopefully, she still recalled how to flirt—if she ever knew how, that was. She was pretty sure she could pull it off.

The soldier, keeping his eyes on her, cautiously backed into the little booth by the gates. Suddenly, she felt vulnerable. If she got caught now, it would end poorly. Her mind raced, desperately trying to think of a backup plan to a primary plan she didn't have in the first place.

Every instinct told her to run, to bail out of the truck and make a dash for some cover. She could probably get away fast enough to disappear. At worst, she could leave the compound altogether. But this was her best shot. If she fled now, they would tighten security and the next time would be much more difficult.

As much as she'd like to, she couldn't shoot her way in and out of this. No, subterfuge was the only way. If only

JASN could access their computer and add her to whatever list this guy had.

But this soldier was taking an awfully long time. She could almost see him mentally wrestling with his choices. Ellyne batted her eyes at him one more time.

"Come on, already!" the guy from the truck behind shouted. "It's hot out here!"

Just as Ellyne was about to jump out of the truck and make a run for it, the soldier pushed a button and the gates slowly swung open on their creaky hinges. She suppressed a relieved sigh as they drove through and on into the Ilserate compound. She still had to fool this clueless soldier next to her.

Her luck was holding out, but there was still a long way to go. She just hoped the drive chip Derek gave her did what it was supposed to do—whatever that was. There was no choice but to trust him, but she still had a niggling fear that he could be setting her up for failure. What if the damned chip set off the alarms or trapped her in there or, worse, activated the security systems? There were a million possibilities.

Still, he seemed genuinely concerned for Nicole's well-being, even if he wasn't all that happy with Ellyne herself. They both wanted the same thing, so there was no reason he would purposely sabotage this mission, was there?

The truck lurched forward, passing through the gates. "Finally! It's about time!" the soldier behind her yelled. "Thought I was gonna see my next birthday, and I just had one!"

Ellyne had never felt gratitude toward a loud-mouthed jackass before.

"You headin' to The Citadel?" the man beside her asked.

"Affirmative," she replied, hoping to sound official. She figured that's where she needed to be. After all, it was the hub, and it was where most of the important functions took place. The rest of the buildings served more mundane purposes like barracks or basic storage.

"Cool. I'll just drop you off out front. Gotta take my supplies to the warehouse."

"Understood. Much appreciated, Private."

They passed simple, one-story structures, office buildings, and warehouses on their way to The Citadel. Nothing much had changed since Ellyne's time in the Ilserate army. Well, nothing much had changed here in the compound. Pretty much everything *else* about life had changed. But being back among the government buildings brought her instantly back into the moment. It was something she'd never thought, or hoped, would happen.

But here she was.

"Nicole had better appreciate this," she absentmindedly muttered.

"I'm sorry ma'am, what?"

"Oh, nothing. Just going over the day's tasks out loud."

Of course, the girl was in this predicament *because* of Ellyne. She'd be lucky if Nicole didn't sling a fireball at her once she found the girl.

When they reached The Citadel, the truck stopped, and she slid out. "Thanks again," she said. The man saluted as she stared up at the towering, shiny building. Before the Flocia Wars, The Citadel had more of an industrial look to it. Now however, it appeared some changes had been made so it looked smoother and sleeker—more elegant.

"Magic really *can* do anything, I guess," she muttered, passing through the automatic glass doors. Several soldiers on their way out immediately saluted as she walked past, providing her with a smug sense of satisfaction that made her want to laugh.

But Ellyne held it together as she briskly walked past them and approached the front desk. It was a rather large, ornate structure situated in the middle of an open rotunda which, as far as she could see, extended all the way to the height of the building itself. Above her, people moved about on the various floors, some of them using magic to basically fly across the open space from one side to the other—apparently in too much of a hurry (or too lazy) to walk around.

For a moment, she wondered if anyone had ever collided with another person in mid-air. The thought brought a smile to her lips. She'd pay several tiks to see that.

"How can I help you, miss?" one of the ladies behind the desk asked as Ellyne stepped close. She pulled one of two pens from her short, curly hair.

"Oh yes, hi." Ellyne tried her best not to fidget but, truth be told, she was nervous. Even when she *was* an officer in the Ilserate military, she never acted the part. "Yes, I've been on field duty stationed in Karakon for a while and just got back. I need to find a computer to . . . log some field reports."

That sounded official, didn't it?

Immediately, she wanted to take some of those words back. This desk jockey didn't need all that information.

"Second floor, room two-ten is the nearest computer lab, dearie." The woman pointed up and behind her.

"Thank you," Ellyne replied as she headed for the curved staircase that ended on the second floor. She didn't particularly remember what the inside of The Citadel looked like before—she'd only been inside a handful of times—but she knew it hadn't looked like this. "I guess the government *does* update some things after all."

She climbed the stairs until she reached the landing. Each floor was just a walkway with door after door along the outer wall, giving the illusion of an open, welcome building but it was really a glorified office space.

Several people passed by her, engrossed in a conversation and staring at some papers as they walked. Ellyne made her way around the landing until she found room 210. Looking identical to all other rooms, it had a frosted glass panel next to the door. She tried to peer in but couldn't make out any details past dark, fuzzy blobs. It felt a bit overzealous, being so suspicious, but it'd kept her alive thus far.

The door swung open as she pushed it inward, revealing a rather plain room beyond. In the center was a table with two computers. One of them was currently occupied by a man staring at the screen a mere inch or two from his face.

Ellyne sat at the terminal across from him, hoping to go unnoticed. She didn't need anyone nosing in on what she was about to do, whatever that may be.

She fumbled in her breast pocket briefly before pulling out the drive chip. After a few seconds of inspecting the computer, she found the proper slot but fumbled with the chip a couple of times until she found the right way to insert it.

She waited for something grand to happen but was met with disappointment.

"Come on, you damned machine."

"Try turning it off and turning it back on," the man said. "It's what technical support will tell you to do first if you contact them."

Ellyne thought she heard him mumble the word "ass-holes" at the end, and smirked. She waited a few seconds more, then hunted for the power switch. Just as she found it, however, her screen changed, briefly flashing The Keeper's familiar symbol.

She reclined in the chair and waited, now relieved that something was indeed happening, even if she didn't know what exactly. The same symbol flashed several more times as Ellyne became impatient. She would rather not stay in one place too long. It made her feel exposed and vulnerable.

"Whatever you're doing, I wish you'd hurry up," she muttered under her breath, looking around the room nervously. If the man across the table heard her, he showed no sign of it. In fact, she could only see a few wispy tufts of red hair poking out above the screen from time to time, accompanied by his noisy keystrokes.

She watched several shadows pass the frosted glass window, each time wondering if someone was going to barge into the room. She still hadn't ruled out the possibility of Derek betraying her.

After what felt like an eternity, the screen flickered and displayed a map. She watched as a blue dot made its way across the map, leaving a trail behind it until it finally stopped in a room. Once there, it blinked. Ellyne did her best to memorize the dot's route, but the map itself was a maze of corridors, rooms, and elevators.

She wondered if this was an intentional design. Maybe the Ilserate wanted to hide their secrets so well that not even they themselves could find them without a ridiculous treasure map. Even *with* a map she suspected it would be difficult.

"I hope you've done what you needed to do," she muttered, pulling the chip out and hiding it in a pocket. Then she took a deep breath and stood.

While she wasn't sure exactly how she was going to find her way to Nicole, one thing was for sure—if this map was accurate, the girl was deep beneath The Citadel.

CHAPTER
TWELVE

ELLYNE MADE her way to the elevator, trying to act normal for one of her rank. She would have been happy enough to be wearing a business suit instead of an officer's uniform. The constant salutes were annoying.

Finding the elevator was the easy part, though. Even though she'd only been in this building a handful of times in the past, she almost always needed to take the elevator because there were so damned many floors and no stairs.

And she'd been in the basement before, but only the first level. The problem currently was Nicole was apparently being held in sub-basement level four.

She didn't even know there *was* a sub-basement level four, let alone how to actually get there. If she remembered correctly, the main elevator only accessed the first basement level, which meant the other three levels (and any that might exist deeper) would be difficult to access.

Because, of course they would be.

There was a reason the Ilserate buried their secrets. Ellyne knew of only a few Ilserate mysteries—powerful magical arti-facts, documents, and even a couple of prisoners. For Nicole to be on the presumable lowest level of The Citadel meant she was extremely powerful or the Ilserate were very afraid of her.

Or both.

The elevator doors opened and several people stepped out, laughing. They brushed past Ellyne and headed down the walkway towards the main staircase. She slipped into the elevator after they left and quickly pressed the button labeled "B". The doors shut but soon opened again. Ellyne never got used to the near-undetectable motion magic created. She fondly remembered the jerky starting and stopping of the old, mechanical elevators.

Fondly in a way that she was thankful the elevator ride no longer made her want to vomit.

"Well, time to wing it," she muttered, stepping out and into the hall. Unlike the ornate rotunda, the basement was a series of stark catacombs made of concrete. In fact, it appeared the lighting was all still legacy fluorescent bulbs not powered by magic. That could be some kind of cost-saving measure or maybe they just never got around to caring since it was, after all, a basement.

That was some sketchy reasoning, though. The government had a reason for virtually everything they did. Oftentimes, those reasons were bullshit, but they were still reasons nonetheless.

Two guards immediately turned to greet her. One of them was about to speak but noticed her commander's insignia and snapped to attention, saluting. The other followed suit almost immediately. Ellyne saluted back and slowly walked away from the elevator, unsure where she was headed, but trying to look confident about it.

"Right, then. First order of business is to find the way down." Ellyne looked to her right and to her left. Each direction was a nondescript hallway much like the one straight ahead of her. This place looked no different than when she was last down here many years ago.

"Well, that wasn't here last time," she grumbled, spotting a small, solitary screen down the hallway to her left. "Okay JASN or Derek or whatever, I hope you're planning on helping me somehow."

She cautiously strode in the direction of the screen. It flickered briefly as she approached and displayed an arrow pointing to the right before going dormant. Having no better option, she followed it, eventually finding a door. Through the little glass window, she could see stairs leading down.

"Simple enough," she whispered, slipping through the door and hurrying down the stairs. Hopefully it would all be this quick and easy. Sure, she wanted to break Nicole out of here, but she was also tired of carrying this damned duffel bag.

The one flight of stairs ended at the next level labeled "B2" as indicated by a sign next to the door.

"Are you kidding me?" she sighed as she opened the door and stepped out into a hallway that looked identical to the one she'd just exited.

As annoying as it was, she had to admit that a setup like this was smart. It made sense to keep it as difficult as possible to escape should someone, say, try to bust out a prisoner and flee. And try as she might, Ellyne was never going to remember how to backtrack out of here. The good news was, she'd be with the world's most powerful magic user. At least Nicole could simply teleport to safety or something.

In any case, there was no use worrying about getting out until she finally got in. But Ellyne knew that wasn't entirely true. The best strategist would always be three moves ahead.

She didn't have time for planning. She improvised. She improvised about improvising, and when things went sour, she had a gun.

"Well, let's see where the next flight of stairs is. Probably on the opposite side somewhere."

She made her way through the halls, evading several

people, some in lab coats and others in business attire. She couldn't be sure she was headed in the right direction but stopping and looking confused wasn't an option.

Eventually, she found an outer wall and began methodically making her way around it, kicking herself for not thinking of this in the first place, but it was still slow going. She'd never realized how particularly immense the basement was, but it shouldn't have surprised her. Most of the actual work that mattered happened down here—the work the Ilserate preferred to keep away from the public as governments were wont to do.

She wondered if the Kithrak had a similar setup. Maybe they experimented on humans in a dark room tucked away somewhere. Derek may have been an exception (and she was still on the fence about him), but she still didn't trust the Kithrak.

Or humans, for that matter.

"Hey!" came a woman's voice from behind her.

Ellyne froze and slowly turned around to see a soldier approach, her boots clacking on the concrete floor. She had a wand at her hip and a gun slung over her shoulder—a curious combination.

The moment the soldier noticed the rank insignia on Ellyne's jacket, she snapped to attention, saluting. Ellyne returned a half-assed salute. She'd never been fond of the ritual. She was always tempted to give the middle finger instead.

"My apologies, Commander. I thought you were trespassing."

Ellyne relaxed slightly and felt her heart rate settle just a smidge. "At ease Corporal."

Ellyne hadn't paid attention to military ranks since she exited. She hoped she remembered them well enough to appear knowledgeable.

"Never been to the basement before and I'm trying to get

to level three. You wouldn't happen to know where the stairs are, would you, Corporal?"

"Without an escort?"

"They said it was urgent. Something's crawling up the brass's ass or something. I'm sure it's going to be supremely disappointing when I get down there."

"Yes, ma'am," the soldier replied, stifling a laugh. "The stairs are this way."

Ellyne followed the woman down the hall for what seemed like an eternity. Not only were the stairs on the opposite wall, they were apparently as far from the other stairs as they could possibly be. Another idea Ellyne thought was smart.

"Here we are, Commander."

"Thank you, Corporal."

"I hope it's not too boring down there."

"What? Oh, right. Me too, Corporal. But hopefully not overly exciting, either, given the, uh, nature of the area." She laughed and nudged the woman with her elbow.

Ellyne ducked inside the door and waited a moment, eventually peeking out to make sure the soldier wasn't hurrying to sound an alarm. Once she was satisfied, she descended the final staircase.

"I feel like I should be leaving chalk arrows or a trail of paper or something. This place is the worst."

She knew, after today, she'd probably never be allowed back unless she was captured and returned to The Citadel, but that was a matter for later.

Traversing Sublevel Three had been easy enough, made easier by the fact she never encountered anyone else and found the stairs quickly, hurrying down them and hoping her luck held.

Breathing deeply, she pulled on the door and stepped out into Sublevel Four. She was immediately surrounded by four guards—two pointed wands at her while the other two had their hands out in front of them, ready to cast spells.

"Stop!" one of them shouted. A husky man with a haircut that looked like it was self-inflicted stepped forward slightly, his eyes looking her up and down. His gaze lingered on her longer than necessary, but she resisted the urge to react. Now was not the time to cause problems, no matter how satisfying such a thing might be.

"What business have you down here?"

"I'm . . ." She hadn't expected to encounter anyone, especially official guards who were going to ask questions. But as she looked around, she saw a bevy of activity as people moved about the hallways, talking, looking at documents, and transporting objects she couldn't identify. Consequently, she hadn't devised a proper lie.

"Well?"

"I'm here to . . . interrogate the prisoner." She was getting better at this.

"Fine then. Which one?"

"The girl. You know the one. She's about twenty years old, won't shut up, kind of a bitch."

"Yeah," he laughed. The other three soldiers laughed as well. "I know the one." He held out his hand behind him and one of the other men placed a clipboard in it, which he then inspected. "What's your name?"

"Commander Vantz."

He flipped through the papers on the clipboard quickly enough to convince Ellyne he wasn't even really looking.

"I don't see you on here, lady."

"Commander."

"Whatever. The point is, you ain't on this list, which means you don't have clearance, which means I can't let you on the floor. You'll have to turn around and go back upstairs."

Ellyne kept her anger in check . . . barely.

"Of course I'm not on the list," she replied calmly.

But why was she not on the list? That was the question. She'd already surpassed the first level of lies and moved onto lies within lies. Hopefully, she wouldn't need to remember them all.

"I'm not on the list," she continued, now leaning in and whispering, "I'm from the military's Magical Research Division." She had no idea if the military even had a Magical Research Division, but it sounded solid.

"I've never heard of that."

"Of course you haven't. I've already told you too much. Make sure you watch your back from now on. I've put you in unnecessary danger."

"Wait, what?" He looked genuinely worried. The other guards stood around awkwardly, but visibly concerned.

"We're so top secret that we don't exist. So, if I were you, I'd forget you ever heard of us unless you want to deal with Marik Kalamoor."

"Shit, *he's* in it, too?"

"Forget I said that." She leaned back, satisfied with her lies. "Now," she continued in a normal tone, "may I pass?"

"Absolutely, ma'am! My apologies for holding you up."

The guard snapped to attention. The others followed suit soon after.

"Thank you." She took two steps past the man and stopped, turning to him. "So where, exactly, would I find her?"

"Oh, uh," he fumbled with the papers on the clipboard for a moment, then pointed to something with his finger. "Looks like she's in Block D4. Oh, *that's* what's in there! She must be special, since that's the one with the most guards."

Ellyne nodded and walked away, looking at the walls for any kind of identifiers.

"She is."

While this floor was just as confusing as the previous basement floors, it was far busier. Sometimes she found herself having to brush past someone just to get by. She knew the risk of being recognized was nearly nonexistent, yet she still felt exposed. It was time to find Nicole and get out.

After that . . . well, they'd figure it out.

"D4 . . . I'm only at A2? Ugh." She hurried down the current hallway until she eventually got to the A four block, then she turned right, hopefully heading toward the D block. She passed several open doors beyond which things happened she couldn't explain and others she would rather not have seen. It was in her best interest not to pay attention or linger.

Despite this policy, something caught her eye and she stopped to take a closer look into the room beyond a particular open door where two men faced off against something Ellyne immediately recognized.

Her heart raced as she watched the feral humanoid lunge at one of the men. Her hand went for her gun which was, fortunately, not currently at her hip. Shooting her weapon right now would most likely turn this whole situation sideways, given she was supposed to be laying low.

The creature charged one of the men who waved his right hand in the air, producing a glowing energy rope which he then threw at one of them. It snarled and drooled as it struggled to move but was fixed in place, entangled in the cord.

"See?" the other man said. "I told you it would work against a *grika*!"

Ellyne ducked to the left of the door frame, her back against the wall. "What in every hell imaginable is a grika?"

"This is amazing!"

"Now if we could just find a way to command them off a leash. The boss is going to be super happy when we tell him about this!"

Ellyne nodded to several people who passed her in the hall. She could feel her heart thumping in her chest having merely looked at the creature, but she continued listening while she pretended to guard the room, hoping that was actually a thing down here.

"I can't wait to let a few loose in Technician territory and see what happens," one of them laughed.

"Right? But not yet. Marik said we can't let them out to play for a while. But when we have enough of them . . . it'll be glorious! Freakin' Techs won't know what hit 'em!"

"And then, if we can turn them against the Kithrak!"

"I know, right?"

Ellyne briskly walked away, now determined to find Nicole even more quickly and get the hell out of this terror-filled dungeon.

How did officers wear these uniforms without constantly scratching every inch of their itchy bodies? Ellyne couldn't wait to get into clothes that weren't spawned straight from the deepest pits of despair. Maybe this was the reason most government lackeys were insufferable jerks.

"Marik's involved," she muttered. "I should've known. I wonder how many asses he's had to kiss to climb so far up the Ilserate ladder."

True, she hated the man. He double-crossed her and he still occupied her thoughts. But what was he up to? Marik was many things but foolish or stupid were not among them. He was always calculating and careful.

The fact the Ilserate knew about these . . . grika . . . was a disturbing development. But the fact they planned to use them for their own purposes . . . that was terrifying. And there was still the question of where they came from in the first place. The government was great at exploiting resources, but not necessarily understanding them, so questioning anyone around here about the grika's origins would most likely be a dead end—at least with the rank-and-file.

As much as she'd like to stay and find the answers, she came here for a different reason, and it was time to be on about it. She hurried past doors and windowless rooms, nodding to guards, employees, and several soldiers, and keeping her head low until she finally found what she sought.

This wasn't just a nondescript, closed door like most of the others. This particular block was a vast open area and appeared to be completely cordoned off with guards and soldiers everywhere—both stationed at various locations and patrolling the area.

In the center was what looked like a small concrete bunker, maybe no larger than one of the apartments back at the murder shack. Nicole's prison couldn't be any more obvious.

She adjusted her ugly cap, took a deep breath, and strutted up to the nearest guards, creating her plan with every step.

"Good day, gentlemen," she said, as emotionless as she could. "I'm here to interrogate the girl for official military business."

Ellyne didn't know if her words sounded official, but she hoped her rank would eliminate any curiosity or doubt.

One of them nodded subtly and motioned her through. She walked toward the bunker, surprised it was that easy. She watched the door get closer as her mind raced to try and think of a plan. Most of her current plan involved just getting past that first checkpoint. Hopefully, Nicole would have some magic-related insight into how they were going to escape.

That was it—that was the best idea she had. After lying and sneaking her way through this whole damned fortress of a building, her best hope was to rely on an eighteen-year-old girl to get them out?

"Shit."

She stopped in front of the final two guards who stood just outside the bunker. Their attention immediately went to the duffel bag.

"What's in the bag?" the woman asked.

"That's classified," Ellyne responded. "I'm here on official military business to interrogate the girl."

A bead of sweat trickled down her back. If they didn't buy her story, this could go badly.

"I have no record—"

"Look, I know I'm not on the list or schedule and I have no invitation to the party. I really wish the process were different but I'm from a department that doesn't make reservations. Believe me, it would make my life so much easier if I could just plan ahead, but my superiors don't operate that way. You have no idea how many times I've had this conversation, soldier."

The two guards stared, dumbfounded. They looked at each other, obviously hoping the other had any idea what was going on. Ellyne once again couldn't believe how good she was at this acting thing. She thought maybe should make a career out of it.

"So . . . can I . . . " Ellyne gestured to the door after a moment of severe, awkward discomfort.

"Oh, uh," the guard on the right stammered, "yes ma'am! My apologies . . ."

"Commander Vantz, soldier."

"Right, please, head on in. Let us know if you need anything."

"Thank you. Keep up the good work."

Ellyne opened the door and slipped inside, exhaling deeply once the door shut behind her. What she was met with was absolutely the opposite of what she expected. What appeared as a small bunker from the outside belied the spacious interior which was at least ten times larger. The room was empty save the hospital-style bed in the middle on which Nicole lay motionless.

"Where the hell am I and what have they done to you?"

She approached the bed, shedding her officer's jacket and duffel bag along the way while loosening several buttons on her shirt. The relief she felt was nearly instant, but there was no time to dwell on it.

Well, maybe just for a second.

She scratched her itchy arms and stood over the bed, watching Nicole's chest move rhythmically up and down as the girl slept.

"Nicole," she whispered. "Nicole, wake up."

The girl didn't so much as stir even a little.

"Come on, Nicole. We've got to get out of here! I didn't risk my ass and walk through the most boring building in Karnascus just to watch you snooze!"

Nicole remained unresponsive.

"Shit." Ellyne ran a hand through her hair and paced around the bed. "They didn't know how to control you, so they must have put some kind of sleeping spell on you, didn't they?" She kicked the side of the bed, jostling it, but Nicole still didn't move.

"Hey! Wake up loser!" She grabbed Nicole's shoulder and shook her. Though Nicole didn't wake, the intense burning pain she felt caused her to quickly pull her arm back. She gasped and inspected her hand, seeing no injury. The burning calmed to a tingle and dispersed throughout her body, eventually vanishing altogether.

Nicole stirred but didn't wake.

"Are you serious?" She looked at the palm of her hand, scowling. She knew what she had to do but in no way did she look forward to it. In fact, she was unsure if it would even work. "I hope you appreciate this."

She put her hand on Nicole's shoulder again. This time, pain shot through her entire body. Every inch of her felt both as if it were on fire and freezing at the same time. She tried to scream but could produce no sound, nor could she pull her hand away. She was frozen in a moment of unending torment that felt as though it would last forever.

When the torture ended, she collapsed on the floor, desperately catching her breath and barely conscious.

Sweat stung her eyes and dripped off her chin as she struggled to stand. She expected to see Nicole fully awake and her spirits sank when she saw the girl hadn't moved. Just when she thought she was beginning to understand things, she was met with disappointment.

"Damn. I'm sorry, Nicole. I thought that would . . . I thought that would work. I guess I still haven't figured things out."

She wiped sweat from her brow and touched Nicole's shoulder again, bracing for the excruciating pain. But when nothing happened, she sank down, sitting on the cold concrete and leaning against the side of the bed.

"I thought I could somehow dispel the magic. I thought that's what the pain meant. I don't know why I thought it . . . it's just, I didn't want this to happen to you."

She felt tears replacing the perspiration on her face. It was only now that she realized just how badly she'd messed up. Everyone treated Nicole like an asset or a weapon. Ellyne thought she was different but now she knew she was the same as everyone else.

"I mean, yeah, you can be chatty and annoying and, at first, I wanted to throw you out a window . . . but you only wanted someone to help you." She wiped her cheek on her sleeve and sniffed. "And now, I'm sitting here in this damned uniform, crying at the bedside of someone who just wanted a friend. But I screwed that up, didn't I?"

"Yeah, you did."

Ellyne gasped and jumped to her feet, only to nearly collapse again, but she steadied herself on the bed. Nicole slowly sat up, rubbing her eyes and smirking.

"Sonofa—"

"But you came back for me." She swung her legs over the

edge of the bed, then hopped off. "So, I guess I can forgive you. This time, anyway."

Ellyne wasn't prepared for the hug, nor did she feel she deserved it, but Nicole threw her arms around her and squeezed.

"I'm sorry," she whispered.

"Thank you," Nicole said at about the same time, her voice quivering.

"I was stubborn and selfish." She gently stroked Nicole's dark hair to try and calm her but also to calm herself. "And don't thank me yet, because we still have to get out of here."

She hurriedly opened the duffel bag and got to work, shedding the officer's uniform for her familiar leather jacket which she'd packed with ammunition. Sliding her weapon back in the holster at her hip felt like welcoming an old friend.

While she changed, Nicole did something with magic or, at least, that's what Ellyne assumed. "Getting out of here might be tricky," she said, staring at something Ellyne couldn't see.

"Well, we're not sneaking out—I'm sure escorting the mage breaker out of a secure facility would go over marvelously. Can't you just teleport yourself out or whatever?" At the very least, she hoped Nicole could get herself to safety, even if she couldn't go with her.

"Not out of here."

"What do you mean?"

"I don't know how you dispelled the sleeping spell they cast on me—thank you again for that, by the way. That was a pretty strong spell. I was out like a light. Did I snore? I'm pretty sure I did. I think I even might have drooled on myself at some point because—"

Ellyne smiled at her ramblings, but knew time was of the essence. "Nicole, focus."

"Right. Anyway, just as they cast the sleeping spell to keep me here, they've also cast enchantments on the area to keep me from using some forms of magic."

"I assume that means blinking and teleporting?" Ellyne shoved the officer's uniform into the duffel bag and threw it across the room. It slid across the floor and eventually stopped close to one of the corners.

"Now you're catching on. But they were sloppy. Apparently, whoever cast the enchantments isn't very good at it. They're powerful spells, but someone seems to have forgotten a few."

"Huh. Well, that's a mixed bag, I guess."

"So, what do we do?"

Ellyne drew her revolver. She pulled back the hammer and grinned.

"What we do best."

CHAPTER
THIRTEEN

"SO, YOU HAVE A PLAN THEN?" Nicole asked as they calmly exited the bunker. Leave it to her to ask the one question Ellyne had no real answer for.

"Nope. I'm improvising. Just keep walking and let's see how far we get."

"Then what?"

"You ask too many questions."

"Hey, stop! Where are you taking her?" Two guards rushed toward them, hands gripping the wands hanging on their belts.

"Well shit, that wasn't as far as I hoped."

With a still shaky hand, Ellyne reached for her gun, about to draw it, but Nicole grabbed her hand and pulled it away. At the same time, she waved her other hand in the air and mumbled something Ellyne didn't understand.

Both guards stiffened, as if standing at attention. "Right! Important business! Carry on, ma'am!"

Nicole grinned. "You do what you do best, and I'll do what *I* do best."

"You'll get no argument from me. Does that include

making yourself invisible or a disguise or something? Because it'd be much easier to get you out of here."

"I can't. Someone's cast an awful lot of wards in the area to block magic—not just mine. They're really powerful. I'd bet they involved many mages to make them this strong."

"I guess they'll be sitting in their T-Helms for a while then."

Ellyne gazed around at the guards stationed about the area. Many of them were beginning to take notice and pointed at the two of them. Had there been this many on her way in? She suddenly wished she'd taken a little more time to observe her surroundings before trying to escape.

"So which way is out?" Nicole asked. "We're beginning to attract attention, and not the good kind—like a boy wanting to ask you out to a dance. Not that I know much about such things except what I've read in some—"

"Yeah, I get it. I don't know which way is out because every damned hallway and room in this place looks exactly the same. But we should at least pick a direction, because anything's better than being out in an open space like this."

They hurried ahead, out of the area with the bunker, and moved through a series of hallways until Ellyne stopped.

"I think we're going in circles. This place is a maze of frustration."

"And things just got worse." Nicole pointed to a group of guards who, upon seeing the two of them, sprinted from the other end of the hallway.

"Shit." Ellyne drew her gun and ducked as spells flew overhead.

Nicole wasted no time fighting back but she had a difficult time finding magic that she could use. She blocked several spells before settling on an adequate counterattack, immediately felling one of the guards.

"This is tougher than I'd expected," she growled, lobbing a blob of orange energy at their enemies. Just as Ellyne felt confident they would make it, she spotted more guards closing in from other directions.

"You won't escape!" one of them shouted, firing off a spell that collided with the wall above her head, raining concrete chunks and dust down on her. "Surrender now, and no one will be harmed!"

"This would be no problem without these wards," she grunted, obviously frustrated and probably taxed from the effort.

"To hell with it."

Ellyne fired a shot at the guard who spoke. The area around him shimmered and deflected her bullet.

"Shit. Nicole, they've got barriers around them. My bullets won't harm them!"

Rarely had she seen this effect. It was powerful magic and there probably were only a handful of mages who knew how to cast it.

"Marik, that asshole," she mumbled. "He knew I'd eventually come for her. He knows how to create those barriers."

"What?"

"Nothing. Just keep doing what you're doing." The groups of guards were cautious, but they slowly closed in from all sides. It would take just one successful spell to knock either of them out or, worse, kill them. And while Nicole seemed to be holding her own, even with her restricted magic ability, she couldn't hold out forever. These idiots would probably just keep throwing more guards or soldiers at them until they got lucky, and Ellyne didn't want to wait around for that.

Still, watching Nicole in action was impressive. The girl's hands moved furiously and with an incredible speed and fluidity Ellyne had never witnessed. She was not only blocking spells from all directions but also casting them without even looking.

Another guard slumped to the floor. Ellyne had no way of

knowing if she was stunned or sleeping or dead. It didn't much matter to her, but she assumed Nicole wasn't the sort to instantly resort to lethal methods.

Not like Ellyne would.

"We can't do this all day, Nicole!"

"Is that what you think?" Nicole laughed, knocking down two guards and redirecting incoming spell at another guard. "This is kind of fun! Most of these guys are terrible, though. They probably only know a couple of spells and most of them are throwing simple stunners which are, like, so last week!"

Ellyne let Nicole ramble while she considered their options. More importantly, she thought she heard the guttural growl of a . . . what did that man call them? Grika? It didn't matter. What mattered was, Ellyne suspected the room behind her held at least one of them.

"The enemy of my enemy is . . . a mindless ghoul?" she mused. "I mean, you've had worse ideas, sure. Coming back to get Nicole may have been one of them, but so was letting the Ilserate have her in the first place." She dodged a spell that missed her by probably less than an inch. "What could go wrong?"

She tried the door behind her and, unsurprisingly, found it locked.

"What are you doing?" Nicole asked.

"I've got an idea. It's probably the worst idea I've ever had, and I doubt you're going to like it."

"When has that ever stopped you?"

"Exactly! Now you're catching on!"

Ellyne fired two rounds at the jamb where she estimated the lock was, sending wood splinters and bits of concrete everywhere. When she tried it again and found it still locked, she emptied the remaining six rounds into the door. She then slipped the empty cartridge out of the cylinder and replaced it with a full cartridge.

"Hope that did it," she whispered, slinging the gun sideways to snap the cylinder back in place. "Nicole!" she shouted, grabbing her and pulling her to the side of the door

"What?"

"This!" Ellyne first rammed into the door but quickly realized it opened outward. She pulled hard on the door, and it swung open. She hid behind it while Nicole continued her defense, dropping another guard in the process. "Suck it, government losers!"

But when nothing happened, Ellyne growled and swore under her breath. She wondered if she'd just opened the door to an empty room or an office or a bathroom. Certainly, the latter would be hilarious if they weren't in their current predicament.

She peeked around the corner of the door, pulling back quickly to dodge a mote of magical energy that exploded in front of her. Her brief glimpse showed her the room was indeed inhabited by a writhing mass of beasts climbing over one another to feed on something.

The urge to vomit was strong, and Ellyne gagged several times at the smell that hit her like a train. Couldn't someone invent a spell for that or was magic really that useless? It seemed simple enough, yet here she was.

"Hey, grika things!" she yelled, quickly poking her head around the corner and pulling back. She waited for the onslaught of ravenous, mindless rage but was disappointed when none came.

Nicole continued blocking spells and retaliating, but the guards poured in from everywhere, slowly making progress. She seemed to be having fun, giggling and shouting puerile insults. Maybe, to her, it was a game.

The walls around Ellyne, now pocked with divots and holes, continued to rain tiny bits of debris on her head as errant spells collided with them, chipping paint and concrete with each burst.

"Oh come on! These things couldn't wait to dig into me

last time. What the hell is so important this time that they won't leave the damned room? You know what? I can't wait around."

Something hit her in the back. Her body tensed up, as if paralysis was setting in, but it quickly dissipated into a warm, tingly feeling which disappeared altogether.

She ducked around the door and fired her gun twice into the crowd. It didn't matter if her bullets found bodies, because it was more than enough to get the creatures' attention.

Several grika looked up, snarling through blood-soaked, jaws, and saw Ellyne who ducked around the door again as they followed close behind, spilling out into the hallway in a frenzy of claws and gnashing teeth.

"Hey, Nicole. Run!"

Ellyne grabbed the girl's sleeve and darted down the hall, covering her head and trying to dodge spells at the same time. Nicole ran with her, lagging a little as she blocked every spell she could along the way. Ellyne wondered if she even knew what pursued them.

"Quick, down here!"

She dragged Nicole down a hallway to the right and watched as a steady stream of grika passed them by, presumably headed for the tasty guards. Shortly thereafter, they heard screams that were quickly drowned out by savage shrieks.

"You let those things out?" Nicole asked, gasping for air.

"Yeah. One of my better ideas," Ellyne laughed. "I'm just glad they don't really care who they tear apart or else we'd be ass deep in them right now. On second thought, it was a terrible idea that just happened to work out as intended . . . for once. At least, for now. You know what? Just go with it."

"Why did they have those things locked up?"

"I think I know, and it's not a great answer. My bigger question remains—what the hell are they?"

"Come on, let's find the stairs up."

"I think they're this way." Ellyne pointed further down the hallway and they hurried in that direction but it wasn't long until they saw another group of guards. "In here!"

Ellyne pulled open one of the doors and pushed Nicole inside. She shut the door and they both leaned against it, waiting and breathing heavily, but trying to be quiet about it.

"How many guards does the Ilserate have?" Nicole whispered.

"Good question. How many secrets does the Ilserate have?"

They heard the hurried footsteps and hushed voices of the guards as they passed and breathed a sigh of relief.

"Hopefully, everyone's more concerned about the grika than us right now. Should give us the advantage to slip away unseen."

"Grika? Those things have names?"

"Sort of."

Someone coughed. Ellyne whipped around and pointed her gun at several frightened Ilserate employees who had apparently been present the entire time. Slowly, they all put their hands up, shooting glances at one another but saying not a word.

"Oh, hell." She holstered her gun. "Sorry guys. I can see you're busy here, and we didn't mean to barge in on your . . . uh, clerical work?"

They all kept their hands up.

"Two things. One, we'd appreciate it if you forgot you saw us. That'd be great. Two, I'd recommend *not* leaving the room. In fact, you might want to lock the door behind us."

Nobody said a word as they all stared at Ellyne and Nicole.

"Good talk." She slipped out the door, followed by Nicole. No sooner had it latched shut when she heard the lock slide into place. "Come on, this way. Quick!"

"Do you think they sounded an alarm?"

"Yep. But I'm not sure who's going to respond at the moment."

"Well, I hope this is the door to the stairs, because look what's behind us!"

Ellyne glanced behind her as she ran. Grika poured through the hallways like a flood of flesh and teeth. They ran everywhere, loping on all four limbs, climbing the walls, scurrying over one another, and attacking anything in sight.

"How many of them were in that room, Ellyne?"

"At least two."

"Not helpful!"

"Come on!" The door looked familiar. She pulled it open and they slipped inside just as the grika lunged for them. They pounded on the door, hurling their bodies at it and screeching savagely as she watched through the window. "Up the stairs. I'm not sure if that door will hold them."

Ellyne truly hadn't gotten a good glimpse into the room—how big it was or how many grika were in it. Certainly, she'd expected a few and got dozens. Probably loads more. How many more were there? How many other rooms contained these monsters and, still that nagging question—what actually were they?

"Let's hope they don't know how to work a doorknob." Nicole quipped.

They darted up the stairs and used the tiny window to peek out. "Looks clear," Ellyne said, scrutinizing her narrow field of view. "Let's go. Hopefully we've seen the last of the beasties."

She opened the door and immediately knew she was mistaken, judging from the trail of smeared blood on the floor that led down the hall and around a corner.

"Let's not go that way," Nicole laughed nervously.

"Agreed."

They hurried in the opposite direction. This time, she

made sure to stick to the exterior wall and keep an eye out for the trademark window in the stairwell door.

"The stairs are at the other end of this floor. Let's just move quickly and not get lost."

"And not run into any of those . . . grika."

"Too late." Ellyne pointed down one of the halls where a grika was chewing on a body in a blood-soaked business suit. It noticed them immediately and lumbered forward, quickly galloping on its hands and feet.

"I got this." Nicole stepped forward and conjured a horizontal plane of brilliant light that shot forward, bisecting the creature which seemed unaffected as it continued advancing. "Uh, maybe not."

"It's immune to magic? How is it immune to—you know what? Never mind. Let me handle it."

Ellyne drew her revolver and fired a shot, catching the grika squarely in the chest. It tumbled across the floor and came to a stop, motionless. "It's about time I got to kill something. But let's hurry. My guess is we just attracted more of them."

"More of them? How did it even get up here?"

"Well, they made it up here somehow—probably busted down a door or two. And where there's one, there are probably more."

Ellyne exchanged ammo cartridges while they moved. She always felt safer with a full cylinder. It would do little good if they ran into a horde of grika, though. Nicole looked genuinely scared. Ellyne surmised it was much the same feeling she herself felt when her bullets bounced harmlessly off guards with shields. Such a thing was no surprise to her, though. This was probably new for Nicole and was most likely terrifying.

"Can you blink or teleport yourself out yet? Or maybe just blow a hole in the ceiling and fly out?"

Nicole concentrated but shook her head, a look of defeat on her face.

"Whatever wards they've cast still affect this level, too. But I sense they're not as strong. But it's not an option anyway, if you're not coming with me."

"Well, that's sort of good news, I guess. Maybe they'll get weaker the higher up we go. Let's keep moving."

Several times, they saw either multiple grika or evidence of them but somehow managed to avoid a confrontation. They apparently operated on instinct, but what drove that instinct was a mystery. Sure, they liked to eat but Ellyne suspected, more than anything, they enjoyed killing. She didn't expect they would like to sit down and enjoy a good book.

They climbed the stairs to sub-basement two. One more level and they could take the elevator up. Hopefully, though, Nicole would be able to get herself out magically before that. If the wards were weakening the further up they traveled, it could be possible. Of course, she knew shit about magic, so it was just a guess.

They hurried straight through the main hallway toward the opposite end of the basement level, once again preparing to look for the telltale door to the stairs. There were no signs of grika on this floor, and they passed employees going about their business who gave them confused looks as they ran by.

"Just like any corporation," Ellyne laughed, "their communication skills are abysmal! Hopefully they don't know anything about us!"

"Ellyne Thandaral!" a familiar voice shouted. "This has gone far enough, don't you think?"

From all directions, guards and soldiers emerged and clogged the various hallways. Some had wands at their hips but there were several with guns and they were all aimed at Ellyne.

Marik Kalamoor emerged from the crowd wearing a familiar smug, shit-eating grin on his face.

"I wondered when you were going to show up," Ellyne growled. "I thought I recognized the smell."

"Yes, well, you've caused enough trouble for one day, don't you think?"

"Oh, you mean your little pest problem?" Ellyne smirked.

"We'll deal with the grika quickly enough. They will no longer be, as you say, a problem."

"I was talking about you."

From the sounds of several people in the crowd stifling laughs, Ellyne could tell Marik was treating everyone around him as well as usual and garnering the standard level of respect he deserved.

"It was a nice effort, but you've lost. Not only does the Ilserate still have the mage breaker, but we also have the number one troublemaker in Karnascus."

Ellyne put her right hand over her heart and smiled. "I'm number one? I mean, I'm flattered! It's a great honor. I'd like to thank all the little people—"

Marik rolled his eyes. "You always were annoying."

Ellyne laughed. She wanted nothing more than to bury all eight bullets in his soft flesh, but she knew he'd be more heavily protected than any of the guards. His personality may have been the worst, but his skill in magic was among the highest in the city. Her tongue ran over the metal in her jaw, conjuring her usual hatred for the man.

"Funny, I was about to say the same about you." She tossed her blonde hair back in a minor show of defiance, then leaned against the wall and shut her eyes. Marik was a talker, but not in the same way Nicole was. He did so enjoy gloating, especially when he wasn't aware of his disadvantage. Now was the best time to get whatever information she could.

"Still got a mouth on you, I see."

"There was a time when you enjoyed kissing it." Ellyne

retorted, holding back the bile rising in her throat at the thought.

"Wait," Nicole interrupted. "You two . . . were a thing?"

"Briefly," Ellyne replied. "I didn't mean to bring it up. It's not really something I prefer to remember, because of the nausea associated with it."

"Take the girl back to her cell," Marik commanded, motioning to Nicole. He then pointed to a group of soldiers. "Take your team and fan out. If there are any grika on this level I want them apprehended, preferably. But kill them if you must."

"Oh, the grika," Ellyne mused, opening her eyes. "I probably shouldn't have let them out, but they were hungry, and I just couldn't deny the poor bastards."

Yes, well, they're a minor annoyance and we'll get the situation cleaned up. If we must kill them, so be it. We've got more. If they die, we'll *make* more."

"Make more? You're *making* these things? What the hell, Marik? What are your mad scientists doing? They were people, damn it!"

"People who didn't follow the laws, Ellyne. Nobody will miss them. Besides, they have a greater purpose now. You, on the other hand are the same, petty malcontent you've always been."

"Your flattery is . . . flattering? Crap, I messed that up. Anyway, we were once on the same side, Marik. Never forget that."

"Take the girl back downstairs and post more guards around her—inside this time."

"Yes, sir," one of the soldiers replied. "What about her?" he asked, pointing to Ellyne.

"Kill her."

"No! You can't!" Nicole shrieked.

"You're right, Nicole," Ellyne replied. She felt fear bubbling to the surface. There were far too many enemies, even with Nicole at her side, to find a way out. And even if they weren't protected by magical barriers, she only had eight bullets. "Marik couldn't kill me before, so he's having his sycophants do it for him."

She watched Marik disappear in the crowd without uttering a response. She didn't want to die, but it bothered her even more that she as going to die without getting her revenge. Her mind scrambled to come up with a solution—some way to escape—but it failed at every turn.

This wasn't how she ever considered it would end. At the very least, she would have gotten back at Marik first. Even alcohol poisoning was better than this. If they fought, they would probably both die. This way, maybe Nicole could live and escape again.

Two soldiers grabbed Nicole's hands and pinned them behind her back. She struggled, screaming and shouting, but to no avail. Her screams quickly turned to sobs as soldiers moved in and pushed Ellyne to her knees. She wanted to resist, to kick the guy in the crotch and shoot her way out, but hopelessness took over and she could do nothing but obey. Her gun was useless against magic and the sheer number of bodies. Marik had obviously been waiting for the right time, and she fell for it.

"You can't do this," Nicole shrieked through her sobs, choking on her own cries. "You can't kill her! Don't do what that asshole said! Let me go!"

Ironic that magic, the one thing she'd worked so hard to avoid, would be her end. If it were up to her, she would've done away with it the moment it was discovered. Filthy, vile magic. The world was better off without it. Without the Kithrak.

"It's okay, Nicole," she said, trying to sound calm. "It's okay. Just don't give up. Don't let them have whatever it is they want. You can escape again and hopefully find someone who can actually help you."

"Ellyne, I'm so sorry! I never should have gotten you involved in this!"

"You're right," Ellyne sneered. "But I . . . if I had . . ." The words got stuck in her throat. "Just take care of yourself, Nicole."

She shut her eyes and exhaled waiting for the end, as the first spell caught her in the chest. It stung and her lungs burned but the sensation subsided.

Another spell hit her in the head and another in the chest, followed by another in the arm. Each time, she felt a piercing, stabbing pain that eventually vanished.

"What the hell?" she heard a woman shout. "Hit her with more!"

Her entire body was on fire as countless spells penetrated her body, each one a pin prick on her skin that set every nerve in her body ablaze with white hot pain. She felt every spell hit her, she pushed through every intended effect, and she felt each spell wane, yet she still knelt, waiting for it to all be over.

It wasn't until she recognized a familiar sensation beneath it all that she realized today was not that day.

ELLYNE SLOWLY GOT to her feet, realizing she was no longer in danger. Though the spells kept coming, colliding with her body and causing intense pain before dissipating, they didn't appear to cause her permanent harm. Her arms and legs tingled—minor at first, as if they'd fallen asleep. And with each spell that hit her, the sensation grew, but she remained otherwise unaffected.

"How is this possible?" someone shouted.

"Our spells have no effect! What kind of magic is this?" another guard shouted.

With each spell that hit her, Ellyne felt the tingly warmth within her intensify. She should have been dead countless times by now and, while she didn't understand how or why she still lived, she wasn't willing to stand by and watch. She knew an opportunity when she saw one.

Ellyne remembered feeling this very sensation just before she'd clobbered the grika back at the murder shack. Although she still understood none of this, she knew it was her best chance.

It was her only chance.

"This had better work," she growled just before she

charged one of the groups. They still lobbed spells at her from every direction, but now she saw uncertainty in their eyes. And, as she closed the distance, they tried to back up.

They felt fear. Ellyne felt rage.

There was nowhere for them to go and, as her fist collided with the first man's face, a wave of force rippled outward, cracking the concrete and catapulting the group into the air. Men and women were thrown in all directions, slamming violently into the walls, the ceiling, and the floor.

If they were dead, she had no idea, but she couldn't linger to find out. She did know, however, that the other bastards still chucking spells at her were about to get the same treatment.

"Holy crap! Did you see that?"

"What was that? What happened?"

"What do we do?"

"Use your guns! Shoot her!"

Ellyne was on them before anyone could act. She was a flurry of kicks and punches as she darted, dodged, and attacked anyone nearby. Bones and wands snapped as she fought furiously, unable to differentiate between the two as each attack was fueled by a power she didn't understand but thoroughly enjoyed.

She drew her sword and pressed the button to extend it. Now that she knew her fists could hurt them, she assumed her sword could, too.

Each guard or soldier froze with a look of terror and confusion painted on their faces. Ellyne breathed deeply and concentrated. The inner warmth had dwindled but was still there. If Nicole was right, and this was all fueled by flocia, then she needed more.

Unfortunately, for these poor slobs, she was surrounded by it.

She could feel it in the spells around her and in the very structure of the building. Everything was flocia and flocia was everywhere. And as she felt it, she embraced it—she *absorbed* it. Painful warmth trickled into her body as she and her assailants stared at one another.

Even the two men holding Nicole were transfixed as she struggled in their grips.

"I told you to use your guns! This bitch can't deflect bullets!"

Guns. Yes, guns. Now that was a fantastic idea!

Before any of them could act, Ellyne drew her revolver and fired, catching one of Nicole's captors and knocking him back. She held the trigger and rapidly fanned the hammer seven more times with her palm, felling seven more enemies, including Nicole's other captor.

"How did she do that? What happened to our wards?"

"Shit! I don't want to die! We need to retreat!"

"The mage breaker is loose!"

The ranks failed and soldiers and guards alike fled. When others noticed this behavior, they, too, retreated. Ellyne watched and dropped another loaded cartridge into the cylinder, quickly flicking it back into place. The moment she looked up she was met with a hug.

"I thought you were going to die!" Nicole wept into Ellyne's shoulder. "I thought they killed you! But then . . . but then you did all that—whatever it was and you're alive!"

It had been a long time since she'd not only enjoyed human contact but had any at all. Unless you counted punching or kicking someone. In that case, it was just a few seconds ago, and she enjoyed that as well.

She was surprised at how quickly she returned the hug.

"Wait." Nicole pushed away a little so she could look Ellyne in the eyes. "Why *aren't* you dead? They hit you with, like, probably a hundred spells. Stunning, sleep, explosive, even *death* spells! I saw them! I saw them all!"

"It's complicated," Ellyne said as she shrugged.

"How complicated?"

"I'm not sure I fully understand it myself. Whatever happened, it can wait. We need to get out of here. Word travels fast, so I'm guessing the reinforcements who haven't pissed themselves will be arriving soon."

Nicole snickered, then looked embarrassed.

"And the floor above us will be crawling with stooges."

"Can't you just, you know, do again what you just did?"

"I don't know how I did it in the first place. I prefer to have a maximum of one near-death experience per day."

"Then what?"

Ellyne looked around them. The hallways were empty, but that wouldn't last long. Marik would probably come back to finish the job personally this time and, while she enjoyed the thought of showing him the business end of her gun, this wasn't a fight she felt she could currently win.

"I need you to teleport us out of here."

It was a bold idea—one she was unsure would work on her, given her resistance to magic. At best, she hoped Nicole could escape.

"I told you, I can't—"

"I know. You can't teleport with the wards or whatever in place. I'm going to weaken or remove them for you."

"Wait, what?"

"I mean, I'm going to try to weaken or remove them. Hopefully enough to give you a chance to blip us out of here or whatever."

"How are you going to do that?"

Ellyne looked around. The halls remained empty. She expected a wave of grika or worse—if there was worse. Which, she suspected, there was somewhere.

"I have no idea."

"You're not making sense."

"Just stay quiet and keep an eye out for any bozos or monsters or . . . whatever else, okay?"

Ellyne closed her eyes, breathed deeply, and tried to relax.

Or wait, should she try *not* to relax? Maybe she needed to concentrate instead of relaxing. Or maybe she needed to reach out with her thoughts and try to feel the magic.

Just thinking about it gave her a headache. She had no actual idea how to do this or if it would even work. It was almost as if her body took over, adapted, and did what it needed to do without her control.

"Whatever you're going to do, you might want to hurry up. We're about to have company."

"Great," Ellyne growled. "That really helps me relax."

She remembered how it felt, the times she was surrounded by magic. Not just the times she was out and about and walking past people on hoversticks or casting their spells. She remembered the feeling she got when in the hallway leading to JASN's cortex, being surrounded by overwhelming amounts of magic. She now knew that tingly feeling she got was related. More accurately, it was produced when she fed off flocia.

She simply needed to do that again only, in this case, feed off a specific ward. Or maybe she could feed off *all* of them. Or, as things were going, none of them.

"Come on, damn it," she growled, balling her hands into fists.

"Ellyne, whatever you're going to do, please do it soon!"

She touched something. Not literally, but it felt physical—as if her hand had reached out and gently brushed a finger over something. It felt warm and tingly and she reached out for it again.

This time, she didn't just barely touch it. She grabbed it.

The moment she did, she felt a connection and its power, whatever it was, seeped into her as if she were a sponge. It was simultaneously terrifying and invigorating and, while she had no way of knowing what was happening, she felt certain this was right.

Suddenly, she felt empty.

"Ellyne, you did it!"

Ellyne opened her eyes to find they were no longer in The Citadel's crummy basement.

"Whatever you did, it worked!" Nicole continued.

"Awesome! I wasn't positive what would happen and I'm not even sure how you were able to teleport me out but—wait, where are we?"

The room's curtains were drawn, allowing only slivers of light in, but it was more than enough for Ellyne. She recognized this place, and she didn't want to be here.

"What the hell, Nicole? You brought us to the murder shack?"

"I know, right? They'll never think to look for us here! I mean, we'd be fools to come back here, right?"

"Yet here we are."

"Wait, what? What's wrong?"

"We can't stay here. This place is dangerous, Nicole."

"Why? You mean those things? Those . . . grika? We just busted out of The Citadel! We're bad asses, Ellyne! This place can't be worse. A few monstrosities got nothing on us."

"More than a few, Nicole. Bringing us here was a mistake."

"Wait, what? What do you mean, more than a few? How many more?"

"Don't ask. Just come with me. I need to show you something—something I wasn't entirely certain of until just recently."

Ellyne led Nicole into the hall and down the stairs to the basement. She flicked on the light and waited for it to groan to life, revealing the piles of broken and disassembled T-Helms contained within.

"What is this?" Nicole gasped, staring in disbelief.

"Busted T-Helms, Nicole. Broken by someone and deliberately stashed down here behind what was once a locked door before I . . . unlocked it."

"But why?" Nicole bent down and picked up a piece of plastic and shredded wires. "Why would someone destroy a bunch of T-Helms and then store them? There must be hundreds of them down here!"

"Well," Ellyne sighed, "I've got a wacky theory about that. Would you like to hear it?"

Nicole nodded, turning over in her hand the broken T-Helm part.

"This apartment building isn't a standard living situation. The term 'murder shack' was more appropriate than we thought."

"What do you mean?"

"I think this place was an experiment, Nicole. These Tara-noms—I think they were taken from the residents and stored down here. Someone broke them in case the occupants came looking and somehow gained access to this room."

"But why? Why do that? What good is taking magic away from someone?"

"They didn't take magic away from anyone." Ellyne gestured to one of the piles. "They took away their ability to pay for magic."

"That's horrific," Nicole gasped. She staggered backward and leaned against the wall, bumping a shelf and causing several broken T-Helms to slide off and clatter onto the floor. "All these people . . ."

"They were locked in this prison from the outside. Their lust for magic consumed them and they had no T-Helms available."

Nicole dropped the piece of T-Helm she'd been holding. "I hate to ask . . . what happened to them?"

"I think I just let a bunch of them loose in The Citadel."

"I feel sick." Nicole looked ill.

"Well, you'd better get over it pretty quick." Ellyne dropped the empty cartridge from her revolver and slipped it in one of her jacket's many pockets. She replaced it with fresh ammo, snapping the cylinder back into place. "We've got company; I can hear them."

Nicole gasped and, attempting to shut the door, grabbed for the doorknob.

"Yeah, it's not going to stay shut," Ellyne said, pulling the dagger out of her pocket. "My lockpicking skills are bullets."

"It seems *all* your skills involve bullets," Nicole sighed.

"I don't suppose you can blink or blip or teleport us out of here, can you?"

Nicole concentrated for a moment and grimaced. "Nope."

"That would make sense. I doubt the Ilserate would want their lab rats escaping."

"Or us."

"Yeah . . . especially us. This place reeks of Marik. It's got his name written all over it. Actually, I wouldn't be surprised if it *literally* had his name on it somewhere. I bet the words 'Marik Was Here' are inscribed on one of the toilets."

"So, what are we going to do?"

"Are there any other wards limiting your magic?"

Nicole concentrated briefly, then shook her head.

Ellyne extended her sword and cocked her revolver's hammer.

"Then let's misbehave."

Nicole smirked as they exited the room. The first grika to appear received a bullet and tumbled down the stairs to rest at the bottom. Immediately thereafter, three more charged them and met the same fate.

"Are you taking a nap or something, Nicole?"

"I just wanted you to have some fun before—"

"Before what?"

"Before this."

Nicole cupped her hand, palm up, and summoned a tiny flame in it. It assumed a vaguely humanoid shape and quickly grew to her size as she tossed it to the ground in front of her. She uttered a word Ellyne didn't recognize and pointed ahead of her.

The fiery shape charged forward into the fray, pummeling two grika and setting them ablaze before moving onto the next enemy further up the stairs. When it was vanquished, the fire entity continued climbing, disappearing from Ellyne's view.

"Fancy," she joked. "And incredibly useful. And I see the grika aren't completely immune to magic."

"Thanks! I made it myself. I mean the spell—it's a Nicole original."

"Yeah, well, don't get too cocky. We're not out of here yet. Something tells me there are a lot more of them upstairs and probably some Ilserate goons who let them loose in here."

"Relax, Ellyne. You shoot some things, I'll shoot other things, and we'll be out of here in no time!"

"It's that plucky, 'can-do' attitude that makes me feel all warm inside," Ellyne laughed. "Well, that and squama juice."

They moved up the stairs, gagging as their noses caught the smell coming off the multiple charred grika husks they passed—stepping carefully around or over them. Nicole accidentally kicked one, snapping its crispy arm from its body.

"Looks like your spell was effective enough."

"And sort of gross."

Just as Ellyne emerged from the stairwell, she ducked back in, narrowly dodging a spell that impacted harmlessly on the wall.

"Yeah, that too . . . and there's our welcoming party."

Ellyne knew she was resistant to spells—maybe even immune at times—but even after all these years, she still didn't understand her unique ability and how it functioned. And these newly discovered applications were even more of a mystery. The truth was, she knew she could still be harmed by magic. Nicole had proven that much when she threw her into the wall back at the apartment. Not only did Ellyne not trust magic, but she also didn't trust her ability against magic. And if Nicole could harm her or teleport her, maybe other spells could get through.

"Looks like several mages, a bunch of bots, and a whole slew of grika in cages," she whispered. "I didn't get a good look at what weapons they have."

"They train them as pets?"

"Attack dogs, I imagine. But, judging from how they attacked their masters back at The Citadel, I'd say that concept doesn't seem to be going too well."

"This place is an experiment? To breed monsters?"

"Seems that way," Ellyne sighed.

"That makes me so angry!" Nicole had an evil scowl on her face. "I'll make them pay for this!"

Another spell impacted against the door frame near Nicole's face.

"Whoa, there," she said, holstering her gun. "Hang on a second."

"Ellyne Thandaral!" a man's voice shouted. "You will give up the girl now!"

"This again?" Ellyne emerged from the doorway. She quickly surveyed the enemy force—four mages, ten bots, and three cages full of drooling, snarling grika. "This is getting really old."

"Yes, it is, isn't it?"

He was clad in red robes and his black hair poked out randomly from underneath the silly cap on his head. Definitely the idiot in charge of all this operation, as the other three mages had on standard street garb. Ellyne vowed to kill the dude wearing the Transgressors T-shirt last if only because he might have had decent taste in music.

"I think we both know I'm not handing over anyone to you."

"Oh," the mage chuckled, "I absolutely do. This was all a formality. I was told—"

The bullet from Ellyne's gun pierced his eye. He was dead before he hit the ground.

"Shit!" one of the others yelled just before her next bullet caught him in the neck.

She dropped the third before he could fire his spell.

She laughed, firing her last bullet. It caught the final mage in the shoulder and flung him backward, but he remained alive. "Crap," she muttered, dropping the empty cartridge from the cylinder.

Before she could reload, the mage waved his hand and the grika cages opened, releasing the snarling monsters, several of which descended upon the mage and tore him apart.

"Well, that's justice . . . or something." She ducked back behind the door to finish reloading as the bots opened fire. "Hey, Nicole, your turn."

"Fun!" Nicole giggled as she exited the stair well, firing off spells as quickly as Ellyne fired bullets, and dropping enemies just as fast.

Ellyne couldn't begin to understand the machinations of magic or what spells Nicole used, but she had never seen another mage so comfortable and relaxed in the middle of a chaotic combat situation. Nicole was quick and deadly, often felling multiple enemies with one casting.

"That one was mine!" Ellyne felt rather useless, targeting whatever enemies she could. "And that one!"

"Apparently not," Nicole laughed, waving her hands and tearing a bot in half. Not only was she casting spells but she was blocking incoming spells simultaneously. Most mages Ellyne had encountered seemed to have trouble doing both. She heard it took years of training to be able to block incoming spells at all.

Several spells struck her in the chest, and she dropped to one knee. Pain shot through every part of her body, quickly dissipating into a tingly warmth, and then disappearing altogether. She stood and shot back at the bot but her bullet bounced off its sturdy armor.

Grika attacked everything in sight. If they weren't devouring bodies or trying to kill Ellyne and Nicole, they harassed the bots which paid them no mind.

"Fists, then," she growled, holstering her revolver and sprinting at the bot that shot her. She felt pricks of pain as spells pelted her, but she shrugged them off, feeling their effects for only a few seconds. Every hit was anguish, and she yelped several times but finally reached her target.

When her fist collided with the bot's thick metal hide, she braced for pain. If this didn't work, she'd probably break every bone in her hand, so she desperately hoped she at least remotely knew how to use her new power.

She was not disappointed.

A jolt of energy raced down her arm the moment she hit the bot's thick armor, and she squinted through the resulting flash of brilliant light. There was no explosion, no clattering of bot parts hitting the floor. Instead, she found herself elbow deep in the bot's mechanical body.

It flailed, wildly shooting spells from its two appendages in random directions while sparking and making odd sounds. Ellyne tried to extricate her arm, but found herself stuck.

"Sonofa . . . figures."

She yelped when stabbing pains covered her body as the other bots hit her with more spells. Sensations of fatigue, confusion, and paralyzation momentarily took hold, but the effects were brief and when they wore off, she tugged at her arm to try and break free.

"Let go!" she shouted, angry at a now nonfunctional Ilserate bot. She finally pulled hard enough to free herself, sending the dormant hunk of metal careening into another bot and crushing it. "I'll be damned," she murmured, inspecting her arm and flexing her fingers. It didn't look any more muscular than normal.

But it certainly felt stronger.

She charged another bot and rammed it with her shoulder, sending it into the wall. It threw spells at Ellyne and floated toward her, but she took the hits and grabbed its arms, roaring as she ripped them off the metal beast.

Then she impaled it with its own appendages and left it to float and sputter. She quickly moved onto the next bot but, before she could strike, several spells ripped into its armor, tearing it into four pieces.

"That one was mine!" she shouted, glaring at Nicole. The girl was grinning wildly.

"I disagree!" she laughed, firing off a volley of spells at various targets, felling most of them.

Ellyne, not to be outdone, drew her revolver and dropped eight grika as Nicole destroyed the remaining bots. Between the two of them, they cleaned up the stragglers and found themselves standing amidst a grisly scene of death and destruction. She nudged a grika corpse with her boot, then sighed.

"That was so violent." Nicole's voice sounded shaky, and her mouth was agape as she came to stand next to Ellyne, staring at the carnage. "I'm not used to . . . killing."

"Don't worry," Ellyne replied, pointing to the four human corpses. "I took care of the messy ones for you. Well, except that poor slob." She pointed to the half-eaten corpse. "His own grika did the job for me."

"Does it ever get old?"

"Does what get old?" Ellyne asked, working to calm her breathing and her pounding heart.

"Killing. Does it wear on you? Weigh you down?"

Ellyne waded through the corpses and still sparking electronics, nudging body parts and machine parts with the tip of her boot as she went, making her way toward the front door she knew was locked. Nicole followed her, gingerly avoiding what Ellyne so callously disturbed.

But she said nothing, not until she leaned her back against the wall and slid down to sit, exhaling deeply, her arms resting on her bent knees.

"It depends on who I'm killing."

This was where they spent their first moments after fending off the grika outside. Ellyne hated this place but, right now, it was possibly safer than most. Her muscles ached, and she was pretty sure her right shoulder was going to be one big bruise later.

Nicole sat next to her and, for a brief moment, it was like the first time they'd seen this place. She remembered how complicated she believed everything to be. Past Ellyne had no idea back then. In just a short time, life had gone off the rails in the worst way.

"To be honest," she continued, "I might feel worse about killing grika than I do Ilserate or Kithrak. The grika had no choice. They're what people become without T-Helms—savage monsters to be used as attack dogs for the government. Their plight is awful. It's almost like killing innocent people."

"Who want to kill everyone."

"Yes, but innocent nonetheless. They have no control over their actions." Ellyne ran a hand through her hair and checked her remaining ammunition. She combined several half-spent cartridges together and grimaced. She was almost out of bullets.

"Do you keep track of how many you kill?"

"Younger me did—during the war. I racked up quite a Kithrak kill count, thought it made me a hero. Younger me had it wrong and didn't learn that lesson until later. But I didn't have the luxury of maiming or disabling."

"Why not?" Nicole looked tired. No, not tired—spent.

Ellyne could see her quivering slightly. She'd used a lot of magic today between The Citadel and murder shack. She wondered what cost power like that demanded of a person—especially one who didn't use a T-Helm.

"You shoot someone in the leg and they can still shoot back. Bullets don't stun or paralyze or knock out. Bullets kill. It's the only thing they do."

"If you used magic, you could—"

"I can't."

"Sure you can. I mean, everyone's had to learn how to use it at some point—even skabs can use magic devices. If they can learn, why not you? I'm sure you'd catch on quickly. I mean, it's a lot different than a gun but—"

"No, Nicole, I can't. I mean I physically cannot use magic. I tried several times out of curiosity and several more during the war when it would've been easy to use a wand I found. I've always hated magic, but it was preferable to death in need."

"You can't use it at all? Not at all?" Nicole's eyes were wide. Ellyne could see the myriad questions building up within the girl's head, fighting for dominance to see which question would emerge first.

"I've loathed magic for a long time, fought to contain it, then fought to keep it out of government control. During the war, I was hit with a spell—I don't know what kind of spell—but it should have killed me. Instead, it simply washed over me without any lasting effect. I couldn't explain it, but I kept it a secret."

Ellyne fiddled with one of her empty cartridges, tinkering with it and shining it with her thumb. Reliving the past wasn't something she relished, and talking about it with someone else was something she never did.

"I got caught out in the open with no backup," she continued. "I saw the spell come at me and I closed my eyes, waiting for death. The spell hit me, and I felt it's terrible pain but nothing else happened. Somehow, I knew, and I used it to my advantage. I executed some of the most successful campaigns during the war because of it—charging furiously ahead and shrugging off magic like it was a mosquito. Rumors made the rounds about how powerful a mage I must have been, but the truth was, I never really knew what I was doing or even what I . . . was."

"That's quite an advantage."

"Except it wasn't enough and the Ilserate acquiesced to the Kithrak who, despite what they said, apparently *do* control the flow of magic with their damned T-Helms." She threw the cartridge in anger. It bounced off the opposite wall and rolled back to her. "We still lost when we thought we'd won," she said, picking it up and slipping it into a pocket.

"Would you use magic? You know . . . if you could?"

"Shit no. I still hate it. It's unnatural. There's something . . . very wrong about it. Maybe I'm the only one who can sense it because of my ability or curse or whatever. But you . . ."

Ellyne trailed off. Telling all this to Nicole was almost therapeutic.

"Me, what?"

"Since the day I found you in my apartment, certain things have been very different."

"Like what?"

"Well, for one, you were able to affect me with magic. You threw me against the wall, remember?"

Nicole's eyes sparkled a bit at the memory. "Oh, yeah. Sorry about that."

"And you managed to teleport me out of the Spire along with you."

"Oh yeah! But how—"

"So maybe I'm not completely immune. I can't be sure anymore. To be fair, you're the most powerful mage on the planet, so that possibly has something to do with it, I guess."

"What else has changed?"

Ellyne stood and worked her shoulder a bit, trying to

move her arm to keep it from getting stiff. She wasn't sure if it felt better or worse.

"Magic sometimes goes haywire around me. As far as I can tell, it's always when there are a lot of enchantments or effects or whatever—whenever there's a dense concentration of magic. And I usually can't suppress it."

"Haywire? How so?" Nicole also stood, but on shaky legs. She used the wall to support her, trying to play it off as nothing, but Ellyne could see her level of exhaustion.

"I crashed a metro once."

"What?"

"I mean, I didn't crash it myself. It crashed because of me. A lot of people died, again because of me. Only, I didn't fully realize what had happened until later, when the same sensation came over me. That was when I first knew."

"That's horrible. And you think it's your fault, don't you? But it's not your fault, Ellyne. I mean, well, it *is* your fault—"

"You're really terrible at consoling people."

"No, I mean, you didn't do it intentionally. You couldn't have known. And the fact you've taken such careful steps to avoid another catastrophe means a lot."

"But this whole magic absorption," she sighed, "creating shockwaves, and that punching through bots thing . . . that's new. What else don't I know about myself? What if I get more people killed?"

"You mean, aside from shooting them?"

Ellyne smirked, then sneered and rolled her eyes and fiddled with a tiny pebble she found on the floor. "If I shoot someone, then they deserved it. I'm at peace with that."

"Well," Nicole said, leaning her head back against the wall. "This does explain some things . . . and raises so many more questions. I bet, if the Ilserate knew of your disconnect from magic, they would die to get their paws on you."

"Why do you think I've laid low for so long? They know —Marik made sure of that. He found out during the war and couldn't keep his trap shut. But the government's also terrified of me, so we have a tenuous alliance." Ellyne sighed. "Well, *had*."

"I can't imagine they're super happy about losing the epitome of magic *and* anti-magic at the same time. I bet this Marik guy is so mad."

"Nope. Brings a smile to my face, though."

Silence overtook them as Ellyne tried to relax and stave off the oncoming wave of fatigue. Nicole's breathing soon became calm and rhythmic as Ellyne felt herself also nodding off.

"Hey, Nicole?"

"What?" Nicole mumbled, obviously mostly asleep.

"I'm sorry. I'm sorry I just handed you over to the Ilserate. It was a dick move, and I'm not proud of it. I was only thinking of myself."

"Yeah, it was totally a dick move." Nicole shifted, trying to get comfortable. "But you came back. I knew you would."

"How did you know?"

Nicole smiled and her entire face lit up. "Because we're friends." She rested her head on Ellyne's shoulder and moved close.

When Ellyne eventually awoke, the sun was clearly setting. She yawned, stretched, and poked Nicole's shoulder, eventually getting a response.

"We need to go. It's nearly nightfall, and that's when this place's residents come out to play."

"Oh wow. We must've been out for a while," the girl yawned.

She stood and dusted herself off. Nicole joined her, looking steadier on her feet now.

"So, what now?" Nicole asked.

"I aim to get some answers."

CHAPTER
FIFTEEN

ELLYNE CHECKED the front door and found it, unsurprisingly, still locked. Before she could ask, Nicole waved her hand in front it and it swung open. They slipped out into the dying light, hoping to put some distance between them and the murder shack.

"Answers are great," Nicole said, "but what are the questions?"

"The Ilserate and the Kithrak both fear and covet you. They may be working together, but I bet we've screwed that up, and I would also bet they're now secretly at odds."

"That makes sense. Neither wants the other to have such a weapon. Ooh! And now that they're probably both aware of your abilities—"

"They're probably not only at odds, but in competition. They simultaneously want to control and destroy us both. It's like we're rock stars and wanted criminals at the same time."

They hurried through the overgrown, decrepit garden and stopped at the fence.

"That's awfully confusing."

"Indeed, it is," Ellyne agreed. "Which means we need to

figure out our next move before they both figure out theirs. Hang on."

Ellyne breathed deep, attempting to relax enough to allow herself to connect with the pool of flocia she knew lived inside her.

"You know I could teleport us. Wait, or maybe I can't. I don't even know."

Ellyne wasn't sure whether flocia strengthened her legs or she somehow used it to launch herself over the fence. Either way, the result was the same. She cleared the barbed wire, easily sailing above the fence and landing awkwardly on the other side right before she lost her balance and fell, laughing.

"Are you alright?" Nicole appeared next to her, having effortlessly teleported to avoid the fence.

Ellyne sat on the sidewalk, still laughing. She lay back, looking at the darkening sky as the sun's last rays tickled the tops of the skyscrapers in the distance.

"I guess that's a yes, then." Nicole offered her hand. Ellyne took it and stood, clapping her hands on her pants. "So, do you like magic yet?"

"Nope. Still hate it. But, as you pointed out, that's not really magic now, is it?"

"Well, no. So, how about channeling flocia? Do you like that?"

"Hate it just as much. But, I'll admit, whatever I just did was super fun."

"It was fun to watch, too," Nicole laughed. "You looked like a chicken trying to fly."

"That graceful?"

"Well . . . I mean, was being nice."

Ellyne sneered at her, still giggling. "Yeah, well, I think I did all right for my first time. At the very least, I didn't break anything—me or the fence."

"So where to now?" Nicole asked, almost as if they were going on a spontaneous adventure.

"I think you know the answer to that already. Before I sprung you from Ilserate jail, I gave JASN access to their network. Hopefully Derek's been putting that access to good use and has got some answers for us by now."

They headed back into the city, the streetlights eventually flickering to life, casting their radiant, flocia-powered glow upon the pavement as the last stragglers of the day hurried home to be with their families—probably to cook dinner, watch a screen together, and plug into their T-Helms.

"I'm not even sure I know what our questions are," Nicole said.

"I'm not either, but we can't keep running."

"Are you suggesting we—the two of us—take on both the Ilserate and the Kithrak? Because that sounds like a terrible plan," she said, looking disappointed.

"Shh! Keep it down! No, I'm not suggesting we go up against both the Ilserate and the Kithrak. That's ridiculous."

"Good. Because, for a moment, there—"

"Okay, yeah, that's basically what I'm suggesting. Wait, before you say anything, just hear me out."

Nicole remained silent, obviously skeptical. Ellyne didn't blame her—it was a ridiculous notion. But they also couldn't run and hide forever. They would never truly be safe.

"Okay, then, what's the plan?" Nicole whispered.

"I don't need a plan. I'm not big on plans because they usually fall apart. I improvise. It's not perfect but I'm also not dead yet."

"So . . . you have no plan."

"Not really, no—short of just walking in, guns blazing, I have no plan."

"That's a terrible plan!" Nicole yelled, throwing up her hands.

Ellyne looked at her before stating the obvious. "Well, yeah, that's because it's not a plan."

Two people approaching ahead of them must have heard

the argument and promptly crossed to the other side of the street, hurrying past Ellyne and Nicole. Ellyne saw the odd looks on their faces as they stared at the two of them.

"Which is why we're going to pay Derek a visit. If the Ilserate is afraid of us and *if* the Kithrak are also afraid of us, then we're obviously dangerous. I suggest we use that to our advantage and see just how far it takes us—before they start working together again and figure out how to neutralize us. And, you know, I'd like to donate a bullet or two to Marik."

They turned a corner, heading towards a park. Ellyne had hoped to get JASN's attention by now but, thus far, all the screens were either dark or showing their usual commercial signs.

"You really don't like him, do you?"

"That's putting it mildly. If he were on fire, I wouldn't piss on him to put him out."

"Ew." Nicole grimaced.

Ellyne sighed. "You get the idea. He double-crossed me. We fought together to try to destroy magic, then he sold out to the Ilserate to bring magic under their control. Then he knocked me out." She pointed to the metal in her jaw where her tooth used to be. "Then he shot me and left me for dead."

"Well, I guess I can't blame you. He sounds like a dick. Oops, sorry. Language."

"The worst. We used to be close, but he sold me out for rank and for power within the Ilserate. He only cares about himself and his status and does whatever it takes to get what he wants. I'm not sure he was ever my friend. I doubt he's ever been *anybody's* friend."

Nicole pondered Ellyne's words for a few moments. "So, do you still want to abolish magic? You know, get rid of it entirely?"

"I'm not going to lie, Nicole. If I could, I would destroy magic right now. Magic is vile. It's an unnatural element that corrupts worse than money."

"You speak as if you feel magic is evil. It's just a tool, Ellyne."

"A hammer is a tool, Nicole. It's made from wood and steel, and it hits things. It's not some mystical force that allows anyone and everyone to lob fireballs at one another."

"But magic *is* a tool. Magic shapes and uses flocia to create specific effects and outcomes. It's basically a drinking straw that moves the liquid."

"Then the liquid is foul and rotten."

"I guess I still don't understand," Nicole sighed.

Ellyne stopped and turned to Nicole. "Look," she said, gently grabbing the girl's arm so she would also stop. "If you had a straw and you found a puddle of unidentifiable liquid, would you drink it?"

"Ew, no. Gross."

Ellyne paused a moment to let it sink in.

"Wait," Nicole continued. "I think I understand. You trust a hammer because you know how it's made and what it's made of. You don't trust magic because you don't know anything about flocia."

"Exactly. Flocia just shows up and everyone begins using magic as if it's totally normal. Shortly thereafter, the Kithrak arrive. Through all of this, I never once saw anyone question flocia or perform any research on it. People were so happy to use magic that they never stopped to figure out what it was."

"Probably because the Kithrak shook things up with their arrival?" Nicole offered.

"Precisely." Ellyne resumed walking with Nicole next to her. The streets had largely emptied out and there were only a scant few individuals out—probably the homeless, scurrying off to whatever refuge they could find. "Before anyone could get a grasp on what magic was, the Kithrak came in and tried to take it. Suddenly, everyone's attention shifted to controlling it rather than analyzing it. Seems really convenient, don't you think?"

"Surely someone's done the research by now, don't you think?"

"Magic gained universal acceptance immediately after the Kithrak arrived. I think any research was quickly forgotten and replaced with wonder and power. I'm still amazed by how quickly everyone jumped on the bandwagon. Well, except the Techno Guild. But even they use magic despite how much they protest to the contrary. And the Teranyne Order worship it like a god or something. Magic makes fools out of people."

"But magic is wonderful," Nicole argued, creating a sparkling, translucent butterfly that fluttered from her open palm. "It allows us to do so much and brings such delight to the world!"

This from a girl who didn't know the world before magic —the Legacy Age. Ellyne thought it difficult to appreciate something Nicole had possessed all her life, never having gone without. The truth was the world had plenty of wonder before magic. The great airships that traveled the skies, for example. Ellyne hadn't seen one in years. Magic travel replaced the need for them.

Was that all this was? Was she simply bitter because magic changed her way of life—a life she'd been comfortable with? No matter how much she loathed to admit it, that element was truly there. And maybe that was originally why she fought so hard against it years ago.

But her feelings truly went beyond that. The reasons for her animosity toward magic were abundant and, no matter how they started, they were grounded in very real problems. Magic corrupted people. Everyone who used it was dependent upon the Kithrak, save one. Nicole was the obvious exception. Everyone else who didn't pay their dues, as Ellyne recently found out, met with an awful fate—one she saw as yet another reason to despise magic.

"Magic does allow for great things," she continued. "I

can't deny that. But, while this is true, everyone's being taken in by the illusion. There's a price for everything, and magic's price is higher than anyone even knows. I bet they wouldn't even care if they did."

"What do you mean? Are you talking about the grika?"

"Yeah. That's part of it. Look, magic's very existence has started wars and brought destruction and strife."

"But it helps people have better lives."

"If they use it. Those who don't use magic are shunned and fall through the cracks. Those who can't afford a T-Helm or, for some reason, can't use theirs . . . they end up even worse. And I believe both the Ilserate *and* the Kithrak are misusing their authority. I don't trust either of them."

Nicole sighed and shook her head. "I'm not sure I understand any of this."

"I'm not certain I expect you to. You've never been without magic, nor must you use a T-Helm. You've also been firmly planted in the Ilserate's pocket. You've never known anything else."

They walked in silence again for a spell. Ellyne could almost see the gears turning within Nicole's head as she wrestled with everything they'd just discussed.

"You wondered what answers we'd get when we didn't even know the questions. As it turns out, we have a lot of questions to ask."

"Wait. If Derek is a Kithrak, then wouldn't he have some of these answers?"

Ellyne clapped her hands. "Now you're catching on."

"Do you think he double-crossed us?"

"I don't know. I don't think so, but he *is* Kithrak, and I trust them less than I trust the government. Maybe. Shit, I don't even know."

"You don't trust anyone, do you?"

"I trust Victor," Ellyne chuckled. A strong drink sounded perfect.

"Do you trust me?"

Ellyne should've seen that question coming a mile away, draped in blinking lights and blaring klaxons, yet it still blindsided her.

The truth was, she didn't entirely trust a person she'd known for only a few days, even if that person was Nicole. What if the girl was a spy or an Ilserate tool—even, possibly, an unwitting tool? Did *anyone* lend their trust so willingly?

"Listen, Nicole, I . . ."

"You what?"

Ellyne pointed to a screen ahead. The advertisement for toothpaste vanished.

"Keep Right." An arrow pointing to the right flashed several times before the screen changed back, now showing an advertisement for glue.

"Looks like JASN finally noticed us," Nicole said.

"Indeed. Come on, let's hurry."

Their journey took them once again through the largely deserted city streets, dodging shady figures and watching carefully for patrols which had obviously picked up. Ellyne expected, on a normal evening, to encounter one or two or *maybe* three. Tonight, it was no surprise the Kithrak and Ilserate were out in full force, scouring the city streets.

If they knew their attack at the murder shack had failed, then they also knew Ellyne and Nicole were on the move. It wasn't a shock to see the Kithrak working with the government anymore. She'd long accepted the fact that the two entities had a tenuous alliance, but she figured it was even more strained now.

She would have liked to take wagers on who would be first to betray the other. In fact, she was shocked it hadn't happened yet. When it did—and it *was* a when situation—it would produce another war.

"Where are we going?" Nicole finally asked.

"Either to find Derek or to hide somewhere . . . then find

Derek. I suspect he knows something he's not telling us. Or maybe he's discovered something after I gave JASN access to the Ilserate network. Or maybe he can simply find a place for us to hide."

Nicole gave Ellyne an all-knowing look. "That didn't work out so well last time."

"No," Ellyne chuckled, "it most certainly did not. But we discovered the Ilserate's making feral attack dogs out of people, so I guess that's worth something."

Had Derek directed them to the murder shack for that reason? Had he known about the grika?

"I'd almost rather forego that knowledge except we met one in the sewer, so that kind of ruined it."

"Just a bit, yeah."

Ellyne poked her head around a corner and watched as two patrols met up further down the street. She was unable to hear any of their banter from this distance, but several of them pointed their fingers in her direction.

"Looks like trouble heading this way," Ellyne said, ducking behind the building and drawing her gun. Her last wish was to get sucked into a pointless street brawl, but it paid to be prepared.

"I'm pretty sure I can handle them," Nicole's voice was filled with determination.

"I'm pretty sure you can, too. But the moment they find us, they'll just call in more of their cronies and we'll be surrounded. No, we need to avoid them, I think."

Ellyne had to admit the thought of leveling two patrols with the relative ease Nicole could muster was a satisfying thought, but she wasn't wrong. The moment the fight began, Ilserate and Kithrak forces would blip in from all over the place and eventually overwhelm them.

But remaining concealed was becoming more difficult. Another peek around the corner revealed both patrols approaching their position.

"Come on," Ellyne said, tugging the girl's arm. "We need to leave."

Nicole pointed across the street where another patrol had just rounded the corner.

Fortunately, the two of them weren't near a streetlight so Ellyne believed they hadn't been spotted yet, but the situation was becoming more difficult with every passing moment.

Even more so once another patrol approached from a different direction.

"You may have to teleport yourself out, Nicole."

"And leave you here?"

"I'm probably unable to come with you, and I'd rather not have you back in government custody. There's no guarantee you can take me with you."

"Ellyne, I—"

"Don't argue with me. There's no need for us both to be captured."

Nicole said nothing. Instead, she sniffed and wiped her left eye.

"Don't get sappy on me. I handed you over to them once. Just think of this as payback."

"I hate you."

"That's the spirit. Now get going before this all gets messy."

Nicole gave Ellyne one last sad look as she stepped back and made several sweeping motions with her hands. But just as she was about to finish her spell, the wall behind them shifted from a storefront to thin air, revealing a dark, empty alleyway beyond.

Before Nicole could utter a sound, Ellyne shoved her into the alley and followed as the wall quickly replaced itself behind them.

"Well, that was nice," Nicole squealed, obviously ecstatic. "Looks like payback will have to wait for another day!"

"I can't say I'm disappointed," Ellyne agreed. "But it

would've been nice to maybe help us out a little sooner!" she yelled, looking around for a camera. The hum of an overhead drone faded until she could no longer hear it. She shrugged as they followed the alley to its end which, as expected, opened into another one of JASN's chambers.

"Yeah yeah," Derek sneered, "I was late on the uptake. Sometimes I have my own problems, you know? I'm a busy guy. Anyway, you can thank JASN for this one—he noticed you before I did."

"I'd simply prefer to not be in need of a hero to save us, machine or no." Ellyne sighed and slumped in one of the two chairs provided. It seemed as if this would never end. How long could someone actively be on the run when *everyone* was looking for them?

"Then you should probably stop trashing the place. You really did a number on the Ilserate back at The Citadel. That Marik guy—he's super pissed off at you."

Nicole sat in the chair next to Ellyne, obviously relieved they'd escaped, but her face still held a considerable amount of worry. Ellyne would be remiss if she didn't admit to feeling much the same way.

"Looks like the Ilserate's out in full force looking for you guys," he continued. "Kithrak-led patrols, bots, and those grika things—which, if I'm being honest, are totally new to me."

"Us, too," Nicole agreed.

"I watched you fighting inside The Citadel. Man, that was chaos! Letting those things loose was brilliant, Ellyne. But I lost you at the apartments. JASN spotted you guys emerging from the building, but he has no visibility inside."

"That 'apartment building' is the Ilserate's grika factory."

"Wait, what?"

"She's right! There's a room full of smashed Taranoms locked away in the basement and people who don't use their T-Helms somehow become those grika things. The government is using that building to create their savage, feral experiments and they're really gross and they smell awful."

Nicole sounded almost excited about the situation, but Ellyne knew the girl was simply rambling due to nerves and fear. Or maybe it was simply because she was twenty years old and tended to do that.

"That's disturbing, and not something I expected."

"You're a Kithrak and you didn't see this coming?" Ellyne was skeptical, and why shouldn't she be?

"Despite what you think you know about my people, you don't know much of anything. Simply because I'm Kithrak doesn't mean I know everything about us, our plans, or our capabilities."

"You mean to tell me you, the guy who oversees The Keeper, don't know everything?" Ellyne began that question as a joke but really was a bit surprised Derek was in the dark about the grika. Of course, if he'd previously known and hadn't told them, she probably would've shot him, so it was wise to play dumb even if he knew.

He wasn't far off, though. She could've used a refresher on her Kithrak studies.

"Very funny," Derek sneered while he typed something on the keyboard Ellyne once again couldn't see. "I'm pretty low on the Kithrak power ladder. In fact, the more human you look, the more shunned you are. They don't trust us with much information or access. I really don't even know much about our heritage."

"Is this why you help us, then?" Nicole asked. "To get back at them?"

"Maybe a little. Mostly, I don't like what I'm seeing. The way things are going, I fear everything will collapse eventually—magic, society, all of it. I think you're the final piece, but I don't know how you fit into the puzzle yet. It's something I've observed for a while now."

"What do you mean?"

"When one has the visibility I do, you start to see patterns, then you begin to see cracks. I've been waiting patiently and watching. You and Nicole appear to have accelerated the chaos."

"What happens if you're discovered?" Ellyne asked.

"Rest assured, if my people or the Ilserate figure it out, I'm toast. Thankfully, I know what I'm doing, and for some reason, they trust me. Besides, I do a lot more than tell JASN to run traffic signals."

Ellyne wasn't sure she would ever fully trust Derek, but he hadn't let them down yet. It made her nervous, though, to rely on someone so heavily—especially when that someone was a Kithrak. She was careful to remind herself, however, she'd been burned by humans, too.

"So," Nicole chimed in, "what now? Yeah, we've figured out the Ilserate's making mutant attack soldiers and I'm the mage breaker and whatnot, but what does it all mean?"

Derek reclined in his chair, scrutinizing something Ellyne couldn't see. She smirked at the thought he might be looking at porn. Didn't everyone at some point?

Her thoughts then turned to what the Kithrak variant of that would be like. She'd never seen the "purest" Kithrak—presumably no human had—but they were rumored to take on different forms, all of which were far from human.

The humor quickly drained from her thoughts when the visuals set in.

"Nicole's right. Where do we go from here? We can't run forever."

"I've been thinking about that." Derek waved his fingers in the air and some images appeared. He sifted through them until he located what he was looking for, then turned it around and enlarged it.

"What's that?" Nicole asked.

"It's a gazebo," Ellyne joked.

The image was that of a great circle of pillars situated

under a shadowy roof. Indeed, it did resemble a gazebo but, as Derek zoomed out, Ellyne saw that it loomed over Karnascus—a giant structure that dwarfed even the city's great skyscrapers—even The Citadel.

"The Sistix, as your language would translate it. It's my people's base of operations," Derek replied. "Where most Kithrak live and operate. It's a fully functional city within one structure that, oh, also happens to be a starship as well as a portal to many different worlds."

Ellyne and Nicole gasped simultaneously but, Ellyne figured, for vastly different reasons.

"But, sure, you can call it a gazebo if you like," he grumbled and shook his head.

"Fair enough," Ellyne stood and examined the image closer. "Wait, I recognize this area. It's largely warehouses, but I've clearly never seen this thing before."

"Nobody has. Even I haven't."

"Wait, how is that possible?"

"It doesn't exist. Or, well, it does, but it also doesn't. I've never seen it because I was born here on Seralune, but not in this facility."

"Oh, wow!" Nicole jumped up and inspected the image as well.

"That's definitely not what I expected," Ellyne continued, "but also not what I meant. I've been to this area once or twice and that giant-ass gazebo wasn't there."

"No, as I said it was there . . . but it also wasn't. I've spent a long time inspecting it—with JASN's help of course. And if my theory's correct, it exists in two places at once—both on Seralune, and on another world."

"Your home world?" Nicole's eyes lit up with curiosity. "Please say it's your home world!"

"I wish I knew. It's possible Kithraki is the other location. I have no way of knowing."

"They really keep you in the dark don't they, Derek?"

Ellyne carefully scrutinized the structure. The mysticism and magic of the situation confused her and the concept of how something could exist in two places at once but also not at all further muddied any understanding she may have had. "Doesn't that annoy you?"

"It's the way it's always been." Derek shrugged. "It's really all any of us have ever known. Kithrak society is very compartmentalized."

"Have you ever wondered why?"

"Of course, but I seem to be an exception. Most Kithrak don't give it a second thought. Or maybe they already know. They wouldn't tell me if they did."

"It just seems . . . I don't know . . . so secretive, to be kept in the dark like that."

"Does your government not do the same? I would argue The Citadel is much like the Sistix—most people have no idea what goes on inside and would probably rather not know. Your people, like mine, go about their business daily without questioning the actions of those sitting in their lofty offices doing whatever they do."

He had a point.

"How did you come to find out about this?" Nicole asked. "I mean, if you're not supposed to even know about it but you do know about it, but they don't know you know about it and—"

"Slow down," Derek laughed.

"Good luck there," Ellyne smirked.

"JASN, of course, is a robust AI with many capabilities. And I, of course, am constantly looking for new upgrades. The specific camera and analysis system that detected the Sistix was part of an upgrade I performed a while ago."

"Wait." Ellyne held up her hand. "How long exactly have you been aware of the Sistix?"

"Several months."

"And you're just now telling us about this? If we'd known

earlier, we may have avoided some of the events of the recent days. Maybe we could've gone straight there."

"I had to be sure I could trust you," Derek growled. "Besides, despite what it may look like, I don't have all the answers."

"So, let's say I understood all of this," Ellyne scoffed, "what now? We know this . . . Sistix exists. What do we do with that information? Blow it up?"

"That's so you," Nicole laughed.

Derek paused, poring over some invisible information. She walked behind him, curious to see what had him so enthralled, but still saw nothing. Either JASN was somehow broadcasting it directly into the boy's brain or Derek had visual capabilities Ellyne didn't understand. Either way, she wanted badly to know what it was.

"The *Skarash Ascalore* prophecy mentions something called *Golgolonar* which is the Kithrak word for 'reckoning', I think. If I read it right, the script tells of the mage breaker bringing about *Golgolonar*." He pointed to Nicole as he spoke.

"I don't suppose," Ellyne interrupted, "it says *how* we're supposed to bring about this . . . Golgola-whatever it is."

"*Golgolonar*," Derek repeated. "And, no, the *Skarash Ascalore* isn't an instruction manual for bringing about peace between our two races."

"Of course," Ellyne scoffed, "how convenient."

"Are we not at peace now?" Nicole asked.

"I think it very much looks that way . . . to humans." Derek waved his hand in front of the image of The Sistix, causing the building to vanish from the cityscape. "But I think appearance is far from actual truth."

"Well, that's dandy," Ellyne grumbled. "Just once I'd like to be wrong."

"Magic can't exist without flocia," Derek continued, "and flocia can't exist without a source. And what better place to park your interdimensional base of operations . . . than on top of the thing you most covet?"

"The source of flocia is in The Sistix?" Nicole clapped her hands and bounced with excitement. "I would *love* to see it!"

"And I hope you do," Derek continued. "Because I believe you can take control of it—wrest it from Kithrak influence, and free humans from those Taranom monstrosities."

"What exactly will that accomplish?" Ellyne asked. "Aside from putting the T-helm companies out of business."

"My people consider themselves the owners and stewards of flocia. Despite what they say, they can't shut out any magic-using creature from using it, but they can, in subtle ways, control how it's used and even profit from it or live off it."

"This is all confusing," Ellyne sighed, sinking back into her chair. "Can we skip to the part where it gets interesting again?"

"As I was saying, if Nicole can basically steal control of flocia from the Kithrak, then my people and you humans will be on even ground. I believe, at that point, many unseen truths will come forward. Life on Seralune will change just as drastically as when the magic was first discovered."

"I remember that time." Ellyne sat up. "There were full-scale wars across the planet. It wasn't a great era."

"Right. It was chaos until the Kithrak made first contact and took control of flocia. With the sudden fear of magic being taken away, humans settled into their new roles—roles as unwitting slaves, prisoners, and workers."

"Do you think, if humans gain unfettered control of flocia again, there will be wars?"

"Possibly. You humans are an unpredictable lot, but I believe you're more mature now than you were back then. There may be some rough patches in the beginning, but I believe, eventually, great things will result."

Derek paused and moved his fingers furiously in the air, swiping a few times and then what looked like typing.

"Besides," he continued, "you'll then have control over flocia, and you can reshape it how you see fit."

"That seems an awful lot of responsibility for a twenty-year-old."

"I'm twenty-five!" Nicole pouted. "But I do agree some-what—how will I even know what to do with it?"

"I'm afraid I don't know," Derek shrugged.

"Okay, then," Ellyne interrupted, "you said we need to get into The Sistix."

"Correct."

"So how do we do that?"

"Iksillix," Derek grinned.

CHAPTER
SIXTEEN

"SO, WHEN WE GET THERE," Nicole whispered, "what exactly are we supposed to do?"

"This Iksillix guy has something we want—something that'll get us into The Sistix. We get him to hand it over, maybe kill him, then we make our way to the mothership or whatever."

Nicole chewed a fingernail in thought. "It would've been nice if Derek had more for us to go on."

"Now you're sounding like me." Ellyne said, smiling a bit. "I'm beginning to understand more why you don't trust him."

Ellyne looked around the corner of a building. Upon seeing no patrols, they swiftly crossed the street, passing two women quickly walking the opposite direction.

"It's a combination of him being a Kithrak and not having the information we need. Even if he is truly on our side, he's only giving us half the picture—intentional or not. I don't like going into any situation that way."

"I think I see what you mean," Nicole agreed. "I mean, he didn't even tell us *what* this guy has that will help us. How do we know he knows if . . . if he doesn't know? You know?"

"No." Ellyne's head hurt just trying to puzzle out what Nicole said. Was she like this when she was younger?

Her thoughts meandered to memories of her parents. They were magic lovers, of course. Who wasn't? They tried to dissuade her from joining the fight, but not because she was only sixteen years old at the time. They wanted magic to be taken from the hands of the public so only those they considered worthy could wield it. Oh, how they would've laughed had they known how badly Ellyne had been tricked by the Ilserate.

But none of that mattered, because she hadn't had any contact with them since the day she left. Not that they cared, of course. Once she chose her side, they chose theirs and any attempts at living in harmony would've been futile.

She often wondered what became of them, if they still lived outside Oakford, if they still wanted to regulate magic, or if they even understood magic was indeed already regulated to some extent.

Ellyne had long since stopped keeping tabs on Oakford itself. When she left, barely fifteen thousand people lived there. The last time she checked—years ago—there were about fifty thousand. Sometimes, she was tempted to go back and visit but she knew that was a supremely terrible idea.

"Whatever it is," Ellyne muttered, trying to keep her concentration, "he'll know. I'm sure it's not standard Kithrak procedure to give just anyone entrance to The Sistix, but hopefully he's as sympathetic to our cause as Derek thinks he is."

"And if he's not?"

"We'll persuade him."

Nicole giggled. Ellyne wasn't sure what this particular instance of the word "persuade" actually meant. They would get what they needed, no matter what it took.

"So, we get . . . whatever," Nicole continued, "then we get into the Sistix. Then what?"

"Then you take control of the source of flocia, and we put this whole disaster to rest."

Nicole frowned, looking dubious. "You really don't think it'll be that easy, do you?"

They hurried across another street, dodging the gaze of a group of Technos who were obviously out for more than just an evening stroll.

"It's getting crowded out here. And, no, it's not going to be that easy. I probably just skipped over five-hundred and one other steps I'd rather not think about. You understand magic best, so I'm relying on you to know what to do when the time comes to steal control of flocia from the Kithrak."

"I'm not sure I know how to do that. What if I can't figure it out?"

"I have every confidence in you, Nicole. You'll figure it out."

That wasn't entirely a lie—just *mostly* a lie. The truth was, Ellyne had too many problems and options to consider, and the endgame wasn't even on the horizon yet. Nicole was a gifted mage—Ellyne could easily see that, but she did have her doubts. How much about magic had Nicole actually studied while under the care of the Ilserate? And was there even a way to prepare for something like this?

As far as she knew, no human had ever seen the Teranyne — flocia's source. If that were true, then how could anyone teach Nicole how to manipulate it. A crucial part of being a mage, as Ellyne understood it, was being able to feel magic and work with it as a welder worked with metal. Or, well, as welders *used* to work with metal . . . before they could simply use magic to shape it.

If Nicole was truly in tune with magic and flocia, then she would have no problems taking it from the Kithrak. Nobody would be able to stop her because she was the mage breaker. Of course, all this relied upon a Kithrak prophecy that even Derek admitted to only barely comprehending.

Ellyne put zero trust in prophecies.

"Quick, in here!" she whispered, pulling Nicole onto a house's shadowy porch. "Stay quiet."

They huddled together in the cramped, dark space as a large group of people from the Teranyne Order passed them, chattering but obviously looking for the two of them.

"They can't elude us forever," a woman said. "It's a big city but we will find them, and the Teranyne Order will be blessed by the Kithrak and by Ilocia. We shall have our moment when the dirty mage breaker is brought low!"

"How do they know about me?" Nicole whispered.

"They're zealots, but they're also resourceful." Ellyne stopped and waited for the group to travel further down the street, then continued. "I wouldn't be surprised if they have contacts all over the place—Ilserate and Kithrak. Both the Teranynes and the Technos may be misguided, but they're formidable. Many of them are just skabs wishing to belong to something larger."

"Skabs? You mean untalented, right?"

Nicole's kindness toward all people made Ellyne roll her eyes.

"Yeah. Now let's get moving. We're almost there and the last thing we need is to run into any more people hunting for us. I must admit, this would all be so much easier if we could just teleport."

"We could try."

"Trust me, it wouldn't end well. I'm pretty sure we got lucky last time. Besides, we don't want the Kithrak picking up on your magic. Now come on."

When they arrived, they found themselves standing on the porch of a simple, two-story house resembling many of the others in the neighborhood, with a bush growing in a tiny patch of grass that served as the front yard.

"Well, this looks quaint," Ellyne quipped, arching a brow

and smirking. "I don't know what I was expecting, but I guess this makes sense."

"Do we knock or ring the doorbell or what?" Nicole searched around for a sign of life looking herself a bit dumbfounded. "It's really weird—a Kithrak living like a human. I thought it'd be different somehow."

The curtains were drawn, obscuring any vision into the house, but Ellyne inspected the window anyway, hoping to catch a glimpse of something inside.

"What exactly are you two hoping to find?" a voice said.

Nicole gasped while Ellyne looked around for the source from which the voice could've emanated.

"Are you Iksillix?" Ellyne asked, unsure of where to direct her gaze. "We require something from you."

"What are you doing?" Nicole whispered, exasperated. The look on her face was a mix of confusion and irritation. "That's not how you ask for help! Besides, this guy's a Kithrak. We should probably bow or something shouldn't we?"

"We don't have time for pleasantries. Or maybe you'd like a cold drink and some finger sandwiches while we wait out here for someone to spot us?"

"I'm sorry," Nicole said, also a bit confused as to where to direct her attention. "What my friend means is, may we come inside and talk? We think you can help us with a . . . problem."

"And why would Iksillix do that?"

"Oh great," Ellyne whispered, "he refers to himself in third person."

"Because," Nicole stammered. She gave Ellyne a quizzical look.

"This is your thing, kiddo," Ellyne replied, shrugging. "I would've already shot my way in."

"That's horrible."

Ellyne shrugged. "I mean, it usually works."

"Because . . . Derek sent us. He said you could help us."

"Derek? Who is Derek?"

"Shit," Ellyne muttered. "I think Derek sent us a false lead. This guy's about as worthless as a discount wand."

"Pardon me, ma'am," the voice replied, sounding mildly irritated. "But Iksillix is *not* worthless. Besides, it was you two who came and bothered me, so—"

"Okay, look bozo," Ellyne interrupted, drawing her weapon. "I'll make this quick. Perhaps you've heard of the mage breaker, yes? All-powerful magic-user who can single-handedly destroy the Kithrak? Sound familiar?"

"How do you know about—"

"Okay, good. You're familiar with the concept. Well, this is her." Ellyne pointed to Nicole who looked rather out of place. "This is the mage breaker. Her. Right here. If you don't let us in, we'll come in anyway and get what we need from you one way or another and burn this place to the ground. Am I clear?"

There were several moments of awkward silence while they stood in front of the house nervously, waiting for something to happen while simultaneously trying to stay hidden. Ellyne fully expected a ball of fire to erupt where they stood, or for every patrol in the city to converge on their location.

Instead, however, the door opened, and a blue-robed figure beckoned them inside. They quickly, but cautiously, obliged.

"You won't need your weapon here," he said. His voice was drippy, as if distorted by water in his mouth, and Ellyne had a difficult time understanding him at first.

"I'll be the judge of that," she replied, still holding it.

"As you wish. Please, come sit in my living room." Iksillix motioned them into the next room with his three scaly green arms and gazing in the same direction with all four of his eyes.

Iksillix's home may have appeared very much like the

other houses on the outside, but its exterior belied what lay within. Ellyne marveled at the bizarre art hanging on the walls and the alien devices sitting atop the bookshelves. Never had she seen anything like it, nor could she even compare these foreign wonders to anything. They were, in every way, very alien.

Nicole sat on the stark, gray couch that would've looked out of place in any standard living room. From the look on her face, it didn't appear to be very comfortable.

"Please, have a seat," the Kithrak said, motioning to Ellyne and the couch.

"I'm fine standing."

"You don't trust Iksillix?"

"Not particularly. But don't take it personally—I generally don't trust anyone."

Iksillix blinked all four eyes at once. Ellyne couldn't decide which was more unnerving—when they blinked in unison or randomly, one at a time.

"You've never seen a Kithrak before, have you, gunslinger?"

"Not one of your caste. I'm used to the more . . . human-looking variety."

"Ah yes." Iksillix relaxed in a plush chair on the other side of a small glass table, opposite the couch. "We either don't mingle with your kind or we change our appearance to do so —on rare occasions."

"Why is that?" Nicole asked.

"Well," Iksillix laughed, "our natural state can be . . . disturbing to some. There are others of higher castes who barely keep a humanoid shape. Imagine them walking about Karnascus's streets."

Ellyne inspected one of the trinkets—a small metal object with a lens on one end, but no hole to look through. It was just one of the many curious artifacts about the room, but what struck her as even more odd was the lack of screens—she hadn't seen one anywhere. Not one. Funny how these aliens had been around for years, but everyone actually knew so little about them. Even many Kithrak were kept in the dark about their own heritage. How could one live that way and not distrust their own species?

"I suppose I can understand that," Nicole joked. "I mean, not that you're scary or anything. I would never think that. I think you look great!"

"I know our appearance can be unnerving. It's well within human nature to shun what is not thought of as normal. We discovered that fact early on. The Kithrak have worked diligently to live alongside humans, but some things just cannot be overlooked—even with magic as an aid. But enough idle chatter. You said you needed Iksillix's help?"

Ellyne almost spoke up but thought better of it and caught herself. Instead, she decided to see how Nicole would handle such a situation while she continued admiring the strange objects strewn about the room. While she did eventually slip her gun back in its holster, her right hand never strayed far from it.

"Our friend Derek," Nicole continued, either taking the cue from Ellyne or simply taking the initiative. "We were told you have something that will allow us entrance into The Sistix."

The Kithrak merely sat and stared at the two of them, his four eyes blinking at different intervals. Ellyne knew they had just entered delicate territory. She wasn't sure what came next, but her gun could be back in her hand in the blink of an eye.

"The Sistix," Iksillix mumbled. He stood and paced while rubbing his chin and pensively gazing at the floor. "Tell me, how is it you know about The Sistix?"

"I, uh," Nicole stammered. She shifted in her chair and

began to fidget with her skirt, tugging on it and picking at the fabric.

"She had a dream about it." Ellyne pointed to Nicole. "Several nights ago, she saw it in a dream—the Sis . . . whatever." When Nicole gave her a confused glance, Ellyne winked.

"The Sistix? You . . . dreamt about it?"

Nicole and Ellyne exchanged looks. Ellyne nodded slightly, hoping Nicole would pick up on her cue and play along.

"Uh," Nicole stammered, "yes. Yes, I did dream about it. It's the large building with the pillars in a circle, right?"

Iksillix paced in silence for a moment, alternating his gaze between Nicole and the floor. Ellyne easily read the confusion on his perplexed face. She hoped that was a boon and not a hindrance to their goals—whatever those were. Several times he paused as if to say something but merely resumed pacing instead.

This was it. This was the moment Iksillix would either let them in or turn on them. Ellyne's hand slowly moved to her revolver.

"There are only a handful of humans who even know about the Sistix," he finally said. "I can count on one hand the humans who have been allowed entry. For you to have simply dreamed about it is . . . nothing short of miraculous."

"Well," Ellyne replied, "she *is* the most powerful mage on the planet. There's no telling what she's capable of."

She walked closer to Iksillix, still admiring the strange items and pictures, but also hoping to get a better look at his facial expressions.

"And if it came to her in a dream," she improvised, "then it must be important for some reason. Hence, we need to get in there."

"Iksillix can't allow you entry to my people's most sacred

structure based on a silly dream. You'll have to do better than that, I'm afraid."

"Flocia's unstable," Nicole shouted, just as Ellyne was about to say something. The girl stood, a stern look on her face. If she was nervous, it no longer showed. "My dream—in it, flocia was . . . corrupted somehow, and it was hurting people. It's a danger to us all, but I can prevent it from happening."

"Iksillix feels nothing wrong with flocia. Surely, if there were something wrong with it, others would know about it."

"No, they wouldn't! There isn't anyone—Kithrak or human—who can feel what I'm feeling. No one else is sensitive enough to detect it. If you don't let us repair flocia, magic will be lost to us forever."

"I wouldn't ignore what she says," Ellyne added. She wasn't aware Nicole could lie so convincingly. She herself would've believed it. "After all, it's her that everyone's searching for. It seems to me she might know what she's talking about. Me personally, having seen her in action . . . I'd trust what she says."

Nicole beamed, grinning ear to ear.

"Don't let that go to your head, kid." Ellyne returned a wry grin while Iksillix looked away.

"If this is true," Iksillix said after several moments of contemplation, "then why not just go to your Ilserate and tell them? Surely, they would inform my people of this problem and try to fix it."

"Except," Ellyne interrupted, all too excited to perpetuate this elaborate lie, "the Ilserate has no intention of fixing the problem. They've been using Nicole as a weapon of sorts. It's possible the Ilserate might in fact be the cause of this particular problem."

"Iksillix finds that highly unlikely. Still, what you say makes a modicum of sense. But, if it's true, then we should report this to a Kithrak Elder."

"That's the last thing we should do," Nicole interrupted. If Ellyne didn't know better, she might have thought the girl, too, was having fun with this tall tale.

"What do you mean?" Iksillix's face told Ellyne all she needed to know. He was hooked.

"The Ilserate's got some of your people on their payroll. We don't know who to trust. If we tell the wrong individual, we'll have everyone descending on us. No, we need to do this covertly. If we succeed, then nobody will know except the few Ilserate agents and who can they complain to?"

"But if we fail," Ellyne added, "society could experience an epic collapse and possibly widespread death. The ramifications would be far-reaching and ghastly. Humans would blame Kithrak, and war would erupt."

"You're sure of this?"

"Iksillix," Ellyne said, putting down another curious Kithrak item, "your people are the custodians of flocia. What do you think would happen if something goes terribly wrong with it? Who do you think people will look to first when assigning blame?"

A look of concern washed over Iksillix's face and Ellyne knew she'd struck a chord with him. While there currently was no actual problem with flocia, for all she knew, whatever Nicole was going to do to it could create this outcome. At best, once the Kithrak no longer controlled its flow, there could still be massive problems. Trading one known problem for possible unknown problems was a gamble.

Hopefully those problems were preferable to being unwitting Kithrak slaves, feeding on everyone's minds.

"You make a good point," Iksillix admitted, exhaling a conflicted sigh. "Iksillix can only believe there would be large-scale wars and destruction. Peace would be a thing of the past."

"Now you're catching on! You understand why Nicole

and I need to get into The Sistix undetected. So, will you help us?"

"Perhaps we can come to an arrangement," the Kithrak chuckled, returning to his chair.

"What kind of arrangement?" Ellyne asked.

"Well," he continued, leaning forward, propping two of his elbows on his knees. "Currently, Iksillix findds himself unable to leave this house for . . . reasons. Several weeks ago, I loaned something to a friend, and he has yet to return it. As Iksillix is unable to go get it himself, I would ask you two to retrieve it for me."

"Sounds easy enough," Nicole said.

"Except," Ellyne countered, "you know, everyone and their grandfather is patrolling the city, looking for us."

Nicole cocked her head to the side. "Right, there is that."

"How far away does this individual live? Are they Kithrak too?"

"He's human, actually. He lives by the docks."

"Crap," Ellyne shouted. "That's all the way across the city. Some dude still has your . . . whatever it is, can't it wait a little while longer?"

"For me, it cannot."

Ellyne growled, balling her fists at her sides. She felt they were lucky to have made it this far, but there were probably going to be at least a dozen patrols between them and the docks. And that number didn't even include the Techs and Mages looking for them.

"Look," the Kithrak continued, "Iksillix will be risking his own life getting you two into The Sistix. If anyone finds out I helped, I'll either be killed or separated from flocia permanently which, admittedly, is worse than death."

"They can do that?" Nicole asked, her mouth agape.

"Yes. As stewards of all magic, the Elders can sever connections to flocia temporarily or permanently. It's a punishment worse than death."

Nicole looked sick. Ellyne found this information supremely intriguing.

"I see by your silence," he continued after several awkward moments, "that we're in agreement, yes?"

Ellyne and Nicole remained silent still.

"Excellent. His name is Garriak Fontage. His house is 152 Wendaro Street. I loaned him a . . . well, it's a Kithrak device that looks like a smooth, multicolored stone—about the size of your fist. You humans call it a tyrome."

"Those are used for communicating over long distances, right?" Nicole asked, obviously excited.

"Correct. But it's a device Iksillix never should've had in the first place. You can understand how embarrassing it would be to me if my superiors found out I not only had one, but also loaned it out."

"Sounds like you'd be up shit creek," Ellyne replied.

"Whatever that means, it sounds unpleasant, so I believe you understand Iksillix's plight."

"I understand this'll delay us."

"Well, then, you'd best be on your way." Iksillix grinned, yellow teeth peeking out from behind his thin lips. "Return to Iksillix with the tyrome and he'll give you the means to access The Sistix. After that, you're on your own."

"We've heard that before," Nicole laughed, rolling her eyes. "But that's the way we like it, right Ellyne?"

"Hmm," Ellyne grunted, staring at the Kithrak suspiciously. His grin didn't diminish, but neither did her scrutiny. "Fine. We'll be back."

"I'll be here, of course."

They stepped out onto the dark porch, the front door promptly closing behind them. Ellyne sighed, thoroughly annoyed and resisting the urge to barge back inside and force what they needed out of Iksillix.

"That went well."

"If you enjoy being a Kithrak's errand girl, then yes,"

Ellyne growled. "But we'd better get moving if we're going to find this Garriak guy. We're on the clock."

"The sooner we get this tyrome thing, the sooner we can get into The Sistix."

"Yep." Ellyne stepped off the porch and hurried onto the streets once again, with Nicole in tow. "And then the real fun begins."

"HOW CLOSE ARE WE?"

"Not close enough." Ellyne found the incessant "are we there yet" questions to be a minor annoyance compared to the groups of Technos and mages, as well as the plethora of patrols. The factions were all still looking for them. "The docks are past the Metro hub. You'll see them once we crest the hill."

"I've never seen docks before! Come to think of it, I've never seen the ocean before! Or even a lake. Ooh! Or the Metro hub!"

Ellyne often forgot Nicole hadn't spent any time outside the Ilserate compound until now. She couldn't imagine what it was like—to be filled with such curiosity and childhood wonder, and to marvel at even the smallest things.

It sounded rather annoying, actually.

But what was more annoying was the three patrols and group of Technos all converging on their current location. They'd been fortunate for a while, managing to deftly avoid any contact and often not seeing any danger at all. But it seemed their luck had run out.

Unfortunately, JASN hadn't been any help. The screens

they encountered broadcast their usual advertisements and text-based news bits as normal which contributed to Ellyne's suspicions of a double-cross. Despite Iksillix's lack of familiarity with Derek, what if they were working together? Maybe one or both of them had alerted the Ilserate?

She could think of a billion scenarios where the two of them were betrayed by any number of individuals. She was tired of feeling as though someone was always turning on her but, she had to admit, it seemed to happen more often than not.

Was it something about her? Did she have some sign on her that screamed "please, screw me over, I'd really appreciate it"? Or did she simply fall in with the wrong people? Anymore, it seemed *any* people were the wrong people.

Nicole wasn't. She was trouble, that was certain, but she seemed genuine. And she stuck with Ellyne even after she handed her over to the Ilserate.

Nicole had come to her begging for help. That wasn't a sign of someone who would double-cross someone else. Well, probably not. The girl still needed her help, especially now. If this was a scam, Nicole was a supreme scam artist.

"Do you think you can handle them all?"

Nicole looked around, barely moving her lips as she quietly counted the people approaching them. "I'm not sure," she said, still counting. "I can take down a lot of them but . . . I hate to say it, probably not—especially since a few of them have some hefty enchantments about them."

"Crap. Okay, then, backup plan."

"What's the backup plan?"

"You're going to teleport out of here—to this dude's house or wherever—and I'm going to stall them."

"Stall them? How? No, you're not going to surrender!"

Nicole must have read something in her expression because that was precisely her intent.

"If they waste their time with me, then you can get away

and, hopefully, they won't be able to follow. They'll still be on your trail, but if you can get to Derek, maybe you two can formulate a plan of some kind. At the very least, you can get out of Karnascus and possibly find someone sympathetic who can help you."

"No!" Nicole gripped Ellyne's arm. "I need *you* to help me!"

"Listen to me," Ellyne growled, grabbing both Nicole's shoulders. She saw her wince and loosened her grip slightly. "I *am* helping you. If any of the factions get their hands on you, I'm not sure they're even going to let you live this time. The stakes are too high on this one. I'm slowing you down and I'm . . . unimportant."

"And you think they'll leave you alive? Ellyne, this is suicide!"

Ellyne knew the answer, but she held onto hope that she could somehow escape.

"If we both go out there, guns and magic blazing, we'll both end up dead. My part in this is over. Find Derek and finish this. You can do this, Nicole."

"Ellyne, I . . ."

She saw tears forming in the girl's eyes as she herself fought to hold back her own. She didn't want to die but the thought of taking out as many of them as possible gave her some solace. It was funny, eminent death. She'd faced the end countless times during the Flocia Wars and still came out of it with her skin. Now, however, she was staring death in the face and somewhat willingly welcoming it.

She also still believed she had decent odds of living. Either way, it was time to test just how far her abilities went.

"I never meant for this to happen when I came looking for help. I never meant—"

"You couldn't have known how deep this goes. Even I didn't really expect it to blow up like this. But if everyone else is willing to go all out in their efforts to find you, then you're their greatest fear and, along with that, their greatest enemy. Use that to your advantage. Make them fear you even more. See if you can rally followers to your cause."

"Another faction? You want me to become a faction?"

"Now you're catching on, kid." Ellyne grinned and let go of Nicole. "I'm sorry I couldn't help you any more than this. Now get your ass out of here."

Nicole grabbed her, hugging her tightly and sobbing into her shoulder. Ellyne found herself returning the hug, still fighting back her own tears. She couldn't remember the last time she'd *truly* hugged someone. A hug wasn't something she thought she'd been missing but now she knew different.

This was, perhaps, the only instance she wished magic would affect her reliably. Even now she battled the urge to have Nicole try to teleport them both to safety, but she knew the outcome, at best, would be failure. At worst, something terrible could happen to them both. Whatever relationship existed between her and magic, it was complex, unpredictable, and wildly unreliable.

"You're the key," she whispered. "You're the only hope nobody knows they need."

Then she pushed Nicole away and walked out into the street. As she glanced behind her, she saw Nicole disappear, having teleported somewhere safe . . . hopefully.

"Well," she muttered to herself, "this was a brilliant idea. A gunslinger's last stand, I guess." As confidently as she could, she strode into the street, emerging into an open plaza, and watched as patrols, Technos, and Teranynes all converged on her location. They flourished their wands and guns and waved their hands, eyeing one another suspiciously as they closed in, mumbling.

"Ellyne Thandaral!" a husky-voiced man shouted. "Your crimes against the government are many." A rather rotund man clad in bright green robes stepped forward, both hands out ready to cast a spell if necessary.

The Technos and Teranynes all remained silent, shifting their gazes nervously but standing their ground. Ellyne knew they were a few mere insults away from fighting one another. She always used this to her advantage.

Unfortunately, tonight, there were simply too many of them. Playing them off one another wouldn't work this time.

"Look at me, still trying to find a way out of this mess."

"Where is the weapon?" a haughty voice from somewhere in an Ilserate group asked.

Ellyne badly wished she understood her magic aversion. Now of all times would have been a great opportunity to know her odds. Could she possibly be immune to every one of the thousand spells about to be cast at her? If just one got through this was all over.

And she believed most of them wouldn't be aiming to incapacitate her this time.

"I asked you a question," the man continued. He, too, stepped forward. His brown robes nearly fell off his thin frame. His kimler was an obnoxious, bright orange. "Where is the weapon?"

"The . . . weapon has a name," Ellyne growled, sneering. "Her name is Nicole. She's . . . she's twenty-five years old, her favorite color is red, she has terrible fashion sense, and she would enjoy long walks on the beach if she'd ever been to one. Also, she's not here. She's far more powerful than you can imagine, and she will be your undoing."

"Is that so?" the plump man asked.

"Yep. Everything you know about magic is going to change, and you're sitting here wasting time with me."

"Nonsense!" a woman shouted. She was a Teranyne mage. "Nobody can alter magic."

"Are you sure about that?" Ellyne grinned. The longer she stalled, the longer Nicole had and the longer she might be able to devise a plan to save her own skin. "I've seen her in action. I've seen the knowledge she has. Even the Kithrak themselves fear her. You and your. . . cult vastly underestimate her."

The look on the mage's face changed from confidence to question. The Technos remained silent. Their purpose was obvious—to kill Nicole who was an abomination with dominion over another abomination. They probably had no idea they would be hurt the most from Nicole's efforts, should she succeed. The Teranyne, on the other hand, might actually benefit. The Ilserate and the Kithrak stood to lose the most, however, and they quite obviously knew this.

"If the girl is no longer with you," the brown-robed man continued, "then we have no need of you."

"I did suspect that might be the case," Ellyne laughed, hoping it came through as confident and not nervous. "That's why I always bring this."

She drew her gun and fired a shot, hitting the thin man in the chest. Several gasps were heard as he fell to the ground, unmoving.

Ellyne immediately dove over a bench and crouched behind it as spells flew wildly through the air, colliding with everything around her, sending grass, wood, and chips of concrete sailing in all directions.

"Like I said, brilliant idea Ellyne," she muttered to herself, "but that conversation was going nowhere."

Chaos erupted with shouting and people barking commands at one another.

She peeked over the back of the bench, fired a shot, and dropped someone. At this distance, she couldn't be sure what faction they'd belonged to, but it didn't matter. The longer she kept them focused on her, the more time Nicole had. With teleportation, she was hopefully already close to Garriak's house.

But this bench wouldn't survive long. Even now it was disintegrating as spells chipped away at it. And if there happened to be a more advanced mage in the group, they'd be able to cast far more powerful spells.

A three-eyed Kithrak appeared several feet away and threw a ray of light at her. Searing pain raced through every nerve, setting them all on fire. She yelped and gritted her teeth but calmly aimed her gun and fired, killing her.

Her body tingled and the pain disappeared, but Ellyne could feel the tiny glint of flocia within her. Though it was neither pleasant nor painful, it felt foreign—as if it didn't belong there. She experienced no small amount of frustration by not knowing what to do with it—especially how to get it out of her.

"Go flocia!" she shouted and leaned out, thrusting her hands in front of her and hoping to cause some magical effect. Instead, several spells impacted close to her, sending debris into the air.

"Damn it!" she swore as two spells hit her hands. One felt cold and the other was a stabbing pain. She massaged and flexed her fingers as the pain wore off, followed by a tingle which disappeared.

The well of flocia within her grew slightly.

"Did we hit her?" someone asked.

"I thought we did, but she's still moving!" another replied.

"If she's moving, then don't stop!"

Ellyne couldn't see much from behind the bench, but she thought she saw them fighting amongst themselves while also attacking her.

"Shit!" she growled and scurried to safety as a vehicle dropped from the air, almost crushing her. She rolled to her feet and ran toward a house, hoping to bust through the front door but she was immediately hit with several spells and knocked to the pavement, barely able to move. She screamed as the pain raced through her and a variety of effects threatened to overtake her.

"We got her!" someone shouted.

"Don't let up!" another voice cried. "Keep her down!"

"How is she not dead?" yet another voice chimed.

"Back off, Technos! She's ours!"

"I don't think so!"

Ellyne felt them—every spell that impacted with her body. She convulsed and writhed as each effect hit her, dissipated, and wore off. It was a mixture of many different effects all at once, and she'd never experienced so many at the same time. Any one of them would have presumably killed a normal person.

And her ability didn't do her much good as she was essentially immobilized, able to do nothing but scream and experience unbelievable pain while her enemies approached, still casting their spells at her. If anyone had an actual firearm, they could effortlessly end her life.

She lay on her stomach and could only see she several pairs of boots standing around her. One of them kicked the gun from her hand. She could still hear people shouting and spells being cast—only some of which were directed at her.

She also felt the large, growing well of flocia within her, but it was useless now. They could essentially do whatever they wanted with her. But she helped Nicole escape, which was the most important thing. She would've laughed if she could have.

"So, what do we do now?" someone asked. His accent was thick enough to where Ellyne had trouble understanding him.

"Magic won't kill her, apparently," someone else growled, punctuated with a particularly painful spell to the back of Ellyne's head.

"How can that be?"

"No idea. But Marik said this might be the case. He said to bring her in if we couldn't dispatch her normally."

"Maybe she's got some really powerful protective enchantments around her? Either way, we were at least able to immobilize her."

Despite the fact she was prone and surrounded, Ellyne still felt the spells they lobbed at her. She convulsed, balancing the pain of every spell with that of the flocia that overwhelmed her from inside.

She was hoisted to her feet and held upright by many sets of hands—a good thing because she didn't think she could stand on her own. She was barely able to wipe the drool off her chin as it was.

"This is a nice gun," the man with the accent sneered, inspecting her revolver. "An old weapon from the Legacy Age that should have been left behind a long time ago. Still, it's shiny. I think I'll hang onto it." He tucked her weapon in his belt and laughed.

"I'll certainly let you keep one of the bullets," Ellyne spat, her words slurred. She squinted through blurred vision. They'd stopped assaulting her with magic, apparently confident of their situation. Though her body still protested as the flocia within her threatened to erupt, she felt control of her limbs quickly returning.

"Charming. Let's get her to The Citadel. Let everyone else fight one another. Hopefully we can put down the Techno and Teranyne garbage permanently—wrap it up with a bow and all that shit Marik likes to say."

Ellyne chuckled.

"What are you laughing at?"

"That really does sound like Marik."

"Well, you can laugh at him to his face in just a second. Torval, are you ready to teleport us?"

Ellyne chuckled again.

"What's so funny now?"

"I'll tell you in a minute."

"Alright, Torval, let's go."

"Yes sir!"

Ellyne gently closed her eyes and breathed deeply, listening to the man mutter his incantation. His deliberate and careful pronunciations were a stark contrast to Nicole who simply teleported on a whim—as effortless as blinking her eyes. The Kithrak, too, were more skilled at certain types of magic, though their ability came nowhere close to Nicole's. For a brief moment, Ellyne wondered if Nicole really could have beaten everyone here.

It was an interesting thought—a thought that was interrupted by hot, searing pain erupting from every part of her body. She opened her eyes and screamed, feeling as if she would be torn apart.

"What's wrong?" someone asked.

"I . . . I don't know!" Torval replied. "The spell failed! Why's she screaming?"

"What the hell is going on?" someone else shouted.

Ellyne would've liked to see the looks on their faces, but she only saw spots across her vision as the pressure within her mounted, came to a head, and burst outward with a deafening explosion.

The hands supporting her fell away and she slumped to the ground, her vision dark and her ears ringing. She wasn't sure how much time had passed, her trying not to pass out, and she was fully prepared for someone to hoist her back to her feet and drag her away at any moment.

But as her vision began to clear and her hearing returned, she neither saw nor heard movement. There was no magic battle, no shouts or yells, no flashes of light from spells being cast—nothing. The sound of her own breathing was deafening by comparison.

As she struggled to her feet, standing on shaky legs, she began to see what transpired and wasn't sure whether to laugh or be appalled. She staggered forward, stumbling but catching herself on the bench she'd just a few minutes ago used as cover. It was now bent, the metal having been twisted and shattered.

"It's like the Metro all over again," she muttered.

Scattered everywhere were bodies, immobile and motionless. Bushes and trees were flattened, windows were shattered, and she could see people cowering inside several houses.

She hadn't expected devastation on this scale.

"We need to go," a familiar voice said from behind her.

"Coming back for me was a mistake."

"Friends stick together, Ellyne. Besides, you already took care of everything yourself.

Ellyne felt a hand on her shoulder and cracked a small smile before she saw what she'd done.

"I don't . . . are they all dead, Nicole?"

"I don't know. I doubt it. I'm sure most of them had rudimentary protective enchantments cast on them to lessen any effects. Well, except the Technos possibly."

"The Technos," Ellyne chuckled. It was morose laughter, filled with both disdain and sorrow. "They would never admit it, but they most likely had some protections—protections produced by devices. And those devices run on magic."

"Ellyne, we—"

"I couldn't control it, Nicole. I didn't know it would be this devastating. I thought it would just knock out the nearest targets so I could escape."

"There was nothing you could do."

"It was like the Metro hub all over again. I could've warned them . . . told them not to. Instead, I encouraged them. I basically *dared* them to try and teleport me. I just . . . I can't control whatever this is. You shouldn't have come back for me. I'm putting you in danger just by being near you."

"Listen." Nicole's voice took a stern tone—something Ellyne had never heard before. "The very fact you're remorseful tells me all I need to know. And I came back for you because, like I said, that's what friends do. You did it for me. Now if you'd like to wallow in your self-pity, do it on your own time."

Ellyne turned to face Nicole. Just seeing the girl brought a smile to her face. She had to admit, however, Nicole's words made sense. Though she found it a bit of a shock—those words coming from her lips.

"Where'd you learn that speech?"

"I made it up. It sounded like something you'd say—especially the wallowing part. Did you like it?"

Ellyne didn't answer. Instead, she hugged her friend tightly. "Thank you," she whispered as she stepped back, trying to compose herself. "You're right—about all of it, but especially about the part where we need to go."

"I enjoy being right," Nicole giggled. "But before we go, you're going to need this."

Ellyne gently took her gun from Nicole and slipped it into the holster on her hip.

"Right," she said. "Let's go."

"SO IKSILLIX IS MISSING his tyrome, is he?" Garriak chuckled as he fiddled with his mustache. It was the same color as his floppy hair—either a very dark brown or black—Ellyne wasn't sure. "I was wondering if he would remember I had it. He can be a bit absent-minded sometimes."

"He didn't seem that way to me," Nicole retorted.

"In fact, I've got several other items of his that I've long since lost the use for, but I'm waiting to see if he'll come knocking to reclaim them."

"Yes, well, he finds himself . . . unable to come claim anything right now."

"Oh," Garriak laughed, "yeah, that whole home confinement thing. I guess that's what the Ilserate does to you when they're investigating you for murder. I find it all amusing, really."

"Murder?" Ellyne perked up.

"Oh, you didn't know?" Garriak strutted around the dining room, grabbed a pitcher of water and three glasses from a kitchen counter, and set them on the table. "I figured, being friends of his, he would've told you."

"He's . . . a man of few words."

"You're right, there!" he laughed, holding a glass of water out to Ellyne. She shook her head. Instead, he set it in front of Nicole. "Sometimes, I wonder why we're even friends. We argue a lot but, in the end, I guess we respect each other enough. Either that or he's just waiting until he gets all his things back from me."

Ellyne shot Nicole a quizzical look which Nicole quickly returned. This man was . . . odd. But he was an afterthought. The fact Iksillix was a murder suspect greatly intrigued her. Her curiosity demanded she know more but decorum dictated she keep quiet about it.

Though, this man's loose lips could offer up the information without her trying. She almost wished she could spend more time here and pry some tasty tidbits from him.

"I remember when I first met Iksillix." Garriak poured himself some water and sat, staring wistfully into the glass. "He hasn't changed a bit. He was my first Kithrak friend, you know. When they've got more than two eyes and two arms it's a little disconcerting—takes some getting used to."

"Hey," Ellyne interrupted, "I'm sorry if this comes off as rude, but Iksillix was very specific about his wishes and didn't want us wasting any time. He was very insistent."

"Oh, yes," Garriak laughed. "I bet he was. See, I'm probably not supposed to have a tyrome, not having the proper access to such things, and especially being an untalented and all."

"It really sounds to me that Iksillix tends not to play by the rules a lot."

"Iksillix and I have been friends for a long time." Garriak stared into his glass, turning it and sloshing the water within. "But one thing has always been true to me. He values research and knowledge over any protocol."

"And what were you trying to do with it?" Nicole asked.

"Long-distance communication, of course. Only, in this case, *very* long-distance communication."

"How do you mean?" Ellyne suddenly found herself intensely curious.

"Well, tyromes are tricky objects. You can communicate with another tyrome halfway across Seralune as easily as talking to someone standing right in front of you. But I think tyromes could be powerful enough to span much more vast distances."

"You mean, like, another planet?"

"Well, yes, another planet is certainly not out of the question, of course. I'm sure such a thing is what the Kithrak have done traditionally to keep in contact with other settlements."

"Wait," Nicole interrupted, "other settlements?"

"Well, of course!" Garriak laughed. "The Kithrak aren't native to Seralune! They inhabit several other planets from what I understand. Tyromes would be a convenient way for them to communicate rather than opening a portal or using a spacefaring vessel."

Ellyne's mind worked furiously to make sense of what she'd just heard. She assumed they had a home world, but it had never occurred to her that the Kithrak would have colonized other planets. Now that she thought about it, it made sense.

"So, wait," she said. "I thought they traveled in their Sistix together. Why are the Kithrak living on multiple planets? What's their purpose?"

"Ah," Garriak chuckled. "He told you about the Sistix! How intriguing. But isn't it obvious? The Kithrak are the stewards of flocia and, therefore, the keepers of magic. They follow flocia across the stars. Once they detect magic use, they seek it out and help the creatures trying to use it, so their society doesn't collapse into ruin. At least, that's what I've gathered from the things Iksillix has said. I'm pretty sure much of it is information I'm not supposed to know—like the Sistix itself."

"And the tyrome?" Nicole asked.

"And the tyrome."

"So, what then?" Nicole was playing with a few drops of water on the table. She slowly passed her hand over it and the water changed shape into a tiny dog that ran around the table before jumping into the pitcher. "You want to talk to Kithrak on other planets? Or creatures on other planets?"

"Oh, no," Garriak laughed. "Nothing that mundane. Besides, the creation of a tyrome is a closely guarded Kithrak secret and they shouldn't be used by anyone other than a Kithrak." He was grinning, obviously proud of having gotten around that constraint.

Garriak rose from his chair and held up his index finger. "One moment," he said and disappeared down the hallway.

"Did you know any of this?" Ellyne whispered.

"Absolutely not," Nicole whispered back. "I doubt anyone but a handful of people in the Ilserate know any of this, and I bet they don't know the full story."

Ellyne suddenly felt she was in well over her head and she wondered if Nicole felt the same. She'd only ever been concerned with Karnascus. She rarely ever thought about the whole planet. Certainly, she'd neglected to consider the bigger picture—a situation which seemed to expand with each new day.

"This is a whole lot more than I'd ever considered."

"You think that's bad? Before tonight, I'd never seen the ocean!"

They both quietly laughed in unison.

"Ah, here we are," Garriak said, returning. He set on the table a smooth, palm-sized stone that shimmered and pulsed with different colors.

Nicole gingerly picked it up, turning it over in her hand and running her fingers over it. "You said you weren't attempting to contact other planets."

"Right you are! Why would I need to do that when it's already the function of the tyrome itself?"

"But you said you were using it to attempt to communicate vast distances."

"I did, didn't I?" The humor disappeared from Garriak's face, and he leaned in close to Ellyne and Nicole. "Planets are not so vast a distance when considering other galaxies, realms or universes entirely."

"I'm afraid I don't understand. Other realms? Other universes?"

"It is a bit mind-boggling at first, I'll admit. It wasn't something I'd intended when I first borrowed the tyrome. You see, I'm a very curious sort and, being a . . . well, a skab, I don't have a whole lot of magical insight the way most mages do. So, I experiment with artifacts I get from Iksillix from time to time. Of course, being a human in possession of Kithrak artifacts . . . both Iksillix and I would be in serious trouble if anyone found out."

Garriak chuckled and took a swig of water, pausing as he admired the tyrome as it pulsed with a warm, green glow.

"Anyway, I've been experimenting with this tyrome for a while and, well, let's just say I don't think even the Kithrak know its full potential. Or maybe they do. They wouldn't tell me one way or another, and I'm not about to ask." Garriak laughed again but, this time, it was a nervous laugh.

"Wait," Ellyne interrupted, "you . . . found something, didn't you?"

"Something. I'm not even sure what or where it is. But, yes, I reached out and something responded. If I had magical talent, perhaps I would be able to determine more. And I can only tell Iksillix about it, but I doubt he'll care. I'm the curious scientist and he's the pragmatic . . . well, something else."

"So why are you telling us all of this?" Nicole asked. Ellyne had to admit, it was a good question.

Garriak laughed again and pushed the tyrome closer to Ellyne. "The Golden Gunslinger has paid me a visit, and she's brought the Mage Breaker with her. Yes, I'm acutely aware who both of you are and, whatever you're doing, I have no doubt you have the best intentions. Iksillix may think he's sent you on some silly errand, but I assure you tyromes are powerful objects."

Ellyne plucked the tyrome from Nicole's grasp. It felt like cold, wet glass in her hand, and she was convinced she could almost feel it thrum with every pulse of light. Just having it nearby disturbed her, and she swore she almost felt a connection of some sort. Ellyne slipped it into a pocket inside her jacket, wishing to be rid of it as if it were some festering evil she now carried with her. She considered letting Nicole take it, but the girl had no pockets. What good were clothes with no pockets?

"Thank you, Garriak." She stood, reached out, and shook his hand.

Nicole did the same.

"Good luck with whatever you're attempting," he said as he led them both to the front door. Upon opening it, he paused a moment. "Listen," he said in a hushed tone, "whatever Iksillix has promised you, ensure he makes good on his word."

Ellyne returned a confused look.

"He may be one of my best friends as well as an exceedingly brilliant mind," Garriak chuckled, "but he can also be a colossal ass, and he's double-crossed me on more than one occasion."

Ellyne nodded and smiled. The moment Garriak mentioned he recognized them, she thought things would turn sour. Thankfully, not everyone was out to get them, apparently. "I think I can see that side of him," she laughed.

Or he'd simply alert the Ilserate once they were gone if he hadn't already. But that was the cynic within. She made a practice long ago of rarely giving anyone her trust. On the positive side, at least there would be fewer people chasing them after what happened earlier.

"Thanks again," she said, slipping out the front door with Nicole behind her. She could hear the locks click into place the moment the door closed, but the magical security wards she assumed were in place were undetectable to her.

The sultry air wafting from the docks was a stark contrast to that of the house they had just left, and Ellyne sighed as they walked back into the city.

"Thank you, by the way."

"For what?" Nicole asked.

"For ignoring what I said and coming back for me. I mean, it's annoying that you unnecessarily put yourself in danger for me, but it means a lot. I mean, you shouldn't have, but I'm glad you did."

Nicole giggled quietly. "You're really bad at this, aren't you?"

"Is it that obvious?" Ellyne laughed.

The sun wouldn't be up for another few hours, but it was going take time for them to make their way back to Iksillix's house. They left the docks behind them and wound through the streets, avoiding patrols and strangers alike, and making sure to steer clear of the area Ellyne had destroyed earlier. That place would be crawling with all three factions trying to determine what happened and . . . well, cleaning up.

"Listen, Ellyne," Nicole said meekly, finally breaking the silence. "What happened earlier tonight—"

"Was awful and I'd really rather not talk about it. Let's just get this tyrome back to Iksillix and then we'll be one step closer to this all ending . . . I hope."

"Well, too bad."

"Fine," Ellyne grumbled. "What do you want to talk about, then? How I lost control and basically slaughtered a couple hundred people or more? Listen." She stopped and turned to face Nicole. "I can't control whatever ability this is. If I can't control it, people could die. First it was the Metro, now this. And don't get me wrong—every last one of them was probably a deplorable stain on this city, but I only kill those who I intend . . . and sometimes the occasional rage bullet escapes. The point is, I didn't mean to kill most of those people no matter how much I wanted to."

"But that's what I'm trying to tell you! Ellyne, you *didn't* kill them! Well, not most of them anyway. The people closest to you, yeah, they're totally super dead, but most everyone else is probably just going to wake up with a really bad headache and maybe some scrapes."

"Wait, how do you know this?"

"I watched it happen. I saw the awful things they were doing to you, and I saw the shockwave you released. I mean, it was really impressive—there was a whole lot of power that came out of—"

"Focus, Nicole."

"Right. Anyway, after it happened, I immediately whipped up a spell that could detect which ones were alive. It was pretty simple, actually. I'm sure most hospitals probably use something similar to monitor patients. I mean, if they don't, they're doing a lousy job, right?"

Ellyne gave Nicole a stern glance.

"The point is, Ellyne, almost all of them are still alive. The good news is, they'll probably be out of commission for a while due to broken bones or other injuries, which makes our lives easier."

"That it does," Ellyne smirked. "Until it happens again."

"You just need to learn how to control it is all. Everyone with innate magical ability goes through the same thing, albeit on a smaller scale. Skabs are fortunate, because they just have to learn to use magic devices instead of accidentally setting a room on fire or, you know, phasing through a wall or something."

"Sounds like you have some experience in that area," Ellyne chuckled.

"More than I care to recall, yes," she grinned. "At some

point, we just need to figure out how you can control this ability—probably, you know, after we figure out what it actually is."

"Which should be super easy, given that I am apparently the sole individual on the planet who possesses it." Saying it out loud, Ellyne wasn't sure whether she should laugh or cry . . . or, well, maybe just get mad and punch some things.

"Then maybe we find someone else on another planet who has the same power."

"Do you think that's likely?"

"Well . . . now that I think about it, no, probably not."

Ellyne was again suddenly aware of the tyrome in her pocket. Was there a way to use it to connect with someone else with her same situation? She had to admit, the prospect certainly piqued her interest.

"Maybe not likely, but do you think such a thing is possible?" she asked, seriously intrigued. With everyone around her constantly using magic, she assumed she was an anomaly and had long since abandoned any curiosity. Sure, at one time she wondered and believed, but that was long ago.

"Honestly, I don't really know. No one understands what would cause such a . . . condition? I don't even know what to call it. I mean, even the untalented aren't *completely* cut off from flocia's source."

"So, I'm a freak is what you're saying," Ellyne laughed. She was honest with herself, and she had never once regretted not using magic. She hated it before she even knew of her . . . condition, as Nicole had just called it.

"I mean, I'd hate to put it that way, but . . . maybe?" Nicole laughed, too. "Surely, someone else out there—whether on Seralune or another planet entirely—must also be disconnected from flocia like you are. Disconnected, yet able to absorb it."

"I'd like to believe that, but I'm not sure I do." She sighed wistfully, not actually sure whether she cared if someone else shared in her plight. It wouldn't change anything for her, and her loathing for magic would always remain.

They reached a major intersection that was thankfully deserted, but they kept their guard up and Ellyne made absolutely sure there wasn't another individual in sight before they scurried across the street to the median, then across the street again to the sidewalk.

It was almost eerie how deserted the city was. Surely, she hadn't incapacitated every single person belonging to each faction. If not, then what? Were they scrambling to regroup and tend to any wounded? Were they making plans? Maybe they were afraid of her, having seen precisely what she could do. Most likely, none of them had any idea what had happened, so that prospect was feasible.

No doubt word had reached Marik by now. He'd be fuming. At the very least, that was a delicious thought Ellyne could take solace in. She now knew he wanted her dead—officially, anyway. His hubris, however, was wanting to do the deed himself. She wondered if his minions had learned their lessons, or even if he had.

"So, Marik really wants to kill you that badly?" Nicole asked, as if she were reading Ellyne's thoughts.

"Apparently he does, which makes me happy."

"Why would that make you happy? It sounds rather dangerous to me, someone wanting you dead. Or is this what you deal with daily? Ellyne, how many people want you dead?"

"Probably a dozen or so," she chuckled. That was most likely a low estimate. "Marik's the only one with the power and resources to attempt it without himself ending up dead . . . maybe."

"Why is this a good thing again?"

"It means I've pushed him to his limits. I've become such a nasty thorn in his side that it's eating at him constantly. I know him well enough to understand that he must be truly pissed off. Plus, as an added bonus, I'm making him look bad to his superiors—whoever they are. He's got to be furious. I'm probably consuming his entire existence right now."

"And what if he sends out forces to come after you? What if he comes for you again?"

"I don't think he will—at least not for a while. He'd need to come up with some different tactics and that'll take a while, so I think we've got some time before that happens. The Technos and Teranynes . . . well, they're both disorganized so I wouldn't put anything past them. In any case, it looks like we're blessed with little to no resistance right now."

"Right. Let's get this tyrome back to Iksillix, get into the Sistix and . . . what exactly comes after that?"

Ellyne frowned. "I was sort of hoping you'd know, actually."

"Yeah, no. If this were The Citadel and the Ilserate we were talking about, I'd know a whole lot more but this Sistix thing or place or whatever . . . I think we're both in the dark."

"We'll figure it out."

Truthfully, Ellyne had considered the problem but refused to put much of her focus on it until they actually got there. They still had a long way to go and, no matter what Ellyne assumed was going to happen, she knew full well the very real possibility of everything going sideways in a heartbeat.

"We should take it step by step," she continued. "And the next step is delivering this tyrome to Iksillix."

"Then, we only need to get into the Sistix, find our way to flocia's source and somehow wrest control of it from the Kithrak, all while avoiding detection by the hordes of Kithrak who are supposedly inside."

"Well, when you put it that way, it sounds super easy."

Nicole gave Ellyne a scowl.

"Let's just get back to Iksillix first." Ellyne smirked but crouched behind a dumpster and motioned for Nicole to do the same as a human enforcer and three Ilserate bots passed the alley in which they hid.

"It looks like not all patrols are canceled," she whispered.

"They'd be fools to attack us."

"You're right. I don't think they will. I bet they're merely trying to find us."

"What does that mean?"

"I think, maybe, Marik's worried."

Ellyne still hadn't even the slightest inkling what official position Marik held within the Ilserate, but he was heavily embedded within the Kithrak ranks. He commanded a lot of power within both organizations, which meant he had a lot to lose. And desperate people often took desperate measures.

"I think he wants to regain control of the situation," she continued. "We escaped and we also proved how dangerous we can be. He knows we're up to something—only a fool would ignore it. He truly *is* afraid of us."

Ellyne couldn't help but smile. She should've been concerned, and maybe she was, somewhere deep down. The joy she felt outweighed any apprehension she may have had about the situation. Truly, she had never feared the man, even though she knew what he was capable of. Her hatred blanketed any fear she may have had, causing it to remain unnoticed.

But just knowing how angry and frustrated he probably was . . . that was not only encouraging, but also motivating. It was absolutely the wrong motivation, but if this all resulted in Marik's complete disgrace, it would all be worth it. It was petty, but then, so was he.

Killing him would be preferable.

Still, that last encounter shook her. Not only were her abilities unpredictable, but she'd been incapacitated under their weight. Magic may not traditionally affect her, but it *did* affect her. Whether it could kill her was still unknown, and that was worrisome. Marik probably knew everything by now, and that was more concerning.

"Come on," she said, tugging on Nicole's arm, "we should be safe."

They emerged from the alley and made their way back into the shadows, seeing no sign of the patrol.

"If we stay in the dark," Ellyne said, "then hopefully we'll keep Marik in the dark."

"Take him by surprise? Sounds like a good idea to me."

"He'll never see us coming."

"IT'S US, IKSILLIX," Ellyne said, looking around. She wasn't sure where the camera was or in which direction she should talk. Hidden cameras always unnerved her—more so when she knew they were there but couldn't locate them. At least, with JASN, she could usually spot them and avoid talking at nothing.

To further punctuate her statement, she held the tyrome aloft, waving it around to make sure the concealed camera would be able to see it before slipping it back into her jacket's inner pocket. Eventually, the door opened and Iksillix motioned them both inside, quickly shutting it behind them.

"Very good," he muttered, motioning them again into his living room where, once again, Ellyne stood while Nicole sat. Iksillix also sat, looking both comfortable and somewhat relieved, but also conspicuously antsy. "Good work indeed. Iksillix will be happy to have his tyrome back where it belongs. He shouldn't have loaned it out in the first place."

"And not to a human, right?" Ellyne asked.

"Indeed. So, may Iksillix have it, then?"

Ellyne pulled the smooth, pulsing tyrome from her jacket and set it on the small table between Nicole and Iksillix. On the one hand, she was glad to be rid of it. On the other hand, however, she felt a nagging urge to keep it.

All four of the Kithrak's eyes lit up at once as he abruptly snatched it up from the table and turned it over in one of his three hands. He grinned as he stared at it, then he made it vanish with a quick hand motion.

"Iksillix thanks you both. You have done him a very important service for me. I hope Garriak wasn't too put out with returning it."

"He seemed like he would've preferred to keep it longer," Ellyne replied, "but he willingly gave it to us. I'm sure he didn't want to be caught with it in his possession just as much as you didn't."

"Indeed," Iksillix agreed, "that would have been bad for the both of us. Iksillix has already lost some favor with his superiors as it is. He'd hate to lose more and drag him down with him. He's a brilliant scientist but, unfortunately, very untalented."

"Of course," Nicole concurred.

Ellyne was more skeptical. She had a feeling Iksillix would rat out Garriak and throw him under the Metro if he had to save his own neck.

"Thank you both for returning the tyrome." Iksillix stood. "You probably have lots to do so Iksillix will let you get to it," he said, motioning toward the front door.

Nicole stood but Ellyne didn't budge.

"You're welcome," Ellyne said, still firmly planted in place. "But there is the tiny matter of our payment. We did what you asked."

"Payment?" Iksillix shifted his weight and Ellyne could clearly seem him fidgeting with one of his right hands. "Iksillix doesn't recall discussing any payment."

"You cheat!" Nicole shouted.

"Now why would we come knocking on your door and run your errand for you without any reason?" Ellyne asked.

"Altruism? Maybe we were bored? Perhaps we just really enjoy fetching objects for random Kithrak like yourself?" She leaned in close, her nose nearly touching his. "Or maybe we were promised something in return by someone who's going back on his word," she growled.

Iksillix moved his arms but, before he could fire off a spell, Ellyne's revolver jutted into his chest. He must've felt it because he immediately stopped his spellcasting.

"I'll put a bullet in you. I've shot people for far less."

"Then you will never get what you seek." Iksillix's voice nearly cracked.

"Something you're apparently not planning on giving us anyway so, let me ask you then, why would I keep you alive if you have nothing to give?" She stepped back slightly and looked around the room. "Perhaps you have something of value I can sell . . . maybe live a comfortable life for a while."

Iksillix slowly backed up a few paces, putting space between himself and the angry gunslinger. Ellyne allowed him to do so, but she still kept her gun trained on him. The only mage who *maybe* could cast a spell quicker than Ellyne could fire a shot was Nicole. Iksillix, being Kithrak was assuredly good, but not *that* good.

"Look," the Kithrak stammered, "please . . . don't take this personally. Iksillix knows what we agreed to, but he was hoping we could come to some other arrangement instead. What you ask—"

"There is no other arrangement we're interested in. The only thing we need from you is passage into the Sistix. You give us that, our asses will be happily on our way. You *don't* give us what we want, however, things get messy."

"I know Iksillix said he could give you access to the Sistix, but he really can't."

"Can't or won't?"

Nicole looked horrified—whether by Iksllix's actions or her own, Ellyne didn't know. The only thing she was sure of was that this deal had gone sideways in a heartbeat. She would get what they required, whatever it was.

"Won't. Can't. Both." A bead of sweat formed on Iksillix's forehead. "Listen, you did Iksillix a great service and he truly *is* grateful but what you're asking for . . . my superiors would not only kill him, but they'd most likely do so with the greatest pain possible. It would be considered treason against Iksillix's people of the highest order!"

"They don't ever have to know you were involved." Ellyne quickly grew tired of this game. Why must everything be so complicated? "You let us in, then you can scurry off and hide under your rock. If we're caught, I promise we won't mention you. It's as simple as that."

"But it's not as simple as that!" All three of his fists were clenched aggressively, but there was distinct fear in his quivering voice. "Iksillix have to go with you and the security would see him letting you in!"

Ellyne sighed. This was going nowhere, but she wasn't about to give up. They were too close.

"Then give us whatever key there is to let us in. You can say we stole it, or you lost it or whatever the hell you want, I don't care. It obviously wouldn't be the first time you gave a Kithrak artifact to a human, right?"

"Iksillix . . . can't do that either. The access device isn't something he can just *give* you."

"What does that mean? Why not?"

Nicole looked worried, as if she wanted to say something to defuse the situation but also as if she knew there was really nothing she *could* say.

"It's . . . it's sort of attached to him. Iksillix can't just give it to you."

"Oh, for the love of . . ." Ellyne sighed. "This just keeps getting better." Although it was frustrating, she now completely understood why Iksillix resisted so adamantly. She lowered her weapon.

"Thank you," Iksillix said, relieved.

"So . . . which body part?"

Ellyne emerged from Iksillix's house and grinned, exhaling happily. Things were coming together and, for once, it seemed they finally had a shot at both not only figuring out what was happening, but also putting an end to it.

The very thought of her life returning to normal was exhilarating. The past few days had been far more chaotic than she was used to and, right now, listening to some Transgressors at high volume while downing a few shots of squama sounded perfect.

Never mind the fact they still had possibly the most difficult part of this journey still ahead of them.

"What did you just do?" Nicole shouted, dashing out the door and into the yard. "What was that back there?"

"It's simple. We got what we came for, now let's go before—"

"You cut out his eyeball!"

"He's got three more, Nicole. He'll be fine. Besides, it's not like he was awake." Ellyne held up a clear plastic bag, the contents of which were one eyeball. "This eye is our ticket into the Sistix—assuming he was telling the truth. I mean, if he wasn't . . . anyway, it would've been a whole lot easier if he'd cooperated."

"You cut out his eyeball!" Nicole reiterated loudly. "How could you do such a thing? Not only is it super disgusting, but it's . . . you mutilated him!"

"Shh! Keep it down, kid." Ellyne grabbed both of Nicole's shoulders and pulled her in close. "I did what needed to be done," she whispered. "Besides, I told him what was going to happen. It's not like he couldn't see it coming." She accidentally made herself laugh. Nicole, however, wasn't laughing.

"There's a lot more going on here than he was divulging," Ellyne continued. "And it was abundantly clear he wasn't going to help us. Is it unfortunate that I had to cut out a body part? Yes. Is it a good thing he still has three more eyes? Also, yes."

"I just . . . I can't believe—"

"I'm not proud of it, Nicole." She let go of Nicole's shoulders and put the eyeball back in her jacket pocket. "But we're short on time and just as short on options. Besides, I'm pretty sure there's some kind of high-level magic that can grow back an eye. If not, then he can probably find a really badass eyepatch or some magic fake eye device or whatever. Hell, I'll even give this one back if he still wants it when all this is over —if we survive."

"I just wish there had been another way. He's not going to be happy when he wakes."

"So do I. It's not like I wanted to cut out an eyeball today." Ellyne stepped into the street, inspecting the area for any enemies. Once Nicole followed, they disappeared back into the city as the sun glinted off the very tips of the tallest buildings. "We need to get somewhere safe. Hopefully, we'll be able to blend in with the crowds until we find somewhere. The whole city will be looking for us soon if they aren't already."

"Iksillix was going to double-cross us, wasn't he?"

"Oh, he already had, I'm sure of it." Ellyne turned down an alley and Nicole followed. She was hoping to make it safely back to Victor's and hide out upstairs but kept her eyes open for any closer alternative options. "Not only did he use us to get his tyrome back, and not only was he not going to help us, but I'm pretty sure he was planning on reporting our location to the Ilserate."

"How do you know?"

"Just a hunch. I'm used to dealing with individuals of his position. They're usually similar in their beliefs and actions. With him unconscious, we've got a head start. How long will that spell last?"

"He should be out for a day or so, but that's for a human. I don't know how long it'll work on a Kithrak."

"Then we'll have to make our move as soon as possible—before word spreads. If we're lucky, we'll be able to move freely about the Sistix and nobody will even think we're not supposed to be there. It sounds like their security is based largely on keeping threats out."

"Here's hoping he stays asleep, then. You're right—we don't need him blabbing."

"Plus," Ellyne smirked, "it'll be just a bit tougher for him to do any significant communication without this." She produced the tyrome from her pocket and tossed it in the air.

"You *stole* the tyrome?" Nicole sounded shocked as she caught the shimmering object.

"Oh, come on," Ellyne laughed, "don't sound so surprised. "You didn't think I was just going to let him keep it and tell all his buddies about us, did you? Besides, if we have it, then maybe we have leverage over him, and maybe over other Kithrak."

"I do *not* approve."

"Hey," Ellyne said, snatching it from Nicole and slipping it back into a pocket. "At the very least, maybe you can study it and learn some things."

It was amazing how quickly the shock disappeared from Nicole's face, to be instantly replaced with curiosity as her eyes widened at the thought. "I'd absolutely love to!" she squeaked. "Do you think I'll get the chance? When can I start?"

"Easy there, tiger. Let's focus on our next task. Besides, present circumstances aside, I'm not normally into stealing. Also, it's probably not a great idea to hang onto it forever and, frankly, I'd love to be rid of it. For now, however, it's ours, so we may as well use that time wisely."

"Assuming there *is* any time."

"Well, yeah, there's that."

The streets eventually filled with people, all hustling to fulfill their morning routines. Vehicles traveled the streets, and the Metro traveled the city, casting its familiar whisper as it carried countless individuals to their destinations along its rails. Karnascus was alive with the breath of a new day. To many, mornings were a beautiful thing but, to Ellyne, they were often burdensome. Today was a particularly pertinent example of the latter.

"Try to blend in," Ellyne suggested, "it doesn't appear there's any kind of public arrest warrants out for us yet."

"How do you know?"

"Because, if there were, everyone and their mother would be trying to apprehend us. So far, nobody seems to care. But that doesn't mean we're not being watched or tracked, so keep your eyes open for anything unusual or dangerous."

"Like what?"

"Like *that!*" Ellyne grabbed Nicole's arm and pointed to a patrol—two enforcers and three bots. It was a routine patrol that most likely wasn't specifically looking for the two of them, but that was no reason to get sloppy.

She dragged the girl into a nearby shop, faking interest in the various items of clothing.

"Pretend we're shopping," she whispered as she feigned interest in whatever was on the rack in front of her.

"This is men's underwear," Nicole whispered, her face turning beet red.

Ellyne stifled a laugh. She pretended to browse the rack but, instead, was watching Nicole who couldn't have been more of a fish out of water. Her gaze darted to the window several times to keep an eye on the patrol which passed by harmlessly.

"Can we go now?" Nicole's face was still a shade of red that nearly matched her clothes.

"Just a few more seconds. I mean, I don't want to rush you and force you to pick out the wrong underwear."

"Very funny," Nicole sneered, moving toward the door. "Let's go."

"Okay, okay, come on." Ellyne couldn't stop giggling as they left the store, still wary of their surroundings. The patrol was nowhere to be seen, but they still needed to exercise caution. All it took was one person to spot them and everything would become a lot more difficult . . . and messy.

The various screens she saw broadcast their standard messages—news bits, traffic, temperature, and various other useless bits of information. They couldn't expect help from JASN during the busy daytime activity, but she was still curious why he was so quiet lately. It had to be the increased patrol activity. Derek was smart and would try to avoid discovery.

His assistance would've been helpful last night, though. Maybe Ellyne could've avoided that massive showdown and just *maybe* her head wouldn't be aching right now. She needed some rest soon and something decent to eat.

And a strong drink. Maybe two.

"So, we get somewhere safe, then what?"

"You love to ask questions, don't you? I'd figure, by now, you'd know full well I have no idea what I'm doing."

"I was hoping, by now, you would at least know slightly more what you were doing than before."

"Nope. Though it's not like I haven't had time to think about it. I guess our next move is to find the Sistix."

"Well, yeah. That much is apparent." Nicole's face had returned to a much more normal shade.

"My normal plan would be to shoot some things and burn it down, but that's not going to apply to this situation, I'm afraid."

"Your plans always involve shooting and destruction, don't they?"

"If you can consider them actual plans, then yes."

"How is it you came to command such a successful force

during the Flocia Wars?" Nicole asked. "I mean, if you're such a terrible planner . . . it just seems to me one would need to exercise strategy and, well, planning."

Ellyne remained quiet.

"I mean, I read the history books—even the books the Ilserate tried to keep from me."

"Let's just get under cover. Right now, I don't like being out in the open."

They left Iksillix's house far behind them and continued moving about the city, winding and pushing their way through crowds and trying desperately to blend in. Several times she could've sworn she heard whispers and saw people pointing at the two of them but, even if they were, there was nothing to do about it except continue moving.

Besides, it was possible her reputation would afford them some safety. She was, even to this day, considered not only a hero, but also dangerous.

Ellyne's feet were suddenly heavy, with each step taken more difficult than the last. Her boots were nearly dragging along the ground, and it took all her effort to stay upright. With as little as she knew about whatever ability she possessed, she was now learning about the consequences the hard way.

"You look tired," Nicole said, obviously reading the signs. "Actually, you look beyond tired. You look like what tired would be if tired could actually be tired."

"How nice of you to notice, if I even understand that correctly." Ellyne attempted a laugh but instead uttered more of a sigh. "Apparently, becoming a weapon of destruction takes it out of a girl."

"Who knew?"

"But, yes, I could really use a nap . . . or three."

"It's too bad you hate magic. I could probably use it to relieve some of the fatigue you're feeling."

"Just like tea only without the annoying need to drink

something? And even if I didn't hate magic, I'm pretty sure there's still a chance it wouldn't work on me anyway. So, I guess it's a pretty good thing I hate magic, then."

"You don't know what you're missing. Magic is wonderful."

"It still sounds a lot like an addiction to me."

"For some, I suppose it might be. That's an intriguing comparison."

"Ever wonder how people would get along without it? What if magic were suddenly taken away? What if the Kithrak decided to shut off flocia entirely from all humans?"

"They couldn't do that!" Nicole gasped. "Could they? Or would they? My gosh, that would be horrible!"

Ellyne noticed the look on Nicole's face alternate between exasperation and curiosity as she pondered the ramifications of Kithrak control over flocia. It was something Ellyne had always assumed—that magic could ultimately be taken away if the Kithrak wished it. After all, they hoarded their secrets and guarded them closely. Any human who thought they knew everything about magic was kidding themselves.

"I don't know. It seems likely, though, that they could and would if it fit their desires," Ellyne continued.

"The Ilserate would stop them, though, wouldn't they?"

"I'd like to think they have the citizens' best interests in mind, but I've never really been convinced of that. Besides, they're essentially at the mercy of the Kithrak too, no matter how much they deny it."

"It's weird . . . to imagine a world completely without magic."

They turned a corner and forced their way past a crowd walking the opposite direction, bumping shoulders with several people in the process. Ellyne's stomach growled as she caught the scent of breakfast from a nearby restaurant.

"I can see how you think it would be weird, but you just described my childhood."

"What was that like?"

"It was crap," Ellyne laughed. "Not unlike now. But we still had things like vehicles and the Metro and screens. They weren't operated by magic, of course."

"It sounds archaic." Nicole grinned, obviously trying to get a rise out of her.

Though she wasn't a fan of magic, she did have to admit the mechanical methods of the Legacy Age did feel a bit outdated compared to the Age of Magic.

"If anything, it was louder and dirtier, and smelled worse. But it was far less chaotic and far more peaceful. The fact we didn't have the Kithrak to deal with was also a bonus."

"Would you go back to those days if you could? To the Legacy Age with no magic?"

Ellyne paused, having never seriously considered the possibility—because it *wasn't* a possibility. Sure, she'd made many proclamations about how she would love nothing more than to return to what she saw as a simpler time, but those were usually through clenched teeth or shouted to the sky out of frustration.

And most often while someone was lobbing magic her direction.

Would it level the playing field for her—a world without magic? Absolutely. She couldn't deny such a situation would make her feel better, but her newfound abilities themselves seemed to accomplish that without the abolition of magic.

And it was true—she hated magic long before she realized she couldn't use it and even longer before she discovered her immunity, however partial or complete it was. Magic was unnatural. Magic was an abomination, accomplishing things in ways that broke the laws of what she considered reality. When laws were broken, there was a price to pay—whether one knew what that price was.

"Probably . . . most likely," she finally said, not entirely confident with the answer she'd given. It was the best answer she could produce.

Nicole said nothing, but Ellyne could tell her answer was not what the girl wanted to hear. She paused as Victor's bar came into view and inspected it to make sure it was clear to proceed.

Aside from the bustling crowd of people cramming their way past each other on the sidewalks, it didn't appear the bar was being watched—at least not by anyone in official Ilserate garb.

"We'll go in the back way," she whispered, turning back, and heading down an alley. "It'd be easier to spot undercover agents at night with less of a crowd, but we can't really afford that luxury right now."

"Then what?"

"I really hate that question."

"FINALLY!"

Ellyne urged Nicole forward. They skittered across the street and into a now empty alley. Waiting for the two drunks to stagger out of view was a test of her patience but the two men eventually vacated, leaving them with a perfect opportunity to sneak into Victor's undetected.

She gingerly pulled down the metal ladder to the fire escape, wincing at each squeak produced by metal grinding on metal during what seemed like an hour-long ordeal. Finally, the ladder extended fully.

"Could you have been any louder?" Nicole joked, giving her a phony glare of disapproval.

"Probably. I could've just lowered it quickly—you know, like tearing off a bandage all at once." Ellyne climbed the ladder to the first landing. "Trust me when I tell you it's loud and ear-piercing. I like to lower it slowly even when I'm not evading . . . well, everyone."

"I thought you always kept a low profile," Nicole said, reaching the first landing.

"I do," Ellyne replied. "But, ordinarily, only a handful of people want me dead." She climbed the ladder to the second story and, once there, slid the window open and slipped inside. Once Nicole was also safe inside, Ellyne shut and locked the window, then drew the curtains. "We should be safe in here, at least for a little while."

"So how long do we wait?" Nicole sank into the sofa, looking rather uncomfortable at first, but adjusted herself and leaned back.

"At least until nightfall. Oh, wait . . ." Ellyne pried open a barely visible panel on the wall, pressed a button, then closed it again. "That'll let Victor know we're up here. Anyway, I figure it'll be easier for us to get to the Sistix under cover of darkness."

"That seems to be our calling card," Nicole smirked. "Everything's easier at night."

"Indeed, it does. Unfortunately, we can also probably expect everyone else to be looking for us again. I'm sure, by now, they've regrouped, collectively scratched their heads, and want answers or revenge or whatever. At this point, I don't really care. It all ends the same if we get caught."

Ellyne moved the short distance into the kitchen, riffling through the cabinets until she found an open bag of chips, which she immediately dipped into. They were stale, but that didn't bother her. She found another bag and threw it at Nicole.

"Hey!" she shouted as the bag pelted her on the head.

"Sorry. I thought you were ready for that." Ellyne snickered quietly.

"Well, obviously, I wasn't." Nicole ripped open the bag and sniffed the contents before holding one of the potato chips aloft and scrutinizing it. "I didn't set any protective wards against snacks."

"It's a potato chip," Ellyne laughed. "You eat it. Good food, yum yum!"

"Ha ha, very funny."

"Wait," Ellyne gasped, "you've never had a potato chip before, have you?"

"Well, no, I haven't."

Ellyne slammed her palms on the countertop and gasped. "Are you serious? What the hell did the Ilserate feed you all those years?"

"Not potato chips, apparently."

"No potato chips? Those bastards are more diabolical than I imagined."

Nicole giggled and put the chip in her mouth as her eyes widened, lighting up with joy. After a mere moment, she was aggressively devouring the salty snacks. Ellyne could do nothing but watch her and giggle.

Unfortunately, less happy thoughts seeped back into her head, and she was soon trying to puzzle out their next moves. It was an impossibility, of course—trying to plan for a situation about which she had no knowledge.

And she was a crap planner to begin with.

Countless times, she'd waded into a battle with no real plan—no strategy or even an inkling of what was going to happen. On the few occasions she'd devised some particular strategy, things usually went sideways, and she'd had to improvise anyway. Things always seemed to work out. At least, that's how she remembered it.

But her comrades trusted her implicitly. Even when she and her soldiers met with failure on several occasions, they stuck by her, confident they would succeed.

And, eventually, they did. Every time.

Nicole was no different than any one of the men and women who fought with Ellyne during the Flocia Wars. She placed her unquestioning trust in her for reasons Ellyne didn't understand. What was it about her that exuded such confidence or knowledge when she was making it all up as she went?

Her reputation was far more prestigious than she really

was. The legends all had her winning in every endeavor and never losing a fellow soldier, but the truth was less positive and far bloodier.

"Nicole," she said, trying to keep her voice calm and not too dire. "You realize I have no idea what we're getting into, right? We could be walking into a trap. I don't even know what we'll find in the Sistix. We may never make it out."

"Of course I know," Nicole laughed, dumping the crumbs from the bag into her mouth. "Though, it would've been nice if we were able to get more information out of Iksillix before . . . well, you know."

"I have a feeling he wasn't going to offer up any more information than he already had but, Nicole, that's not the point. I mean, this is serious. We will have no allies inside the Sistix. If you thought everyone was gunning for us now, just wait until we get in there. I have no plan for this."

She bowed her head and stared at the ugly gray countertop, ashamed. She felt responsible for Nicole now, even though she'd spent the past few days trying to avoid doing just that.

Nicole's hand soon slid over hers and squeezed gently. When she looked up, Nicole was smiling wide, apparently not having heard a word she'd said.

"Ellyne, don't worry. I know the danger we face. If we fail, it's not your fault. But we're *not* going to fail."

"What makes you so sure? Because I'm not."

"Look how far we've made it—you and me! Look how far we've come! We're where we are right now despite not having a plan of any kind. Or, maybe, we're where we are simply *because* we didn't have a plan of any kind. Through all we've experienced, I'm beginning to see what made you such a great leader during the wars. We stand a better chance together—as a team."

"I just hope things go smoother than they have been," she chuckled nervously. She hadn't had so much at stake since the war, and it had been at least that long since she had anyone she even remotely considered a friend besides Victor.

"I asked around and kept my ears open for a long time while the Ilserate had me. One name came up a lot, even when I didn't ask. Your name. Well, okay, once or twice someone would mention some guy named Borland, but it was your name almost always. I'm pretty sure they may have been joking whenever they mentioned him, actually."

"Ha! Borland's a coward. I mean, he's good with tech and I hear his enchantments are powerful, but he's not a fighter in any sense of the word. Come to think of it, he probably can't spell the word 'fight'."

"You were the clear choice, Ellyne. I chose correctly." Nicole slid her hand off Ellyne's and walked around the counter into the kitchen. "Now, is there anything else to eat in this place?"

"Search the cabinets and see what you can find. I've been lazy about restocking supplies lately. You know, on account of being dragged around the city while the Ilserate chases us." She winked at Nicole who didn't see it but was obviously amused.

Despite her jocular tone, Ellyne couldn't shake her apprehension. Fear crept into her mind, nibbling at the edges of her conscience, and replacing confidence with doubt. Her growing fatigue compounded those negative emotions. She would've given anything to simply be done with this whole mess.

"You tried that once, didn't you? But you just had to go back for her." Ellyne smiled as though she had made a funny joke.

"What?"

"Oh, nothing. Just muttering useless things to myself. Did you find anything to eat?"

"I found some candy, so I guess that's something. Oh, and ketchup. Seriously, Ellyne, is this all you ever eat?"

"And squama juice."

Nicole gave her a disapproving glance as she tore open the bag of fireblossom-flavored treats.

"Don't give me that look. You're not my real mom!"

"Age logistics aside, I should be thankful for that." Nicole laughed as she passed Ellyne and sat down on the couch again.

"Definitely don't send me to my room . . . where all my stuff is!" Ellyne continued. "That would be terrible."

"Do parents really do that?" Nicole asked. "Send kids to their rooms as punishment?"

"Yep." At first, Ellyne dismissed the question, thinking nothing of it. Her parents had often sent her to her room, which was where she preferred to be anyway. "Wait," she continued. "You were never sent to your bedroom as a punishment?"

"Who was going to punish me? Certainly not parents."

Ellyne immediately wished she could take the words back, feeling about two inches tall. Given Nicole's childhood situation, of course the girl had never been sent to her room.

"I'm sorry, I didn't mean to—"

"It's okay. I'll admit, even now, it's a bitter subject but I try not to be too sensitive about it. We're all given a lot in life, but it's what we do with it that matters."

"I guess becoming the mage breaker isn't such a bad fate, then, right?"

"It has its perks. Everyone did their best to not make me angry, so that was nice. I had a great living space filled with all kinds of nice things. Sometimes I felt as if every day was my birthday. It was just, you know, I had no parents."

"I had parents." Ellyne fidgeted with a hand towel on the counter, picking at a stray thread until it snapped off. "Hell, I probably still have parents somewhere, not that I particularly care. If your parents would've been anything like mine, weren't missing out on much."

"You and your parents didn't get along?"

"Let's just say we didn't see eye-to-eye on most things. But, if I'm being honest, I probably don't see eye-to-eye with a lot of people." Ellyne laughed, both admitting to herself how true that statement was and then recounting the myriad of people who fit into that box.

"You don't seem all that disagreeable to me," Nicole countered. "Maybe cranky and a little rough."

Ellyne left the kitchen and sat on the couch next to Nicole, snatching one of her fireblossom candies and popping it in her mouth. It was a strong flavor that made her mouth water instantly just before the heat hit her tongue. She hadn't had one of these in a while and it seemed hotter than she recalled. She almost spit it out.

"Yeah, well, I'm not disagreeable probably because I'm not trying to kill you," she laughed. "That tends to put people in a bad mood."

"Why do you do it? Why do you kill?"

Ellyne fell silent. She wasn't sure if it was the question or the person asking it, but she felt shame the moment the words left Nicole's lips. Her ears burned and she wiped her moist palms on her pants before she got up and paced.

"I'm good at it," she said, averting her gaze. "I've always been good at it. I started fighting in the war and I just . . . never stopped, I guess. Once the war ended, I found myself without much of a purpose but one day I overheard a lady at Victor's talking about a man who wouldn't leave her alone and I . . . helped her."

She chuckled for a moment, kicking at a ball of dust and hair with her boot.

"And she paid you?"

"Paid me? Nope. She probably still has no idea what happened to the creep. But, after that, I looked for similar jobs that did indeed pay. If I'm coming after someone, rest assured, they deserve it."

"But why—"

"And, no, I don't *always* kill. I mean, okay, it happens more often than not . . . but not always."

Nicole appeared puzzled and sad. Ellyne held no illusions as to her own true nature. She'd killed a lot of people and even some Kithrak. Her actions often weighed heavy on her, but the state of the world itself also added to that weight and she tried to justify her actions through crooked reasoning.

She walked to the window and stared out at the cityscape beyond and the streets below. The setting sun painted many of the buildings in reds and oranges, glinting off clouds and metal alike. She watched as people still scurried about, heading home or to a restaurant for an early dinner, or perhaps just for a drink.

"They don't know the truth," she muttered. "The people down there. And how could they? The Flocia Wars took a heavy toll on those who fought in them, but they also bestowed knowledge and insight upon anyone who merely opened their eyes to see the surrounding world."

"What do you mean?"

"I think you know what I mean," Ellyne sighed, running a hand through her hair. "Those people down there . . . they all kiss their families, go to work, come home, eat dinner, go to sleep, and then do it all again the next day. To them, it's like drinking water. They use magic on a whim without even the slightest thought about the price or the consequences."

"You mean the T-Helms and the grika?"

"Yes and no. I always wondered if we were all being played—by the government, by the Kithrak, and maybe even by the other factions. I've suspected a darker side to magic since its discovery but until now—until what we've uncovered—I was never able to be sure. What else don't we know?"

Nicole sidled up next to her, gently gripped Ellyne's hand, and stared out the window. She could tell Nicole was uneasy as they stood in silence for a moment. "I think I understand," she whispered. "I'm one of the Ilserate's biggest secrets."

"That you are. And when we've done . . . well, whatever it is we're about to do, there's no telling how the world will be when we're finished. Those people down there, well, their lives may never be the same. And I have no way of knowing if that's a good thing. But I hope it is, because people are being used and they at least deserve to know. At least, then, they'll have an informed choice."

There was a long pause before Nicole spoke again.

"Ellyne," she said meekly. "You do realize that magic doesn't take a side. There is no good or evil to magic or flocia. It's a tool just like a wrench. You can choose to use it for its intended purpose, or you can hit someone with it."

"A wrench doesn't often come with strings attached."

"Precisely my point."

Ellyne moved to the couch and shut her eyes. Her body suddenly felt heavy and sluggish. She wanted nothing more than to set out later tonight, but sleep was demanding and, despite her wishes, Ellyne knew she would have to rest.

"I would point out there's still a whole lot about magic and flocia we don't know. The Kithrak guard their secrets closely."

She felt Nicole snuggling next to her as the girl put her head on Ellyne's shoulder and sighed. A few hours of sleep wouldn't hurt, would it? The world would still be waiting when they woke up.

Yes, the world could wait.

"So," Nicole mumbled, already half-asleep. "What's our plan?"

"We show everyone the price they're paying to use their wrenches."

CHAPTER
TWENTY-ONE

ELLYNE RECLINED against a rock and closed her eyes, listening to the familiar babbling of the creek as it sang its unique song—a song she'd heard countless times before. The forest was always welcoming each time she visited. The canopy of leaves above filtered the sunlight to just the right amount, the ground was soft, and the water was cool and refreshing.

Somewhere above, a bird squawked, momentarily shattering her melodic tranquility. She was unsure exactly what type of bird it was but suspected it was a blue wriggler. There was simply no explanation how a bird with such an offensive song ever got laid.

Each time the bird yelled, she twitched, wishing she could find it and shoot it so that she wouldn't have to hear its terrible voice again. As a child, she'd heard its song many times, but she didn't recall it being this awful. Of course, having lived in Karnascus for so long, she normally didn't hear many bird songs. There simply wasn't much nature in the city for animals to cling to.

Thankfully, it only spoke up sparingly which left Ellyne able to enjoy the forest's natural beauty largely uninterrupted.

It would be so easy to stay here and enjoy a life of solitude, let the world deal with its problems, and enjoy life for once. Solitude in Karnascus was an illusion—she knew that now. In fact, she'd always known it; she simply refused to acknowledge it.

Here, in the forest, she need not worry about the Ilserate, Kithrak, magic, or the damned Technos and Teranynes. There were no politics or battles out here, and certainly no Marik.

There was also no alcohol, which was regrettable. And existing off berries or whatever she could hunt didn't sound so appealing, either. No, this place wasn't perfect.

"It would certainly be closer to perfect if that damned bird would shut its beak."

Ellyne sighed and tried to relax, focusing on the sound of the water dribbling over the rocks. The forest was just like she remembered—it always was. As a child, she would come here to get away and build a fort or pretend she led a life of adventure and intrigue. Whatever problems life threw at her always melted away and flowed downstream to eventually end up somewhere else.

She knew it was a dream. She always knew. Most dreams she didn't remember but this place was so entrenched in her memory, so vivid, she always recalled them. And it wasn't that her childhood was so terrible that she had to escape but, rather it was so . . . mundane.

Of course, now that her life was far less ordinary, she almost wished for the humdrum days of doing chores and obeying her parents. Almost.

Except her parents were government-supporting drones. There was always that problem. Thankfully, they stopped being a factor when she left, only to be replaced by Marik, which was a far more painful subject than her parents ever were.

Such thoughts were intrusions and had no place here, and

her mind quickly put Marik and all other negative notions out of her head.

The blue wriggler above squawked again as Ellyne drank from the stream and splashed the refreshing water on her face. It was chilly and clean and, when she gazed into the stream, she could see the trees above flawlessly reflected on the surface.

The serenity was a far cry from the chaotic, cramped streets and sidewalks of the city where trees were scarce. Karnascus's allure diminished even more given hers and Nicole's recent discoveries and the tarnished interior was laid bare for them. Trees kept no secrets and harbored no enemies, except maybe a blue wriggler or two. But the city . . . it held all kinds of unsavory surprises.

The bird shouted again.

Ellyne looked up, hoping to catch a glimpse of the noisy bastard but, unsurprisingly, was unable to locate the bird. Would it be considered animal cruelty to kill a bird if it was in a dream?

When her gaze returned to the shimmering waters, something was amiss. She could still see the trees but she saw something else in the reflection—something both simultaneously familiar and new.

"The Sistix."

Ellyne looked behind her, as if expecting the structure to be on the horizon but all she saw was the usual trees and bushes. She gazed back into the water and there it was, clear as day and looming in the distance.

The blue menace above squawked again.

She hurried through the woods, weaving around trees, shrubs, and rocks as she made her way to the tree line. She'd never done this before—at least not in her dreams.

The forest was real—a memory from her childhood. Her parents' house was at the bottom of a hill just outside the tree line. However, when she emerged from the woods, she saw something quite different.

Instead of her house, the town, or even the hill, she emerged into Karnascus at night. The quiet, deserted streets starkly contrasted the constant yet soothing forest noise she just left. Instead of forest animals and water, there was only silence—more so than she was normally accustomed to. Ordinarily there was *some* ambient noise or activity, but not here. Was this how she wished Karnascus to be, or was it how she feared it would be?

The Sistix loomed over her like a giant. With its thick, towering pillars and massive dome, Ellyne couldn't fathom how this structure had gone unnoticed. Not only did it rise high above the tallest building in Karnascus—it dwarfed even The Citadel—but the architecture was. . . vastly older. It should have stuck out like as . . . well, like a blue wriggler in the heart of the city.

The bird squawked again but, this time, it wasn't just one burst. It shouted repeatedly without end. Ellyne searched the area for the pest and finally located it, perched atop The Sistix at the very highest point of the dome.

Something moved in her jacket pocket, and she grabbed for it. Iksillix's eye wriggled and rotated in her hand, its gaze darting wildly in every direction as if it were looking for something specific.

"Well, that's gross." She grimaced, resisting the urge to drop the eyeball on the ground and squash it. Instead, and she had no explanation why, she held it in front of her and pointed it toward The Sistix. Trying to ignore the noisy bird's banter, she squinted and gazed through it.

A piercing light nearly blinded her, and she dropped the eye, gasping and blinking wildly to regain her vision. Her knees buckled and she collapsed on the ground, unable to see anything but a blur as the bird above screamed even louder.

This time, however, instead of its shrill, ugly shriek, its voice sounded out a word.

"Unite."

"What?" Ellyne asked, as if the animal would answer her.

The bird flitted nearby and alighted onto a garbage can. It pecked at a lamp post and then chewed on one of its blue feathers. "They're coming. Wake up!"

Ellyne opened her eyes to see Nicole standing over her, shaking her.

"Wake up! We have to get out of here!"

Ellyne's mind struggled to keep up, still in a hazy fog of sleep and stuck somewhere between reality and her dream. She sat up on the couch, rubbed her eyes, and ran her fingers through her hair. "Who?"

"The Ilserate, I think." Nicole hurried to the window, then she quickly ducked away. "I got nervous, so I set some wards around the area just in case." She kept low as she made her way back to the couch. "And several of them were just tripped. We don't have much time."

"Right," Ellyne growled, "because, of course we don't." Her mind was still fuzzy from the dream, and it churned incessantly, trying to make sense of it. "But maybe we'll get lucky and they don't actually know where we are."

"Do yourselves a favor and give yourselves up," a voice from outside yelled. "We know you're in there!"

"You were saying?"

"Well, crap."

Ellyne slid off the couch and sat on the floor with Nicole sitting next to her.

"Someone must've seen us and snitched," Nicole whispered.

For a moment, Ellyne wondered if Victor could have done it. Would he turn them in? They'd known each other for a while, and she felt she knew him well enough. He didn't strike her as the kind of man who had any allegiance to the

Ilserate but, still . . . maybe they offered him a lot of tiks. Money could make people do terrible things. But she had to believe Victor wouldn't betray them, though that didn't mean she wouldn't exercise caution in the future.

"So . . . what's the plan already?"

"Follow me."

Still keeping low, Ellyne led Nicole across the room to the door. They hurried down the stairs and into the bar. Even though the windows were shuddered, they carefully crept behind the bar and hunkered down there.

She grabbed a bottle of serafun and inspected it.

"Ooh," Nicole gasped. "Serafun's super flammable! Are going to make a firebomb with it and blow things up? Because that would be super cool and also terrifying!"

"Nope."

Ellyne grabbed the cork in her mouth and yanked it out before drinking deeply from the bottle. She offered it to Nicole who grimaced and rolled her eyes.

"Really? You just needed a drink? That's the plan?"

"Relax, kid. These Ilserate stooges are always overconfident." She took another pull off the bottle. "With more of their goons over here looking for us, we'll have fewer of them bothering us where we're going."

"And where exactly are we going?"

"To the Sistix, of course." Ellyne corked the bottle and peeked over the counter at the front windows. The movement outside was easy to spot. "Thanks, Victor," she whispered, taking one last look at the bottle before returning it to the shelf.

"And how are we supposed to get out of here, then?" There was no mistaking the urgency in Nicole's voice.

"Through there." Ellyne pointed to the now closed door to Victor's back room and office.

"That door looks too sturdy to break down or shoot, though."

"You're not wrong. So, it's a good thing I know how to get in." Ellyne flipped open a tiny panel and exhaled into it. Several lock mechanisms behind the steel door clicked and she pushed it open, gesturing to Nicole. "After you."

Once they were through, Ellyne turned on the light and shut the door behind them, resetting all the locks. Victor's "office" was a cramped space littered with boxes full of liquor, glasses, and various other equipment the man used to run his business.

"Now I see why he's got this room locked down," Nicole said, looking around.

"He's got loads of tricks, like a breath sensor that unlocks the door, but only if it detects serafun."

"And here I thought you just wanted a drink."

"Oh, I did," Ellyne laughed. "Whose idea do you think it was to install that particular mechanism in the first place?"

"Charming . . . but I have to admit, also quite imaginative."

"And convenient." Ellyne pulled aside a rug on the floor and opened a hidden panel leading down into darkness. "Again, after you."

"Why am I going first again?"

"Because you can conjure a light for us to see by—as long as I don't get too close, I assume."

"Right, okay." Nicole muttered a few words and waved her hands. Shortly thereafter, a floating ball of light appeared next to her. She took a deep breath and climbed down the ladder into the tunnel.

Ellyne waited until she was clear of the hole and hopped through the opening, falling only a few feet and landing next to her. "It's been a hot second since I last had to use this tunnel," she smirked. "I'll admit, it's much dingier down here than I remember, but I never really had a good light source either."

"It's . . . cozy," Nicole laughed.

"This'll reset everything up there, including the rug." She found a button on the wall and pressed it, causing the panel above to creak shut. "Now let's go. This tunnel eventually opens out into a safe house. From there, we can make our way to The Sistix—hopefully before daylight, and hopefully before the Ilserate goons catch on."

"Victor really seems to have thought of everything."

"He's very thorough. I never asked him what he did before he opened his bar, and I'm not even sure he'd tell me. I don't ask him about his past, and he doesn't ask me about mine. Though, I guess, my past is unfortunately a bit more well-known."

"I wouldn't be surprised if children in school learn about you."

Ellyne winced. Her? A historical figure? "Well, that's awkward," she said, pointing ahead of them and heading in that direction.

"Your name came up several times during my life under Ilserate control."

"That's not only awkward, but disturbing. Come on, we need to put some distance between us and them."

"I never really understood who or what you were. Nobody really talked about anything important in front of me but there were times when they didn't know I was listening."

"Great," Ellyne muttered, stepping over a small pile of trash. Or rodent droppings. She wasn't about to stop and inspect whatever it was. "The Ilserate's infatuated with me. I hope they don't expect me to be flattered."

Nicole stifled her laughter. "Flattered? Probably not. But you're important to them somehow."

"Probably because Marik still wants me dead. I had no idea he'd worked himself so far up the Ilserate sycophant chain. I wonder how many asses he's had to kiss to get that far."

"All of them?"

They both laughed. Ellyne made certain to stay at least several paces ahead of Nicole in case she somehow counteracted her magic. The floating light produced more than enough illumination to see down the tunnel, so there was little reason to stay close.

There was no danger down here. According to Victor, this particular tunnel was part of a much older system and, when he appropriated it for his own purposes, it hadn't been used in years. He'd simply blocked it off and connected it to a safe house. No, the only danger down here was stumbling over something and ending up with bruised pride.

"So how far is it?"

"I don't remember."

"What do we do when we get there?"

That was a good question. It was *always* a good question—every time Nicole asked it. If only there were an answer she could give. She wasn't even sure Nicole expected a solid answer at this point, but maybe the girl just wanted to know she wasn't alone in her confusion.

"I think you know as well as I do, the answer to that question."

Nicole sighed.

CHAPTER
TWENTY-TWO

DAMP, dusty air invaded Ellyne's nose the moment the hatch at the top of the ladder creaked open, and dust sprinkled down on her. She sneezed and wiped her face, emerging into the building above. Nicole soon followed, waving her hand in front of her face as if that would clear the lingering dust particles.

"Home sweet home," Ellyne laughed, helping Nicole through the hatch. Once they both surfaced, she pressed a button on the wall and watched the hatch close, then the rug replaced itself. Sure, it was all powered by magic and Ellyne still despised that but, as with the setup in Victor's back room, it was immensely convenient. She wondered if that reasoning was how the Technos explained their usage of magic devices.

"It's," Nicole muttered, "um . . . it's unique."

"That it is. Snuff the light."

Nicole waved her hand and the ball of light vanished.

Though the room was dark Ellyne remembered it well enough, having made use of it several times in the past. It was fully furnished and, like her apartment above the bar, Victor usually kept it stocked with the essentials. But it certainly was nothing fancy—your basic, two-story nondescript house in the guts of Karnascus that could have contained a single family just like so many other homes.

"Is there a light switch somewhere?"

"Yeah, but leave the lights off. I don't want to attract attention."

"Aren't you being a little paranoid? Houses have lights that people turn on. It's what normal people do."

Ellyne moved to a nearby window and peeked through the drawn curtains. The streets beyond were lifeless.

"Normal people who aren't wanted by every faction in the city." She sighed. "Paranoia's kept me alive this long, why stop now?" She chuckled a little, still gazing out the window. Somewhere, in this tangled mess of a city, lay a giant, yet invisible interdimensional structure they were supposed to somehow infiltrate and then do . . . well, they didn't even know what.

Through this particular window, she could see what was colloquially known as "Storage Central" or, more directly, the warehouse district. It was only such a thing in name, since at least half the structures lay empty. The Ilserate had a hand in building many of them and used the location until they eventually moved much of their equipment into the compound. They stored the rest of their resources in concealed locations throughout the city. Some were obvious while others were not. She figured there were reasons for both.

"It's out there," she continued. "The Sistix."

"How do you know?" Nicole stood next to her now, catching a glimpse out the window. "I don't see anything."

"I can feel it."

"Can you really? That's amazing! Is it, like, a tingle? Or a hum? Can you sense it better when you get closer?"

Nicole looked as if she would dissect Ellyne right there if that would give her the answer. The girl really was ridiculously excitable sometimes . . . well, all the time.

"I'm joking," Ellyne smirked. "Keep your boots on. I can't sense a damned thing, though that would be convenient."

Nicole wilted, the disappointment on her face was obvious even in nearly nonexistent light.

"But don't worry. I'm sure there are all kinds of discoveries we're about to make . . . while we run from all the Kithrak and Ilserate trying to kill us."

"Or . . . we *fight* everyone trying to kill us!"

"Look at you," Ellyne laughed, "ready to take on the world!" Outside, the city slept, waiting for the sun's first rays to bring it to life. "Believe me, I share your motivation, but not your optimism."

Nicole left her side, emitting a growl or some other kind of annoyed noise Ellyne could barely hear.

"I'm just tired of running. Running is all I've done since I escaped the Ilserate."

"And running is all I've done since you broke into my apartment." Ellyne turned from the window to see Nicole's shadowy outline seated in a chair. "So, believe me when I tell you, I know how you feel."

"Do we ever get to stop running? What happens if we succeed in . . . whatever we're about to do?"

"Probably more running or hiding or fighting . . . or all three." Ellyne found a simple wooden chair, set it down across from Nicole, and sat in it. "I've done a little thinking and I believe I have an idea. Well, I believe I have the beginning of an idea."

"An idea for what?"

"For what we need to do, of course."

Ellyne paused a minute, both to tease Nicole and to determine exactly what she was going to say. The truth was it was barely even the beginning of a plan.

"The source of flocia is somewhere in the Sistix, right?"

"According to Derek, yes. That is, if you trust him."

"Still not sure I do, but we have nothing else to go on."

Ellyne leaned forward, closer to Nicole, and propped her arms on her knees. "So . . . if the most powerful mage on the planet and whatever the hell I am can somehow wrest control of the source from the Kithrak then neither they nor the Ilserate will have control of Karnascus."

Nicole fidgeted in her seat. She looked excited as always, but Ellyne could see hesitation behind her boisterous exterior.

"After that," she continued, "I would hope everyone is too preoccupied with more important things than us."

Neither spoke for a few moments. Ellyne tried to flesh out more of her plan, quite unsuccessfully to her chagrin, as Nicole also appeared to be lost in thought.

"What you're suggesting," Nicole finally said, "sounds a lot like anarchy to me. Chaos."

"Yes, it does. And before you ask, no, I don't know how we're going to accomplish this or what comes after it."

"Well, that *is* what I was going to ask, actually."

"I only know the first step, which is to leave this house. And it's probably best we were on our way soon. Hopefully nobody who's looking for us is expecting us to waltz right through their front door. . . wherever it is or if it's even a door at all. And, speaking of front doors . . ." She got up and opened the door, motioning Nicole through.

The door shut and locked behind them as they stood on the front porch. Ellyne breathed deeply to calm her nerves while she pondered what they were about to do.

And how they would do it.

And what they would do after.

Or what if they failed?

"Come on," she said, "Let's just start walking and see where it takes us, I guess."

To Ellyne's surprise, no one was about—not a patrol, not anyone loitering—not even the homeless. The only signs of life in this area were Ellyne and Nicole.

It made sense for several reasons. Nobody simply hung

out among a bunch of warehouses. There were no restaurants or bars here—no reason for anyone at all to be wandering about, especially at night. Of course, if the Sistix was indeed around here, somewhere, there would be enough Kithrak to keep everyone at bay.

The street ahead descended gently, losing itself in the myriad of warehouses below, which were broken up by the occasional abandoned factory or industrial building. Some structures truly were empty while others, Ellyne suspected, were probably just meant to appear that way.

"Well," Nicole said with obvious frustration, "we're where we are supposed to be, but I see nothing."

"Maybe there's a spell to reveal it or to be able to detect it?"

"Or maybe one has to be Kithrak just to be able to see it." Nicole squinted, then moved her hands methodically in front of her, mumbling words Ellyne didn't understand. When she was done, she sighed, disappointed. "I don't think a spell is going to reveal it," she said, obviously disappointed. "At least not one I know of. I just tried all the revealing magic I could think of, which is pretty much all of it in existence."

"Damn." Ellyne paced, never taking her eyes off the scene before them. "So how do they do it? We know there are a few humans allowed into the Sistix, including Marik, so how are they getting in?"

"There are always a few rats that sneak into even the most secure buildings," Nicole laughed.

Ellyne joined her.

"Likening Marik to a rat is insulting to the rat. Besides, rats are sort of cute if they're not infesting your basement."

"Ew, no thanks. I'm a cat person."

"The Ilserate let you have a cat?"

Nicole laughed again. "Absolutely not! But that didn't mean I couldn't find a way to smuggle one in once or twice. Everyone was pretty upset when they found out, though. I wasn't allowed to leave my quarters for a month after! Not that they were able to stop me."

"Oh?"

"There are many mages in the Ilserate with a pretty good grasp of magic. Their wards and enchantments were solid, and they took time to circumvent but all it ever took was time. I think most people who use magic simply do so through habit."

"I don't understand."

"Well," Nicole continued, "it's the difference between knowing something works and knowing how or why something works. Sure, you can use the machine because you remember how but, if it breaks or you want to improve on it, you're stuck."

"So," Ellyne said, "most people don't know how magic works; they simply know it works. So, we have a bunch of idiots running around using magic but not *understanding* magic."

"Pretty much."

"Well," Ellyne sighed, "I can't say I'm surprised, but that basically confirms what I suspected."

"You don't believe people should use magic if they don't understand how it works?"

"I think people who don't *respect* magic shouldn't be allowed to use it. It's powerful and dangerous, and if everyone's running around using it without some knowledge and awe, we end up—"

"In the predicament we are now." Nicole chuckled, but it wasn't out of humor.

"Right. Everyone uses magic, but nobody considers the cost. Nobody except those poor individuals who've become mindless, drooling savages."

"The grika," Nicole muttered under her breath.

"We're all firmly planted in the pocket of the Kithrak, and nobody's stopped to question it. Everyone willingly submitted to the power of magic without considering the cost."

"So that's what we're here to do? Free everyone?"

"I'm still not sure what we're here to do, Nicole, but we first need to find the Sistix in order to do *anything*."

"Maybe you need to be a Kithrak to see it? Or maybe you must have more than two eyes?"

"Eyes!" Ellyne exclaimed. "Maybe all we need . . . is another eye!"

"I'm afraid I don't understa—" Nicole paused, mid-sentence, as Ellyne produced the bag from her jacket pocket, the plastic rustling as she pulled out the eyeball. "You're joking, right? That's so gross."

"Nope," Ellyne replied, holding the slimy orb in her hand, "no joke. I'm out of ideas." Holding the eye aloft, the iris pointing away from her, Ellyne squinted as she lowered it in front of her own eye and the world changed.

She gasped, unable to explain what she saw. The city sprang to life in pulsing colors and clouds of. . . well, she didn't know what. Mere simple lamp posts sparkled with different hues while the ubiquitous screens were engulfed in swirling colors.

She shut her eyes and lowered the eyeball, blinking several times only to gaze out at a drab, boring field of warehouses once again.

"What did you see?" Nicole asked, excitedly. The restraint she exercised must have been considerable, as she was unable to stand still. "Did you see anything?"

"Here," Ellyne replied, handing the eye to Nicole, "see for yourself."

Nicole's excitement overwhelmed her revulsion and she gingerly picked up the eye, a grimace plastered all over her face. She, too, squinted through the orb.

"There, see? Isn't it weird?"

"I mean . . . no? It's the city. Karnascus is definitely weird but all I see is . . . normal weird."

"You don't see all the swirly colors and clouds of sparkly crap?"

"What are you talking about? I don't see anything."

Ellyne grabbed the eye from her and peered through it, greeted again by vibrant flashes of color mixed with swirling clouds. She shut her eyes, feeling nauseous.

"When I look through the eye," she said, reopening her eyes once the world stopped spinning, "I see flashes and clouds of swirling colors surrounding virtually everything. Is this how you and every other magic-user sees the world? If so, I count myself lucky."

"No, not at all! That sounds wondrous but awful! I can only speak for myself, but I definitely don't see anything like that."

"So, what do you see?" Ellyne asked, disbelief consuming her.

"I can see flocia but it's muted. It's subtle, really, and I usually don't notice it. It's like a sock or a glove—you know you're wearing one, but you don't actively feel it. I suspect many people don't notice it at all. Maybe it varies with magical ability? I never thought about it before and certainly never asked but it's possible—"

"Well," Ellyne interrupted, "I don't like it at all. The eye didn't change the way you see the world, but it goes completely wonky for me. What does that even mean?"

"I would guess your brain has no idea what to do with the information you're seeing. You yourself can't use magic but Iksillix's eye can—er, sort of. It's almost like it's an enchanted item, only it's alive. Well, mostly alive anyway—for now. This might explain why you can use it at all."

"It's disturbing. But maybe my plan will work after all." Ellyne exhaled forcefully, trying to relax but failing. "I just need to find the Sistix in that colorful disaster soup and then we know where we're headed."

Trying hard to focus and calm herself, Ellyne took several deep breaths and slowly brought the eye in front of hers. The city once again sprang to life in a stomach-churning canvas of colors, swirling and popping, flashing, and blinking.

"Ugh," she muttered, "it's like . . . someone vomited a rainbow all over the city."

Ellyne struggled to keep her balance as she peered through the eye. Trying to stay upright was enough of a chore, let alone attempting to locate the Sistix. Confident the disorientation would not subside, she slowly scanned the area, taking care not to shift her gaze too quickly and cause even more nausea.

"I wish I could see what you're seeing!"

"No, you don't. Trust me." Beginning from the left, Ellyne slowly turned her body to gaze across the city, watching the myriad of colors swirl and bloom everywhere she looked. There was so much magic! It was embedded into the very fabric of Karnascus—more so than she had ever suspected.

"I wonder," she said, still slowly looking from left to right, "what would happen if magic were just to . . . quit."

"I would guess total chaos. But that would never happen, right? The Kithrak are just *stewards* of flocia. They don't actually own it or control it!"

"I suppose that's what we'll find out if we make it into the Sistix which, if it doesn't show itself soon, will be a moot point."

"No luck, then?"

"Not yet, but I'm moving slowly so I don't throw up or pass out."

"Well, this is certainly intriguing magic. And even more interesting how the eye works for you but not me and that you're seeing magic for the first time and then wouldn't it be . . ."

Nicole's voice trailed off as Ellyne concentrated, fighting to remain standing. She wished she could somehow expedite the process and just get it over with already but, no, that would be easy, and nothing was ever easy.

The slimy eyeball nearly popped out of her grasp as she stumbled slightly. If she were to drop it, there was no telling how far down the hill it would roll or where it would end up. She was also trying not to think about the fact that she was holding a Kithrak's body part in her hand in the first place.

And then she saw it—something shimmering. It was only a part of something, and it wasn't the sickening, swirling clouds of color. In fact, there appeared to be no magic flowing in or out of it. Because of this, Ellyne was able to get a better look and see more of it quicker than the rest of the city.

It appeared to be a pillar. Yes! And there were more of them!

"This is it!" she exclaimed. "Found it!"

"Really?" Nicole asked.

"There." Ellyne pointed ahead of her, not really paying attention. She was still moving over the edges of the Sistix and its towering pillars. The entire structure shone brightly, sparkling with a benign, golden hue instead of the chaotic, shifting colors of the magic surrounding it.

It also seemed to pulse in and out of sight, barely visible at its apex. It was simultaneously amazing and confusing and she suddenly wished she were back in her apartment, oblivious to all of this.

Ellyne returned the eyeball to its bag and stuffed it back into her pocket, waiting for the disorientation to finally subside while Nicole fidgeted impatiently next to her, mumbling under her breath.

"Are you ready to do this?" Ellyne asked.

"Yes!" Nicole replied, unable to contain her enthusiasm. "Wait, do what?"

CHAPTER
TWENTY-THREE

THE WAREHOUSE AREA of Karnascus was just that—a jumble of warehouses and maybe a building or two that served some other purpose. And while they encountered a handful of people walking the streets, the area was indeed largely deserted, as Ellyne surmised. She herself had been to this area only once before, and that was to shake a few Ilserate pursuers off her trail. That was also years ago. To think the Sistix had been here all along . . . it felt eerie.

From what she recalled, the area hadn't changed much . . . or at all. And why would it? Warehouses held stuff and there was no real way to improve that or give it a facelift. No real reason, either.

Nicole, apparently seeing this part of the city for the first time seemed captivated by it somehow—as if it was the most wonderous thing she'd encountered—at least today. Given the fact that she knew so little of the world outside the Ilserate compound, Ellyne couldn't fault her even though she was amused. She wasn't paying much attention to the girl's babbling, but Nicole appeared to be fascinated with what might be inside the structures.

As they hurried past the buildings, each structure looking

much like the next, Ellyne's mind raced, trying desperately to formulate some hint of a plan to fix everything. Since discovering the grika and the side effects of the T-Helms she had long decided the goal had to be to wrest control of magic from the Kithrak, but her brain had never settled on a method of how that was possible. Even Nicole, who might know more about magic and flocia than anyone on Seralune, had no input.

Nicole did, however, have faith. Why the girl felt so certain they would succeed without even knowing *how* they would succeed was a mystery to Ellyne. Was there something Nicole knew and wasn't telling her?

Ellyne didn't consider herself talented in anything, but she was a master of second-guessing herself and being suspicious of everyone around her. She liked to think it kept her alive but there was an equally good chance the only result of that mindset was indigestion and odd looks from others. Sometimes she wondered what it was like to be oblivious to the things she knew.

And it wasn't just the current situation. She saw and discovered things during her campaign in the Flocia Wars that she would rather forget. If they were all common knowledge, everyone in Karnascus may not have such a rosy view of the Kithrak and, more importantly, their own government.

Most people woke up, showered, used whatever method they had available to get to work, worked, traveled back home, and did whatever they wanted in their spare time. To them, nothing was amiss. To those unfortunate inhabitants of the murder shack, nothing could've been further from their fates. They knew the truth.

At least, they did at one time, before they were turned into rage-filled monsters. The grika were something Ellyne couldn't stop thinking about but wished she could.

She scanned the area for possible threats as was her standard habit. There were very few screens in this part of

Karnascus. The warehouse area traded most of the informational screens for large, towering billboards that spewed soundless commercials endlessly. Many of them loomed high above the short buildings, urging citizens to buy their products while others barely cleared the roofs.

Ellyne would've felt better if the obnoxious signs weren't casting so much light. Fortunately, the area wasn't a hotbed of activity, so their chances of being spotted were still low.

Just when she was feeling like they could relax a bit and stop looking behind them every five seconds, one of the shorter billboards changed. It was brief, but the message was clear.

"*Warning: Impending Severe Weather. Seek Shelter Immediately.*"

"Move," she growled, getting Nicole's attention. "Now!"

They scurried into an alley, Ellyne looking for anything they could hide beneath and Nicole trying to stay calm.

"Where are we going?"

"We have company."

Just as Ellyne finished her sentence, she heard the gentle hum from somewhere overhead—most likely an Ilserate skiff quietly searching for the two of them. And she knew there were others not far behind.

"Did they see us? How do they know we're here?"

"I don't know. Maybe Iksillix finally woke up and blabbed or maybe they're blanketing the whole city. It doesn't matter." Ellyne kicked at a door which, to her surprise, swung open. "Quick, in here!"

They quickly slipped into the warehouse, slamming the door behind them, and ducking beneath the windows while simultaneously trying to catch a glimpse outside. Ellyne didn't expect to see anything. The skiff would be hovering somewhere above the rooftops and the view out the window afforded little visibility into that area. She slumped down and sighed, her back against the wall.

Nicole, on the other hand, couldn't sit still. She fidgeted and shifted, looking at Ellyne from time to time before averting her gaze into the darkness. The city's ambient light filtered in through the dirty panes of glass but did little to illuminate the blackness beyond.

"What now?" Nicole asked.

"Let's see what the eyeball sees, shall we?"

"That thing gives me the creeps," Nicole admitted as she shook with a chill.

"I don't know why, it's only an alien organ I dug out with a spoon and have been keeping in a plastic bag like some weird trophy. What's so creepy about that?"

Nicole giggled. Ellyne had to admit it was gross, but she was thankful it actually worked—not only because, yes, it would hopefully allow them access to the Sistix, but also because she would've hated to take Iksillix's eyeball for no reason.

Mostly.

She nearly dropped it as she slipped the slimy orb out of the bag and into her palm. She briefly wondered how long the eyeball would remain functional or, at the very least, how long they had before it simply rotted. That thought nearly made her gag.

Ellyne reluctantly held it close to her right eye and peered through it.

"Kithrak can see in complete darkness," she said. "This answers several questions I had."

"Oh really? Can I see?"

"Sure. Here, take the eye."

"Uh, on second thought, no. No thanks. I'll just let you handle all the eyeball-related tasks."

Ellyne laughed and scanned the area. "I figured that would be a deal breaker for you."

This warehouse was a large, open room filled with crates stacked high and piles of mundane supplies—furniture, rugs, and what appeared to be vehicle parts. She didn't know if she expected to find some scandalous Kithrak contraband or Ilserate secrets but, admittedly, she was a little disappointed.

Until she scanned the far end of the warehouse and saw something that obviously didn't belong.

"There," she said, pointing off to her right.

"There what?"

"I think one of the Sistix's pillars is in this warehouse."

"Wait, what do you mean? Like, it's built into the warehouse or something?"

"No, of course not." Ellyne got up and slowly walked in the direction of the pillar, using the eye's vision to see. "I mean, yes. Well, sort of. It doesn't appear completely solid. It's hard to explain, but if you want to see for yourself—"

"Nope. No thank you."

Ellyne grinned.

Several times, while winding around pallets and between rows of assorted junk, she nearly dropped the slimy eye. Her heart skipped a beat every time, knowing how difficult it would be to find it in the dark. Sure, Nicole could conjure some form of a light but that might give away their location, even through the dusty windows.

Behind her, Nicole stumbled and tripped over something but kept up, keeping her hand on Ellyne's shoulder as they made their way to the other end of the warehouse.

The ghostly pillar encompassed a large area, superimposing itself over the contents of the warehouse. How could such a thing be there but also not be there? She could obviously see it, but she could also see *through* it.

"Where is it?" Nicole asked.

"We're standing right in front of it . . . sort of."

"What do you mean, sort of?"

"Look, I can't explain it. Take the damned eyeball and see for yourself."

She grabbed Nicole's hand and carefully placed the eye in

her palm, making sure the girl didn't drop it. Then she waited for the inevitable flurry of excitement and disgust to bellow forth.

Nicole gasped and Ellyne giggled as she watched her head swivel to look at everything around her. The scene was similar to a cat playing with string.

"I've never seen anything like this," she said, gingerly reaching out her hand to touch the pillar Ellyne couldn't see but knew was there. "Do you think there might be more of these in Karnascus—buildings or other things we can't see but the Kithrak can?"

"I hadn't thought of that." Terror filled Ellyne as she considered the prospect of more than one invisible Kithrak secret hidden in the city. Just how pervasive were they? "It makes sense, though. If they can hide a structure this large in plain sight, what other secrets are they hiding."

Nicole lowered the eyeball. Even in the scant illumination, Ellyne could see the concern in the girl's eyes. "The Kithrak have a tighter hold on us than anyone knows, don't they?" She held out the eyeball.

"It seems that way." Ellyne took the eye from Nicole, grimacing at its slimy texture. "But hopefully we're going to fix that."

They had no proof there were any other Kithrak constructs hidden throughout the city, but it wasn't a stretch to believe there were. And even if there weren't, she was certain they concealed other secrets. Everyone had been so eager to embrace magic they never stopped to dig deeper into its origins and especially its relation to the Kithrak. They surrendered to it willingly, and without a fight.

"We'll expose the Kithrak to the world," she muttered, gazing through the eyeball, and inspecting the pillar more closely. It penetrated the ceiling as if it wasn't there at all, somehow existing but not existing at the same time. Where it connected with the floor, there were no crates or equipment stacked in the area, though Ellyne surmised it really wouldn't matter since it would just pass through them.

But there must have been a reason for the space around it to be free of junk. The Kithrak were deliberate so, if this area was clear, it was meant to be.

"What's so special about you?" she mumbled, scrutinizing the pillar further. Though she couldn't touch it to feel its surface, she could see it was made of a foreign substance. There appeared to be no texture—no grooves or seams. It might have been metal, or maybe some strange combination of materials, but it certainly wasn't anything with which she was familiar.

She badly wanted to run her fingers over the structure, to feel its texture, but such a thing wasn't possible. Though that didn't stop her from trying, even if just out of habit. She was, of course, met with disappointment when her hand passed through its surface as if it were the air itself.

"Under different circumstances," she mumbled as she slowly circled the pillar, "this would be fascinating."

"What do you see?"

"The same thing you saw," Ellyne grumbled, slowly circling the artifact, "nothing." A dull throb surfaced in the back of her head leading her to wonder if using Iksillix's eye this much might be harmful or, at the very least, have some temporary adverse effects.

Undaunted, she continued her inspection, squinting through the orb and resisting the urge to touch the structure that was clearly in front of her, but also wasn't. That was a conundrum her brain still vigorously worked to understand, even while she scrutinized the pillar.

"Maybe we should find another pillar? This one seems like a dead end."

"Not necessarily."

"What do you mean?"

Ellyne ran her fingers over a rough spot on the pillar.

While the rest of the structure was smooth and seamless, this one small spot appeared to have an almost imperceptible, rectangular joint at eye level.

Her fingers touched something solid.

"Found it!"

"Found what?"

Ellyne was focused on the pillar, but she could sense Nicole's excitement as the girl literally bounced up and down beside her. "I'm not sure," she said, "but I can touch it."

She ran her fingers over the surface of the small area. Not a second later, it vanished, revealing a red light behind it. Ellyne gasped.

"What is it?" Nicole asked.

"A light of some kind. There was a panel that . . . dissolved or something." The moment she leaned in closer to inspect the light it flashed rapidly and something beeped. "Something's happening."

"What?"

"I don't know. Hopefully something good? But I'd be ready to run just in case."

After the beep, the red light flashed three times before emitting a beam that began at the top of Ellyne's head and worked its way down to her chin. It then crawled back up her face and disappeared. The panel reappeared, obscuring the light.

"I think it was some kind of scanner, but I'm not sure if it liked what it saw."

"Facial recognition, maybe?"

"Maybe. But it looks like it didn't work." Ellyne backed a few steps away from the pillar, keeping her eyes on it as she did so. "I think we should leave."

"What do you mean? Why?"

"If the scan failed, then I would assume someone's been alerted to—"

She was interrupted by a whooshing sound as the pillar

shimmered and distorted, soon obscured behind a sparkling, dark portal.

"I've seen one of these before," Nicole gasped. "Sometimes the Kithrak that visited the Ilserate compound would use them."

"What is it?"

"It's a gateway, I think."

"To where?"

"Good question."

CHAPTER
TWENTY-FOUR

THE NAUSEATING disorientation lasted only a few seconds. Shortly after, the cold, wet feeling subsided and Ellyne could properly inspect her surroundings. Nicole appeared to have recovered at the same rate, and looked around in both awe and confusion.

"So," she said, "we're back in Iksillix's living room then?" Ellyne still clutched the eye.

"It kind of looks like it."

Ellyne couldn't help herself. She reached for one of the baubles on the small table, but her hand passed through it, causing it to distort and briefly flash. She waved her hand through it several more times, watching its image disrupt each time.

"Except maybe not," she muttered.

"It definitely *looks* like his house." Nicole passed her hand through a chair and watched as it, too, shimmered and distorted, then reappeared when she pulled away. "This is weird!"

"I have to agree with you there."

Ellyne noticed the rest of the house was . . . missing. This living room was the whole of it, bereft of any other rooms, windows, or interior doors. Most importantly, there was no obvious way back home. No, the only way out was through the front door.

"How do we get back?" Nicole asked, obviously looking for the same thing Ellyne herself sought.

"I was sort of hoping you'd have the answer to that question."

"I . . . I don't see any portals or devices to take us back. What about the eye?"

Ellyne squinted through the eyeball, scanning the room for anything out of the ordinary. She spent several minutes slowly inspecting everything, walking around the room to do so, but the outlook was bleak.

"Nothing," she said, happy to slip the orb back into the plastic bag in her jacket. As she did so, she could feel the remaining two ammo cartridges in her pocket. Both were full and, when combined with her already loaded weapon, meant she had only twenty-four bullets. Hopefully, she wouldn't need any of them, but she was aware how things usually went.

"Surely Iksillix has an easy way to get back. It wouldn't make sense otherwise."

"I agree with you." Ellyne wanted to sit and think a moment but the chair she was eyeing was most likely an illusion along with the rest of this room. "Maybe this is meant for one-way travel and, to get back, they must go somewhere else? After all, nothing in here is real, so having a portal in here might not be possible."

"Of course! That's probably it. You know more about this than you give yourself credit for."

"I'm just lucky. I could be talking out my ass." She pointed to the front door. "You ready to finish this?"

"Do you mean am I ready to maybe start to figure out how to possibly finish this?"

Ellyne chuckled, laying her hand on the doorknob. It was

solid, which half-surprised her, but made everything feel more real. They were close. For a moment, she felt giddy, almost hopeful.

"While, yes, that is more accurate, it doesn't roll off the tongue as well." She took a deep breath and exhaled, trying to relax. "Are you ready? There's no telling what's outside this door."

While Ellyne felt fear and apprehension, Nicole was the opposite—giddy and unable to contain her excitement. She wished she had the girl's enthusiasm, especially now.

"Yes! Let's do this!" Nicole laughed. "Was that better? Was I convincing?"

Ellyne rolled her eyes and held her breath as she turned the doorknob. The door quietly opened to reveal a wall of swirling, dull colors. "Well, that's unexpected," she said, disappointed, but also more anxious. Not being able to see what lay beyond didn't sit well with her.

"Another portal," Nicole gasped.

"I don't like this."

"It's not like we have a choice, Ellyne."

"Now I like it even less."

Several moments passed with no words spoken between the two. Ellyne still gripped the doorknob as all kinds of thoughts raced through her head. In front of her, the dull grays and blacks swirled in a chaotic dance that held no pattern.

Nicole, too, remained silent, but Ellyne could see the excitement bubbling up within her. She was about to explode. Ellyne wished she shared the girl's enthusiasm.

"Well," she sighed, "as my father always said, 'sometimes the only way to find out what's wrong is to stare up the cat's ass.'"

"What does that even mean?"

"No idea. He's an idiot. Anyway, here we go."

Ellyne stepped through the swirling gray portal, instantly

feeling a rush of cold as if ice water coursed through her veins. The sensation was only momentary—lasting for just a split second before it subsided and left her gasping for air on the other side.

"Are you alright?" Nicole asked, appearing next to her.

"I don't think that type of travel agrees with me," she said, quickly catching her breath.

"Add another item to the list!" Nicole laughed.

"It's a long list." Ellyne looked behind her and noticed there was no swirling gray and black exit. She was unconcerned, however, since any portal would have probably led back to the facsimile of Iksillix's house—a place they already knew held no way back to Seralune. "Quick! Behind there!"

Ellyne grabbed Nicole's arm and pulled her around the corner of a black dome, trying desperately to keep out of sight. "We need to keep a low profile until we are where we need to be."

"And where is that?"

Ellyne peeked around the dome of the building and gasped, speechless.

The scene before her was so alien it was difficult for her brain to puzzle out.

They were on the edge of a city—at least, that's what she thought. Before her was a chaotic jumble of buildings. Some were tall, elegant spires that glimmered and shined while others were ornate, shorter structures that looked as though they were made of lace.

But it wasn't the variety of buildings that was difficult to comprehend. No, it was the fact that they pointed all directions in seemingly impossible feats of construction and physics. While some structures jutted up from the ground, others floated in mid-air—pointing sideways or downward.

The city was teeming with bright colors and lights and each building radiated a different hue. But it was all a distraction because, once she looked past it all, she saw what she knew to be their goal.

"There," she pointed ahead of them.

"I see it too. It's beautiful!"

Behind all the colorful floating buildings was a bright beam of light that reached high into the air. It flashed and pulsed, changing color with each burst.

"I'm going out on a limb, here, but I think that's where we're supposed to be."

"I'd say you're right. I mean, I was getting pretty comfy cowering behind this building, but I guess I could be persuaded to leave if that's what you think is best." Nicole shot Ellyne a wry look.

The ground shook slightly and the dome moved, rising from the ground slowly as they both backed away. Ellyne could see insect-like legs appear underneath.

"Not a building!" she said as she ran toward the city with Nicole in tow. Looking behind her, she watched the giant crablike creature lumber away in the opposite direction. They didn't stop running, however, until they reached another building behind which they hid. Ellyne looked it over carefully to ensure that it was, in fact, not another monster.

"There don't appear to be any, uh, city streets."

"There also doesn't appear to be anyone walking the nonexistent city streets, which is good for us."

"You don't think they'll let us just waltz up to the source of flocia do you? I mean, that's just rude."

"You're certainly welcome to ask them." Ellyne stared at the pulsing energy in the distance. If it truly was the source of flocia, then they were close. It wasn't something she believed they would leave unguarded but, then again, why would they feel the need to do so? If it was this difficult just getting to it, then surely, they felt it was safe just by obscurity alone.

Ellyne was neither a Kithrak nor a security expert. Her hand went absent-mindedly to her pocket, checking her available ammunition. Twenty-four, same as the last time. It paid to be over-prepared, but this was more of a comfort issue—as if her bullets were her closest friends.

That wasn't all that far from the truth.

"So," Nicole whispered, even though there was nobody else around to hear her. "We just walk into the city, saunter up to the source and do whatever we need to do?"

"Until it all goes to hell and things start exploding, yes."

Nicole had a look of utter confusion on her face. She fidgeted with her fingers for a moment, obviously trying desperately to think of another plan.

"There's no way it's that easy, though, right?"

"Look," Ellyne continued, pointing ahead of them. "That's the source, right? Do you see anyone between us and it?"

Nicole shook her head.

"Obviously, the Kithrak don't hang around outside. If they're going to do us the favor, then we should be grateful for the gift. They obviously don't expect interlopers running around their little Sistix."

"But what if they spot us? This is their *home*. Saying we're outnumbered is the understatement of the year."

Ellyne left the relative safety of the building's shadow, confidently strolling out into the open. "We're not going to make it easy for them, but I also think we don't need to skulk in every shadow or jump at every noise. Come on, we're not getting any closer cowering and talking."

Nicole, looking dubious, emerged from the shadows as they made their way further into the city. Ellyne felt countless questions building up inside her, the least of which was how the hell this city worked. How did the Kithrak operate in such a chaotic, seemingly random environment? How did they get from one building to the next?

Obviously, the answer was magic. That was the answer to nearly all questions. She wondered what Kithrak life resembled before magic. Was there a before magic? Surely, as with

Seralune, there was a time the Kithrak didn't command flocia.

She wondered if even the Kithrak knew. How many generations had passed since they first discovered it? Did any of them know the history or were they alive during that time?

She didn't even have a solid grasp on how long an average Kithrak's life span was. But given how secretive they were, even amongst their own people, she doubted many—if any—knew the full story.

Nicole went from apprehensive to fascinated in the blink of an eye. She constantly looked around, gasping and pointing while mumbling to herself. Ellyne suspected this was the proverbial kid in a candy store moment—as if her fears had been completely assuaged, replaced with wonder and awe.

Ellyne herself was a bit taken by the landscape, but her fascination was more logistic than wondrous. Still, she had to admit the Kithrak city was fantastic. It was also paradoxical, confusing, and seemingly impossible.

A silly question popped into her head, and she almost laughed—what, if anything, did the Kithrak think of human cities and their ordered buildings . . . that were stuck in the ground? If they ever reconnected with Derek, she would have to ask him his thoughts . . . if he had any. After all, they now walked where he'd never been. Did that mean he'd never truly been home?

Meeting back up with Derek was skipping past the endgame, though. Every step forward brought them closer to flocia's source and, at that time, they would have to decide what to do. Nicole was the mage breaker which hopefully meant she could wrest control from the Kithrak and end their silent tyranny.

But Nicole herself would need to know how to do this and, so far, she hadn't offered up any suggestions. It sounded just like every other plan Ellyne had ever come up with. If she were being honest with herself, every one of her plans was basically "travel to where you need to be, then shoot stuff."

Maybe it would work one last time. Going up against the Kithrak was no small feat.

One last time. Why did it seem that way? Why did she have a nasty feeling this was the end of the line? But this wasn't a new outlook, was it? She'd been feeling this way for a while—since the altercation with the factions.

At that time, she'd thought it was her end, and she'd felt remorse that she didn't get to finish what Nicole had started.

Now she was on the precipice of doing just that, and she believed there was a strong chance she may not make it out alive. She didn't fear death; she simply wasn't ready for it yet.

Or maybe she was concerned for Nicole? Perhaps both of them. This whole operation began harmlessly enough but, with each step, slowly felt like a "sacrifice yourself for the greater good" type of mission.

They passed several large structures, each a different color and not one window among them. Ellyne couldn't even see a door. Nicole was captivated by every little thing she saw, gasping and pointing incessantly while Ellyne tried to wrap her head around their situation.

She wasn't accustomed to looking out for someone else's safety. The two of them hadn't known each other for very long, but the girl was the closest thing Ellyne ever had to a friend. Or maybe a sister—she could be irritating like a sister. At least, that's what it felt like.

Yes, a friend. It was a welcome feeling but also complicated everything. And, no, Marik didn't count. They were companions in a war, not friends. She might have felt differently at the time, but she knew better now. And, besides, he played her. He was a friend to no one but himself.

For a moment, Ellyne questioned if she were any different. For the longest time, Victor had been the closest thing she'd had to a friend. Otherwise, it was just her. She was also a friend to no one but herself, wasn't she? At least, until now. Maybe that was the difference.

"Let's go over there, behind that statue." Ellyne pointed to a towering, metal statue that looked to be two creatures locked in an embrace. It seemed an odd thing for the Kithrak to have a statue of such a thing and Ellyne not only believed it would provide good cover, but she was curious.

Nicole nodded, probably excited to see more of Kithrak culture, and they hurried over to it.

At this point, there was no hiding *behind* objects. They were in the heart of the city. Structures surrounded them—both on the ground and hovering above. They were exposed from every direction, yet Ellyne felt no sense of urgency. This was going far easier than she had anticipated.

"What is this?" Nicole asked, staring at the statue.

It was a good twelve feet tall at least, crafted from a dark metal. Ellyne circled the artwork, carefully scrutinizing it and discovering what she thought at first was two Kithrak was something a bit more alarming.

One of the two figures was indeed Kithrak with six eyes and five arms. But the other figure was something she'd never laid eyes on.

The other figure was some kind of winged, humanoid lizard. And the two were not embracing; they were fighting—locked in a struggle of some kind.

"Maybe it's some kind of victory memorial," Nicole said, running her fingers over the base of the statue. "Possibly a war from the past?"

"I wonder if there's a similar statue with a human."

Neither spoke for a moment after her chilling comment.

"Another race conquered by the Kithrak?" Nicole finally asked.

Ellyne was shaken inside. Just this one statue shone a whole new light on the Kithrak as a race. This monument proved beyond a doubt they were the conquerors she believed them to be.

"Most likely," she replied, her resolve now strengthened. She was even more determined, now, to do whatever must be done to stop them. They weren't benevolent. They had enslaved the people of Seralune, and nobody knew it. "Come on," she said, "we've got a hostile occupation to end."

TWENTY-FIVE

EVERY HAIR on Ellyne's body stood up and her skin tingled. It was as if every part of her thrummed in the same rhythmic pattern, synchronized in harmony with the light emanating from the source of flocia. They were close, and Ellyne felt the familiar sensations she'd come to know all too well lately.

Fear and anger invaded her mind. She was both afraid of accidentally causing a disaster but, at the same time, almost hoping she would. Certainly, there was no better way to go out if this was their last stand.

Nervously, she felt around her jacket. Twenty-four bullets including those in the gun. That habit would never die. Maybe it was an obsession, but it was reassuring, nonetheless. Twenty-four bullets. She hoped that would be enough.

But no amount ever seemed enough, did it?

Nicole appeared to know the way but then, the multicolored pulsing pillar of light was difficult to miss.

They moved to a red building and skulked around the perimeter. The structure jutted upward at a disorienting angle —certainly not the straight up and down Ellyne was accustomed to on Seralune. The air was still and quiet, which unnerved her, and every footfall may as well have been a parade of thousands, and every breath a scream. The only other sound was a hushed, ambient noise that reminded her of vehicles on a distant highway. Well, vehicles before they were powered by magic.

So far, however, there hadn't been anyone around to notice, but that did little to allay her fears. She suspected someone was watching them.

She always suspected that, and she was seldom wrong.

Even Nicole, usually vibrant and loquacious, was mostly quiet. She spoke only in whispers and not often. It was apparently a feeling that permeated everything, and she didn't like it.

The real question was, if they were truly being observed, what was the plan? Surely the Kithrak would want to apprehend them as soon as possible, wouldn't they? It seemed logical but, thus far, they hadn't seen a single living creature other than themselves.

Well, and that crab thing they thought was a building.

They moved to the next structure—a squat, square building with three towers jutting from the top. It was the closest Ellyne had seen so far to a more familiar type of construction, but definitely still alien and bizarre.

"You think we're being watched, don't you?" Nicole whispered, leaning against the rough, abrasive wall.

"It seems the most logical theory."

"I was hoping you'd say no."

"In this case, I'm sorry to disappoint."

Ahead of them, just up a hill and past several more buildings, lay what Ellyne believed to be the source of magic— what the Kithrak called The Teranyne. Flocia itself! The radiant pillar of pulsing light was surrounded by wisps of energy which swirled and wound upward into the sky. Some winked out of existence, resembling momentary stars while others simply traveled out of sight.

Captivated, Ellyne found herself staring at the spectacle. She felt every part of her body humming in unison with whatever was happening. This was it. This was definitely the source of flocia. If the light show wasn't enough to convince her of this, the connection she felt certainly was.

And it was both terrifying and liberating.

She likened the sensation to standing at the bottom of a great dam with a bomb in hand. How long could she hold back the torrent of energy within her? How long did she *want* to? Could she even stop the bomb from exploding if she had to?

"It's amazing and beautiful and . . . just miraculous." Nicole appeared completely enthralled. Her eyes were wide and her mouth agape as she gasped in awe.

"I mean, it's neat and all," Ellyne teased, "but I think a really good sandwich is better."

"Shut up," Nicole sneered, elbowing Ellyne in the side.

"Okay, okay, it *is* pretty amazing. But wait a minute." Ellyne snapped her out of her daze. "How can this be *the* source?"

"What do you mean?"

"Well, we accidentally unearthed it on Seralune years ago, right? So how can there be two sources—one on our planet and one here? Or did it get moved? How do you even do that?"

Nicole looked perplexed as she considered the conundrum. "I . . . don't know," she finally said, still obviously struggling to find an answer. "The most likely conclusion being that there is more than one source, I guess?"

"How does that work, then? Obviously the Kithrak travel and they've done this before, so where are the other sources? Are they here?"

"I don't really know."

"This is going to get complicated if we have to steal multiple flocia sources from the Kithrak."

"We'll . . . we'll think of something. Right now, we need to focus on that." She pointed to the light show at the top of the hill. "We start there and then figure it out."

"Now you sound like me," Ellyne laughed.

Nicole's calm lucidity was both a surprise and a refreshing change.

They moved to the next building, beginning their ascent up the hill. As they got closer to the source, Ellyne found it increasingly curious and worrisome that they still hadn't encountered anyone else. Maybe the Kithrak were just that confident in their security?

Maybe. Ellyne still couldn't shake the feeling they were walking right into a trap. It certainly wouldn't have been the first time. Historically, her track record of avoiding traps was spotty, but she was still alive.

Just one more time.

The journey up the hill continued. Ellyne stopped taking any precautions to conceal herself, knowing full well their half-assed attempts at subterfuge probably hadn't done any good. Plus, she was impatient and preferred a fight to sneaking around and hiding. At the very least, she believed she was much better at the former.

The question on Nicole's face was painfully evident, but the girl knew not to ask it because there was no answer. Neither of them knew what to do when they got to the source. It was something Ellyne had asked herself time and again. It was unfortunate she couldn't just shoot something. That solution worked in most situations.

What once sounded like distant traffic was now like rushing water. It still wasn't loud or overwhelming, but the resemblance was unmistakable.

"It smells like . . . it might rain?" Nicole said, unsure of herself and sniffing the air.

"Not rain, but it does smell similar. Does flocia have a scent?"

"I can't be sure. But I've never smelled this before and it can't be mere coincidence. This is fascinating, Ellyne! If only we could study it closer!"

"Oh sure. I bet, if we tell the Kithrak our interests are purely academic, they'll totally just let us wander around, inspecting things." Ellyne smirked.

"It's a shame. There's so much to learn from it!"

"I suspect the Kithrak have good reasons for keeping everyone in the dark. Come on, let's keep moving. We've been lucky so far, but I bet everything for us now is going to be uphill."

"You mean in addition to this actual hill we're climbing?" Nicole giggled.

"You're funny."

The ascent was neither steep nor arduous. There were no crags, no debris or scree to hinder their climb. Ellyne briefly wondered if there was some Kithrak groundskeeping crew that manicured the area in reverence to their magic source.

"I guess it takes magic to make magic," she mumbled.

"What?"

"Oh, nothing. Just making a terrible joke to myself."

Every thought imaginable swirled through her mind. When they first arrived in . . . wherever they were, those thoughts centered around confusion and fear—fear of the unknown and, ultimately, the fear of dying here. She liked to believe she was never afraid but, in this instance at least, that was merely a façade.

Nicole was rambling, but Ellyne paid no attention. It was background noise while she wrestled with her emotions. The fear was still there but it was a different kind of fear, having morphed from fear of death to . . . fear of failure. At least, that's what she thought. Had she really become so wrapped up in this mission that she didn't care if it was her last?

She wasn't even sure if that fear extended beyond just keeping Nicole safe at this point, but she supposed it did. She wanted badly to end the Kithrak's grasp on flocia not only for possible human salvation, but for revenge.

And revenge was a powerful motive. Ellyne herself had been fueled by revenge for so long. In fact, that may have been a part of her current apprehension—would she die here, before being able to pay back Marik for his treachery?

She had to admit, that was a ridiculous train of thought. Yet still, she had to wonder if the only reason she was helping Nicole was to get back at him. She liked to believe she'd grown a bit recently and maybe her motives weren't so selfish but that required some deep introspection—the kind which, at the moment, she hadn't time for.

Most likely, revenge was still in the mix.

She ran her tongue over the metal in her jaw, absolutely sure she still felt the ache of the wound in her left shoulder— gifts from him to remind her always. Yes, revenge was very much still in the mix. There was more to it, now, but that didn't mean she couldn't hold onto her most primal motive. If she managed to somehow ruin Marik's life, this operation would be successful. But she believed she could both have revenge *and* free the source. She believed, in fact, the two were related.

Nicole would know what to do. When the time came (and it was rapidly approaching) Nicole would figure it out. Her innate ability and close relationship with magic would be the keys. In fact, Ellyne had a hunch the girl already knew what she had to do and simply wasn't revealing it yet.

The hill leveled out and they found themselves at the edge of a vast, flat circular area at the center of which was the massive column of energy. Nicole gasped and Ellyne fought the urge to cover her ears, the once gentle rushing sound was now almost painfully loud.

"Ellyne, can you hear it? Can you hear the flow of flocia?"

She could barely hear Nicole's words over the din of raw

power that pulsed with various colors. "Yes!" she shouted back. "It's a little loud!"

"What are you talking about? It's beautiful . . . peaceful and harmonic—like a song on a gentle breeze."

Ellyne took a step forward. When her foot touched one of the pavestones, it sprang to life, illuminating a pattern of yellow light that snaked its way across the area and ultimately ended at the pillar of flocia before disappearing.

"Ooh!" Nicole gasped. "That's cool! Let me try!" She put her foot down on a stone, gasping some more when the same thing happened, only in blue and not as bright. The disappointment was painted all over her face.

"Maybe mine's brighter because I've got a bunch of it stored up inside me right now?"

It wasn't a lie. From the moment Ellyne set foot in this place she could feel her body absorbing flocia. She tried the entire time to shut it out, to keep herself from soaking it in but the truth was, she still had little to no control over it.

Which added another level of fear. Bad things happened when she lost control. Though none of this was new information, she had no idea what would happen in this place with a seemingly unlimited supply of power. Maybe that was the key, though. Perhaps she could . . . destroy flocia *with* flocia?

She took another step and the ground responded in kind; tracing lines which zig-zagged across the floor until disappearing at the source. It was in her head—not just the sound but the energy itself. She felt as though she were an extension of the source. It was both exhilarating and terrifying.

Through brief concentration, she quelled the roar down to a dull hum.

"That's better."

Every methodical step produced the same effect, but the pattern of lines differed each time. Regardless, they always began at her feet and ended at the source. She almost wished for more time to play around with it. If she had more time, perhaps she could discover more about herself.

Time. How much more did they have? Here they were and neither of them had made a move to end this. Her hope that Nicole had a plan was quickly slipping. And their time could be running out.

"So, what now?" Nicole asked. She was busy staring at the light her feet created in the stones.

"I . . . don't know. I was hoping something would become apparent or we'd have a big fight or something—anything. Certainly, I hadn't envisioned this."

"And it took you two long enough," Marik's voice said, coming from all directions just as a sparkling portal opened.

CHAPTER
TWENTY-SIX

"SHIT," Ellyne muttered, her hand resting on her gun. Her left hand was ready to pull her blade if necessary, but it would probably do little good here.

Marik emerged from the portal on the other side of the circle, his red robes flowing in a breeze that must have come from wherever the portal led.

"Magic is a truly wonderous thing," he said. "Even more so here than most other locations, since right here at the source is where magic is most powerful." He gestured around them. "You must have felt that, am I right?" His gaze settled on Nicole.

"Duh," she snorted.

"We really figured you would arrive here sooner though. There are mixed emotions among the others about this development but, I must admit, it was foolish for you to come."

"I brought the most powerful mage in history—the Mage Breaker—to the most powerful place of magic, which just makes her even more badass, and I'm the foolish one?"

If she hadn't been looking closely, she may have missed it —the slight crack in Marik's calm façade as he, for the quickest of instances, looked concerned while he contemplated the weight of Ellyne's words. It vanished as quickly as it appeared, but Ellyne would make sure she remembered that one moment for the rest of her life—no matter how long or short that was.

"You do feel the power of this place," she whispered, "right?"

"Very much, yes."

"You can't win, Ellyne," Marik laughed, slowly making his way closer to them. His lackadaisical movement annoyed her—walking as if she was of such little consequence to him. "There are two of you, here in the Kithrak's domain. You are hopelessly outnumbered. I don't even know what you hope to accomplish but it's a fool's gambit."

He laughed again. Her anger rose. He knew what he was doing because he knew how to get under her skin. But what annoyed her the most was, he wasn't wrong.

"I think you underestimate us," she sneered.

"Do I?"

"Yeah!" Nicole shouted. "You do! We know what we're doing!"

"And what, exactly, would that be then?"

Ellyne pulled her gun and aimed it at him, slowly cocking the hammer back for effect. "She's taking the source of flocia from the Kithrak, and I'm taking back my life from you."

"Oh, really?" Marik laughed again. He didn't seem concerned, yet he stopped his approach. Ellyne's trigger finger twitched. "I wasn't aware I owned your life."

"You've been in my head for far too long. I think it's time I got rid of you."

"Now now," he said, slowly raising his palms in front of him, "you should already know your bullets can't—"

Ellyne fired a shot. The slug ricocheted off a shimmering barrier surrounding him.

"As I was saying, you should already know your bullets

can't hurt me. My wards and enchantments are far too powerful to succumb to such an archaic weapon."

"This gun saved your ass many times."

"I wasn't referring to the gun."

Ellyne fought her anger. She wrestled with the urge to scream, to tackle him and pummel him to a bloody mess. Chances were good she'd never get close to him anyway, but the sentiment was still there.

"You've already lost," he laughed again, lowering his palms. "You can't hurt me."

"No, I can't," Ellyne growled, lowering her gun. Before she fired that bullet, she knew the result. Metal was never a match for magic, and that was only one reason Ellyne hated it.

"Yes," Marik agreed.

"But *she* can." Ellyne grinned.

Nicole immediately went to work, creating a swirling mass of energy that she promptly directed at Marik. He struggled to counter it, moving his hands frantically and muttering quiet words but he couldn't keep up and was enveloped.

He screamed as the blast launched him backward, his body rolling several feet across the pavestones before eventually coming to a stop.

"How are those wards and enchantments working for you?" Ellyne jeered.

He moved slowly but finally rose to his feet as Nicole readied another volley. There was no competition, here. His wards would fail, and Nicole would destroy him. In fact, she looked absolutely ready to take on anything that came at her. Ellyne had never seen her so determined, so . . . angry.

It was as if something inside Nicole had awakened. Determination and fury filled her whole being. Maybe it was their proximity to the source, or maybe the girl felt some of Ellyne's anger. Regardless of the reason, it didn't bode well for Marik.

"Fine," he growled through clenched teeth. "I see I should've made sure you were dead when I shot you years ago."

"You should've had better aim."

Ellyne unloaded the remaining seven bullets from the cartridge, each one bouncing harmlessly off his shimmering barriers before they could reach him.

"It's not wise to waste your ammo, Ellyne."

"It was worth it!" She quickly reloaded, counting sixteen bullets remaining.

As she finished, Ellyne noticed numerous shimmering portals appear. A split second later, Kithrak flooded the area, throwing spells of all varieties in their direction. Before she knew it, Ellyne was hit by numerous sensations at once as she took the brunt of the attacks.

Nicole moved quickly, summoning a glowing, translucent red barrier in front of them that blocked every incoming spell. As they hunkered behind it, the ground shifted around them, creating obstacles of stone around the area and providing cover for the Kithrak that continued to pour out of the portals.

Ellyne and Nicole followed suit, each ducking behind a different wall across from each other. Nicole peeked out over her barricade, then ducked down as spells whizzed past her head.

"There's a whole lot of Kithrak out there," she said, dismissing her energy barrier.

"Well, that's to be expected. After all, we *are* on their turf. I'm just glad this didn't happen when we first arrived."

"Just as long as we're not fighting that weird crab creature thing we saw earlier. That thing creeped me out."

More spells flew by overhead, some impacting the stones and sending chips into the air. Then came the shrieks and feral cries that sent chills down Ellyne's back.

"Damn it!" she growled, "grika! They're really pulling out

all the stops for us!"

"I think they like us."

Ellyne raised a suspicious brow at her counterpart. "Not the word I would choose."

Nicole laughed. Even under fire against incredible and overwhelming forces, she still found the ability to laugh. Ellyne wondered if it was confidence in her abilities or naivety about the dire situation that allowed her to feel such mirth.

Ellyne could still laugh too, but for her it was simply because she gave no shits. This mess was going to end one way or the other—right here, right now.

"Are you ready to do this?" she asked.

"Only if you are."

Together, they stood, Ellyne with her gun and Nicole wielding magic. Without a word, they tore into their enemies. Ellyne focused on targets she thought would be vulnerable to her bullets which included mostly grika and lower-ranking Kithrak. One by one they fell, and she reloaded the new cartridge before the empty cartridge hit the stone by her feet.

She emptied the next eight bullets just as quickly, dropping grika and Kithrak without remorse while dodging fire, lightning, energy and whatever they threw her way. She couldn't avoid them all, however, and she felt the pain and the effect of each spell. Some burned while others slowed her down, but she always recovered and fired back.

A quick glance at Nicole and she was in awe. The girl truly *was* a master—tossing out spell after spell quicker than the Kithrak could respond. She created marvelous effects to both counter and attack simultaneously, all with fluid hand motions and movements. Whereas the Kithrak were uttering words, Nicole's spells were wordless. The Kithrak looked like clumsy children when compared with her. The mage breaker was truly a sight to behold.

Marik was largely holding his own, as Ellyne suspected.

After Nicole (way after Nicole), he might have been the most magically gifted human. Unfortunately for him, however, none of his attacks came close to harming her, which is why he focused primarily on Ellyne.

Well, either that reason or hatred. Probably the latter. Truth be told, she herself was no different. If she could gun him down right now, she would gladly spend all her remaining bullets on him.

If she had any.

"I'm out of ammo!" she yelled to Nicole who nodded but showed no concern as she collapsed a stone barrier down onto a horde of grika. "So, uh, no problem! Don't worry about me! I'll just be over here . . . uh . . ."

Ellyne holstered her gun and pulled out her blade. She pressed the button and it telescoped out into a full sword.

"I guess just stabbing the living crap out of every damned Kithrak in sight," she mumbled. "At least the Kithrak who suck and can't muster up any protections." She stood, exhaled deeply, and hopped over the barrier behind which she'd been hiding. "Here goes nothing."

This was going to be painful. But she told herself she had nothing to worry about as long as the Kithrak weren't carrying guns.

Ellyne charged into the fray, striking at several grika and clumsily dropping two of them. Her skill with a blade was nowhere near as good as her skill with a gun, but it was acquired in the same fashion—experience.

She often wondered how deadly she could be with formal training. People seldom fought with blades anymore and they weren't often seen as a threat. That was usually their mistake. In the end, she suspected it didn't matter. She was still alive after all these years, so her skill had served her well enough.

But she knew, this time, a simple blade may not be enough.

Her blade effortlessly ran through a Kithrak as he was

trying to cast a spell. She kicked the body off and planted her dagger in a grika to her right. She dodged several spells but a few connected, causing her to stagger backward and fight just to remain standing. The pain dissipated along with the effects just in time to avoid several more spells as she ducked behind a barrier. She was still not used to the feeling of her body absorbing this much magic.

Nicole had also moved up to try and stay close as she continued her attack. Both her left leg and left arm had what appeared to be serious cuts on them but either she didn't notice or didn't care. Either way, her spellcasting didn't seem to be hindered by either, and she continued her onslaught, laughing.

Two grika approached Ellyne but turned to charge when they saw Nicole.

"Not today," Ellyne grunted, running them through before they could lunge at her friend. Searing pain wracked her right arm as she pulled out her blade and her hand spasmed, throwing her weapon and sending it clattering across the stone ground somewhere behind her.

"Shit! Nicole! I lost my blade!" The spell dissipated and she could feel a trickle of it collect within her.

"Well, go get it!"

"Can't you just wave your hands or some shit and bring it back to me?"

"I'm a little busy right now!"

Nicole moved to block several incoming spells, a few of which were headed for Ellyne.

"I guess, as far as excuses go, that's reasonable. Also, there are grika coming up behind us!"

"Well, do something about them!"

"What the hell am I supposed to—"

She had an idea. It was a *bad* idea. It wasn't *just* a bad idea, though. It may have been the worst idea in the history of bad ideas—especially this close to the source.

"What's the old saying? If you're going to make an omelet, you've got to blow some shit up."

"What?"

"Never mind. That sounds about right. Let's do this."

"Do what?"

Ellyne took a deep breath and calmly walked out from behind the safety of her barrier. Spells immediately connected with her. Every part of her body screamed out as if it were on fire or frozen and she struggled to move but, with concentration and overwhelming effort, she arduously plodded forward slowly. Each step was a struggle and if the grika got to her, they would tear her apart.

Searing pain filled every bit of her, tingling and throbbing, and she was barely able to resist the urge to scream. But for as much as it hurt, it wasn't enough. She felt magical energy well up inside her, but it was mere drips and she needed more than that. Was it possible for the Kithrak to attack her, but with lower-powered spells? There was so much about magic she didn't know, but she absolutely knew she needed more than what she was siphoning.

Fortunately, she had already thought of that.

"Nicole! Hit me!" she yelled.

Ellyne dared not look back to see how much distance she'd put between the two of them, but she hoped it was enough . . . if there even was a safe distance at this point.

"What?"

"Hit me! Full blast or whatever you want to call it!"

"But Ellyne—"

"Just do it and then run for cover!"

Ellyne saw Marik and focused on him just as the excruciating pain threatened to overwhelm her. Then she felt Nicole blast her in the back with something and she yelped.

She felt more spells hit her from behind.

Whatever Nicole was throwing at her was potent and pure—more powerful than anything she had ever felt. She thought she knew how powerful Nicole was before, but she now realized she had no idea.

"I just hope she knows not to actually harm me," she grunted, remembering the one time Nicole's spell had penetrated her immunity.

She felt every blast of magic. And each of Nicole's barrages threatened to consume her in fiery pain. She fought it, remembering her failure earlier when she lost control and killed so many people.

But she couldn't lose control now. Not yet. She kept her eyes focused on Marik and struggled to make her way over to him. The best part of it all was the worry she saw on his face. He knew he couldn't stop her and his fear increased with each step she took. She tried hard to take a moment and enjoy it but found it difficult to concentrate on anything other than putting one foot in front of the other.

Nicole hit her in the back again. Yes, there was pain but also reassurance—her friend was still alive and fighting.

"Just a little further." Ellyne gritted her teeth as tears rolled down her cheeks. Breathing was a chore only slightly less difficult than suppressing the battery of energy she held within her.

Everything was a monumental effort.

Were her hands glowing?

This was it. She was going to explode. There was no containing the power any longer. This could be the end of everyone—even her.

Ellyne screamed with sweet, excruciating release as the flocia within her burst forth in all directions, leveling the barriers, turning enemies to dust, and still flinging others far into the distance.

With one last gasp, she slipped into darkness, her thoughts dwelling not on herself and not on Marik, but on her friend's safety.

CHAPTER
TWENTY-SEVEN

THE VOICE WAS MUFFLED at first, as if someone was speaking underwater, but without the gurgling noises. After a moment, it got clearer, louder, and more coherent.

"Ellyne!"

Colors. They swam in random vectors, swirling and sometimes pausing. They were often accompanied by stars or flashes of light, some that seemed to almost have their own sounds.

Soon there was a sensation. Not altogether pleasant—like something impacted. Actually, not pleasant at all.

"Ellyne!"

It happened again, then again. The swirling colors started to fade while the flashes of light increased.

"Ellyne!"

"Stop!" Ellyne shouted, shielding her face with her hands.

"Holy crap, you're alive!"

Ellyne felt something on her, something heavy but soft and warm. She opened her eyes and, through blurry vision, saw what appeared to be Nicole draped over her. The soft blob was a red hue, which matched the shade of Nicole's clothing and, though it took Ellyne's mind a while to catch up, she was finally sure.

"If I'm going to have a headache like this ever again, then it's going to be from drinking too much squama juice and not from exploding." She sat up slowly, which prompted Nicole to back off. "Did it work?"

"If by 'work,' you mean leveled everything in sight and killed everyone around us then, yes, it worked."

"You're hurt," she said, pointing to Nicole's left side which appeared to still be bleeding. But red blood on red clothing made it difficult to determine which was which.

"Oh, it's a scratch," the girl replied, but her hand went to the wound, and she winced. "So, um, I conjured a pretty strong barrier, but some debris hit me from behind."

"Shit, I'm sorry. We need to get you medical help." She was about to get up and then noticed Nicole's mangled left leg.

"Yeah," Nicole replied, obviously noticing Ellyne's gaze. "My barrier failed when I was hit, and my leg was crushed under more rubble. Ours is not going to be a speedy exit, I'm afraid."

"Nicole, I—"

"You did what you had to do and we're both still alive because of it. That's all that matters, Ellyne." Nicole sat next to her, grimacing as she did so. "Besides, whatever you did closed off all portals to this area. It may be a little while before we see any more Kithrak. It looks like you broke . . . well, everything." She mustered a smirk.

"Nicole, I'm sorry. If only I could control this . . . whatever it is. I never meant for you to get hurt."

"Don't blame yourself. I'm not dead. I mean, it hurts like a son of a bitch, and you owe me a drink when we get home, though."

"Oh, look at you," Ellyne laughed, until it turned into a

cough. "Wanting to do naughty stuff—what would the Ilserate say?"

"Well, if you'd like to ask Marik his thoughts, he's—"

"Still alive?"

"Yep." Nicole pointed to a lone, motionless body in red robes lying at the edge of the circular area. "His magic was strong, but it wouldn't have held up against that blast. I gave him a little help to keep him from being vaporized."

"Why would you do that?"

"I figured you . . . might have some choice words to say to him before he dies—I mean, if that's the choice you make for him. I'm not sure I would blame you. He really is kind of an asshole."

"Nicole, language." It was Ellyne's turn to smile. "Right now, I'd say that's what I'm leaning toward. It'd be no different than if he'd perished in the blast. We also still have to figure out what we're doing about the source, now that we have time to think. You're the mage breaker. What does your intuition tell you?"

"My intuition tells me Marik's awake." Nicole nodded in his direction.

"Stay put."

"I'm not planning on going anywhere," she said, motioning to her leg.

Ellyne pulled her weapon and, keeping it trained on Marik, walked cautiously toward him on shaky legs as he struggled to stand. After failing several times, he rolled over and propped himself up on his elbows, at which point she stopped just about ten feet away.

"Well, look at you," she said, staring down the barrel at him.

"I've felt better."

"You've looked better. Not much, though. It was a pretty low bar to begin with."

"What are you going to do?" Marik asked, sitting up with great effort. "Are you going to shoot me?"

"I thought I might," she replied, making sure not to take her gaze from him. "It's only fair to pay you back for everything you've done to me."

"I suppose so," he laughed.

"And what's so funny then?"

"I think," he said, slowly getting to his feet but keeping his palms out in front of him, "you're going to have a problem with that."

"And why is that?"

"Because Ellyne," he laughed some more, "you can't shoot me with an empty gun."

Ellyne looked at her gun as if she thought he were lying. Unfortunately, she knew she had expended her ammunition early in the fight. He was right.

But he was also wrong.

"I heard you gripe about it during combat. If you want me dead, she's going to have to do it for you. It's sad, really. You've waited all these years and you still screwed it up."

Ellyne truly had waited years for this moment—to wipe that shit-eating grin off his face permanently, and it looked like she would miss her chance.

Except she knew something he didn't.

"That's what has always impressed me about you, Marik."

"Oh yeah? What is that?" he asked, still grinning.

"Your attention to detail. How you can always be so sure you're right but still be so very, very wrong. You may have duped me in the past but, this time, I'm one step ahead of you."

"I don't understand."

"Do you think I would plan revenge for years and not have a bullet saved especially for you? I saw this moment coming years ago and I made damned sure I would always

—*always*—be prepared for it. I've waited a very long time—too long to, as you say, screw it up."

Marik's smile turned into a look of concern and confusion.

Ellyne reached into her mouth and felt the metal tooth—the metal that replaced the tooth Marik knocked out of her jaw years ago. She grabbed it and pulled hard, plucking it out and wincing as she did so, then she held it aloft for Marik to see briefly before sliding it into a slot in her gun's cylinder.

"I had this little beauty crafted shortly after you knocked the real one out. You probably don't recognize it, but it's the very bullet you buried in my shoulder years ago."

She turned the cylinder, so the bullet was properly loaded, then she aimed the gun and slowly cocked the hammer.

"How beautiful," he said, trying to exude confidence and his usual attitude. Ellyne, however, could sense hesitation and fear in his voice which betrayed his attempted cool exterior. "But you know full well your bullet can't past through my wards."

"Normal bullets can't," she said, squinting through one eye, aiming down the barrel. "But this one can. You see, I loathe magic, but I loathe you more, so I was willing to make one concession—just this one. I had this bullet—your bullet—enchanted long ago. Its magic was suppressed by my condition . . . until now."

She pulled the trigger. The gun fired with a brilliant flash of multicolored light and a louder than normal explosion. Marik's defenses faltered and winked out the moment the bullet passed through, burying itself in his shoulder.

He screamed as the force knocked him back and onto the ground where he now lay, clutching his shoulder and bleeding profusely.

"Now we're even. You can rot in hell for all I care, Marik." She holstered her weapon.

She hurried over and knelt by Nicole who appeared to be

getting worse. She was pale and her normally bright red clothes were a much darker shade in many spots.

"We need to get you out of here," she said, trying to disguise the worry in her voice.

"Yes, but not yet. We first need to finish what we started."

"Nicole, you're dying. We—"

"Aren't done yet, Ellyne. We can free flocia and, with it, the people all over Seralune. We're so close Ellyne!" She coughed into her hand and Ellyne noticed blood when she pulled it away.

"You're in no condition to do that, Nicole. And, besides, we don't even know how. The source is *right there,* and we still don't know what to do with it."

"I do," Nicole said weakly.

"You what?"

"I know what to do." She sat up slowly and with great effort, wincing from the pain. "I think I've known for a while, but I didn't really want to admit it because I'm not sure it's survivable."

"What do you mean?"

"The way to free flocia is to unite with the source. To do that means almost certain death."

Ellyne's knees gave out and she sat next to Nicole who, if she was right, probably wouldn't survive—especially not in her weakened state. It wasn't something she was accustomed to, but she wasn't ready to say goodbye to her friend.

"There has to be another way," Ellyne said, fighting back tears. "We can come back. I've still got the eye!"

"If I'm right, to complete this prophecy thing, the mage breaker has to enter the flow of energy and surrender to it."

"You mean run into *that*? You're right, that will definitely kill you. No, we're not doing that. We'll find another way."

"There is no other way unless you want to kill every Kithrak in existence."

"Then I will!" Ellyne sobbed.

"I believe you," Nicole whispered, shifting to sit more comfortably. "Listen, this is our only chance, Ellyne. It's now or never. We're never coming back here and if we don't do this now, the Kithrak won't stop until we're both dead. At least, this way, one of us gets to live. It's just . . ."

"It's just what? I don't like it when you say that."

"It's just the real kicker is," Nicole continued, tears welling up in her eyes now. "It's not me who has to go in there. It's you."

"Me? I don't understand."

"Ellyne, you have no connection to magic, yet you can command flocia somehow, even if you can't control it."

Ellyne gasped, trying to puzzle out everything Nicole just told her, feeling elated—happy her friend would hopefully live, but still unable to comprehend the situation.

"Ellyne," Nicole said. "I'm the most powerful mage, but I'm not the mage breaker."

"This makes no sense, Nicole."

"You are."

Ellyne stood on shaky legs and looked around her, pacing nervously. The rush of flocia was in her head, beckoning her near. She knew that now. She understood it. It sounded almost like millions of voices mumbling and calling to her. She had tried to shut it out before but now she succumbed to it, and she knew it was true. What once was simply a cacophony of chaos now spoke clearly to her.

She wiped back tears and sniffed. This all happened so fast. How could Nicole be sure either one of them had to go running into the source? Her brain worked furiously to figure something out—to come up with an alternative plan where they both lived but, the more she did so, the more she was sure.

"I have to go," she whispered.

"And I have to say goodbye to the first and only friend I've ever had, and I don't want to."

"Then don't," Ellyne replied. She embraced Nicole in the tightest hug she could, hoping to avoid most of the girl's injuries. "Don't say goodbye."

"Ellyne," she sobbed, "I knew I chose right. I knew, when I sought you out, that you would help me. I can never thank you enough, my friend. I will miss you!"

Wiping the tears from her eyes and blinking furiously to clear her watery vision, Ellyne charged at the pillar of energy, running as fast as she could. Each step was powered by sadness and rage. She would do this, and Nicole would go free.

And Marik got what he deserved. That alone made the entire journey worth it. But it was time to bring it to an end—all of it.

She leapt into the pillar of energy, and it consumed her. She felt every pulse and, somehow, every color as the overwhelming noise filled her ears.

"I . . . I understand it now!" she shouted, though she had no body left to produce a sound. "This is too much power! And it shall belong to the Kithrak no more! Your time is over!"

She forced her will upon the column of energy—upon the very source of magic itself—and it bent. She pushed against it again, this time harder and unrelenting.

And it acquiesced. It invited her in; it accepted her. It *welcomed* her!

No longer adversaries, she felt a part of it—completely in sync with every pulse and color. There was no more fighting, no resistance.

Flocia cooperated and they worked together, now acting in unison both in color and rhythm.

"And now," she roared, "I will talk and you will listen."

There was silence. The pulsing stopped and the deafening noises ceased. Flocia waited.

"Good. Now let's get started."

EPILOGUE

NICOLE COLLAPSED ON THE COUCH—
ELLYNE'S couch. This was where it all began, just a few
days ago, when she broke into Ellyne's apartment . . . when
she met the famed Golden Gunslinger for the first time.
Fitting, she thought, that the whole thing should end in the
same place. If only Ellyne were here to share in it.

She had nowhere else to go. For the first time in her entire
life, she had no direction and no one to watch after her . . . or
protect her. And that wasn't all that had changed in the blink
of an eye.

She reclined, wincing as she recalled every injury. Each
bruise and laceration screamed in agony as she tried to
pretend they weren't serious. Sure, she'd managed to heal
them up just enough with magic—something she never
attempted until now. Magic wasn't supposed to be able to
heal wounds and, as far as she knew, she was the first to
succeed at it, even if it was only minor.

The city outside was dark and still. Whatever Ellyne did . .
. well, it disrupted everything. It *changed* everything, and the
chaos that followed was absolute. Nicole believed herself

lucky to have escaped and navigated the city safely just to get back to Ellyne's apartment.

Magic was dead.

Except, that wasn't entirely true. She still felt her connection to flocia, but it was much more distant now, and connecting with it was far more difficult. The rest of the city wasn't so lucky. The things she'd seen and heard on her way here . . . she would never forget them.

"If I have such trouble connecting with magic," she wondered, "then what about everyone else?"

She fought back sadness but eventually succumbed to the tears with the realization that she was now truly alone. Her only friend was gone. Nicole told herself again and again that it should have been *her*. She should have been the one to take control of flocia but, in the end, she knew that was impossible.

She shut her eyes and breathed deep, quickly feeling her body relax a bit as sleep began to overtake her. Before she could drift off, however, her eyes snapped open and she sat upright, gasping from the pain and effort.

It was a voice.

"Ellyne?" she shouted, but the empty apartment remained silent.

The muffled, distorted voice repeated.

"Where are you? *Who* are you?"

There was a moment of silence when even Nicole's breath seemed painfully loud. But then she heard the sound again. She slowly and carefully rose from the couch, steadying herself as she nearly collapsed, and removed the cushions.

There, underneath was the tyrome, glowing and pulsing.

"Wait . . . how did that get here? Ellyne had it and—"

The voice emanated from the tyrome. It was louder now, but still distorted. Nicole carefully grasped the object and held it in front of her, turning it over in her hands."

"I don't understand!" she sobbed, tears streaking down

her face. Just clutching the tyrome reminded her of her lost friend. "What . . . what are you saying?"

It was almost as if someone was trying to speak over static —like one of those old devices in the Legacy Age. Nicole brought the tyrome closer to her ear and closed her eyes to concentrate, trying to glean whatever she could until she finally thought she heard a word—just one, single word.

"Golgolonar."

The tyrome suddenly went dark, and she dropped it. She was about to pick it up off the carpet when the screen behind her buzzed, popped, and crackled to life. Her body shook and fear gripped her. She always felt safe with Ellyne; she always had confidence in her mastery of magic. But now, nothing was the same and she was a scared little girl, all alone.

The screen popped again, then made the noise screens normally produced when they powered up. When the message appeared, it displayed only four words.

"What have you done?"

COMING SOON

Last Available
March 2024

Mage Breaker Eight Bullets
August 2024

ABOUT THE AUTHOR

Sean R. Frazier lives in Missouri with his wife and two daughters. He also shares the house with two dogs and three cats. He is the award-winning author of the Forgotten Years fantasy saga. That award was a participation trophy from his elementary school soccer team. When not scribing important tomes, Sean enjoys reading, playing guitar, running, playing tabletop and video games, 3d printing oddities, and he recently picked up archery. He's decent, but don't call him Hawkeye just yet.